Pauper's Child

MEG HUTCHINSON

Pauper's Child

Hodder & Stoughton

Copyright © 2004 by Meg Hutchinson

First published in Great Britain in 2004 by Hodder & Stoughton
A division of Hodder Headline

The right of Meg Hutchinson to be identified as the Author
of the Work has been asserted by her in accordance with the
Copyright, Designs and Patents Act 1988.

2 4 6 8 10 9 7 5 3 1

A CIP catalogue record for this title is available from the British Library

ISBN 0 340 82994 X

Typeset in Plantin Light by
Phoenix Typesetting, Burley-in-Wharfedale, West Yorkshire

Printed and bound in Great Britain by
Mackays of Chatham plc, Chatham, Kent

Hodder & Stoughton
A division of Hodder Headline
338 Euston Road
London NW1 3BH

ACKNOWLEDGEMENTS

Parian is a porcelain imitation of marble from Mount Elias on Paros, a Greek island in the east of the Aegean Sea . . . it originated in Britain, produced there in the early part of Queen Victoria's reign . . . there is a dispute about who found Parian first . . .

Parian Ware by Dennis Barker

Leabrook Pottery was demolished some time after 1930. In the seventeenth century the town was famous for its salt-glazed vessels known as Wedgbury Ware.

Wednesbury Revisited by Ian M. Bott

Seeing no one is absolutely certain as to who it was first discovered Parian, and given Wednesbury enjoyed a long history of producing many types of pottery for use in the home, I have taken the liberty of having the birth of Parian Ware take place in my own 'Black Country'.

Meg Hutchinson

I

'I saw . . . I saw him there and I knew, I knew what he was doing and why! It was her . . .'

Eyes blazing with hatred so intense it burned like black fire, Sabine Montroy glared at the small girl standing before her in a dismal joyless room empty except for the two of them.

'. . . I saw him . . .'

Breath snatched between teeth which hate had almost glued together, the words were a snarl.

'He was there in Stafford Street, I did not need to wait to find out *where* he was headed; but who he was intending to meet, that was what I had to see, that was what I had to be sure of.'

'Please . . .' Violet, eyes wide with fear, stared upwards.

'No!' A long-boned hand shot out, catching the small pale face, the force of its blow knocking the child back on its heels, the woman's lips peeling back from her teeth in fury.

'Did *he* give the chance of saying please? Did *he* listen to any plea? No, he did not. Like a thief in the night he left, no explanation, no apology, no care for the heart he broke . . . and why did he do so? It was because of her . . . her and *you* . . . you, the spawn of his evil . . .'

Callista Sanford opened her eyes to a grey rain-soaked morning. The dream had come again. Like so many other times it had come from the distant realms of a childhood she tried so hard to forget; but in the night's dark hours while her body lay in exhausted sleep the phantoms of memory slipped from the shadows of her mind, bringing with them the fear and the heartache. Turning her head, she watched the rain beating against the window. Why had that child been hated so? Why had she been treated with so much cruelty?

Her body heavy, eyes wanting only to close, weary as if sleep had not come at all, Callista willed herself to rise and wash in the bowl of cold water she had placed on the rickety washstand the night before.

It had simply been a dream; the reality was over. Cold biting through thin clothing, she shivered, her fingers blue as they bound her hair close into the nape of her neck.

The reality was over, but the nightmare went on. As the sounds of muffled coughing reached through the stillness, a stab of fear added to the numbness of her fingers. Her mother's illness, the cough which racked leaving her breathless, got no better with the days but seemed to grow worse. Her mother denied the worries but bright fevered eyes told Callista their own story, and also gave the remedy: she needed to get her mother out of this cold damp house. There was a way . . . a way she had refused until now to take, hoping every day might bring a different answer; now, hurrying to her mother's room, she knew that way was the one she had to take!

'Why are you out of bed?' Concern at not finding her mother in her room echoed in Callista's question as she hurried into the box-like living room.

Ruth Sanford coughed into a scrap of cloth clutched in thin fingers, folding it quickly so the scarlet specks would not be seen.

'I was not tired, my dear, I had rested so long yesterday I could not sleep.'

Her mother could not sleep because of the cold! Callista poked the ash-grey embers of last night's fire. If only they could afford a fire in her mother's bedroom, just a small one to keep the worst of the cold at bay . . . but buying fuel for this one was as much as she could do. Maybe today would be better. Nursing the hope to herself she fetched the bucket from beneath the scullery sink, feeding the last of the coal it held onto the embers. Maybe today she would find a permanent post which would mean not taking the one way left open to her. She had fought against it so long, the thought of that man's flabby mouth lowering to her own, his thick hands . . .

Reaching for the quietly bubbling kettle she scalded tea she had spooned into a fat-bellied pot, trying all the time to rid herself of the thought, but as steam rose from the kettle it seemed to form into a heavy-jowled face, a face which leered.

'I have finished the gown.' Ruth Sanford coughed again, the scrap of cloth no disguise against the rattle in her chest. 'But I . . . I must wait until tomorrow to deliver it. Mrs Ramsey will need to be advised beforehand.'

What her mother meant but would not say was she felt too weak, too ill, to take the gown they had shared the making of to the woman who had ordered it.

Callista added the last spoonful of sugar to the cup she stirred before handing it to her mother, leaving her own unsweetened.

'I think Mrs Ramsey will be eager to see her new gown.' She smiled, trying not to show her worry at the short gasping breaths or the tell-tale red rims of purple-shadowed eyes. Had it been as she had thought, had it been the creeping cold of the bedroom had sent her mother downstairs in the early hours? Or was the truth of it the need for the money it would bring?

Reaching for the small pot of dripping she had saved from the few strips of fat bacon the butcher in the High Street had added to the threepence she had earned scrubbing out the shop, Callista emptied it into the shallow-bottomed pan which she hung from the bracket suspended over the livening fire. They had enough bread for two slices. It would make breakfast for her mother, and the one egg left in the food cupboard would be her dinner. And her own breakfast?

Callista could not deny the hunger pangs gnawing her

stomach as she dipped one slice of the bread, placing it aside while the other fried, the appetising aroma of it causing her mouth to water. Swallowing hard, she placed the egg in the kettle still partly full of hot water and set it to boil.

'I can deliver the gown, I will take it this evening,' she said, handing the plate with its slice of fried bread to her mother.

Letting it rest on her knee, Ruth Sanford watched her daughter busily set another plate with eggcup and spoon, then slice the dipped bread into dainty triangles before rescuing the egg from the kettle. They had tried so hard to make her life happy, and it had been in those first years. Jason Sanford had loved his wife and adored the child they had named from his beloved Greek myths; she had been his beautiful tiny wood nymph; and she was beautiful despite the hardship of their lives now without him. Yes, the hunger and cold had the face drawn, but even that could not detract from the beauty of the flawless skin, the wide violet eyes and gleaming black satin hair. All of Jason's handsomeness was there in their child but it was added to, there was an extra something which at times seemed almost ethereal. The magic of a wood nymph! Ruth sipped her tea, lowered lids shielding the tears glistening in her own soft brown eyes.

It had been difficult convincing her mother that she herself was given breakfast by the wife of the butcher whose shop floor she scrubbed and it was equally difficult to look into those gentle eyes as the lie was told. But it had needed to be told if her mother was to accept the egg and bread being left for her midday meal. Maybe today she would be asked to scrub more of the shop, perhaps the counter and the huge chopping block the man saw to himself . . . it would pay another penny, possibly even two.

Having her mother's promise she would stay close to the fire and rest, Callista left the tiny two-room house, drawing her woollen shawl close against the sharp nipping frost. The people of Trowes Square were good neighbours; though most were poor as church mice with nothing to spare but a friendly word this they gave willingly, and knowing several of the women would find a minute in their day to call in on her mother made her own long absence easier to bear.

Passing the church of St James, nodding and returning the several good mornings of others hurrying to their places of work, Callista entered Barlow's butcher shop.

'There don't be no cleaning I wants doing today.'

The shawl half on, half off her shoulders, Callista felt her heart drop like a stone. Not again . . . it couldn't be happening again; but as she looked at the plump red-cheeked man fiddling embarrassedly with his moustache she knew it was happening again.

'But . . . but yesterday you said . . .'

'I knows what I said and I be sorry . . . but that be the way of it, I've got no call for the shop to be scrubbed, the missis be going to do that herself from now on. I apologises for getting you along of 'ere when there were no reason.'

Releasing the moustache he had twiddled to dagger points he reached a small parcel from beneath the counter, holding it towards her.

'Take the sausages for your trouble.'

Why? She stared at the man, his gaze shifting before her own. Why this sudden change? Every day for a week he had expressed satisfaction with her work and every day of that week had requested she come to scrub out the shop on the following morning. He had been pleased with the standard of cleaning, so much so he added a little bacon or a chop to her pennies each time, yet now, suddenly, he was dispensing with her services.

She could ask the reason, offer to do the work for even less than the threepence he paid but it would do no good. Her being told she was no longer required was merely history repeating itself.

'Thank you, Mr Barlow.' She glanced at the package still held in the plump-fingered hand. 'But I accept only what I have worked for.'

What did she do now? Holding a press of tears in her throat, Callista walked the length of the High Street. Some of the shops had given her employment of one kind or another but every owner had eventually acted as John Barlow had just done, each saying she was no longer required. Why? What did she do that was so unacceptable as to see her dismissed? It was not true that they no longer required assistance, for she had seen other women quickly installed in her place. So what was the truth? What particular Jonas rode on her shoulders?

Brought up sharply by the hoarse shout of a wagoner to get out of the way, she glanced across the space which was the junction of several streets each feeding onto Trouse Lane, the arterial road to Darlaston. Immersed in her own thoughts, she had walked almost beneath the wheels of the heavy cart, bringing the owner's displeasure singing about her ears like a whip. Once the cart had trundled past, she looked at the people stood in small groups, their breath hanging in small white clouds on the frosty air. This was the High Bullen, the place where men, women and even young children collected each morning hoping to be selected for a day's work. She had never stood the line before, hating the thought of being inspected, looked over like cattle in a market. Trying desperately to think of some other place she might enquire for work, she crossed over to the other side of the road. Maybe if she went on to Darlaston? With that in mind she turned and next moment found herself held tight in the arms of a man, the package he was carrying hitting the ground at her feet.

Holding her steady until she found her feet again, the neatly bearded face of a well-dressed man regarded her with amusement.

'My dear.' He smiled. 'It is a long time since I held a pretty girl in my arms and pleasant as I find the experience now I fear it is not quite proper.'

'I . . . I beg your pardon.' Confusion tripping her words, Callista broke free. 'I was not looking where I was going . . . it was purely my fault.'

The face broke into a broader smile. 'Then it is a fault an old man welcomes.'

'Your package, I do hope the contents are not damaged!' How on earth did she pay for whatever might be broken? Picking up the small brown paper-wrapped parcel she held it, all of her inner worry showing in her eyes.

'Ah, the beautiful Artemis.' He took the package. 'Who knows, perhaps her fellow immortals have protected her and she remains in one piece.'

'Artemis, daughter of the Titaness Leto and king of the gods Zeus, and twin sister to Apollo the god of archery, prophecy and music . . .'

'So . . .' The broad smile faded as she broke off but eyes lifted to hers held an expression that was congratulatory and at the same time questioning. 'You are familiar with the gods of ancient Greece. If it is not too personal a question might an old man enquire as to how you came by your knowledge?'

Callista blushed, acutely aware of the logic behind the question. Her clothes, though clean, were shabby to the point of raggedness. How come a girl from her obvious walk of life had any knowledge of Greek mythology?

'My father . . . Oh, I do hope the Artemis is not broken.'

'Tut, child, forget the Artemis,' he answered. 'I too would wish the lovely goddess remains in one piece but should that not be the case then that old rascal Glaze will have the pleasurable and profitable business of hunting down another. But right now I wish to hear of this father of yours . . . he must be a man of some education.'

Profitable! The word stuck out above the rest in Callista's mind. The shop the man had indicated when naming its owner was filled with antiques of all kinds, but none of them within the range of her father, who would often bring her to stand looking in through the window, his voice caressing every object he pointed out, a love of them colouring their naming and describing. 'Expensive,' he would say, 'but their beauty is one that knows no price.' How then could she pay for the one she was responsible for breaking?

'Does he perhaps read the classics? Your father, child, how did he learn of the ancient tales?'

Callista glanced to where people were fast being chosen from the line of hopefuls. If she were to have any chance of employment she must join them now. 'No,' she answered quickly, 'he does not read . . . I mean . . . please tell me the cost of the piece, the Artemis, and . . . and I will pay it, but I must go now.'

She would pay the cost. The smiling eyes followed the direction of Callista's glance. It would never be with money earned by work got from that line.

'Why do we not get ourselves a hot drink and assess the harm we have both done.'

'Both?' Callista's finely winged brows drew together.

'That is unfair of me.' The broad smile returned as he shook the package. 'Our gracious goddess tells me her glorious body remains intact so you have caused no harm while I . . . I have prevented you gaining that for which I think you came. I fear the selection of workers for the day has been completed.'

Shoulders drooping with realisation that the one hope left to her was gone, Callista watched the remaining figures drift aimlessly away.

'Will you allow me to apologise over a cup of chocolate? Really I feel the need of both.'

She could sit for perhaps a few minutes, let the cold thaw from her bones before taking the long walk into Darlaston.

Hiding her shivers beneath the pretence of rearranging her shawl, she nodded. 'A hot drink would be most welcome, thank you.'

She had walked past this place many times with her father, and often since his death, but she had never been inside. Callista hesitated as her companion walked towards the imposing entrance of the George Hotel.

'Is something wrong? You do not like this hotel?'

She had lied once today; she would not lie a second time. Looking directly into the face of the man regarding her with shrewd eyes she answered quietly. 'Liking or not is something I cannot say, for I have never been inside. People of my station can hardly be welcome.'

'Guests of Phineas Westley are welcome wherever *he* is welcomed.'

'No, sir.' Callista shook her head. 'I believe a more accurate word is "tolerated". A valued client can be allowed his foibles provided they do not infringe . . .'

'Hah!' An amused laugh echoed on the frost-bitten morning; he banged a malacca cane on the ground. 'You have more than a knowledge of mythology, girl, you have a shrewd head on those young shoulders; but allow an old man his foibles and accompany me into this palace of social snobbery.'

She had been mistaken in agreeing to his proposal; the offer of a hot drink had seemed a few moments ago something to lift her flagging spirit but now with the glances of women hurrying past she realised the folly of what she had done. Decent girls did not agree to accompany a man unknown to her family. She glanced into the watchful eyes. Had his offer been as innocent as her acceptance or was he planning a more personally rewarding way of her apologising for possibly damaging the contents of that package?

'You need say no more, child. I was thoughtless in my suggestion; I only hope you will overlook my action. You have my most profound apology.'

The smile had gone from his eyes, the curve of laughter from his mouth. Drawing her shawl closer about her shivering body

Callista saw instead the look she had often caught shadowing her mother's face, a look of longing for something gone from her life, of inner sadness, a loneliness which had words tumbling from Callista's heart when she had meant her brain to answer. 'You did not speak thoughtlessly. What you offered was kindness and for that I thank you.'

'That is charitable of you, my dear, but I will not take advantage of it. Maybe some day I will have the privilege of meeting with your father and speaking with him. I feel he shared my passion for the lovely goddess of the chase and her fellows.'

'The Artemis, I had forgotten . . . please!' She ran the few steps the departing figure had already put between them. 'Please, you must allow me to pay.'

If his judgement were anywhere close to correct this girl could not offer a single penny were that penny to save her from a lengthy term of imprisonment! Diplomatically keeping the thought to himself Phineas Westley glanced at the string-wrapped package held in one hand before replying.

'How can I ask you to pay for a statue which may not be broken? That would be tantamount to robbery and that, my dear, is not a foible Phineas Westley enjoys.'

If it were damaged . . . if he demanded recompense; took her before the magistrate! What of her mother? Worries noting in her mind Callista stared at the small parcel.

'I can see I must agree if your mind is to be set at rest.' Above the elegantly trimmed beard Phineas Westley's mouth found again the curve of a smile. 'But it is too cold for an elderly man to stand in the street. I shall examine the piece when I reach my home and if you will trust me with the address of your own I will write to you should payment prove necessary.'

He would write to her. Callista watched as he hailed a hansom. The package had fallen to the ground when they had collided; it had to be damaged if only minutely. But minute or otherwise the result was too awful to think of; an antique of that nature, a genuine piece carved hundreds of years ago, maybe even the work of an old master . . . and there would be no question of its authenticity; her father had always maintained Joseph Glaze was a man of integrity and the antiques and jewellery he dealt in could be relied upon to possess the same. All of which added to the impossibility of her ever being able to repay what that figurine would be worth. Phineas Westley must know that but he had not blinked an eyelid when she gave her address. Not that she had described the huddle of tiny compressed houses each joined to the other, their brickwork encrusted with the soot of steel mill and coal mine; the yard bisected by an open drain, the privies shared by as many as four families, the women who scrubbed and cleaned in the hours they were not engaged in picking coal from the mines waste heaps to sell to a jagger who paid a pittance for each bag; no, she had not described the poverty of Trowes Square . . . for no one of wealth or position in Wednesbury wanted to hear.

The hansom out of sight, Callista turned the corner into Union Street. There would be no employment for her here as there was none elsewhere in the town. She would return home and collect the gown. Delivering it would mean they had money for coal, food and to pay the rent. Thank God they would be able to pay the rent! She would be free for a few more weeks of having to submit to that flabby mouth, to the thick-fingered hands which took every opportunity of touching her . . .

. . . *tantamount to robbery* . . .

The words struck so suddenly she almost tripped. Wouldn't she be doing the same? The money she had helped to earn – it would be like stealing to spend even part of it on herself when it might have to go towards a debt . . . but those hands, that mouth . . . she could not! But even as the shudder passed along her spine Callista knew that she must.

2

He had looked so dreadfully lonely.

The gown on which her mother had spent days and herself long evenings was wrapped carefully in a spotlessly laundered cloth, and Callista hurried with it through the streets overhung with smoke and heavy soot, the dark blood of Wednesbury's veins. The man who had offered her hot chocolate, his whole demeanour had changed as he had detected her sudden withdrawal. The smile had died in his eyes, the curve of a smile faded from his mouth. The picture of his face had stayed with her as she had returned home to Trowes Court, the effects of its look adding to her own dejection and refusing to lift. Had he sensed her rejection? But she had not meant it that way. It was not rejection of him as a person. He had been so kind, insisting she need have no worries for the contents of that package, and she had returned his treatment of her with rudeness.

Skirting the stalls set in rows covering the market place, she walked quickly up the slight incline that was Spring Head. If only she had thought, given him an explanation before the hansom had driven away, but she had not and the chance might never come again.

That same thought must have shown in her face for her mother had quickly asked was something amiss. Passing the gracious old Oakeswell Hall, its blackened timbers standing out boldly against lime-washed walls, Callista felt a rush of admiration and pleasure, the pleasure her father had built in her for the skills of man's hand, admiration for the mind which could conceive beauty then create it from clay, wood or stone. 'Art is present in all of human creation, only a lying tongue or the blackness of an evil heart is ugly.' Those words had often been the finish of his describing a building, a painting or a sculpture and now as the lovely old house fell away behind her they seemed even more significant.

She had lied that morning, saying the butcher's wife gave her breakfast, and again an hour ago when coaxing her mother to eat the egg and last remaining slice of bread. She had forced a smile to accompany the lie which said she was too full to take another bite. But what way other than that would she have got her mother to eat?

'It was a lie, Father,' the whisper trembled beneath her breath, 'but I could think of no other way.'

Could he have heard her whisper would he have agreed or would he have smiled as he often had at a small girl's query why a lie was never the way to choose?

The cloth-wrapped gown warm against her body, Callista seemed to hear the voice she had loved. Deep, musical, full of love, it filled her mind. 'Truth is always a better way, Callista, only truth gives peace of mind . . . only truth eases the heart.'

But in this case truth would not ease her mother's heart; she would fret over taking a meal while her daughter went hungry and that she would not allow. Her mother was not well and worry proved no medicine!

'There be a visitor along of her, been 'ere some time her have; but come you in, wench, and take a cup of tea.'

Accepting the offer, Callista set her parcel on a table which, though three times the size of the one at home, was swallowed by the large airy kitchen of Acacia Villa. She took the chair indicated by the smiling housekeeper. Wood Green could be on a different planet to Trowes Court! Large detached houses with spacious well-tended gardens overlooked the beautiful park laid out two years ago to celebrate the Queen's Diamond Jubilee, while to the further side, were wide fields which each summer saw wheat and barley spread green-gold skirts prettily with scarlet poppies. This was the beautiful world her father had envisaged; thank heaven he had never lived in Trowes Court.

'Be your mother well? I must say her looked fair peaky last time her was to this house.'

'My mother has a cough which is why I have brought the gown instead of her.'

'Ah well, that be sensible. What with this damp weather, don't want to take no chances of catching that there influenza. Take my tip and keep her against the fire.'

There had been almost no fire. Callista's mind flew back to the tiny room where her mother sat. The embers in the grate had showed patches of red beneath a covering of grey ash but they gave no heat. It could have been a description of the woman staring into them. Twin patches of scarlet glowed on the cheeks of a face grey with the spasms of coughing which racked more and more harshly while the hands clutching a piece of white cloth held no warmth.

'There you be and a fresh baked scone to go with it.'

Callista's throat closed as a prettily flowered plate was set before her. All of this – she fought the rising tears – all of this wealth and comfort while her mother . . .

'Now don't let's 'ave you being shy.' The woman's smile beamed as she lowered her ample frame to a chair. 'There be plenty more where that come from.'

Plenty more! Callista swallowed hard. But only for those who already had plenty; what of the likes of the families of Trowes Court and of every other hard-pressed family where even the children worked themselves to a standstill to earn enough simply to keep them alive; where was their plenty?

'I hears there was a bit of a shemozzle up along of the Bullen this mornin', fella had a bump leaving that antique shop.'

Fingers stiff about the china cup, Callista's nerves quickened. News of any sort spread quickly in a town small as Wednesbury and on its travels gathered spice in the telling. This woman's tone said as much now; had her informant also told of the butcher's refusal to have a young woman scrub out his shop?

'Not so much a shemozzle,' she answered, lowering the cup, 'there was no aggravation. It was simply an accident and Mr Westley was gracious enough to see it as such.'

'Phineas Westley?' The woman eased her large frame, spreading it more evenly on the chair.

'That was the name he gave.'

'And comin' from the shop of Joseph Glaze! Then the package a wench knocked from his hand would 'ave something in it which cost more'n a few pennies.'

The woman had gossiped and now wormed for verification of the tale carried to her ears and would not give up until she was sure she had every last detail.

'The wench you speak of was me.' Leaving tea and scone untouched, Callista looked into the rotund face. 'I was the one collided with Mr Westley and the contents of the package was an Artemis.'

'A what?' The housekeeper's brows drew together in a puzzled frown.

'I did not see for myself but was told the package contained an Artemis, a small statue of the Greek goddess of that name.'

'A statue!' The tone held disappointment. 'Oh well, that can be easy replaced, one statue be like another I reckon.'

Not if it were carved by Phidias or Praxiteles, Lycippus or Michelangelo. Works by masters such as these could never be replaced. Callista smothered the reply which had so quickly jumped to her tongue, asking instead could the mistress be informed of the delivery of her gown, adding that due to her mother's ill health she was anxious to be home.

'Would be more acceptable for you to leave it with me, the

mistress won't take kind to bein' disturbed. You need 'ave no fears for it and you can be sure you will be notified as to when you can call for payment.'

Her mouth set in a determined line, Callista rose, meeting the other woman's surprised glance. She would not try to disguise the prime cause of her refusal; one look at her shabby clothes would be enough to decry it.

'I'm sorry,' she said tightly. 'As you can see well enough, payment for the work my mother has completed is needed now, not in a few days hence. I'm afraid I must insist I be taken to see Mrs Ramsey.'

Pushing to her feet the housekeeper smoothed her long brilliantly white apron with offended hands. 'I don't say I recommends it but if you insists then you insists, though I warns herself can be sharp of tongue when her words be ignored.'

Acacia Villa was imposing from the outside but the inside was more so. The gown once more in her hands, Callista followed the dark-skirted figure across a floor set with exquisite turquoise and blue tiles, couch and chairs of inlaid mahogany and upholstered in blue and cream Regency brocade standing against walls hung with gilt-framed paintings while at the centre a mahogany drum table stood proud on a wide central column before tapering into three carved ball-and-claw feet. How her father would have enjoyed looking, touching, exclaiming appreciation of each in turn.

'This be the drawing room.' The housekeeper had already halted before a highly polished door. 'You best wait while I tells the mistress you be 'ere.'

And be told I must call at a more convenient time! That was the message this woman would emerge with but it was one she could not accept. Determination settling solidly in her stomach Callista shook her head stepping quickly forward as the door was opened.

'I be sorry, mum . . . I told her—'

'Your housekeeper advised I call some other time, Mrs Ramsey.' Callista cut across the housekeeper's stammering apology. 'At any other time I would have been happy to do so but not today.'

Sat on an elegant tapestry-covered couch, the taffeta of her lilac-coloured dress spilling over its cabriole legs, Emma Ramsey turned sharply towards the two stood in the doorway.

'*Not* today!' She raised an eyebrow it had taken a steady hand to darken with pencil.

'No, ma'am.' Aware of more eyes turned her way, Callista felt a flicker of apprehension. 'I ask your pardon but my mother is not well and I would rather not leave her any more often than is absolutely necessary. That is why I must ask, please may I be given payment for the gown I deliver to you.'

'Oh, my new gown, then you are the daughter of Ruth Sanford.'

'Yes, ma'am.'

'Then I . . .'

'A new gown!' Emma Ramsey's visitor purred delightedly but the look she shot at her hostess was that of a tigress waiting to pounce. 'Really, Emma, my dear, you must let me see it.'

'But . . .'

'No, Emma, no buts; we are friends, aren't we? And do not friends share their pleasures with one another?' A waft of perfume followed the hand beckoning Callista.

'No!' A lace-trimmed handkerchief lifted to dab Emma Ramsey's thin nose. 'My housekeeper had best open it. We don't want dust on your hands, Sabine.'

It was well meant but brought a quiet tut from the housekeeper and a flush of anger to Callista's cheeks. Clenching her fingers, she waited until the gown had been draped over a matching couch and the housekeeper dismissed from the room.

'It is quite pretty.' Silk petticoats rustling beneath emerald cashmere, wide collar and tight cuffs caught beneath elbow-length bouffant sleeves threaded with sage and gold threadwork, Emma Ramsey's visitor crossed to where the blue silk spread like a tiny glittering lake over the couch. With a smile on her lips, she let her fingers stroke the soft material.

Emma had seen the smile. Was it one of disdain, was her fashionable visitor laughing up her expensive sleeve at a gown made by a local woman?

'Pretty.' She sniffed disparagingly. 'I suppose it may have been thought that twenty years ago but who wears that style any more? It's absolutely archaic.'

'The gown was made to your specific requirements, Mrs Ramsey, you drew the design yourself.'

'I drew a design!' Emma felt her visitor's eyes upon her. 'But the interpreting of it . . . this interpretation . . .' She glanced at the gown glistening in the light of the gasoliere. 'Is more the work of a fool than a seamstress.'

'My mother is an excellent dressmaker, her work is never less than of the highest standard!' Callista's reply burst across the room like a round of pistol shot, the anger behind it blazing with the strength of living fire.

'Emma, my dear, perhaps you should inspect—'

'I do not need to inspect the gown to see it is not what I gave instruction for! I cannot possibly accept that . . . that outmoded creation. You must see that, Sabine, and you know I would not possibly have chosen that material, it is so obviously cheap, and the stitchwork . . .' Rising to her feet Emma Ramsey grabbed the delicate fabric, thrusting the gown towards her visitor. 'Look for yourself and tell me if it is not positively ghastly.'

As she held the gown in her hand, Sabine Derry's expertly painted mouth held its smile. 'My dear,' she said, 'of course the gown is not of the standard of a fashion house but then you could hardly expect otherwise.'

It was there beneath the words: condescension! Emma felt her chest tighten. Sabine Derry thought her not wealthy enough to have her gowns made in some specialist establishment. The thought painting her cheeks with embarrassment, she snatched the gown, throwing it deliberately to the ground.

'I could at least expect the cloth I gave the woman to be the cloth which was used but this . . .' She ground a foot angrily into the silk. 'This is not the material I supplied and as for the design it bears no resemblance to what I drew.'

'But it does, Mrs Ramsey, the sketch you gave my mother is there with the wrapping; you can see the gown follows the design exactly.' Callista's protest was tinged with the worry beginning to trickle along her nerves. Emma Ramsey seemed bent upon refusing to accept the gown, but why? She had not found fault with any of the many she had commissioned from Ruth Sanford in the past.

'It follows the design exactly.' Emma Ramsey's voice was scathing. 'I have little doubt it does, but whose design – yours . . . your mother's, whichever, it is certainly not mine!'

Across the room the grey eyes of Sabine Derry gleamed as they met Callista's but in the same moment the look was veiled as the woman spoke.

'Obviously there has been some mistake. This gown must have been made for someone else and wrongly delivered to this house. We know, Emma dear, you are a woman of more refined taste, you cannot be held responsible if the finished garment is not what you designed, but this girl—'

'Is obviously trying to foist her mother's mistakes upon me!'

Emma turned her glare upon Callista. 'You take the silk I paid for, you take the design I myself drew and what happens? You exchange a costly cloth for cheap imitation, you find the design too complicated for your clumsy brain to follow and the result, this . . .' She stamped her foot on the gown spilled at her feet, twisting her shoe into the shimmering fabric. 'This disaster of a gown you try to pass off onto me. Well, my girl, in thinking to do that you have made an even greater mistake!'

How could anyone behave as this woman was behaving? Callista stared at the foot twisting the lovely silk. She was naming her mother a thief and a liar. Suddenly she felt more angry than she had ever felt in her life but it was fire bound in ice. Head high, she regarded the face, the pink of embarrassment now a dull red.

'Mrs Ramsey.' She spoke quietly, each word having the timbre of breaking ice. 'A moment ago you were spoken of as a woman of refined taste; with apologies to your visitor I have to tell you that is the biggest mistake of all. Taste is a quality you are sadly lacking.'

Emma Ramsey's darting eyes caught the veiled amusement on Sabine Derry's mouth before the woman turned away. It was not a smile but a sneer, the woman would let the whole town know what had gone on in this room, they would all be sniggering.

'What . . . !' She gasped, hurling a look of pure despising at Callista, 'What did you say?'

She should have quailed before that look, lost her courage and run, but instead Callista stood firm. 'I said how can you claim to be a woman of taste when you are so sadly lacking that quality.'

'How dare you!' Carmined lips thinned. 'How dare you speak to me that way you . . . you filthy little guttersnipe!'

'I dare because it is true.' Callista felt her nerves sing but she answered with unshaking calm. 'Not only do you have no concept of the quality contained in that gown, you have none regarding the quality of polite behaviour.'

Slumping to the couch, her cheeks flaring their anger, Emma Ramsey caught her breath in a loud gasp, her mouth hanging slightly open as Callista went on.

'In fact, Mrs Ramsey, any guttersnipe including myself would count themselves unfortunate indeed to possess manners the quality of your own; as for the gown I will inform my mother you find it unsuited to your . . . taste!'

Letting the last word rest on a withering note she bent, snatching the gown from beneath the woman's foot.

'Wait, Miss Sanford.' Emma's visitor turned as Callista straightened. 'Mrs Ramsey, I am sure, had no intention of speaking disparagingly of your mother or of yourself. She can have nothing but regard for a dressmaker whose services she has so regularly employed.'

On the couch Emma Ramsey fumed silently. The sneer was there again; Sabine Derry was taking great pleasure in driving home the fact that while she had her gowns made by an à la mode house Emma Ramsey did not.

'Emma.' Sabine turned her smile to the woman on the couch. 'You should not let your disappointment become anger. I am sure the woman did her best; pay her fee and have done.'

'Pay!' Emma spluttered. 'Pay for that rag, I'll do no such thing!'

Deeply red hair glistening in the overhead light, rouged cheeks a spot of reserved colour against a slightly pallid skin, Sabine Derry moved to pick up a small leather bag set aside on a chair. Opening it she drew out several coins, offering them to Callista with a smile.

'Then you must allow me to pay, my dear; we cannot allow you to return home with nothing.'

'No thank you,' Callista answered, not looking at the coins glinting on the outstretched palm. 'The work was not done for you, therefore no payment can be accepted from you.'

Turning then to look at the woman who for so many years had gowns made by her mother, Callista laid the dress beside her on the couch.

'As you well realise, Mrs Ramsey, but for reasons you refuse to acknowledge, this gown is made from the silk you supplied and the design adheres exactly to the specification you gave and the sketch you supplied, therefore it belongs to you. I wish you both good afternoon.'

She had not waited for the housekeeper to be summoned to show her from the room. Reaction trembling in every vein,

Callista hardly noticed the woman already standing beyond the door, face beaming as she looked at the shaking girl.

Reaching the kitchen the woman laughed. 'Eh, wench, I enjoyed that more'n a glass o' stout. Done my heart good it has hearin' you tell Emma Ramsey what you did. Ever since that there visitor of her'n took to callin' her ways have got more fancy and highfalutin' by the day; but you told her, wench, you told her good and proper. I only wish there had been more of her fancy friends in that room to have heard it!'

Her father would not have approved. Callista felt the first wave of regret for her outburst. He would have told her rudeness in one's self does not counteract rudeness in another. It was right, of course, but she had not given thought to right or wrong but only to her mother who had worked so long to make the gown that woman had walked on . . . a gown she now had no hope of getting paid for.

'You take this along 'ome with you, I be sure your mother will find a use for it.'

The housekeeper had bustled quickly about the roomy kitchen and now handed a basket across the large table. Half of her mind still locked upon the recent scene in the drawing room, Callista looked blankly at the round smiling face.

'It be nothing but a cut of ham and a few bits and pieces but your mother . . .'

'No thank you.' Her mind suddenly together, Callista glanced at the basket. 'It is a kindness on your part but my mother and I cannot accept what we have not earned.'

There had been food in that basket. Walking back towards the town Callista gave way to mounting dejection. What had made her do it, what had made her refuse that food? Not common sense, that would have seen her grab the basket with both hands, but instead she had left it standing on the table.

Pride! Tears pressed behind her eyes. Pride had been the spur . . . but pride would not feed her mother.

3

'The gown was stitched perfectly and the material was what Mrs Ramsey gave to you and she knew it, I could see by the look on her face she knew it. But it seemed she did not want the visitor to know who had made it, that must have been why she said the style was no longer in fashion, that the cloth was obviously cheap.' Callista's voice shook with feeling. 'It . . . it was as if she didn't care about me being humiliated; were it not that it would be letting anger cloud my judgement I might say she was a little afraid of what her visitor might have been thinking.'

Ruth Sanford had sat staring into the ashes of the dead fire while her daughter related the encounter but with the last vehement words she looked up sharply, her tired eyes bright with more than the fevered cough which racked her thin chest with almost every breath.

'This visitor.' She coughed into the slip of cloth. 'What . . . what did she look like?'

'Mother, please, you really must go to bed. It's far too cold for you—'

'Later.' Ruth interrupted here daughter's concern. 'I will go to bed soon, dear, but first tell me, what did Emma Ramsey's visitor look like?'

Taking the iron poker from the side of the fireplace Callista stirred the ashes, searching for any last glowing embers.

'I didn't get but one look at her face and by that time I was too angry to take note of her features, I can't recall . . .'

'Try, dear . . . try to remember.'

What difference did it make what Emma Ramsey's visitor had looked like? Her search for a few hot coals ending in failure Callista returned the poker to its accustomed position.

'You say you got only one look at her face?'

Puzzled by her mother's insistence, Callista turned. Why this interest, was it because the woman had advised Emma Ramsey to take delivery of the gown her mother had worked so hard making? If so where was the use of it? The refusal was made now and nothing could be done to reverse it.

'She had her back towards me almost all of the time I was in that drawing room but there was a moment . . .' Callista paused as memory showed the face in perfect detail. 'Just a quick moment. I told Mrs Ramsey she had no concept of good manners, the other woman turned to look at me, her face . . . her mouth smiled but her eyes . . . her eyes were veiled.'

'And what . . . what else did you see?'

She had not thought of it until now, the look which had been in that woman's eyes, a look that, recalling it, seemed almost a sneer.

'It . . . it's difficult to describe,' Callista answered. 'The woman's features were, so far as I remember, nothing extra-ordinary, except . . .' She stopped short, seeing now what her temper had prevented her seeing at the time: the eyes, cold, unblinking lizard eyes!

'Except?' Pressing the cloth to her lips, Ruth Sanford watched her daughter closely.

'Her face was . . . she . . . she was wearing rouge.' Callista searched for words which would be fair as well as accurate; she would not let her anger of an hour ago colour her judgement now. 'Her hair was deep copper-coloured and perfectly arranged, what I could see of it beneath a green feathered hat.'

'Not her clothing, Callista . . . her face, tell me of her face.'

Her mother had never questioned her so closely about anyone before. Callista's puzzlement deepened. Had there been the slightest reason to think it she might say what she saw on her mother's own face was fear.

'She had quite sharp features, a narrow nose and wide brow gave a hardness, but most arresting were the eyes, they are what I remember most clearly; they were deep-set and their colour . . .' She paused seeing again those piercing ice-filled eyes. 'Their colour was grey like a storm-filled sky yet at the same time they blazed with . . . I might almost say with hostility; but that is ridiculous, you need to know a person before you can say that of them and the woman and I had never seen each other before.'

'Her name . . . did the woman give her—'

A spasm of coughing rising from deep within Ruth's chest ended the question abruptly.

'Mrs Derry . . . now that is the end of it! You have to go to bed . . . please, Mother!'

She had tried to keep anxiety from her voice but the sight of crimson seeping into the cloth held to her mother's lips defied Callista's efforts. Helping her now up the narrow stairs to the small bedroom she felt the bones biting through the thin clothing. Although she would not admit to it her mother's 'cold on the chest' was getting worse. She needed good food, daily nourishment, but how was that to be obtained when every means of employment was snatched away? Yet somehow she must get food and coal to keep her mother warm, without it she might . . .

She would not think of that; could not think of it! Her mother's breath a visible white film on the cold air of the sparsely furnished bedroom; Callista felt the fingers of finality clutch her heart. She must take the one option left to her.

But even that could bring no relief before tomorrow. Callista stared at the pale face, the tired eyes closed in their circles of purple shadows, the fresh cloth already mottling with scarlet spots as it tried to stem the wet rattling cough. Tomorrow was not soon enough, her mother needed food and warmth now.

Tucking the one blanket around the shivering shoulders, Callista kissed the moist brow then quietly left the room.

'Be your mother feelin' better, wench?'

'A little.' Callista tried to smile. 'I think once the winter is done she will recover fully.'

Ruth Sanford would never recover. Opening the parcel placed on his counter Henry Glover kept his thoughts to himself. He had seen so many folk with coughs such as that woman suffered from, the gradual wasting of the body which no amount of medicine nor doctoring had effect on . . . no, Ruth Sanford would see no summer.

'We'll all feel chirpier with the comin' o' fine weather,' he answered, not meeting his customer's eyes. ''Tis the cold o' the wind gives everybody a touch o' the miseries; I knows my rheumatics be achin' summat awful.' The parcel fully opened, he took out the dove-grey jacket trimmed at the front and hem, neck and cuffs with a deeper grey band of soft fur with a line of amber cord frogging to either side. Watching it being shaken free of its folding, Callista wanted to snatch it back, to run with it back to her cupboard-sized room and hang it away out of sight; this was the coat her father had bought for her, his very last gift before . . .

'How much were you thinkin' of asking for this?'

'I . . . I thought perhaps five shillings.'

'Phew, wench!' The pawnbroker shook his head, the muddy light of a sputtering lamp failing to find any gleam among the grey hair. 'Y'might as well ask for the moon, like I told your mother when her pledged her promise ring.'

'My mother pawned her promise ring?'

'Y'dain't know, wench?' Inspecting the coat closely he heard the surprise behind the girl's question. 'Brought it in more than a month since, pledged it for ten shillin' and sixpence.'

Her mother had pawned her ring, the ring given to her on her promise to become Jason Sanford's wife, the one thing she had left of him.

'Like I told her then I 'ave to tell you the same, times be bad and folk don't 'ave the money to spare for to go buying rings nor jackets neither, not even ones so pretty as this be.' Twisting the coat this way and that, squinting at the seams in the sickly light, he pursed his lips. 'No, wench, times be bad. Should you not redeem your pledge . . .' He sucked a thin bottom lip inwards holding it beneath yellowed teeth. 'Mmm, should you not redeem it then I could be left with it on my 'ands, ain't much call in these parts forra fur-trimmed jacket.' The head shook once more as the coat was laid back on the counter.

He had to take it . . . Out of sight of the counter Callista's fingers curled tight into her palms. This was the very last chance of getting a meal and a fire for her mother.

'Please,' she almost sobbed, 'I . . . I have nothing else I could have brought.'

That was probably the truest words had been spoken in this shop for many a bright day! Henry Glover looked again at the coat draped across his counter. It was good quality cloth, pure mohair if he were not mistaken, and the fur . . . that had come from no rabbit, the whole thing was soft, the very best, and even second-hand worth every penny he had no intention of paying. The only question was how had Jason Sanford, a man without tuppence to bless himself with, come by such an expensive item? But it was a question need not worry him; this certainly was a pledge would not be redeemed no matter how little he offered nor would it be put up for sale here in Wednesbury. No, this would go to Birmingham; sales there were more profitable.

'I be takin' a risk lendin' money on a jacket such as you've brought in.' He lifted a corner of the cotton cloth the coat had been wrapped in. 'And times don't be suited . . .'

'Four shillings! Please, Mr Glover, I need the money!'

The wench was desperate. Henry Glover felt a twinge of pity

but it was rapidly exterminated. A man couldn't run a business like his on pity but try to cut too near the bone and the joint could be snatched from his table. Heeding his own caution he looked up, a smile showing dark patches at the base of yellow teeth.

'I knows y'mother be in poor health so though it be goin' against my best interest I'll let you 'ave the four shillin'.'

Writing name and number quickly on the white pawn ticket before his customer could change her mind he passed half to her with four silver coins, pinning the other half to the rewrapped parcel. Watching the thin figure draw a shawl about her shoulders then hurry from the shop Henry Glover glanced at the parcel still resting on his counter. This was one bundle that would not join the forest of others lining his shelves. Freeing the coat from its wrapping he held it to the fragile light, one finger stroking the soft fur. Yes, Brummajum was where he would sell this; there was many a whore in that town would be willing to trade a night's takings for a jacket like this one.

The smile still on his face, he carried it to the living room adjoining the back of the pawnshop.

Yes, a night's takings . . . and a free tumble for the man who sold it!

Outside the dimly lighted pawnbroker's shop, Callista breathed deeply, the smoke and soot heavy in the air preferable to the dank smell of decaying woodwork and the odour of damp bundles emanating from the far side of that counter.

Four shillings! She bit back the tears of disappointment. She had hoped for more but the risk of the man refusing to lend her any money at all had been too great for her to take.

Turning left she walked quickly, a shiver riding her veins as she came to St James's Street. It was there in that tall building with its pointed roofs, there in that school she had suffered so much misery.

I saw . . . I saw him there and I knew, I knew what he was doing . . .

The words seemed to scream from the shadowed street and with them Callista's head jerked with the remembered slap which had always accompanied each one. Of all the girls in her class she had been the only one to be treated that way, the only one that teacher had slapped. But why had she been punished so regularly? Callista drew the shawl tight about her head as if protecting it from the stinging blows of vicious fingers. What was the reason for that almost daily punishment? What had she done, and why were those same words hissed at her? It had been a long year trapped in that classroom.

Despite the tremble shaking her, Callista could not prevent herself from turning to look at the tall windows staring back at her from the rapidly darkening street. A year in which every day after lessons she would run to the church standing only yards from the school and pray God to take her from it. But He had not, nor had her torment ended with that year or the years following. Appointed monitor, she had been required to see the teacher of each class ensuring they had the equipment needed for next day's work before she could go home, and every after-noon had brought those slaps. The woman had been careful; the punishment had never been administered within sight or hearing of anyone either staff or pupil. And she, Callista, had never told of it . . . except to God.

Passing from the tall-windowed building, Callista's stare rested on the long-bodied church further along the street, last light of day slipping silently over grey stone, glinting weakly on the gilded clock face set in its square tower.

The heart of a child had been poured out there in that quiet interior and the sorrows of a young girl broken-hearted at the loss of her father. The exquisite stained glass had played its colours over her, sharing its beauty, but that was all heaven had granted. So why had she not told her parents of that teacher's behaviour, of the cruelty meted out to that same child?

The question had often reared in her mind as she had hidden

her childhood tears and even now on awakening from those nightmares: why? But she could not answer; she only knew now as her heart had told her so many years before, to speak of it would add to the distinct though quickly veiled unhappiness she sometimes caught reflected in her mother's eyes.

'Was you wantin' summat, wench?'

Lost in memories, Callista jumped at the sound.

'Yes.' She brought her glance to the man standing watching her from the opposite corner, a bloodstained apron reaching to the toes of worn boots.

'I was hoping perhaps . . .'

'For tuppence worth o' bones?' The man's rapid glance took in the drawn face beneath the tightly wrapped shawl, the clothes even more worn than his own. 'Well, if it's bones you be wantin' you be in luck, the abattoir took delivery of several pigs this mornin' and the carcasses 'ave been cut and boned naught but 'alf an 'our ago so they be fresh . . . wait you there, wench, and I'll fetch you out a couple o' pennorth.'

Returning a few minutes later the man shoved a newspaper-wrapped package into Callista's hands, his head shaking at the offer of one of her precious coins. 'Tek 'em,' he grinned, 'I reckons old 'Ollingworth won't miss what he don't 'ave the knowin' of.'

It was not honest. Conscience pricking, Callista hurried on along Holyhead Road. When she had the money to spare she would repay the owner of the abattoir but right now she needed every penny she had.

Back at home she checked on her mother, a sigh of relief escaping her throat when she saw she was sleeping. Returning downstairs she glanced at the ashes of the dead fire; she could not cook on that but no jagger would deliver coal at this time of an evening. But there was a way she might get sufficient for a fire tonight. Not waiting to grab her shawl from behind the stairs door she ran from the house, the worn-through soles of her side-button boots rapping sharply on the blue brick setts as she raced across Portway Road and on into Chapel Street.

Called to the door by his pregnant wife a man eyed Callista before answering, 'Ar, I 'ave coal for the sellin', be ninepence a bag or a shillin' an' fourpence should you be buyin' the two.'

'Thank you.' Breathing hard from her running, cold air biting at her lungs, Callista felt in her skirt pocket for the coins she had got from the pawnbroker's.

'You be from them 'ouses along of Trowes Court, it be there I've seen you.' The woman rested a hand on her swollen stomach, smiling as Callista nodded. 'Your mother be named Ruth?'

Again Callista nodded.

'I would 'ave gambled as much,' the woman answered, pleased with her detecting, 'it were her as 'elped me two month back when this one decided it were time to turn.' She patted the lump hardly disguised by a grubby apron. 'In the street I was when it 'appened, fair 'ad me faintin' away so it did; but your mother 'elped me into her own 'ouse and give me a cup o' tea then med me rest 'til I was in me proper senses agen. You remember, Bert,' she glanced at the man bringing a sack of coal from the brew-house, 'I told you, didn't I . . . told you how that woman took me in when I 'ad that turn up along the street, well this be her daughter.'

'I be beholden.' Letting the sack rest on the ground the man touched a blackened finger to an equally blackened cap.

'An' that don't be all you be, Bert Garbett!' his wife piped sharply. 'You be carryin' that there coal to Trowes Court!'

Thank goodness the man had coal to spare. Callista peeled vegetables she had fetched after paying for the two bags of coal. Her mother had related the story his pregnant wife had told proudly. Her husband had an understanding with the 'cutmen'. In return for a jug or two of her home-brewed ale they 'acciden-tally' dropped several lumps of coal onto the towpath whenever their narrow boat passed this stretch of the canal and every Sunday afternoon Bert took his handcart and collected it. It be fair trade, the woman had added defensively, an' it be good quality coal, my Bert wouldn't stand for havin' any rubbish pushed onto him, and he sells at less than the jaggers ask for a bag.

Both of those claims were true. Callista felt the heat of the fire warm on her body as she added diced carrot and parsnip to the pork bones and barley simmering in the pot. But as for the 'fair trade'! That she was not so sure of. Was it not the same as being given meat bones; the coal did not belong to those bargees any more than the pigs' bones belonged to the man who had refused the tuppence in payment for them. The twinge of guilt she had experienced outside of that abattoir returned. Adding salt and pepper to the bubbling pot, Callista sighed. How many more debts would she be responsible for and how would she ever be able to repay them?

A sharp knock on the street door echoed in the silence of the house as she stared into the coals gleaming red beneath the cooking pot. There was only one way, and the time to take it was now.

4

The knock sounded again, sharp and authoritative, demanding entry. Authoritative! Callista turned from her cooking. That could be a description of the person whose knock she had come to recognise . . . and to dread. There was nothing gentle about that rap to the door as there was none about Oswin Slade, nothing considerate, certainly nothing loving . . . and nothing about him to love . . . yet she had to marry him.

Slowly, every part of her wishing she could call to him to go away, she opened the door.

Inside the room Oswin Slade wore a slightly irritated look. This was not at all what he had expected.

'Good evening, Callista. Your mother is well, I hope.'

Even the voice had no trace of gentleness. Going to stand at the further side of the table, seeking to put space between herself and the man who was glancing at the sparse furniture while making no effort to disguise his distaste, Callista answered, 'Mother is resting.'

Resting! Oswin flicked open the book he carried. Ruth Sanford 'rested' more and more often, which could only mean the illness she was so obviously suffering from was getting worse. All to the good – he thumbed several pages; he did not want the expense of keeping a mother-in-law for any length of time.

'You will give her my regards.'

It sounded more of an order than a request. Callista nodded, watching a thick finger run slowly down the chosen page. But then everything was an order when spoken by Oswin, his whole manner was – how could she be kind – commanding? No, that gave an entirely false impression, as did imperious; there was only one description she could say in truth fitted the man standing across from her: pompous. It had to be admitted, Oswin Slade was a pompous man.

'Have you spoken with her concerning my offer?'

His offer! Something inside of Callista shrivelled. Not a protest at the choice of word, just a quiet dying. It was a proposal of marriage he had made but in his eyes it was a project . . . no word of tenderness, of wanting to spend the rest of his life with her; to Oswin Slade marriage was a contract of business, not of love. She watched him now, one finger still moving slowly, methodically, over the page like some pale bloated caterpillar. Marriage to him would mean no more worry over how to earn money to pay the rent . . . but payment would still be called for. Her glance moving to the jowled face which already showed a tendency to fat, to the lips subjected now to the caress of a moist tongue, her own mouth dried. Those hands would touch her, those lips close wetly over her own; Oswin Slade would not take payment in coin, he would take her body!

She had not allowed herself to think of that part of it, closing her mind each time any such thought began, but now it flooded into her brain. She would be forced to lie with him, to subject herself to the demands the past weeks had shown in his eyes, in the touch of his hand.

The admitted reality bringing a sickness to her throat, Callista's words tumbled out. 'I . . . I have not spoken with my mother.'

'But I told you to do so!'

It was snapped out. An order given to an underling. A taste of her life in the future.

'I am aware of what you told me, Oswin.' At her back the quiet hiss of simmering broth could well have been a hiss of breath coming between lips curled back as anger flashed across that heavy face.

'Then why did you not obey me?'

Again the authority, the demand so apparent in his rap to a door, in his every mode of speech and action. Life would be no partnership with this man, no sharing; it would be give and take with Oswin Slade doing all of the taking.

It would serve only to goad the irritation already so plain in the grip clutching the pencil but Callista could not resist voicing the words. Violet eyes held steady on ones which nature had attempted to colour blue but failed, leaving them instead a washed-out semblance, a pale wintry hint of a sky lost to winter.

'Obey, Oswin?'

'Of course obey!' The quiet irony lost on him, Oswin Slade stabbed the point of the pencil viciously against the book, anger mounting red to his cheeks at the snap of lead.

'I did not understand . . .'

'Understand . . . understand!' Thrusting the broken pencil into the top pocket of his jacket Oswin rolled a fresh one between podgy fingers. 'It was simple enough for a child to understand! "You will speak to your mother," was what I said; surely even you can grasp the meaning of that!'

'It was not the meaning eluded me, simply the fact of your expecting to be obeyed.'

'Of course I expect to be obeyed. Once we are married that is exactly what I will expect.'

'But we will not be married.'

It was the astounded silence which followed a thunderbolt. For a few seconds Oswin Slade's colourless eyes stared blankly at Callista, then as if only just registering her words, a frown drawing brows together, he snapped, 'What was that you said?'

What had she said? Hands folded together across her front, Callista felt a stab of apprehension. Marriage to Oswin would mean warmth and food for her mother; there would be no more walking the streets begging employment for herself. It was not too late, she could retract her words, change them, add to them until it seemed she had spoken merely a part of what she had intended to say. Marriage would mean security . . . marriage to Oswin Slade would mean misery! From the room above the sound of coughing came harsh to her ears and Callista drew a long breath. There was only one choice she could make.

'She is lovely. The nose, the mouth, the lift of the head, the line of the body, everything about her speaks of a quiet, compelling beauty.'

'Yes, she is beautiful.' Phineas Westley nodded agreement but his answer did not allude to the figurine held in the other man's hands but to the picture arisen in his mind. The figure of a young woman whose raven-black hair was drawn back from a pale heart-shaped face out of which gleamed eyes of the most bewitching violet. Her features were shaped as perfectly as was this statue's, the poise of her head and body every bit as regal. Her father had called her his water nymph and maybe as a child that description could have passed as accurate, but now in the first bloom of womanhood Callista Sanford was best described as a Helen, a woman whose beauty challenged the gods themselves.

'Where did you find her?'

'Find?'

'Yes, find. Really, Phineas, I don't think you have heard a word I've said!'

'You said she was lovely and I agreed.'

'True . . . but to a description I feel I did not make.'

Taking a silk handkerchief from his pocket Phineas Westley wiped his gold-rimmed spectacles, using the moment to avoid meeting eyes which had ever been shrewd enough to see more than was held in the hands.

'So tell me what you were looking at in your mind.' His companion smiled. 'Was it perhaps an Aphrodite? Or maybe it was not a woman at all but a man. Have you found some wonderful Heracles or maybe even an excellent Apollo?'

'Neither.' Replacing the spectacles on his nose Phineas met the enquiring, slightly teasing look. 'I was merely daydreaming . . . you must allow an old man his dreams, Michael.'

'If they are dreams such as the one I am holding now then I would not make you forgo them, but at least tell me where you found her.'

'It was not I who found the Artemis, praise for that must go to Joseph Glaze.'

Standing the figurine carefully on the table the younger man nodded. 'An expert indeed but is he not also a collector?'

'What you mean, Michael, is why does a man so in love with antiques as is Joseph Glaze allow such an exquisite object as this to pass through his hands? The answer, my boy, is business. Were Glaze to keep for himself every piece he comes across he would soon have a healthy collection but a dead business. The man, fortunately for myself, has to make a living and so the Artemis comes to me.'

'No doubt to Joseph's chagrin.'

'Very nearly to his advantage, Michael, in the way of profit I mean.'

Michael Farron's blue eyes gleamed sapphire in the light of a crystal-drop gasoliere, his smile echoing their interest. 'Joseph Glaze's advantage. Therein lies a story unless I am sadly mistaken.'

Rising to his feet Phineas took the marble figurine, holding it several seconds before replacing it in a glass-fronted cabinet. 'You are not mistaken.' He smiled. 'Let's go into dinner and I'll tell you all about my little encounter.'

'The girl sounds to have been well educated,' Michael Farron said as Phineas's recounting of his collision with Callista ended, 'but why so poorly dressed?'

'There are some things a gentleman does not ask and questions involving a lady's attire is one of them. You should know that, Michael.'

'Of course . . . I did not mean . . . I was not intending to imply . . .'

'You always did travel a mile before taking a step.' The older man laughed, a rich throaty laugh. 'But I know what you mean and in fairness I have to confess I myself have wondered how it is a young woman so obviously tutored and well mannered should be in the straits Callista Sanford appeared to be in.'

'Did the girl give no clue?'

'She said her father did not read, yet only a moment before, when I asked how she came by her knowledge of mythology, she answered it was her father. But now I think of it she did not say that in so many words, she broke off her sentence before . . .'

'Now who is travelling a mile before taking a step?'

'You are right, my boy.' Phineas's eyes twinkled. 'It seems I've got the horse and the cart mixed up, Callista did not actually say her father was responsible for her own erudition, but nevertheless I find myself intrigued. I would very much like to meet and talk with the man.'

Watching the man he had loved and respected from his earliest years, Michael Farron smiled. His mother's brother had annoyed his own parents by preferring the ancient to the new, the past to the present. He should take interest in that which made money rather than in something which swallowed so much of it and gave nothing in return. Yet Phineas had proved his worth while still retaining his passion. Typhoid had wiped out his family leaving only his sister's son and Phineas Westley had taken him in, rearing him with the full knowledge they were uncle and nephew but loving him as well as any parent could; and the family business? That too had prospered and grown under this man's hand.

Accepting the glass held out to him he glanced into the amber depths. 'It could well be her father was responsible for her learning.'

'Oh?' Phineas took his drink to a wing-backed chair, easing himself comfortably into its depths. 'What makes you think that?'

'The name,' Michael answered. 'You did say the girl called herself Callista, did you not?'

'Delightful, isn't it?'

Was that all his uncle found delightful about the young woman who had seemingly accidentally collided with him in the street or was there something more, something which had taken an old man's fancy . . . something Phineas had not disclosed?

'It is not an unpleasant name though you must admit it is certainly different for . . . for an area like Wednesbury. You might even say it was carefully chosen!'

Looking over the rim of his glass Phineas Westley surveyed the face which had all the hallmarks of his sister. Patrician looks, he would call the straight slender nose and well-cut mouth, the finely arched brows curving over eyes of brilliant blue. Yes, his sister had been a fine-looking woman and her son was a fine-looking man and like her he too showed caution in his characterisation of others, but now this hesitation in choosing his words illustrated clearly his distrust of the girl.

'You could say that indeed.' Phineas sipped his brandy.

Callista! Repeating the name to himself Michael grudgingly admitted he thought it not at all unpleasant, but had it been truly the girl's given name or was it one deliberately contrived to impress an old man devoted to classical mythology? Lifting his glance from the glass he looked into the grey eyes watching him intently.

'Callista,' he said aloud, 'is that not a derivation of the name of one of your beloved Greek goddesses?'

'Of Callisto, companion of the divine Artemis.'

'Ah!' Michael nodded, recalling the stories he had heard so often. 'Callisto, the pretty wood nymph who caught the roving eye of Zeus and by whom she had a son causing his wife Hera to strike in a fit of jealousy which had the nymph changed into a bear.'

'Hera, the queen of the gods.' Phineas smiled. 'But no less a woman and as many have learned to their detriment there is no fury like that of a woman scorned.'

And no man more foolish than one taken in by a young woman's artifice! Phineas Westley was an intelligent man but would that be enough to protect him from a scheming woman? Michael looked again into his glass as the older man continued.

'But our pretty nymph was not abandoned completely by her lover nor do the stories make it certain it was his wife's action had her changed into a bear or whether it was Zeus himself protecting her from the anger of his queen; we are told that Callisto was shot by Artemis in the woods and in compassion Zeus set her among the stars as the She-Bear.'

And where will you place your wood nymph, what will her reward be, money . . . marriage . . . Was that this modern Callisto's aim? Marriage to a wealthy man regardless of love? That aim too was as cruel as the arrow of his uncle's goddess of the hunt. But this was no myth. Michael Farron twisted the glass held between tight fingers. And Callista Sanford was no immortal; she might think Phineas Westley a man she could easily dupe but she would learn his nephew was no man to fool with!

It had not been too late! Alone in the small room, the only sounds those of the simmering pot and tick of the clock on the mantel, Callista gave way to the shudder she had suppressed as Oswin Slade had pressed his lips to her mouth. It had not been a tender kiss, the kiss of a man in love, but a demanding, dictatorial suppressive kiss of a man set upon showing domination. And his touch! She shuddered again, eyes closed tight against the memory. Those thick hands had caught at her, holding her close to his body, a body she had felt pulsing through her thin skirts.

The revulsion of it had been too much and she had pushed free only to hear him laugh, a hoarse gasping sound catching in his throat. 'I can wait.' His eyes had gleamed as he had said those words. 'I can wait, but once the banns are called we will be married and then the waiting will be over!'

Like his kiss the words had held no love but the dark shadow of threat. Once she became Mrs Oswin Slade she would be his property to do with as he would, to treat in any way which pleased him.

She could have told him . . . told him what she felt in her heart, the truth of her feelings for him. She had been almost there, had said, 'We will not be married'; if only she had stood by that one simple statement, had let the words stand as she had spoken them. But she had not! A sob trembling on a mouth she had rubbed sore immediately on closing the door behind the heavy dark-suited figure, she opened her eyes. She had not!

He had demanded to be told what she meant by those words. Callista stared at the two bronze coins lying in the centre of the table. That had been the moment she should have been strong, the moment to repeat her statement, but the sound of her mother's terrible coughing had robbed her of that strength and she had forced herself to apologise, tell him what she meant to say had been, 'We will not be married for a while, it will take time for me to become accustomed to your ways.'

His smile had been cunning, his eyes vulpine. Callista reached for a shallow basin, spooning broth into it. The tip of his tongue had flicked across his flabby lips like a snake's, scenting its prey, and it had taken every atom of her will power not to shout her dislike of him. But to have done that . . . to do it even now would deprive her mother of any chance of health.

'Why?' The sob on her lips became a soft tortured cry none could hear but herself. 'Why did it happen . . . what is it which so annoyed the Fates?'

Placing the basin on a plate she set a spoon beside it then

reaching to the line of string fastened wall to wall above the fire-place took down a piece of clean cloth.

They will not tell you, Callista. It seemed her father's voice whispered in her mind. *The Fates are jealous of their secrets, they keep them hidden.*

As she must keep her own hidden! Draping the cloth over her arm she picked up the plate and basin, walking with them up the narrow stairs. No one must ever learn the secret in her heart. The fact that she held only contempt and dislike for the man she would soon marry must remain forever locked away.

5

'Your mother be bad, wench, her be needin' of a doctor.'

'I know that, Mrs Povey, but I have no money to pay.'

'That be the same wi' everybody in Trowes Court, all works our fingers to the bone but finishes up no better off than paupers.' Ada Povey sniffed loudly. 'There be nowt fair to life in this world!'

It had not been fair to her mother. Callista's thoughts flew to the woman lying upstairs. She was thin to the point of shadow, her face pale as marble, the fine lines of veins showing through the papery skin. But she made no complaint, asked for nothing while each time her daughter entered the bedroom her weary eyes gleamed their love.

'You could go to the Parish.' Ada Povey glanced at the empty fireplace. 'They'll send the doctor.'

'I asked Mother could I do that but she would not hear of it, she said we would accept no charity.'

Ada Povey's head nodded slowly. 'An' that be summat else the folk of Trowes Court 'olds in common! They asks for nobody's charity; but atwixt you and me wench I sees precious little other you can do. You've said y'self you've traipsed the town asking for work while findin' none.'

It was true. Callista drew her shawl closer against cold still chilling every bone. She had spent most of each day walking the streets seeking employment, returning every couple of hours to assure herself of her mother's comfort then resuming the search until late evening. But what comfort did her returning give her mother? She could not put words on a plate, a smile could not constitute a meal or place coals on a fire.

'Look, wench, I knows well how your mother feels about Parish charity same as I knows it will do more harm than it'll do good aforcin' of her to take it, but at the same time her be a needing of a linctus to ease that chest of her'n.' Ada lifted one corner of a dark apron pocked with the tiny burn marks of flying sparks coming from the hammering of hand-forged nails, wiping her nose on it. 'Look,' she said again, letting the apron fall into place, 'I've been meanin' to put this to you for some days since. There be a woman I knows. Me and the others we goes to see her when . . . when we be up the spout.'

'Up the spout?' Callista frowned enquiringly.

'Ar, you knows, wench, when we've took a tumble . . . when we've gone and got with another babby!' The last came on a note of exasperation followed at once by one more shake of the head. 'They needs keepin' do babbies and Trowes Court already has all it can feed. Poverty can do more than bring tears, wench, it brings starvation, I knows 'cos I've seen it on more'n one little face, every women in Trowes Court has, and not wanting to see more of the same be often the reason we visits with Eulalie Ulmar.'

'But what can this have to do with my mother and me?' Callista blushed deeply. 'We . . . we are neither of us pregnant.'

'Tcha!' Ada Povey's exasperation sounded afresh. 'I knows that wench, I can spot a babby in the belly afore a wench sees the first signs for 'erself! But I didn't go saying it were for just that one reason alone women goes to see Eulalie. The woman be skilled with herbs and liberal with kindness, her don't ask for what her sees a woman don't 'ave; but afore you cries "charity" let me tell you there be ways of making payment without the using o' coin, ways such as the mendin' of a roof or a bucket, the cobbling of a shoe or a pennorth of shag tobacco.'

'But I can't mend roofs or buckets nor do I have a penny for tobacco!'

'That don't go to say as you never will 'ave!' Ada retorted. ''Aven't I said the woman be liberal with kindness, her won't turn nobody away 'cos they comes with no payment in their 'ands and no more will her turn you away. Go see her, Callista wench, could be her will 'ave the means of easin' your mother, you can but try.'

She would do anything to help her mother get well, even go so far as to marry a man she did not love . . . what was paying a visit to a herbal woman compared to that? Smiling agreement Callista asked, 'Will you tell me where this woman lives, Mrs Povey?'

'I'll do more'n that.' Ada Povey beamed. 'I'll take you along of her meself . . . we'll go tonight.'

The half-crown he had taken in rent for that house was likely the last money the Sanfords had. Oswin Slade watched an auburn-haired woman run a swift finger over the column of pencilled figures he had marked in his collecting book. He had not expected Callista would have been able to pay on that last call yet she had handed the two shillings and one sixpence to him without batting an eyelid and there had been fire in the grate with a pot of tempting broth bubbling over it. So where had she got her money from?

'Number six Hobbins Street has not paid . . . this is the second time!'

Oswin returned rapidly to the moment as a finger tapped sharply against the page. The woman's head bobbed dartingly. Oswin swallowed. She looked like a blood-spattered crow pecking the flesh from some hapless creature.

'No.' He cleared his throat, nervous of what would come next. 'No . . . they said their eldest was poorly and hadn't worked . . .'

'Eldest, youngest, what do I care if their brat is unwell! Perhaps if a few of their brood died so they did not have the cost of keeping them then they could pay their rent. I tell you, Slade, Mr Derry is not going to be pleased . . . *I* am not pleased!'

'I warned them . . .'

'*You* warned them!' The bobbing head stilled but eyes grey and cold as frozen mud raked cuttingly across the nervous face. '*You* warned them . . . now I warn you, Slade, one more week with an incomplete collection . . . you allow just one more rent to go unpaid and you will be standing the line with the rest of the unemployed. Mr Derry does not pay wages for a job he considers unsuitably done and this . . .' The finger tapped the book again. 'He will most certainly view as unsuitable. You *do* understand, Slade?'

He understood. Leaving Hill House, Oswin stood breathing deeply. That bitch of a woman treated him like dirt! She blamed him when a family failed to pay their weekly rent . . . went over his figures close enough to lift them from the page. And the takings, Lord, how she counted those takings, handling each coin reverently as a priest would the Holy Sacrament. But then money was the god of the master of Derry coal mines and his wife a most devoted acolyte.

Money! Oswin stared across the sweep of the hill to where two church spires rose almost side by side then out across the spread of the smoke-hazed town, winding wheels of collieries ringing it like a necklace. Money was power and he wanted both, deserved both. He had not spent the years of his boyhood kicking a tin can about the streets or swimming in the canal like the others; his time had been given to numbers, adding, multiplying, dividing but always numbers until he could handle them with closed eyes. They had already provided him with a house of his own, small, yes, but then from little acorns mighty oaks do grow and Oswin Slade would be an oak. Edwin Derry's wife could sift the figures he had recorded, go over them again and again before penning them into her own ledgers, enjoy the satisfaction of seeing their total but what she would never see was what was kept for himself . . . the tuppence here and sixpence there, increases he placed upon those rents, money which went into the pocket of Oswin Slade, money which accumulated steadily.

Self-satisfaction a balm, he smiled inwardly. Some day he would have his own coal mine, his own string of houses tenants would need pay heavily for . . . and his own fine red-brick house. One day – soon – Oswin Slade would be a name to reckon with in Wednesbury.

She could not go to that woman empty-handed, ask for her medicines yet pay nothing for them. Sitting beside her mother's bed Callista thought over Ada Povey's offer to take her to the herb woman. Was it the right thing to do . . . would it be the right thing not to do? Should she tell Mrs Povey she had changed her mind, that she would ask instead for the Parish doctor to call? But requests to the Parish took time. 'The Board had to consider, they must enquire into the circumstances of such requests.' That had been the answer given to another family in Trowes Court when the father had suffered arms and a leg badly injured in an accident at the mine where he dug for coal and, while they considered, infection had set in claiming the man's life. Looking at the shadow-circled eyes closed in fitful sleep Callista knew time was an option she could not afford. She must go with Ada Povey.

At the other side of the bed the embers of a small fire settled deeper into their own grey ash. Tomorrow would see the last of the coal she had bought. Why bother with visiting the herb woman? Callista let the sob fall quietly from her lips, dropping her head into her hands. Why bother about medicine when she could not feed her mother or keep her warm, why not just let it all go the way it would in the end?

'Callista, Callista child, don't cry.'

'I . . . I wasn't crying, Mother.' Lifting her head Callista brushed her eyes with a finger.

'Nor must you speak an untruth even when it is kindly meant. Your father taught that lying was not a quality to be admired, especially not in a wood nymph.'

It had been so long since she had been called that, so long since her father had left them. The pain of it rising now like a living thing inside her Callista caught at the wasted hand, pressing it to her cheek.

'Why, Mother?' she whispered brokenly. 'Why did it happen, why did my father take his own life?'

There had been many times in the long years of widowhood when she had known this question must be answered yet each time she had put if off; but now, looking at the pale unhappy face of the daughter she cherished, Ruth Sanford realised it could be put off no longer. She had never spoken of suicide, telling her daughter only that her father had died. But others in Trowes Court had spoken of it. On the day of the funeral they had gathered in their groups, women holding babies on their hips or infants in their arms, while one hand covered the eyes of older children trying to keep them from seeing the spectacle of a coffin being passed from a window down a ladder to ground level, then carried not through a gate but over the wall to the waiting hand-cart and taken to be laid beyond the boundary of sanctified ground. Such had been the burying of Jason Sanford . . . a man guilty only of falling in love.

'He did not intend to hurt you, my love.' Ruth spoke quietly. 'He did not want to hurt either of us.'

'Then why?'

There was pain and heartache in that question, the same pain and heartache she had felt whenever it arose in her own heart. Ruth touched the shining black hair.

'I cannot expect you will understand,' she said, 'and will not blame you but I believe your father ended his life so we could live ours in peace. It began long before you were born. Jason and I met at the Spring Fair; he was handsome with hair and eyes the same colour as your own and when he smiled it seemed you saw a glimpse of heaven. We spent the rest of that evening just walking about the fairground though I heard and saw nothing other than the tall figure walking beside me. Over the weeks . . .' A cough rattling up from her lungs took the words from her mouth and the hand stroking the ebony hair fell to rest on the sheets.

'No more, Mother . . .'

'No!' Eyes fever-bright, Ruth fought for breath. 'No, it . . . it must be told now. We should not have met again, I think deep down we both knew that; but something drew us to each other, something too strong to be denied. It was wrong, wrong to love each other. I tried . . . I tried to stop when Jason told me . . .'

The terrible cough rising again had Callista reach for the glass of water beside the bed. 'Please,' she said as her mother sipped, 'please rest now, I don't need to hear any more.' But even as the glass was returned to the table the weak voice was speaking again.

'Your father told me . . . he . . . he was engaged to be married. I felt as if my world had shattered into a thousand tiny pieces; I ran from him keeping to the house where I was in service, not stepping beyond its doors. My days were a blur and my nights long stretches of heartbreak. Then two weeks later I was sent to fetch cottons from the town and on my return found Jason stood at the gates. He had been there every evening since our parting, he looked so . . . so drawn and tired but when he took me in his arms we both felt life return to our hearts. It was then we knew we could not live without each other. It was decided he would tell his fiancée, ask her forgiveness and we would be married. But it was not so easy as he had made it seem. Julia Montroy would not release him from his pledge; she said she would see to it he lost his position as private tutor. If that happened he would be without a penny so we continued as before except our love deepened with the weeks until each separation became a torment.

'Then it was I discovered I was pregnant. It was like some

terrible nightmare and I was caught in the middle of it. I had to wait a week before my free afternoon when I could see Jason and all of that time I prayed a miracle would happen, that I was mistaken in counting the days since my last monthly, but I was not. I could not look into his face when at last I told him but that wonderful laugh broke out and he swept me into his arms. This was our miracle, he said, this would set us free; on my next afternoon off I must bring the few belongings I had and leave Willenhall. We would be married and find a home somewhere where Julia Montroy's spite could not reach us.

'And that was how it was. The boy he had tutored was to go to Eton at the beginning of the next term. It coincided well with Jason's leaving his position and he was given an excellent reference. We came here to live in Wednesbury where he secured a place as tutor to the son of James Adams, a coach axle manufacturer. For seven years all went well; the house we rented at the foot of the steps leading to St Bartholomew's was small but cosy and we were happy. In the evenings your father would take pleasure in sharing his beloved books with you, telling you stories of gods and heroes, then at weekends we would walk in the park or picnic in the cornfields which border the town and he would laugh when each time you asked to hear again the story of Demeter and her daughter Persephone . . .'

She had loved that story. Deep inside Callista smiled. Her child's heart would break at the sadness of a mother weeping for a lost daughter, then pound at the relating of the girl's capture by Hades, the powerful god of the underworld. Her father had made it all seem so real.

'. . . the classics were his passion . . .'

Recalled by that quiet laboured voice Callista allowed the picture to fade back into the wells of memory as her mother continued.

'But you were his delight, his own little wood nymph. Then of a sudden things began to change. The smile was no longer in his eyes, the laughter not so quick to his lips. He became quiet, withdrawn into himself. His books lay untouched and he was no longer so ready with a story. I asked what was wrong, begged him to tell me, but it was no use. Was it that he had found someone else, was he wanting to leave us as he had Julia Montroy? The thought dominated my mind night and day until I thought I would go mad. After weeks of torment I found the courage to tell him if what I feared was true then he was free to go, he must not let us stand in the way of his own happiness. I remember that look that came to his face, the love in his voice as he held me. We were his happiness, he said, his wife and daughter were the breath and blood of his body, they were his very soul . . .'

Tears sparkled along lashes resting on pallid cheeks found an echo in Callista. Her mother had suffered so much, the death of a husband dearly loved, the struggle to rear a child with help from no one; she had worked herself to a standstill and for what?

'Then no more than a day later he was removed from his post at Hollies House. No explanation was given other than he was no longer required. He was like a man destroyed.' Ruth Sanford's eyes opened but it seemed they watched some scene Callista could not see, her words no more than a whisper. 'For weeks he was without employment, each letter he wrote bringing the same reply . . . it was felt the position was not quite suitable. But at last he secured a post as teacher at St Bartholomew's School for boys and gradually the smile and laughter returned and we were happy again. The bad time was ended, only . . .' A cough rattling in her chest, Ruth paused but would not be silenced. 'Only it was not ended. Almost a year later it returned, a perfect copy of all that had gone before. Your father's position as teacher was withdrawn and he was dismissed with no reason or reference given.'

'But why, what had he done?'

Turning her glance to her daughter, Ruth's eyes glistened their sadness. 'We asked ourselves that question, Callista, but we could find no answer. He wrote letter upon letter seeking a teaching position but to no avail. It seemed the world had turned its back. We had to leave the home we had built together and come here to Trowes Court and Jason . . . Jason took the only job offered him, he went to work at the steel foundry. I knew he hated it and my heart ached for him, but we had to live. He never complained but his eyes told their own story. His heart too was aching. But the months passed and I thought my prayers for his happiness to return were being answered as I watched him with you, teaching you, explaining things to you.

'Then once more my hopes were dashed. Oh, he was not dismissed from his employment, but I knew something was not right, I had learned to read the signs. I saw them become ever clearer but still he would not say their cause and all I could do was pray. I watched him all of those last few years, watched him become even more depressed and then one awful day they brought him home. The men with him told me he did it knowingly. They said he knew what he was doing.' A sob adding to the cough shaking her thin frame she dragged at the cold air, sucking it into gurgling lungs. She held the cloth to her lips with one hand while the other pushed weakly at Callista's as she tried to cover the frail shoulders. 'Now child . . .' she breathed, 'I have to tell you now. The men, they said your father turned away from them, walked some distance beside the railway line which ran through the foundry yard; then when he reached a spot some distance away he stopped walking. They said he watched the engine pulling wagons of ore behind it, watched it coming towards him. Then he stepped between the rails and stood quite still in the path of the moving engine. The driver sounded his whistle and the men began to run but they were too late, as the driver applied his brakes Jason . . . Jason walked straight into the engine. I . . . I could not believe . . . for months afterwards I tried to understand . . .'

A fresh spasm claiming the thin body Callista felt her own

heart twist. Her mother had suffered so much, been hurt so deeply.

'I . . . I lay at night in the bed we had shared.' The cough-racked words came so quietly Callista had to kneel to catch them. 'I tried to find the reason, thought of those men and the words they said as they laid the board with my husband's body across two chairs; it was as if something drove him to do it, to throw himself beneath that engine. If that was true then . . . then it was something he kept from me.'

Strength almost gone, Ruth's eyes closed. What was her mother telling her? Callista remained perfectly still. Was she saying her husband was driven to take his own life, because he saw death as the only way out of a misery so terrible to bear?

Watching the pale face, its dark-circled eyes still closed, she could not hold back the sob thick in her throat. Her mother was the gentlest, kindest woman; why . . . why had she been given so much unhappiness!

'No, my dearest . . .' Purpled lids lifting, Ruth Sanford smiled weakly at the words unwittingly whispered aloud. 'You could ask why was I given so much happiness. Despite the hard times your father and I never ceased to love each other; that was heaven's gift to us, a deep abiding love. Oh, Callista, my precious one!' Her wasted hand catching her daughter's Ruth gazed into violet eyes swimming with tears. 'If I could give you the world's greatest treasure it would be a marriage like mine, a husband with whom you would know the love your father and I knew, but only God can give such blessings. Trust Him, Callista, trust Him and your own heart, go the way it leads . . .'

The last strength spent, the tired eyes closed and there was no resistance to hands being tucked beneath the sparse covers. Pressing a kiss to a brow damp from the exertion of the continuous cough Callista went quietly from the room.

Had her father taken his own life in order to protect his wife and child? But to protect them from what? What could he possibly have done which made his life too intolerable to be lived?

Downstairs in the tiny cramped living room she fed the fire just sufficient coal to keep it burning. Leaving the kettle to boil she carried the near-empty coal bucket out into the yard, staring at it as she set it down.

Julia Montroy! The name hit her brain with the shock of a stone striking between the eyes. The teacher who had made her young life such a misery had the surname Montroy. Could it have been one and the same; the same woman to whom her father had been engaged? The one he had left in order to marry her mother? Maybe it was not something her father had found which had hounded him to his death but rather something which had found him.

Returning to the living room, Callista tried to analyse her thoughts but always they returned to the same question. Was the Miss Montroy of St James's School the Julia Montroy of her father's past? If so, was she in some way responsible for Jason Sanford's suicide?

6

The whole idea was ridiculous! Walking quickly Callista turned along Foster Street, the questions that had plagued her earlier returning to her mind as her path followed the narrow Paget's Passage which ran close to the grey stone St James's church opposite which stood the high-storeyed school. How could a teacher, a woman of education, be responsible for a man taking his own life? It was the stuff of fantasy! But Miss Montroy had not been like the rest of the staff; only she had made a misery of a child's days in that establishment, only she had treated a young girl with nothing short of cruelty.

'*I saw . . . I saw him there and I knew . . .*'

Words which had stayed with her through the years, their returning always accompanied by fear, seemed to whisper from the surrounding darkness.

Why?

The whisper which part of her tried to tell her existed only in her mind, that it was no more than imagination, seemed to draw closer.

'*. . . it was because of her . . . her and you . . .*'

Across to her right the churchyard trees creaked and rustled among the shadows, branches thin and black reaching towards her as a dark-sleeved arm had so many times reached for a frightened child and suddenly Callista was back in that dreaded classroom, a vicious hand grabbing for her.

'No . . . no, you cannot blame him!' Lost in her childhood world Callista cried out. 'He loved her . . . he . . .'

'I'm not blaming anyone.'

Shaken by strong hands Callista was dragged from the shadows of the past; the hands holding her arms were real, the voice clear and distinct.

'I'm not blaming anyone,' it repeated, 'except you! Have you no more sense than to be walking alone at night? I take it you are alone unless the "he" you babbled on about has chosen not to show himself.'

'I . . . I was not aware I was speaking aloud.' Still slightly bemused, the present not yet fully extricated from the past, Callista pulled free.

'Obviously! Nor do you seem to be aware of the risk you take walking alone at night.'

Callista felt the sting of the cynical reply and the resentment it aroused in her marked her answer. 'I am in no danger, people of these streets are no threat.'

'No?' It was quiet, wrapped in a breath of velvet smoothness. 'I am here in this street, can you say I am not a danger, that I pose no threat?'

Suddenly, startlingly aware the narrow street was deserted apart from the two of them, Callista's heart raced. 'Excuse me, I . . . I am in something of a hurry.' Stepping to one side of a figure so tall it seemed to overshadow her she caught her breath as the man moved to block her way.

'Not so fast . . . we are not finished, you and I!'

What did that imply? Drawing her shawl tight about her Callista tried to control nerves beginning to jangle. The voice was one she did not recognise and the face . . . it was kept carefully, deliberately to the shadows; and why prevent her passing, was it because he intended to rob her or was his mind set upon a deed far worse?

Using every ounce of will power in her, Callista pressed her feet hard to the ground. She must not run, she might not outpace him and if he found the depth of her fear then surely he would take advantage; but remain calm and he might just go on his way.

'You are not from Paget's Passage?'

It seemed he stared at her yet she could not be sure; the obscuring gloom was too thick a veil to penetrate with any certainty. Why had he asked such a question, what difference could it make where she came from? But it was best not to anger him. Heeding the caution of her mind Callista answered. 'I . . . I live in Trowes Court.'

Etched black against the deep grey of the moonless night, the head moved. He was taking stock of her. Callista's nerves screamed but she would not let herself give in to them.

'Trowes Court?'

It was quietly said as before but the velvet smoothness was gone, replaced by disbelief.

'I know people of Trowes Court but you are not one of them.'

'Then you do not know as much as you think you do!'

Hearing the intake of breath Callista held her own. Why had she answered so sharply when every sense had told her that was the worst thing she could do?

'Then enlighten me, tell me what I do not know.'

There was a hint of laughter in the reply emanating from the darkness; mockery or pleasure at having someone smaller and weaker than himself to bully and frighten? But she would not allow him to see her fright, that pleasure at least she would deprive him of. Her fingers clutched tightly to her shawl, her throat dry with apprehension of how he would react; but she had already cast caution to the wind by answering as she had so why not speak her mind. She would suffer as much for a pint as for a quart!

'I have no doubt there are many things you do not know,' she said scathingly, 'such as that accosting a woman is against the law. I would also say it is an appalling breach of good manners but then *you* would probably not appreciate the difference between good and bad in anything; but to answer your request

I will tell you: you do not know all of the people living at Trowes Court . . . for example the Sanfords, those who are neighbours to the Poveys!'

'And you are a Sanford?'

'That is none of your business!' Callista's voice cracked like ice. 'Now do what you have set your mind upon and let me be on my way.'

A definite chuckle brushed the space between them before melting into the shadows.

'Do what I have set my mind upon. Now what, I wonder, could that be?'

He was laughing at her! Callista burned beneath a flush of anger. 'You know very well,' she spat. 'It might be dark but not so dark you cannot see my dress and deduce from it that I have no money, therefore I doubt your intention is one of robbery!'

'You are correct.' He laughed openly. 'I am not thinking to rob you, Miss Sanford . . . or should that be Mrs Sanford?'

He intended to take his time, to play her like a cat would play a mouse; but she must get to the market and then home, her mother would be needing her.

Worry for her mother drowning both fear and anger her eyes strove to penetrate the shrouding darkness, to reach the fact at its heart. 'Please.' Both hands dropped, releasing the shawl to fall open. 'Please, I must get to the market, my mother . . . please just take what you want and let me go.'

Once more the figure silhouetted against the night lifted its head sharply, its words when they came a mixture of accusation and demand. 'The market! Why there when only a moment ago you said you had no money . . . or is it there you hope to earn some? The Turk's Head . . . the Green Dragon or maybe you prefer one of the many other establishments plagued by ladies of the night.'

He thought her a prostitute! Callista's cheeks flamed afresh. But what did it matter what this man thought, what did it matter what he did to her so long as it was over quickly. Eyes closing, she clenched her teeth against paralysing nausea as strong hands closed over her arms drawing her close against a hard body.

The market place was empty. Candlelit jars which evening saw strung across each stall had been extinguished. She held a hand to the sharp pain throbbing beneath her ribs, her breathing hard and rasping from non-stop running. That man had enjoyed humiliating her, enjoyed forcing her . . .

From one corner of the entrance to the narrow street, the Shambles, where butchers' stalls sold every kind of fresh meat, a shout of laughter accompanied a group of men approaching the Green Dragon Hotel and Callista pressed into the shadows. Waiting while the group passed inside she stared at the vacant stalls, their poles rising like skeletal limbs in the darkness. She had been freed of those hands at last. He had thought her too spent or too afraid of him to move but as his hands had tightened their grip she had kicked out, her boot striking with a crack across his shin, and as his hands fell from her arms she had fled. His shout had followed her, echoing from the shrouded walls of the church, passing like some tuneless song from stone to stone. Surprise or anger at her escaping him? Callista dragged in a ragged breath. She had not paused to find out but had raced away, dreading every moment of that wild flight to hear his steps coming after her.

But it would have been as well to have run in the opposite direction, to have raced back to Trowes Court instead of the market. She had hoped to be here soon enough to earn a few pennies helping to clear the stalls and carts as trade for the day ended, but both the Shambles and Market Square were empty of traders; the only people to be seen were men returning from their shift at the collieries or iron foundries, boots striking on the cobbles as they passed, while others turned towards the Golden Cross Inn, the light of whose low bow-fronted window Callista could see beckoning from the other side of the Market Square.

He had known she needed to get to this place quickly, she had told him of her need . . . of her mother's need . . . yet still he had held her. Despite the fear that had gripped her then, or maybe because only now would her mind allow the full horror of it to become clear, Callista's thoughts returned to the events of minutes ago. She had begged that man to let her go, sobbed to him to release her, but it had done no good. Intent upon his own dreadful business, mindful only of his own needs, he had simply snatched her closer . . . and now it was too late. But it did not matter what had happened to her; the only important thing was her mother's welfare.

Tears of what might have been anger but were the tears of defeat blurred the empty deserted stalls. There was nothing more she could do. The hope of earning enough to buy her mother a meal was gone and there would not be so much as a bone or even a sausage skin left among the rubbish cast aside by the butchers during the day; they would have been devoured by stray dogs long since. But the vegetable stalls, perhaps the dogs would not have eaten the cast-offs from those. Hope flickering uncertain as candle flame caught in a breeze, she pulled the shawl close. A few vegetables cooked into a broth might not be a feast but it would provide a meal.

Oswin Slade parted his sandy hair down the centre and combed it sleekly towards his temples. Laying the comb aside, he ran the palms of his hands over the thinning drift helped to lie smooth with a smear of bay rum. He cut a smart figure, one any woman would be glad to be seen walking with! Fastening the high-buttoned jacket of the fawn and brown check suit bought from a pawnshop in Wolverhampton he stood admiring himself in the speckled mirror of his bedroom. The close-fitting trousers coming as they did well down over his boots gave a slenderness to his legs while the high starched collar of his white shirt teamed with a large crimson tie gave the whole ensemble a pleasing effect. Yes, Oswin Slade cut a figure to be noticed in Wednesbury. Satisfied, he reached for the brown derby hat purchased from the same pawnshop. It was something of a journey taking the train to Wolverhampton, but in that town he was unknown while in this – he patted the small bowler hat perched on his head – it was not known where his suit had been purchased.

There was just one thing marred his satisfaction. Oswin's reflection frowned among the speckled depths. He had to pay for his pleasure, pay for the services of a woman. But not for much longer. The frown became a smile. A month from now would see him married and his pleasure would cost him no more than the five shillings paid for the licence. A lifetime of taking what he wanted when he wanted it and that for less than it cost paying a prostitute every night for a week. And he liked his pleasure every night; like the feel of a naked body beneath his own, the touch of a moist tongue tracing a line from his navel to his crotch, lips parting to take him into a mouth, and later . . . much later . . . legs opening wide giving him access to that delicious hall of delight. All of this he would get from Callista Sanford: long nights of sensual excitement. And when that particular excitement wore off? He would still get his money's worth. In and out of the bedroom, the Sanford girl would earn her keep.

Full of thoughts of the ease the next month would bring to his pocket, Oswin walked confidently from his house in Loxdale Street, glancing once at the row of small tight-packed terraced buildings. What had bought one of these would buy another and another until they all belonged to him. If only there were a way of speeding things up. He couldn't risk upping those rents again for a few months and the account books . . . those too were best not fiddled with; Sabine Derry had a sharp mind and a vicious one. But there *had* to be a way. Following the way of Camp Street and the Shambles he paused. Should he seek his entertainment here at the Green Dragon or should he go on to the Turk's Head?

The company he sought could be found in either. Mentally debating the choice he stepped back from the road while a heavy cart rumbled past, its driver clucking his tongue encouragingly to his tired horse, then, his line of vision once more unobstructed, Oswin's thick lips jammed hard together, annoyance blazing in pale eyes as he watched a thin figure bend to pick up something from the ground. He knew what was being gathered; he had seen it done many times before, women with no other way of feeding their families grubbing through market waste.. What he had not seen was Callista Sanford grubbing alongside them. Had anyone else seen her; anyone of importance? How would it sound when he was a man of consequence? 'Did you know Slade's wife one time grubbed for food among the rubbish of the market place?'

A hiss of anger pushing his lips apart, he almost ran between the empty stalls, pushing aside several people, ignoring the angry calls that followed after him.

'What the hell do you think you're doing!'

Jerked almost off her feet by the angry snatch at her arm Callista's mind at once sped her back to Paget's Passage with its tall shadowed figure. Fear she had felt then flooded rapidly through every vein and she screamed.

'Stop that, you fool!'

One hand slapped sharply across Callista's mouth knocking her head back on her neck while at the same time the other hand jerked her arm so fiercely cabbage leaves and carrots went tumbling from her grasp.

'Stop your screaming!' Oswin sucked air savagely through flared nostrils, his order no more than a hiss. 'Do you want the whole town to hear you, to see you here rooting through filth even pigs wouldn't eat!'

Senses dulled by fear, her mouth stinging from the blow, Callista stared unseeingly at her assailant.

'Get away from here,' Oswin hissed again, 'get away before anyone recognises you.'

The hand jerking again at her arm seemed to Callista's distraught mind to be snatching at her as before, drawing her closer to a hard resilient body. He had followed her, she had not seen or heard him but he had followed her . . . he intended to do that which her running from him had denied him. Fear mounting higher, she screamed again.

'I said stop that!' Oswin's hand struck again only this time it remained clamped over her mouth, an arm holding her trapped against him.

Held more by her own fear than the strength of that arm, Callista stared at the angry face. Recognition filtering at last into her dazed mind, she twisted her head, freeing her mouth.

'Oswin!'

'Shhh!' Oswin glanced rapidly to either side, seeing other night scavengers watching. 'Not here, you will be seen!'

It was not the same man had accosted her in that dark street but one who repelled her almost as much. As her senses returned quickly she shook away his hold, her voice cold with dislike.

'Is it my being seen disturbs you, Oswin, or yourself!'

'It will be the same thing once we are married,' Oswin snapped. 'My wife was seen grubbing in the streets . . . my wife fighting the dogs for scraps . . . should anyone of significance . . .'

Dormant until now, Callista's grasp of the situation surged like an incoming tide sweeping before it any latent thought of concealing the purpose of her being in this place at such a time, leaving in its wake a cold despising anger.

'That is it, isn't it, Oswin!' Violet eyes blazing contempt, she stared defiantly at the heavy-jowled face she knew beneath concealing shadow would be suffused with wrath. 'Should anyone of significance see . . . It does not matter to you the reason which brings any person here, only that the future wife of Oswin Slade be spotted among them, seen by someone of significance, someone who might prove useful to your future—'

'That will do. You will return home at once!'

There was no request, no offer of walking with her, seeing her safely back to Trowes Court; instead the words had held the familiar order. Keeping her own words quietly clipped Callista answered.

'I will be glad to return . . . once I have what I came for.'

Temper a bubbling mass seeping into his throat Oswin watched her retrieve the spilled vegetables then as she straightened his hand shot out, strewing the lot about Callista's feet.

'I'm telling you to go . . . *now*!'

'And I am telling you, my friend, leave the young lady alone. I fear she does not welcome your advice.'

'Mind your bloody own business!' Oswin's thickset body turned quickly but the hand rising to strike was halted by a slender cane, its tip flashing silver in light spilling from the tavern widow.

'I perceive a young woman being subjected to treatment obviously unwelcome to her as being my business.' Cool and well spoken, a man's voice replied evenly though the cane remained raised.

Taking a moment to swallow this fresh spasm invading his throat, Oswin took in what the dim light of evening allowed him to see. Tall hat, its sheen marking it to be silk, thigh-length dark coat with a single line of buttons showing below it, dark close-fitting trousers, the whole finished off with a white high-collared shirt and dark bow tie. He swallowed, hiding a rising chagrin. This was no man searching rubbish in the hope of a meal, nor was it a collier or foundryman returning from his work. This was a man possibly of note.

'This . . .' he stammered, uncertain of how to reply, 'this girl is my fiancée.'

'Then you are doubly at fault in your treatment of her.'

It was like acid thrown in his face! Oswin recoiled, stung by the sarcasm.

'I . . . this is no place for her,' he replied defensively. 'I wished her to return home.'

The man lowered his cane; a pair of eyes flashed in the gloom and a cultured voice holding no trace of lenience spoke. 'Is that the way you obtain what it is you wish from a young woman, by striking her?'

'I did not strike her, I merely knocked that . . . that rubbish from her hands.' Oswin followed the lie with a stare. His back had been turned to this man; he could not have seen.

'You add lies to your other questionable habits!' Stiff with contempt, the answer met Oswin's account. 'An undesirable trait in any man.'

'Now look here . . .'

'I have looked and must confess I do not like what I have seen!' The head moved slightly to concentrate a look on Callista. 'One can only hope your fiancée sees as clearly.'

The anger Oswin had hastily swallowed regurgitated, flooding his throat with fire. They were all the bloody same, these people of property, thinking they possessed a God-given right to belittle those with less. No longer so careful of his own reply he was sharp. 'My fiancée, sir, has the sense to see I act only in her best interests!'

'You surprise me.' The other man's voice held a note of mockery. 'I would hardly call striking a woman across the mouth acting in her best interests.'

He had seen! Oswin's teeth gritted together. The man could call for a constable, have him charged with assault. If that happened he could kiss any dreams of bettering his future goodbye. Sabine Derry would take great pleasure in getting him dismissed from his job as rent collector, which would mean no more money siphoned into his pocket. In fact it would be another charge to answer when his fraud was discovered – and robbery carried a heavy sentence!

'Please.' Callista intervened, wanting to avoid further un-pleasantness. 'No harm has been done, my . . . my fiancé is right, I should return home.'

'I am glad you understand that, Callista.' Oswin smarmed his satisfaction.

'One moment.'

Callista halted as the tall hatted figure bent to retrieve several of the fallen vegetables, holding them towards her.

'I believe you said you came for these. I would not wish you a wasted journey by forgetting them.'

'She does not want—'

But the man had already turned his back on the furious Oswin, his silver-topped cane dancing in the yellowy tavern lights as he signalled a carriage stood a short distance away.

'When you have retrieved all you require then my carriage will take you wherever you wish to go. That way your fiancé has no need of interrupting his evening by accompanying you home.'

Callista almost felt the wince of Oswin's heavy body at the other man's obvious dismissal of him and she answered quickly. 'I have no need of a carriage though I thank you for the kindness of your offer.'

'Take it.' The cane flashed as it lowered. 'I will not be requiring it for several hours. It will find the man something to do . . . give him a little less time with his fellows in the stables of the George Hotel.'

It seemed to Callista the voice held a smile, a hint of mischief, but Oswin's ears detected only confrontation. The man wanted him to disagree, wanted an argument. A further opportunity to call a constable? He could not afford the possibility of that happening, although it would have given him a great satisfaction to snatch that cane and beat this interfering bugger over the head with it.

Stifling the desire if not the thought, Oswin forced a degree of apology to his voice. 'I do have business that needs my attention, Callista; to go with you to your home would mean missing an important appointment. You do understand?'

Yes, she understood, and judging by the near-inaudible sniff so did the other man. Holding the vegetables in the fold of her shawl, Callista felt the distrust she had often felt when listening to Oswin's excuses. Dislike and distrust. She turned her glance from the heavy face. It was no foundation for marriage!

Helped into the carriage, Oswin's hand painfully warningly clutching her elbow, Callista leaned to the window; but the thanks she intended to say caught on her tongue as the man standing beside her fiancé raised his hat, the light spilling from the tavern windows playing across his face . . . a face she recognised.

7

Out of sight of the market place, Callista called for the driver to bring the carriage to a halt, clambering out almost before the wheels ceased to turn. Asking if he would relay her thanks to the owner, she turned away, disappearing quickly into the night.

It would be seen as unmannerly, probably churlish, but she wanted no favours though to be honest she felt gratitude to that man for relieving her of having to endure Oswin's company and recrimination all the way back to her house.

Clutching the few vegetables, tight boots tapping a rapid rhythm, she ran on. Going by way of Lower Russell Street would get her to Holyhead Road and home more quickly than would her going on to the White Horse and turning there. The decision made, she turned to her right. To one side an uninterrupted line of tiny houses showed dim anaemic light telling of the burning of a solitary candle, the smoke-grimed brickwork of their exterior blending into the darkness leaving only chimney stacks outlined against the sky like giant blackened teeth, while on the opposite side St Bartholomew's School and an opening leading to the chapel broke the same monotonous pattern.

Ahead a pool of stronger light silhouetted a figure in wide skirts and tiny topknot bonnet, a jug balanced in both hands, shuffling into the side entrance of the Market Tavern beerhouse. The nightly fetching of a quart of ale. Callista slowed to a walk, somehow comforted by the sight of another woman.

Had it been a terrible rudeness, her dismissing that carriage as she had? What would Oswin have to say of such behaviour when next he called? If only he did not have to call ever again . . . if only she did not need to marry him. But good fortune rarely made an appearance in Portway Road and miracles never!

You will return home at once . . . !

Oswin had made no attempt to disguise the command, no effort to veil the demand. He saw nothing untoward in speaking to her with such authority while they were yet unmarried. What then would her life be once she became his wife? She would be no more than a possession, a chattel to be used for his comfort . . . a woman with no voice of her own. It would be a waking nightmare, one from which she knew well there would be little respite. But what else could she do but marry Oswin Slade? That was the only way she had of bringing a little comfort to her mother's life.

Emerging onto the wide Holyhead Road Callista glanced at the dark outline of the recently erected municipal buildings and the more elaborate façade of the art gallery which was the bequest of Mrs Edwin Richards, wife of the proprietor of Portway Coach Springs Works. To have even a fraction of the money that building had cost!

Pushing the impossible aside Callista switched her glance to the steam tram lumbering past. Dreams were like the first air of morning, like the scent of fresh-mown meadows, sweet as the fields she had walked with her parents, heady and wonderful; but like air you could not live on them.

After the tram had rattled on its way, she crossed the road, taking care to lift her feet clear of the lines of tram rails. She hurried on, averting her eyes, passing the street which held the church and school of St James without a glance. Dreams did not last forever . . . so why did her nightmare live on?

Who did he think he was? Sir bloody Lancelot! Anger hot inside him, Oswin watched the stranger walk away. They had both watched that carriage round the curve in the road, the echoes of wheels and horses' hooves soon losing themselves amid the rumble of heavier carters' wagons heading for one of the many ale houses; then without a word or glance the man had turned his back and walked away.

He'd had no right to interfere! Callista Sanford was nobody's business but Oswin Slade's, she was his promised wife and as such it was his duty to monitor her behaviour, to see she did nothing which could reflect upon himself, and it was hardly creditable to him for her to be seen scavenging among the rubbish of that market! Yet that man had picked up the scabby cabbage leaves and mouldy carrots, handing them to her with apparently no consideration for the fine kid gloves he wore. No doubt the fellow had expected him to slink away, to leave the field open. Then the real purpose of his interfering would have shown itself. He would have offered Callista more than cabbage leaves and carrots. Only Oswin Slade had not slunk away, he had not allowed Callista to be propositioned, but had given the man a rude awakening. A smile of self-satisfaction touching his mouth, Oswin swung in the direction of the Turk's Head. Whoever it was had thought to provide himself with a cheap evening's entertainment would have to buy himself a prostitute elsewhere.

The thought calming his still-hot anger, Oswin glanced about the hotel bar room then taking his tankard of beer chose an empty table separated a little from the rest. He would take his time in choosing a companion for the evening.

'. . . well, that was what her told me . . . said it were given her.'

'Oh ar, and a body be supposed to believe that?'

'You believe what you likes but that were what were told me.'

'Ar, well, what be told and what be truth be two very different kettles o' fish. It ain't only big tits that there Sally Baker has, her's got a big imagination an' all, if her thinks folk'll go believing that woman gives anythin' for nothin'. From what I hears o' Emma

Ramsey, her wouldn't give the drip from the end of her nose and talk has it that there visitor her entertains so often, that there wife of Edwin Derry, ain't no more charitable.'

The name slamming into his brain with the force of a barbed arrow Oswin glanced towards a glass screen, its surface etched with a frosted design obscuring a clear view of the people sitting on its other side. The view but not the voices. Carelessly pitched a little too loud for privacy they had caught his attention; now he strained his ears, intent on catching every last syllable.

'Huh!' The first voice went on. 'I hears the same, seems Emma Ramsey be got notions of grandeur since taking up wi' the Derrys, her fist be tighter than a duck's arse swimmin' on the Tame, but I seen the frock, blue silk it were an' styled fit for a lady.'

'And Sally Baker don't be one o' them!'

Oswin listened to the shout of laughter following the words.

'Nor do that Derry woman be for all her'd have folk believe otherwise.' The voice quickened irately. 'Now had you 'ave said styled fit for the devil's doxy I might 'ave agreed but then even that be too good for that one. Twice this year her's put three-pence on the rents, takin' money off folk who don't earn enough to keep theirselves. I'd be more inclined to listen should you be tellin' me somebody had done for that greedy bugger instead of some tale of Emma Ramsey givin' away of a frock.'

'There'd be many in Wednesbury wouldn't join in the huntin' of the one who done *her* in . . .'

The talk pausing, Oswin watched the hazy outline of an arm raising a glass.

'But supposin' it be true . . .' The arm lowered. 'Why would Ramsey give away a frock which as you tells it be worth a bob or two? The woman don't be no believer in charity an' it be certain her don't be no saint!'

Pitched slightly lower the answer was clothed in a meaningful chuckle. 'I d'ain't say her given it for nothin'!'

Sat at the other side of the ornate screen Oswin felt his nerves tense. They couldn't begin to whisper now . . . Christ, not now! This was a chance he'd long hoped for, a chance of finding something of use to him, something he could hold over the head of Edwin Derry.

'So how much were paid . . . and more to the point where would money such as that come from? Sally Baker earns her'n the same way we earns our'n, by lyin' on her back or standing against a wall while some bloke pumps away at her, and at no more'n a shilling a go it takes many a night and many a client to earn that kind o' money.'

His own drink forgotten, Oswin watched the hazily outlined arms rise and lower.

'Ar, you, me and a few others beside earns our coppers pleasurin' men . . .'

The voice he recognised as belonging to the first speaker sounded again through the dividing screen. It was not as loud as before. Thinking to edge closer, his fingers gripped about his tankard, Oswin began to rise from his seat. But if they saw his moving as he had seen the lift of their arms . . . should they suspect they were being overheard then those women might leave off their talk. Carefully as laying a newborn into its cradle he eased his body back into the seat. Fingers still about the tankard, he stared into its depths. To any onlooker he appeared oblivious to all around but every sinew of him strained towards that screen. There was something to be told, the cynicism in those voices hinted as much, and if it concerned the wife of the owner of Derry Coal Mines then he wanted to hear.

'. . . ar, Sally gives a man what he pays for . . .'

The voice was speaking again. Breath held in his throat, Oswin listened.

'But that ain't all her does, Sally her be different.'

''Ow do you mean, different? Her be a prostitute same as you and me does!'

'Not altogether . . .'

There was a repugnance in the reply, a disgust which made the speaker spit her words as though they held a vileness on the tongue. Honed to every word, Oswin waited.

'You and me along of the others so far as I knows bowls from only one end of the pitch while Sally Baker her bowls from both ends alike.'

'You mean . . . !'

Oswin heard the quiet gasp his own tension held in check. He must not give himself away now.

'Ar.' The voice resumed. 'We pleasures one sort only while Sally her be different and it be to my way o' thinkin' her paid for that frock by the pleasurin' o' Emma Ramsey.'

Christ, if that were true! Oswin's fingers ached from gripping the pewter tankard but he did not feel the pain, only the surge of excitement that woman's words had soaring along his veins. Emma Ramsey and a woman . . . Lord, what couldn't he do armed with information like that and what if he could involve Derry's wife! But gossip was not weapon enough . . . and gossip was not always based on fact.

'That couldn't be . . . a woman like her, the wife of one o' the richest Wednesbury holds . . . there has to be a fault somewhere along the line; I reckons you been told wrong.'

Had the woman been told wrong . . . was the story a web of lies? Oswin forced his breathing to remain regular as he listened but at his throat a pulse beat wildly.

'Oh ar!' The first woman thickened her answer with cynicism. 'There be a fault all right but it don't be mine nor do I think it her'n as told me. 'Tain't every woman comes to this tavern be on the game and it ain't only prostitutes I numbers among my friends. I growed from childhood with her who be housekeeper to Emma Ramsey and there don't be much goes on in that house as don't get told to me; things such as nights Samuel Ramsey stays drinkin' with his cronies 'til the small hours, them same nights as Sally Baker don't show her face here at the Turk's Head.'

'That don't go to say her be with Emma Ramsey, chances be Sally just likes to tek a night off.'

'Night off my arse . . . !'

Scepticism sharp as a blade sliced from the woman's tongue, adding to the pounding rhythm in Oswin's throat.

'Sally Baker would no more turn down a night's work than fly in the air, her knows the only thing money don't buy be poverty, and like a good many more folk in Wednesbury Sally Baker were reared in poverty but her don't intend to die the same way. No, her don't stay away from this place so her back be rested, reason being her don't come here is 'cos her be at Acacia Villa; and while you be thinkin' up reasons why it don't be as I says then ask y'self this question. . . why is it Polly Burke be given a full afternoon and evenin' away from 'er job as housekeeper when we all knows Emma wouldn't give a blind man a light? Why is it that woman don't want her nowheres near that house the times Sam'l don't be comin' home at a normal hour? But don't go givin' y'self a brain fever searchin' for the answer 'cos I already told it to you. Emma Ramsey entertains a lover on them days, and that lover don't be no man.'

A flurry of movement shadowing the glass screen heralded the departure of the two women but their leaving did not disappoint Oswin. He had heard enough, enough to make him a wealthy man. The only thing now was devising a plan of action; of deciding how this pearl of wisdom could earn him all that he wanted.

All that he wanted! Raising his tankard he drank deep before setting it down. He wanted a great deal, a very great deal. He would have every penny Samuel Ramsey possessed and with it all that Edwin Derry had. Maybe Sabine was not involved; but would the world at large believe that!

★

The man who had stepped from the darkness, the one who had accosted her in Paget's Passage, he had made no attempt to . . . but that was unfair, she must not even think the word rape.

Her breathing laboured and painful from running, Callista allowed herself to slow to a walk.

Strong hands had caught her arms but they had not held on as she shook free; then he had stepped to one side, deliberately blocking her path, and moments later he had grabbed her again, his voice a mixture of mockery and teasing. He had snatched her close, holding her against a body firm and strong, held her against a heart beating powerfully above her own yet he had made no attempt to drag her deeper into the shadows or force her to the ground. Why? Why grab her and hold her if he had not intended to abuse her . . . why let her run from him when he might so easily have caught her?

Thoughts rapid as her pattering feet on the rough cobbles ranged endlessly in Callista's mind as she hurried towards Portway Road.

But the strange event had not been the only occurrence now giving food for thought. One more had followed quickly on its heels, this time a man intervening, disrupting the flow of Oswin's anger; not only that but actually retrieving and handing back to her the vegetables Oswin had knocked from her grasp and then almost insisting she take his carriage home.

Oswin had been so irate but there had been no trace of the same in his adversary. He had spoken as had the man in Paget's Passage, the same cultured delivery, the same velvet tone. Two men, both educated to judge by the way they spoke, both expensively dressed, and though one had frightened her thinking of that fear now she realised that beneath it had flickered something deeper . . . a feeling the man would not harm her. And he had not. In fact he could be said to have helped her by making her aware of the danger of walking alone in narrow deserted streets. Two men, both of whom had shown her a kindness, both well dressed, both seeming to possess a quality of civility and breeding which had showed in the first of them despite his brusque and slightly cynical questioning.

Two men – or one and the same?

Vegetables wrapped securely in her shawl, Callista turned into the heavily shadowed Trowes Court, familiarity guiding her steps past the one privy and on across the unpaved space separating it from the houses.

They had so much in common . . . or was that simply her own imagination? It would mean the man from Paget's Passage had followed her to the market. He did know it was there she was going, she had told him so herself. But then if he had followed her there for whatever reason was it likely he would have allowed her the use of his carriage to take her home alone; would he not have insisted he travel with her? Perhaps that had been his idea but the presence of Oswin had thwarted it.

Oswin! Callista's already laboured breathing snagged as the name entered her mind. He was not a man to forgive or forget. The anger she had known he felt, the displeasure he could not vent on the man who had admonished him, would still be there brewing inside him, growing in energy until it could be released on her. And she must endure it if she were to keep her mother alive. That was Oswin Slade's hold over her and he knew it . . . knew it and would use it in any way pleased him.

Why had life turned so against them? Hand on the door she stood a moment, darkness hiding the droop of her mouth. What had she and her mother done that fate should treat them so? Had it been so wrong, her father breaking an engagement and marrying the woman he really loved? Would it not have been a far more terrible wrong to have wed a fiancée he felt nothing for, to have ruined that woman's life? Some might argue it was not; was fate one of those contenders, was that the reason for the life she and her mother shared now? She had dwelled on that reasoning so many times since her mother telling her of her father's decision, let it play in that time before sleep, but always told herself the whole idea of fate was an excuse used by people who failed themselves. Each person was responsible for their own life, whatever they made of it, whether good or bad was of their own doing; and always in that last moment before the veil of sleep closed off all thought she had known her answer was no answer at all. Just as becoming Oswin Slade's wife would be no answer. Swapping one misery for another was what she would be doing, a misery which would last long after her mother was taken from her. One life. She sighed, lifting the latch and stepping into the house. One life to hold so much unhappiness.

'Thank you for coming in, I'm very grateful to you, Mrs Povey, and I know Mother enjoys your company.' Placing the wilted vegetables on the table, Callista whipped off her shawl, hanging it on a peg set behind the door before turning to the fire-place. The remnants of fire burned low in the bed of the grate. Automatic in her movement she swung the bracket with the kettle over the glow; there would be sufficient heat in the embers to boil water, to make her mother a drink, and the few vegetables would cook in the remaining water.

'I know I'm back late.' She smiled at the woman stood by the foot of the stairs. 'I . . . I was held up, people wanting to talk.'

It was a lie. Turning her back to the next-door neighbour, Callista blushed. But to tell Mrs Povey the truth of what had happened, especially seeing she had not arrived home in a carriage, would have meant long explanations and even then she might not believe it; but then who would? A young woman had been stopped by a man in an empty street, yet had not been assaulted in any way! Then another had come to her defence in the Market Square . . . ! It was hardly believable to herself, so how could others be expected to think it so?

'I have not forgotten our visit to the herb woman . . .'

Callista moved quickly about the small room collecting cup and jug which held a mere trace of milk. 'I hope she will still see us, I would hate for you to walk with me all that way only to have her refuse. But it will be later than expected so she might . . .'

'Eulalie Ulmar refuses no caller to her house no matter the time they comes.'

'You said how kind she was,' Callista answered, pouring bubbling water over the one spoonful of tea left in the house, 'I would not like to return that kindness by disturbing her late at night, nor would I want to keep you from your family, Mrs Povey.'

Eyes following the movements of her busy hands, Callista did not see the look settling over the old woman's face as she spoke on.

'I could not find anything I thought suitable to offer in exchange for medicine, Mother and I have nothing of value but I thought perhaps some pretty covers for her herb pots . . .'

'There be no need.' Ada Povey took a step, closing the door at her back shutting off the narrow stairs.

'But I have to give something and covers would be quick and easy to sew. Mother has a small piece of silk left over from the dress she made . . .'

'Callista, wench.' Ada came to the table. 'There be no need for covers nor aught other, it be too late.'

'I'm sorry I kept you waiting, it truly wasn't my intention; please, Mrs Povey, just give me a moment to take this to Mother and we will go . . . the soup will simmer until I get back, I'll—'

'No, wench!' Ada's hand closed over Callista's, forcing the cup she held to the table. 'We won't be visitin' of Eulalie Ulmar, there no longer be call for medicine.'

Her mother no longer needed the herb woman's elixir, the cough which had troubled her was eased. A wave of relief sweeping through her, Callista smiled at her neighbour.

'Oh, Mrs Povey, I'm so thankful Mother is better. I will just see if she is awake.'

'Your mother don't be awake. Her won't be a needin' o' that tea . . . not no more. Callista.' The firmness of the woman's voice softened but the hold on Callista's hand remained strong. 'Your mother be passed on.'

8

Sitting in the drawing room his wife had furnished so exquisitely, Phineas Westley let the book he had been reading rest on his knee. They had once brought him so much pleasure, this house and its gardens, the paintings and antiques he had collected delighting in the acquisition of each as he might have delighted in the birth of a child. But generous as life had been to himself and Rachel it had not blessed them with a child. There had been no son to bear his name, no daughter to cherish. Wealth had brought him many things, wonderful Venetian glass, the finest Limoges porcelain, carpets from the far Orient, statuary carved by the great masters, but all of this was as nothing compared to having a child of one's own. Consider the father of that girl who had bumped into him; judging by her appearance the man was as good as penniless yet in his daughter he possessed the greatest wealth. 'My little wood nymph.' Phineas whispered the words then fell back into the silence of thought. What were the treasures of this house compared to a daughter?

A blessing or a disadvantage? His glance rested on a statue in a glass-panelled French walnut cabinet, the glow from the fire blushing the ancient marble to pink; he smiled ruefully. Had it been fortunate the Artemis had been undamaged by that mishap or had the blessing worn a disguise, one causing as much disappointment as the other might have given pleasure? Of course it was wonderful for those who in the future would view the undamaged masterpiece, but for Phineas Westley? Returning his glance to the fire he sighed . . . for him it was the relinquishing of the opportunity to meet again with that well-mannered young woman, to meet with her father and talk with him, to enjoy conversation with a man who it seemed shared his own appreciation of the classics, of literature and art of the ancient world. But the Artemis was not damaged; he had been given no cause to write to the address that young woman had given. But only he knew that! He glanced again at the figurine, every line of its graceful form the essence of beauty. It could be worth chipping that beautiful creation, to take a small piece of marble from one of those elegant limbs, perhaps to break a little from the base. It would be an embarrassment to the girl and her father for despite her promise to reimburse the cost of the piece it was obvious they would never be able to meet that obligation.

But there were other ways of meeting an obligation! Phineas smiled at the lovely lifeless face. Not every debt needed to be paid with money!

Your mother be passed on.

Somewhere within the great sound of silence the words whispered.

. . . passed on.

Beneath the other woman's hand Callista's own trembled. There had to be a mistake, she had misheard.

'Sit you down, wench.' Ada Povey spoke quietly as she pressed the unresisting girl to a chair, releasing the cup from her hands. 'It be 'ard for you to grasp at this moment but this be the Lord's way of endin' your mother's sufferin'; her be at peace now along of him her loved and you must try to be grateful her will know no more pain.'

Grateful! The word was like cannon fire blasting the silent roar, throwing the shards of it from Callista's mind. She should be grateful her mother was relieved of half a lifetime of unhappiness! Of a poverty that had taken her health until she had coughed that life away . . . was that a cause for gratitude!

Teeth clenched on resentment rapidly turning to ice within her she spoke quietly. 'Thank you for calling, Mrs Povey . . . I will tell Mother—'

'Your mother be beyond talkin' to,' Ada Povey interrupted. Her words had been a shock but the wench had to be made to understand the truth of them, to accept what were said to her. 'Her last words was for you,' she went on quietly, feeling the tremble of a shoulder beneath her touch. 'It was like her knowed you wouldn't be 'ere in time. God rest her . . . her asked you be told you was the most precious thing her life held, you were the gift of love, the love shared atwixt herself and your father; her said to tell you that so long as you remembers that, keeps it in your 'eart, then the two of them will always be with you.'

Her mother was dead! The cold had grown, encasing mind and body, wrapping her in a shroud of ice trapping thoughts inside. Her mother was dead and she had not been here to hold her, to tell her she loved her. There had been no goodbye.

'I'll hot that cup o' tea, it'll 'elp tek the chill from your bones.'

Ada moved methodically between fireplace and table. She had done these same things many times over, comforting folk left behind, and doubtless would do them many times more. It were never an easy task; death were like a scorpion, it always had a sting in its tail striking it deep into the heart of them who loved. Looking at the girl sat motionless and white-faced as a statue she felt the twist of sympathy in her chest. Life was hard for every family in Trowes Court but for this wench and her mother it had been harder yet. They had both tried, scrubbing the house daily, the mother sewing until her eyes were swollen and red from strain, the girl tramping the town looking for work wherever it might be found . . . Ar, heaven had been kind tekin' Ruth Sanford from her pain but where had that kindness been while her lived . . . where was heaven's kindness for any soul findin' theirselves in Trowes Court?

'Drink that down, you be needin' the warmth o' it.' The wench

needed more than a cup of tea so weak it needed 'elp to come
from the pot, and more nourishment than were to be got from
the waste leaves o' cabbage. Taking the poker from the hearth
she rapped it several times on the wall joining this house to her
own and when a tousle-haired lad came running in told him to
fetch the dish of broth she had placed in the oven. Her eldest
would not object to losing his supper seeing the circumstances.

But tea and broth went untouched. Isolated in her own frozen
world, Callista was oblivious of sound or smell, insensible to the
kindness of her neighbour, mindful of nothing but the stab of
those words, 'Your mother be passed on.'

Hands folding across her stomach Ada stood. The wench were
given to a pain no hands could heal nor could sympathy quench;
words spoken now might find no place in her brain but the mind
would hold them and bring them forth when sorrow seemed it
could be borne no longer.

'Callista, wench,' she said softly, 'there be a special tie atwixt
a mother and 'er child. It can't be seen nor can it be touched; it
don't be med of steel nor yet of iron but it be of a strength death
itself can't break. You no longer sees your mother but her be
near, her will be along of you every day you walk this earth and
be standin' with hand outstretched when you steps into the next.
There be too much sorrow in you now for my words to mek a
mark but I be goin' to say 'em just the same. When days be so
heavy, so full of worry and fears, then speak in your mind, speak
to your mother and listen in your 'eart for her answer. It will
come, wench . . . it will come.'

'Pneumonia!'

So short his balding head appeared almost on a level with an
ornate walnut desk the man squinted through owl-like spectacles
at Callista.

'Was the woman attended by the Parish doctor?'

'No.'

'No?' Behind the spectacles the eyes stared like gobstoppers. 'But this certificate is signed by him.'

'My . . . my mother passed away sooner than . . . than expected.' Fingers twisted tight into the folds of her shawl, Callista used the pain of them to concentrate her mind, to hold back the tears trembling on the brink of every word. There had been no money to pay a doctor to certify her mother's death, to issue the necessary certificate; the only way open to her had been the Parish. Now she was asking the same body to provide burial.

Pneumonia. The man peered through thick glass lenses. Judging by the look of this one the doctor had been generous in stating the cause of death; most like it had been tuberculosis hastened by pneumonia. But it was no surprise to him; he saw paupers many times, all asking relief of some sort or another, though this one was prettier than most.

'You have no money at all . . . no means of providing for the deceased?'

Would she be here if she had? Callista wanted to scream the words but knew she must not. She was asking charity of the Board this man represented; it could be granted or refused on his recommendation. Letting a shake of her head prove her answer she stared at the well-polished floor of the room which was the office of the Clerk to the Parish.

'But you are in reasonable health.' The bald head bobbed, taking owl eyes the length of her body before returning them to Callista's downturned face. 'You are able to earn money. You must use that to inter the deceased, the Parish cannot be held to ransom.'

Callista's head jerked upwards. This man thought her no more than a thief, a liar out to entice the Board to take on an expense she could pay herself. The heartbreak of the night before, the pain of seeing her mother lying dead in her bed, gelled into a terrible anger. Fingers releasing the shawl, she snatched up a pen from the desk. Eyes glittering like liquid stone, breath squeezing through taut nostrils, she stared directly into those condemning her from behind their protection of glass.

'Sir!' It snapped hard and brittle, bouncing across the neatly ordered desk. 'Though your manner tells me you will find this hard to believe I would not be requesting assistance either from the Parish or anyone else had I been able to find work. I have walked the length and breadth of this town willing to accept any employment, however menial, but there has been none; but I will continue to search and when I do secure that employment I will repay the Parish every penny it has spent on my mother's burial. Draw up the bill now . . . write out the note of obligation and I will sign it!'

The Board would provide burial. Sat in the tiny house darkened by curtains drawn close against the daylight, Callista breathed deeply trying to still the tremors rippling her nerves. There had been no note of obligation to repay, but somehow, God willing, she would return whatever was spent. Whatever was spent! She glanced at the rough unplaned deal box in which her mother's body lay. No mahogany and brass would shelter Ruth Sanford, no satin-lined casket would cradle her beloved mother. She had never asked a farthing from anyone in her life, never asked any man's charity, yet now . . . in the quiet gloom of the darkened house memories hurled themselves forward.

'The benevolence of the Board . . . she should be grateful . . .' The owl eyes had held a slightly more respectful look, the Clerk withdrawing in the face of her anger, but still he had not resisted the opportunity of showing her her place. She was the suppliant, the beggar asking charity, and as such must be reminded of her position.

'The men be 'ere, say your last goodbyes, wench, an' come away while they does what has to be done.'

She had not seen Ada come to her side; now at the quiet words Callista rose to stand beside the rough rectangular box. The face was so cold, its colour that of marble, but in its peace it held the beauty of youth. The lines of stress were smoothed from the forehead, the dark circles disappeared from beneath the closed eyes, the marks of suffering gone from a mouth which seemed to wear a faint smile, a first hint of welcome. It was a face such as she had so often seen on the statues displayed in Joseph Glaze's antique shop; those exquisite figures carved of white marble, their serene features frozen in eternal youth, faces which would be forever beautiful. But that would not be the picture of her mother she would keep in her heart, a woman of stone. The mother that would live in her memory would be warm, the laughing vibrant woman who had walked with her husband and child.

With Ada Povey's arm supporting her, Callista let herself be led to wait in the communal yard, feeling every sound of nails being driven into wood as though into her own body.

'The little 'uns med these, got the pieces from Miss Hagget the milliner from up along Lower High Street. We all be sorry they couldn't 'ave been real all the way through; the lads, they did search but there be nothin' in field or hedge, weather's been too 'arsh for 'em I reckons. I 'opes you don't be offended, wench, they wanted to show respect but . . .'

The thin ragged woman come to stand beside Ada in the yard blushed with embarrassment. Much as folk had all liked Ruth Sanford, even respect cost money and that was almost non-existent in Trowes Court. Glancing at Ada with troubled eyes she whispered, 'I shouldn't 'ave brought it. The little 'uns meant no 'arm but still I shouldn't 'ave brought it; the wench will see it as mockery and . . . God forbid . . . I d'ain't want that.'

Perhaps it was the quietness of it, the hush of a whisper trying to remain hidden in the mouth or the soft regret in the woman's words. Callista couldn't say which of those things broke the barrier that had erected itself about her, closing off her mind to all except her misery, but somehow the words rang clear.

'I am so very glad you did bring it. Please thank the children and tell them I will never forget their kindness.'

'I'll say that, wench.' The thin woman smiled her sympathy, wooden clogs clattering on the cobbles as she hurried away.

'They looked for real flowers like Kate said, but it be too soon in the year; still her ought not to 'ave fetched it to the 'ouse, it don't be a proper offerin', I'll get rid of it.'

'It is a beautiful offering, Mrs Povey, one my mother would have been proud to wear on her dress.' Tears clouding her vision, Callista looked at the tiny handmade posy of yellow silk roses nestling among deep green velvet leaves. Each petal had been separately cut from scraps of cloth, then sewn together with almost invisible stitches. The tiny flowers peeped from between the lush velvet leaves, cascading like a spray of sunbeams gathered together and tied with a narrow band of purple. 'It is beautiful,' she whispered, 'my mother would have been so happy to have received such a gift and I will be proud to have it placed on the coffin.'

'She said what?' Phineas Westley's aristocratic features wore a definite smile.

'She said I showed an appalling breach of good manners but then I would probably not appreciate the difference between good and bad in anything.'

'Good for her.' Phineas laughed. 'The girl showed spirit . . . so what happened next?'

'She told me to do what I had set my mind upon so she could be on her way.'

'Did she, by George! And what had you set your mind upon?'

Michael Farron's eyes hid their concern in his wineglass. His uncle was showing more than a passing interest in the girl he had talked with in the town; in fact it might be said he was showing definite interest bringing the conversation around to include her whenever opportunity presented itself, and if it did not occur of its own accord then he manoeuvred it.

'Well, it was not robbery.' The moment of silence following

the answer seemed to weigh heavily. What was the shrewd mind of Phineas Westley making of that? Michael waited.

'Did the young woman deduce that for herself or did you inform her so?'

Eyes lifting to a face which had lost its smile, Michael's thoughts remained concealed. 'I didn't have to, she was way ahead of me. She said the evening was not so dark I could not see her clothing and thus deduce the fact she had no money and therefore doubted my intention was one of robbery. I told her that was correct.'

'Was that when she left?'

'Not quite.' Michael sipped the claret, savouring its bouquet on his tongue. 'She said she had to get to the market place . . . it was then I reminded her that only a minute ago she had declared she had no money and asked so why the hurry to go there? Was it in the hope of earning a shilling or two in one of the establishments plagued by ladies of the night?'

He had not been mistaken in thinking his uncle was interested in that girl; his mistake had been in gauging that interest too thinly! Michael Farron watched the fine mouth harden, the eyes take on the texture of flint. Only a few times in the years of his upbringing had he seen the cold disapproval now registered on that kind face. But unlike as in childhood he felt no regret for his words. Phineas was a lonely man, liable in that loneliness to see friendship where none existed, to misconstrue the false for the genuine and sincerity where there was only treachery . . . to hear on a young woman's glib tongue the promise of affection when that affection was centred not upon the man but upon his wealth.

'You accused her of being a prostitute. Then you are a fool!' Phineas's lips hardly parted. 'That was ungentlemanly of you . . . you disappoint me, Michael, I had thought to have taught you better than that.'

A knife blade could not have cut so sharp as the stab of those words. Michael watched the tall figure of his uncle lean heavily on a cane as he left the room. The old man was annoyed at his behaviour, disgusted at the way he had spoken to Callista Sanford. Staring into the dark red wine Michael Farron smiled grimly to himself. Phineas Westley was vexed at his behaviour, unhappy with what his nephew had said to a young woman. Taking a mouthful of wine Michael swallowed hard. Strangely enough his nephew felt exactly the same way.

9

It was over! Sitting in the tiny living room, Callista felt the silence crushing in on her. She had walked alone along Holyhead Road. Women, shopping in the only hour they could spare from the nailmaking shared with their husbands, flitting like dark birds in the overcast street, had crossed their breasts, lips moving in silent prayer; men going to and from their shift at colliery or iron works had doffed flat caps, holding them against the chest until the cart had passed. She had felt their sympathy, it had flowed from each of them reaching her in some unspoken silent wave. The people of Wednesbury were no strangers to a pauper's burying.

There had been no church service. Tears like chips of ice lay on Callista's cheeks in the freezing fireless room but their coldness was no match for the ice in her heart. Ada's husband had wheeled the cart into the cemetery of St James's church, pushed it to where a dark hole marked a spot in the further corner, then with an apology he could not leave his work for longer had left. It had been a kindness wheeling the cart for her. Callista had thanked him; she had known every minute away from his labours meant a little less food for his family, for children such as those who had made the tiny imitation posy. Closing her eyes she saw again the tiny flowers nestled like silken jewels on a bed of velvet. The coffin, no more than a crudely shaped box, the services of the gravedigger, these had been given grudgingly yet that tiny offering had been given from respect and love, and it would have meant more to her mother than would the most elaborate wreath of lilies.

But what parting gift had her daughter given? Lying in her lap Callista's fingers twisted into each other. She had given nothing, she had not even been at her mother's side to take her hand or to speak a word of love; she had failed, failed the one she loved more than anything else in life: and what was that life without her, where was the use in living it!

'I've just popped in to see you be all right . . . eh, wench, you never drunk the tea I fetched you in.'

Hardly aware of Ada Povey's presence, Callista stared at her fingers twining in her lap.

'I knows how you feels, ain't a woman in Trowes Court as don't know the pain you be feeling now. We've all felt it before buryin' child or husband, layin' a mother or father to their rest; it feels the heart be broke inside of you and I'll mek no pretence . . . you'll carry the hurt of it for many a year to come, but time places a salve on all hurts, and gradually the sting is drawn, the pain eases and though the mark of it never fades complete you finds you can live with it.'

Moving to the window, so small and narrow it admitted little daylight at any time, Ada twitched the closed curtains, pulling them aside two or three inches, a gap which would be widened a little each day until they were drawn fully open.

'It don't serve no purpose you just sittin'.' Ada glanced at the motionless girl. She had spoken no word since coming from that churchyard, made no attempt to move but just sat staring at nothing. It was a wonder the poor wench were not frozen to the bone sitting with not a spark of fire. But there was nothing to make a fire with, the bucket in the yard were empty as the food cupboard. Lord, if the wench didn't find work soon her would be lying alongside of her mother six foot under the sod.

'This don't be what your mother would 'ave asked.' Ada felt the tremble of the thin shoulder beneath her touch. 'Her would want you to be strong, to lift your 'ead and be a credit to her; her wouldn't be happy to think of you givin' in. I ain't sayin' to forget your sorrow but to live you must walk alongside it.'

'I don't want to live, Mrs Povey . . . I don't want to live!'

Her own tears trembling on her lashes Ada held the girl who turned to press her face against her. How many times had she heard that same cry, those same words? How many women had she held while their hearts broke? Nobody in Trowes Court had an easy life and Callista Sanford was no different from the rest, but in every house except this one there was kin to share the sorrow. Yes, life had treated this wench hard and chance was it would treat her harder yet.

Leather money bag fastened about his waist, ledger in the crook of his arm, Oswin Slade reached the end of Foster Street, his nose wrinkling with distaste as he took the right-hand turn which led into Portway Road. Each of the houses he had called at collecting rent had been a twin of its neighbour, reeking of poverty and filled with kids packed in like berries in a jam pot. That was not going to be the life of Oswin Slade; he was not about to let poverty grind him into the dust or work himself to an early grave feeding a bevy of children. One . . . a son, yes, a son he could train, teach to be like himself, a man to make life do as he said, to become a figure this town would take note of.

'Me mother said to tell you 'er ain't in.'

Oswin looked down his nose at the barefoot child who had opened the door of the first in the line of soot-grimed houses. The pattern was beginning! Week after week there were one or two thought to get away with not paying their rent. 'Me mother says to say 'er'll pay double next week . . . my 'usband don't yet be 'ome with his tin . . . will you tek 'alf this week and a week and a 'alf next . . .' They ran like lines in a play, well rehearsed but forgotten the moment it finished – and he had heard them all.

A tousle head tilted upwards, the child's large brown eyes stared blandly from a face showing no sign that the words he had spoken were a lie. They learned at an early age! Letting his glance rest momentarily on the open ledger Oswin snapped it shut then met those so innocent brown eyes with a thin smile.

'Your mother is out, you say?'

'No, mister,' the lad met Oswin's smile with a grin, 'I d'ain't say that, I said as 'er ain't in.'

The boy was young, no more than seven or eight, but brains sharpened early in Portway Road and this little toe-rag was as sharp as they come. Fingers tightening on the pencil held between them Oswin controlled the anger biting keenly at his tongue.

The fading smile denoted his only admittance to the annoyance that had him wanting to slap the grin from the boy's face and he appeared to think a few seconds before answering.

'It is unfortunate your mother not being at home because I have a message for her. But then you and I both know how smart a lad you are so perhaps you could give the message for me.'

Stepping a few paces back from the doorway Oswin looked up at the window of the bedroom where he knew well the mother stood listening.

'Tell your mother.' He raised his voice, letting it bounce from one smoke blackened building to the next. 'Tell your mother she's been given notice to quit the premises . . . the bailiffs will be here first thing in the morning!'

His words had carried like smoke on the wind running before him from house to house and in each women had stood with coins in their hands. They realised Oswin Slade made no empty threat. But those women, lips trembling as they watched their children's keep disappear into the leather bag, would not be long alone in knowing that; soon they would be joined by others, joined by Samuel Ramsey and Edwin Derry.

Emma Ramsey has a lover . . .

The words he had heard in the Turk's Head Inn, the words spoken behind that glass screen, rang in Oswin's brain as he continued his round of rent collecting. They had rung there ever since his first catching them, had taunted him with their promise. He could use them to advantage, they were the stepping stones to the life he promised himself, the foundation stone of the fortune he intended would be his. But how to go about it? Blackmail was not something you shouted like he had just shouted that eviction order, it was a private matter, one best kept between himself and the men he would bleed dry! Samuel Ramsey would find no pleasure in parting with his money and no satisfaction in hiding his wife's infidelity from his friends. And what of Edwin Derry? But it would afford Oswin Slade a great deal of pleasure to see that conceited, self-important poetaster, that wife of Derry grovel . . . and even more pleasure to laugh in that haughty disparaging face!

He would pay her back a thousandfold for the insults she had thrown at him, for all the times she had threatened to end his employment and watch him slide into the gutter along with the rest. But it would not be him felt the slime of the gutter, not his arse would hit the slippery slope; Oswin Slade would climb and if fortune was with him then the shoulders of Ramsey and Derry would not be the only ones he would use as steps.

'The rent man be 'ere, he said to tell you he don't 'ave all night to wait on you.'

Callista's face still pressed close to her middle, Ada looked at her youngest wiping his nose on an already crusted sleeve. It was a losing battle trying to keep the six of them clean while working every hour God sent at the nailmaking, a trade which brought home less every week.

When Callista pulled away, Ada reached a hand to the string tied across a grate which had seen no fire since the night of Ruth Sanford's passing. Taking down a strip of cloth, she pressed it into the girl's hand.

'You 'eard what the lad said, I 'ave to go pay afore Slade busts a gut and he'll be to this house next so you best give your face a swill. Eh wench, 'tis a pity . . .' Breaking off, Ada caught the scruff of her son's neck, marching him from the house; the rest of the sentence silent in her mind. *A pity you've promised yourself to that man.*

Oswin would be here in a few minutes; it took little time to mark an entry in his ledger and then he would come to this house. Callista rinsed her face in the bowl of water Ada had drawn earlier from the pump in the yard. Using the cloth to dry her skin she held its dampness to her eyes. If only she did not have to see him again, if only she could just close her eyes and fade out of existence, be free of cold and misery, be free of Oswin Slade. But the world rarely gave what was wished for.

She was to be his wife. Her movements automatic, her fingers numb with cold, Callista draped the cloth back over the string. She was promised to Oswin Slade, to a man who had not spared the time to attend her mother's funeral. She had told herself the news might not have reached him, that he had not known of Ruth Sanford's death, yet all the time she had recognised she was duping only herself; Wednesbury was a small town, a warren of narrow streets and close packed houses; very little happened in one that was not known in almost every other within hours and Ruth Sanford's passing would have been seen as no secret to be kept. No, it would have been no secret; Oswin would have heard but had chosen not to call. He was prepared to stoop to marry her daughter but to acknowledge the mother, even to pay respect to the dead? Oswin Slade's back did not bend that far.

'Callista, I did not know . . .'

Movements awkward and wooden Callista turned towards the figure entering the house. Already he saw his coming into this house as a right, entering without a knock, not waiting to be bidden, already the master.

'Why was I not informed?'

Where were the words of condolence? Where the softly spoken comfort of a man for a stricken fiancée? Where the feelings of a man in love? Inside the frozen barrier circling her mind the questions hung like spiked icicles.

'You should have sent word to me . . . imagine how my not being present at your mother's funeral must look, the picture it presents! Really, Callista, you should have more thought.'

'My senses were not all they might have been, my mother's dying—'

'Was not unexpected!'

Sharp, and reprimanding, edged with the usual self-righteousness, the words pricked at the shell of ice which through the past days had held her together.

'Your mother's dying cannot have been so much of a shock as to make you forget your duty, you should have . . .'

Duty! It pierced the barrier like a spear. That was all Oswin Slade could think of, her duty. But it was not duty to her mother he had meant, it was Callista Sanford's duty to him, the submissive unquestioned duty she must always pay once she became his wife.

'I should have . . . ?'

Meeting a look he had not seen in her before, Oswin hesitated at the coldness of it. Was she challenging him, questioning his superiority of thought? Maybe not but any hint of such must be nipped at the bud, removed before it had any chance of growth. He wanted a wife who not only knew her place but kept it and with it a quiet tongue.

'Yes, Callista,' he forged on, 'you should have sent word to me.'

'Why?'

'Why?' Disconcerted by the flat monosyllabic question Oswin repeated it while his own mind juggled an answer. 'How can a woman as intelligent as yourself voice such an inane question? You should have gotten word to me so I could—'

'Have sent some excuse not to attend? You were aware of my mother's passing though you pretend otherwise.' Apathy suddenly falling away Callista saw the nuance of expression flick across the pale eyes now watching her with new acuteness and she went on. 'You did not come here nor yet to the church-yard not because of my failings, Oswin, but because of your own.'

'My failings?'

Drawing a deep breath Callista watched the face with its already deepening jowls, the pompous line of the mouth thinned now to mark his offence. How could she ever have thought of joining her life to his!

'Perhaps not the best description but as true as any other.' Frigid as hailstones, Callista's words drummed one after another, rapping into the room. 'You failed to suppose I knew the honest reason you did not come, that reason being you might be seen. You did not want the taint of a pauper's burial touching the name Oswin Slade.'

'There is no need to speak of that!'

It was curt, peremptory, cutting in its sharpness. A week ago, perhaps even yesterday, she would have obeyed the latent command underlying the brisk remark – but yesterday was gone! Holding that pale wintry glance with one she did not realise held all of her own distaste, all her repugnance at this pedantic man, his heavy features drawn into a frown, she let the storm which was building inside her hurl its defiance.

'There is every need!'

Violet glaciers stared undaunted, holding his own answering gaze with a resolution he had never expected to see in the docile, acquiescing girl he had chosen to make his wife, and Oswin felt the first stirring of doubt. But quickly as it had come he dismissed it. He did not make mistakes, her words were no more than the after-effects of that funeral. Tomorrow it would be gone and she would be her normal self again.

The confidence of the thought lending a spark of leniency, he smiled over the ledger he had flipped open. 'The trials of the day have upset your mind.' His look dropped to the column of pencilled numbers. 'We will say no more of it.'

For once he had said something which found an echo of agreement in her heart. The light of a solitary candle glinting on the raven darkness of her hair, Callista nodded.

'Yes, Oswin, the trials of the day have upset my mind, a day which you did not offer to share. But I am glad you did not come to be with me for had you done so my mind might still be in the state of torpor which had me believing marriage to you would be best, that I would still be telling myself you were acting only out of love. Yes, my mind was upset but not in the way you think. The pain of today has burnt it clear and now I can tell you what I have known yet kept hidden in the hope of providing my mother with a few physical comforts. But my mother is dead, Oswin, and so is that hope. In that loss I no longer need to lie, to pretend marrying you would be anything other than anathema, a living nightmare. So you need have no more fears people of quality may see you with a pauper's child for there will be no marriage between us.'

Momentarily stunned, Oswin stared at the small heart-shaped face, glowing velvet eyes gleaming defiance. Callista Sanford would be an asset to his plans and nothing, especially not her, could be allowed to stand in the way of those. It drew his senses together like a magnet. Returning his glance to the page of the open book he forced a nonchalance to his voice.

'That is nonsense, Callista, but I shall overlook it this time. Now if I might have your rent . . .'

'You may overlook whatever you wish but I shall not!'

The definite snap of it tweaked the doubt Oswin thought he had overridden. The pencil hovering, he glanced again at the thin figure staring obstinately across the margin of space the tiny room allowed between them. She was daring to defy him! Well, in three weeks' time he would be her husband . . . and he would take great delight in proving to her he was not a man to be defied.

The thought a morsel to be savoured later, to be rehearsed and lived through again and again while lying in his bed, he smiled. 'Callista, you don't know what you are saying, you are not in your right mind.'

'Oh but I am.' Callista returned the smile but in hers there glowed the certainty of deep-seated truth. 'I have never been more in my right mind. My agreeing to become your wife was simply a means to an end, one for which there is no longer the necessity. The need no longer exists for me to force myself to suffer your touch; I did not and will not ever feel less then revulsion at the thought of sharing my life with you . . .'

Watching her, Oswin's smile faded, but the weak light of the candle burning on the shelf above the empty grate reflected the glint of anger in washed-out almost colourless eyes, and teeth clenched behind lips whitened by seething fury.

'Take care!' The attempt to mask the threat encased in those first words was not entirely successful so he forced himself to pause, to breathe evenly before continuing. 'You wouldn't want to say something you may come to regret.'

'No, Oswin, I would not. But then you see I shall not regret saying what has been in my heart to say for so long. I will not marry you, nothing you could say would induce me to change my mind.'

'Nothing?' The threat did not fade as Oswin glanced again at the book balanced in his hand. 'But what of the rent for this house . . . how else can you keep a roof over your head unless it is by marriage to me? And what of the money owed? You know tenancy operates on the basis of payment at the end of any week, payment which is now due, Callista, a debt you must pay. Do you have that money? No, I see you don't. I could mark it as paid, put the amount in for you . . . but you don't really expect that of a man you no longer intend to marry.'

He was right of course. Callista's fingers twisted the thin cloth of her patched skirts. A week's rent was due on this house, a debt she had no means of paying. Watching the jowled face, the innate menace in the thin twist of the mouth, the sneer in those pale eyes, she felt a cold trickle along her spine. He was playing her as he had often done, using her poverty as a weapon against her, a tool with which to gain what he wanted. It was blackmail, sheer psychological blackmail, a cold-hearted act of the worst sort . . . but then when had Oswin Slade had consideration of any other kind, when had he held feelings of tenderness or benevolence, an interest in anyone's welfare other than that of Oswin Slade? But all of her thinking of him could not deny the truth.

. . . *how else can you keep a roof over your head?*

The words seemed to taunt, to sneer their derision. It was a challenge he had flung at her, a blow which depleted the joy refusal of him had brought. Debts could not go unpaid. Oswin knew her pride and now he waited like a vulture for her to apologise, to beg as he would make her beg . . . then to suffer those hands, that mouth . . . she couldn't . . . she couldn't! She could go to the Parish, ask their help as she had a few days ago. But that was as much a humiliation as pleading Oswin's forgiveness and their answer would still be no.

The thought of life with him sickened her now as it had always done. To be chained to him by marriage vows would be a lifetime sentence of unrelenting misery. But a life of going from place to place, homeless and spending nights sleeping in barns or under hedges, begging every day for work to earn a penny to buy bread . . . was that preferable? Could she live that life any easier than the one Oswin held out to her?

The choice heavy in her stomach, Callista looked again into the pale triumphant eyes.

10

'The chap said 'e knocked a few times but there were no answer but I knowed you was here so I fetched 'im in.'

Light struggling between still partly closed curtains played over the figure sitting beside the empty fire grate.

'Eh lad! Best say the reason of you callin' to this house.' Ada Povey turned to the young man who had followed her into the room.

'Mrs Sabine Derry sent me.' Quick eyes darted in the half light, a shiver rippling as the cold caught him. 'Her said to give you this and to tell you should you be in need of assistance then you may call on 'er.'

Thrusting an envelope towards Callista he glanced at Ada when the girl made no move to take it.

''Er, Mrs Derry, 'er said to give it to nobody savin' a Miss Sanford. This do be 'er, don't it?'

'Ar, lad, this be Miss Sanford.'

'Then why don't 'er take it?'

'You 'eard what he said, wench, nobody but yourself be given leave to tek charge o' what he brings and like as not he were told it must be delivered so best tek it an' let the lad go about his business.'

'I do 'ave other messages to run.'

Twitching the envelope hopefully between his fingers the young man turned as Callista took it from him then was halted by Ada's firm 'Don't you be swannin' off 'til you knows whether or not there be an answer.'

'Mrs Derry d'ain't—'

'Mebbe's 'er d'ain't tell you to wait,' Ada interrupted, 'but Ada Povey be tellin' it so you just stand you there 'til Callista be seein' what it is that woman be sendin'.'

Opening the envelope Callista withdrew the contents, Ada's sharp intake of breath accompanying the young man's soft surprised whistle as they saw the white five-pound note.

'Eh, Callista wench,' Ada breathed, 'it be a gift from 'eaven!'

No, not heaven! Callista too stared at the crisp note. It was a gift from the woman she had seen at Emma Ramsey's house. But why would the woman send her money? Why make her the object of her charity?

'Eh!' Ada breathed again, 'It couldn't 'ave come at a better time.'

It should not have come at all! The thought pushed itself to the front of Callista's mind. There was no reason. Slipping the money back into the envelope she held it out.

'Please thank Mrs Derry for her kindness but tell her I have no need of this.'

'No need!' Ada almost choked. 'You needs that money like a drownin' man needs a towline!'

Flat and lifeless, Callista's tone matched the feeling inside her. 'I have no need of charity.'

'That be bloody daft talk if ever I 'eard it!' Ada snapped. 'Charity it might be but it be given with a good 'eart an' you should be grateful. The easiest way to starve in this world be to pretend you be rich when truth is you don't 'ave two farthings to your name. Take what Providence 'as seen fit to send and thank the Lord for His bounty.'

It seemed Callista had not heard the other woman's outburst. Leaning a little forward she set the envelope in the young man's hand then folded her own in her lap. 'Please do as I ask,' she said as his fingers closed over the envelope. 'Return that to Mrs

Derry. Tell her I could not accept her charity the day we met at the home of Mrs Ramsey and I cannot accept it now.'

'Eh wench!' Ada shook her head as the young man made a rapid exit. 'I've seen money trickle away like water down a drain but I ain't never seen it rush away in a torrent same as I seen now. I knows last night's 'appening left you feelin' fair flummoxed but to turn your back to five pounds! Why, it would feed you for many a day to say nothin' o' payin' the rent. Do my 'eart good to see the face of Oswin Slade next time he comes a callin'.'

The next time he comes calling! Fingernails biting savagely into her palms brought reality bursting fully into Callista's mind. She had refused to think of that, refused to think of anything after what had happened but now, watching her neighbour leave, her brain was painfully alive. Oswin Slade would return to this house and he would do again what he had done last night.

Those eyes had watched her; pale, almost colourless they had held to her face and in them she had seen the gleam of pleasure, a sensual, almost hedonistic pleasure! Numb to all around her Callista remembered the night just past. Oswin Slade had relished his power of the moment, enjoyed watching her knowing she had no alternative but to ask his forgiveness, to plead they could still be married. Yes, he had enjoyed her discomfort and by its showing in his eyes had painted a graphic picture of what her life was to become.

She had breathed deeply, trying to find that inner strength which would enable her to do what he expected and she dreaded and with that breath had come the words, silent unspoken words, yet they had filled her mind. With the sweep of an invisible wave, they had washed it clear and its ebbing had left those words: 'Trust your own heart, go the way it leads.'

They had given her the strength she needed. Alone in this room she had given her answer. 'I will not marry you!'

For a moment it felt like every trace of air had gone from the house, burned away by the heat of his anger, consumed by the passion of fury which twisted Oswin Slade's face to an unrecognisable mask while breath had hissed like serpents behind his teeth.

'So that is your choice,' he had snarled. 'Then this is mine!'

So swiftly she had not seen it coming he had thrown the ledger aside and in the same move had grabbed her blouse, ripping it apart.

'You don't be the only wench wanting to marry Oswin Slade, and soon I'll be in a position to choose among the best, but that don't mean I won't take my due from you. For months you've been promised to me, *this* has been promised to me!'

His head had dropped and she had felt that mouth close over her breast, the wet tongue pulling at her nipple. It had felt like she was bound, fettered with ropes she could not see, and then the hands, those thick-fingered hands, had grabbed the waistband of her skirts, wrenching it loose, tearing away petticoats to grasp at her bloomers.

'You don't make a fool of Oswin Slade and get away with it! Edwin Derry won't be getting his rent but I'll take my payment, there'll be no reneging on that.'

It was the sound of the button popping from the skirt, the ping of it falling onto the brick hearth, that one tiny sound ringing against the sluggish torpor closing her mind, that and not the snarling words had broken the hypnosis, smashing it to fragments, freeing the scream locked in her throat.

But the cry had barely left her lips before a heavy hand smashed against her temple.

'Cry out again and it won't be just your virginity I'll take, it'll be your pretty looks as well! Won't be no more men you'll dangle from your apron strings when that face of yours be scarred.'

'Get away . . . get away from me!'

Her hands pushing at his shoulders had brought another blow sharp and stinging across her mouth.

'Oh no!' Cunning and insidious the words had breathed into her face, a sly vulpine look creeping across his own as he knelt where she had fallen. 'I'm not going away from you, Callista, I'm going to get closer, much, much closer; you will feel me inside you, feel me taking what is rightfully mine. But first we must make certain the cries you will try to make go unheard.'

The smile spreading across his jowled face he had snatched a neatly folded handkerchief – the flaunted hallmark of his being neither nailmaker, steel worker nor collier – and thrust it in her mouth, then had tied her hands above her head with the muffler taken from his neck. Standing up he had leered over her naked body, while thick fingers fumbled with his trousers.

Sickness and loathing had flooded from her stomach, filling her mouth but finding no escape.

'You are thinking how hateful.' Erect flesh was exposed as clothing dropped to his ankles; he had laughed, a malevolent venomous rustle in the throat, the sound of malice. 'But what does it matter how you feel or what I leave in your belly.'

He had lowered himself onto her, forcing her legs apart, the pleasure gleaming in his pale eyes as bare flesh touched bare flesh.

'Not to worry about my leavings . . .'

He had felt the shudder of revulsion tremble along her limbs as he lay across her and again that cold-blooded, ruthless laugh had scraped across his throat.

'No, not to worry, the Workhouse will find a place for paupers and their bastards.'

'The cemetery also finds a place for bastards!'

It had been screamed, the anger of it filling the tiny room, bouncing from its walls, but the loudness of it was swallowed by Oswin Slade's howl as an iron poker slammed across his bare buttocks. 'That be where you be goin', Slade . . .' The poker had fallen again, catching his thighs as he rolled clear. 'Supposin' the church be disposed to tekin' a bastard such as you be!'

White with anger Ada Povey had brandished the poker, jabbing it into the man struggling to climb into his trousers then, as the door banged open, had flung her shawl over the girl sprawled at her feet.

Callista closed her eyes, remembering.

Ada's husband had come running into the room shouting for his eldest son to 'watch the door'. He had glanced once at her hands tied above her head then had grabbed Oswin, dragging him away.

'They'll learn the bugger! 'E's made his bed but I guarantees it'll be many a long day afore 'e lies comfortable in it.' Temper bubbling, Ada had released her then helped her dress. 'I never did trust that dirty little toe-rag, 'tis said a crooked stick throws a crooked shadow and Slade be twisted through an' through.' Cries from the yard had filtered into the room.

Callista's eyes opened, watching fingers writhing together as the emotions of the night before threatened to take over. Cries of anger and sharper ones speaking of pain; Oswin Slade had paid for his treatment of her but it would not end there. Ada had said her husband and son would teach him a lesson but Oswin Slade too would want to teach; he would not forget what was done to him, he would return and when he did Callista Sanford would be his pupil.

It was a strange sort of relationship that existed between that girl and the man who has spoken so peremptorily to her, ordering her to return home. He had called her his fiancée, he had claimed he had not struck her . . . that had been a downright lie but her being promised to him, had that also been a lie?

Michael Farron watched the last of six narrow boats being loaded with steel plate bound for Southampton shipyards.

'*I do have business that needs my attention . . . to go with you to your home would mean missing an important appointment . . .*'

The words of a man to the woman he loved? A man mindful

of his fiancée's welfare, of her safety walking dark alleyways alone at night? Hardly! And the rest, the words which had followed telling her rather than asking if she understood?

After the final batch of steel had been lowered into position on the boat, Michael put his signature to an invoice before handing it to the bargee. Smiling to the man's wife and children waiting to board he called his wish for an uneventful journey then turned, crossing the wharf to where several warehouses stood tall against the day.

The attitude of the man he had reprimanded that evening in Wednesbury market square had irritated him, the man's caution striking the girl had infuriated him. It angered him still. He should have knocked the blackguard down, given him a beating he would not have forgotten in a hurry!

But would having done that have prevented the memories which returned so often, would it have cleared his mind of the picture of a small heart-shaped face, of eyes which looked at him like dark moons? Even more, would it have rid him of wanting to see the girl again?

Alone in the small office he walked to an arch-shaped window, staring down at the busy comings and goings of narrow boats in the canal basin discharging cargo or being reloaded in a hurried cycle which used every moment of daylight.

His uncle had called him a fool and so he must be to still have the girl in his brain; but Phineas Westley was the bigger fool to see friendship where there was none. Maybe the girl Phineas spoke so highly of was not a prostitute but then nor was she in need of a father confessor. It was more likely she viewed Phineas Westley as her way to a comfortable life. And his uncle? Staring hard at the scene below Michael Farron saw nothing but a sad old face. It would be the age-old story, the young woman taking the older man for everything he had while giving nothing but unhappiness in return.

He had seen when talking to Phineas of speaking to the girl in

Paget's Passage, seen the interest in his eyes and, moments after, the anger harden that usually smiling mouth, glisten in those fine eyes.

Phineas had been disappointed in his nephew's behaviour. Turning from the window Michael walked to the desk set to one side of the compact room. But better that than be disappointed by that girl; it would not be so long healing the hurt Phineas felt now as one he would get from marrying . . .

Marrying! Dropping to the leather chair drawn to the desk Michael Farron stared into space. Would he? Was the interest Phineas showed strong enough to have him marry the girl?

His head falling backwards to touch the chair, Michael Farron's eyes closed. He did not want the man he loved and honoured hurt . . . but should he marry Callista Sanford whose would be the deeper hurt: Phineas Westley's or Michael Farron's?

Oswin Slade would return. The thought had not left her mind all of last night. He would want revenge and it would be taken on her.

'There be no need of you leavin'.' Ada Povey looked up from wiping the nose of her youngest. 'You sit you against the fire, this one be off to school and there'll be no one to bother you.'

The woman had been kindness itself, insisting she stay the night in her already overcrowded house, but staying longer could only be an addition to the problem. Every bone shrieking from the tension that had held them during the long hours of a sleepless night and even now refused to release them Callista rose, holding her torn clothing together with visibly shaking fingers.

'I . . .' She paused, searching for a reason to leave which would not hurt the woman's feelings. 'I need to mend my clothes.'

Ada shook a head liberally threaded with grey. 'Ar, I sees that. I'll be in the workshop should you 'ave need o' me though there be no fear o' Oswin Slade settin' foot inside of this 'ouse nor that

of your own agen. My man told 'im that from now on he takes
the rents while standin' in the street and should it 'appen Slade
go against that then he would be sat down to a nice bit o' liver
. . . his own, fried an' dished up on a fancy plate!'

It was meant to reassure, to bring a smile, but Callista could
manage neither. Thanking Ada again, repeating she was feeling
much better, she slipped from the house, halting at the door of
the one she had shared with her mother. Ada's husband might
forbid Oswin Slade entry to this house but Ada's husband could
not be present every moment of the day . . . or every hour of the
night!

Forcing herself to go inside she stared about the living room.
Ada had opened the curtains fully but the light the window
admitted was barely enough to lift the shadows . . . shadows
which as she stared at them seemed to take on the shape of a
figure. It would always be there. Clenched lips stilled the sob
hovering in her throat. Now a second nightmare was joined to
that of her childhood and it would return to haunt her in the same
way. Thought of it adding a shiver of dread to the fear already
trembling in her fingers she opened her mother's sewing box,
pressing a hand to her mouth as she caught the sheen of a scrap
of blue silk.

Why had Emma Ramsey refused to accept that gown? Why
deny as she had the quality of the stitching . . . the fact that both
cloth and design were the ones she had given? Reaching for the
fragment, Callista stared at it lying across her hand. Had she been
influenced by the presence of her visitor, had she felt a gown
made by a local woman would be deemed by her friend to be
inferior to that bought from a city salon?

For all or none of those reasons Emma Ramsey had not
accepted the dress she had commissioned, nor had she paid for
it. The other woman, though, had offered money . . . pity?
Disgust at Emma Ramsey's treatment of a girl so obviously in
need of payment? There had been no call for her to feel either

yet she had offered those coins. Why? And why had she herself not taken them? 'They must take only that which they earned.' Her father's maxim learned in her early years whispered in Callista's mind as she touched the scrap of silk with one finger. But always telling the truth had also been a principle of his teaching and now, standing in the cold empty room, she admitted a truth she had denied her mind. It was not simply the thought of accepting charity had prompted her to refuse those coins, it had been the look she had glimpsed in those grey eyes . . . a look which stayed beyond the perimeter of understanding, which would not step forward into recognition and which for some inexplicable reason aroused a feeling of wariness. But that caution had no basis in reality and she had pushed it away. Sabine Derry had shown her worth in offering yet a second helping hand, sending five pounds to a girl she did not know. The woman was as kind as was Ada Povey.

Slipping the cloth into the pocket of her skirt, she took needle and thread. Sitting in the chair her mother had used, she sewed her torn clothing with neat, almost invisible stitches. She must thank the woman for her kindness; she must thank Sabine Derry.

11

It would be the talk of the whole town. Women would snigger as he passed, gossip behind his back while men would laugh in his face, call out their vulgar remarks, pass some facetious comment. He would be the object of derision, the source of everyone's amusement!

'Ar, 'twere along of Trowes Court, Povey kicked his arse forrim . . . they say it were Povey give 'im a right latherin' . . . belted 'im in the yard did Povey, give 'im a fair old pummellin' . . .'

Phrases he knew would already be passing from mouth to mouth, covering Wednesbury with the speed of a racing pigeon, flitted through Oswin Slade's head as he made his way to Hill House. He would be the butt of men's jokes and snide humour, a regular laughing stock and all because of that bitch!

'Eh up, Slade, where d'ya get them black eyes . . . 'ave an argooment wi' a tram did ya?' Across the street several men returning from work watched Oswin hurrying past.

'Weren't no tram! Slade don't be the sort to act rash . . . 'e just picks on women, they be more his barra.'

'Reckon ya be right,' another answered, 'women be more his style when it comes to usin' his fists, ain't that right, Slade?'

'Ar, well, watch 'ow you goes, mate,' the first man called, his voice raised to follow the scurrying figure. 'Ya might meet a five-year-old, give ya another belloilin' would a babby.'

Roars of laughter followed, smarting like the slash of a knife; Oswin compressed his bruised and swollen lips, flinching from the sting of them. They could laugh now, the whole bloody town could laugh, but Oswin Slade would laugh last. He would make them pay . . . every last one of them would regret having their fun at his expense . . . but that sow Callista Sanford would pay most of all! The thought, still raging as he was shown into the study of Hill House, burned higher as the eyes of Sabine Derry flicked over his face.

'I see there is a deficit in the takings again this week, Mr Slade. Why is that?'

What she really meant to ask was what had given him the appearance of having gone several rounds with a fairground pugilist, a bare-knuckle fighter who knocked any man senseless for being daft enough to challenge him.

'The tenant did not have money to pay.'

'I see.' Sabine Derry lifted her glance from the ledger he had handed across the pristine desk. 'I did warn you—'

'I . . . I've taken steps—'

'Steps?' Grey eyes glinting like ice chips, Sabine interrupted the interruption. She disliked Oswin Slade; disliked the thin sandy hair, the pale eyes almost colourless in the heavily jowled face; everything about the man was unappealing but the thing she relished least was the shrewd brain she knew lay within that unattractive head.

'I have issued notice to quit.'

'*You* have issued notice to quit!'

Oswin's body throbbed with the pain of the beating he had taken but he knew better than to ask if he might sit.

'The tenant is destitute,' he answered, 'it was obvious to me there would be no rent paid again next week therefore I issued a termination of the occupancy of the premises.'

Such fancy words. Sabine returned her glance to the ledger. Such a detestable little man. Had the issuing of notice to quit rewarded him with those bruises? She certainly hoped so.

'The tenant is destitute, you say.' The grey eyes lifted. 'How can you be sure of that? How do you know failure to pay is not simply a ruse on someone's part?'

'Callista is not like that . . .'

An eyebrow shaped to careful perfection rose as the explanation halted in mid-sentence. 'Callista?'

'The tenancy was held by Ruth Sanford.'

'Was?'

The eyebrow had remained raised, the one word flipping the strained silence. Why the hell did she want an explanation? Hadn't he given those notices many times before without her ever wanting to know the reason? Money was Sabine Derry's only interest, failure to pay their rent, anyone's failure, her only concern; what was so different this time? His body screeching for rest he knew he would not get until the woman was satisfied enough for him to leave, Oswin resumed his explanation, missing the tightening of long fingers at his first words.

'Originally the premises were let to Jason Sanford, passing on his death to his wife Ruth Sanford. Several days ago the woman died, leaving her daughter Callista as the sole occupant. I have known Callista well for some time now . . .'

How well is well? Had he tried to increase that knowledge? Was that the reason he was bruised black and blue? Sabine watched the figure trying to ease sore bones without her detection.

'She would not refuse to pay rent if she had the money with which to pay.'

'So you gave her notice. Could the girl not work, earn the money to keep the roof over her head . . . or is it she is still a child, too young yet for employment?'

Her glance steady, giving no indication she already had the answer to her question, that she too knew the girl he spoke of, having met her once at the home of Emma Ramsey, Sabine waited.

'Callista is not a child.' Oswin winced with the pain of moving his lips. 'She is quite capable of work but has been unable to secure any form of employment.'

'Is there any reason for that? Does she perhaps think herself above menial work?'

Christ, what did this woman want! A fully itemised account, a detailed report with every specification of Callista Sanford's history underlined! Anger added to pain chivvied Oswin's fragile patience.

'I would not have given that as a reason!'

He had answered more curtly than intended. Sabine Derry noted the quick look of regret pass across the pale eyes and smiled to herself. The man was not what he thought himself to be.

'Then what reason would you give?'

Keeping a rein on his tongue Oswin shook his head then immediately wished he hadn't, the grievance of the action shooting barbed arrows along his neck.

Teeth clenched against the assault to his swollen mouth, his head held immobile, he replied. 'I can offer no reason. She cooks, she sews as well as her mother did and the house is well scrubbed.'

It seemed he knew this Callista Sanford as well as he claimed. But again, how well was well? Keeping the thoughts to herself Sabine ran a finger over the page of the ledger pausing against one entry. 'This appears to be the first default in payment. I wonder you acted so quickly in ordering the girl's removal . . . that you did not consult me before doing so.'

She was enjoying this, the harridan! Oswin's fingers curled with the desire to smack his fist hard against that rat-trap mouth. *That you did not consult me!* The words rankled, adding to the irritation he was having difficulty controlling. If he had come to her she would have given the same instruction; Sabine Derry would evict the devil out of hell if there was a penny to be got from it!

'However.' The gimlet look lifted. 'The question Mr Derry will be asking is how the unpaid amount is to be recovered? What would you have me say to him?'

You could try telling him about those visits to the Ramsey house . . . Quenching the desire to smile Oswin held the woman's challenging glare . . . no, he would do the telling of that himself and enjoy it. Sabine Derry thought she had him by the balls, that she could squeeze them and watch the man writhe, and for the moment he would let her revel in it, bask in the feeling of power it must give, but revenge was a sweet wine and he would drink deep from the cup.

'The house does not have anything of much value,' he answered, aware of the mockery barely hidden in the cutting gaze, 'but I have alerted the bailiffs. I am sure the proceeds of their work will be enough to reimburse Mr Derry and pay their wages.'

Her eyes still on him Sabine snapped the ledger shut. She could get rid of him now, send him packing while keeping his own wage to offset the loss of rent. There would be no query from Edwin; this side of the business he left in her hands. But she would not end the association just yet; much as she disliked Oswin Slade it amused her to watch him squirm.

Shawl drawn tight against a sharp breeze Callista glanced at the house the bailiffs had stripped bare. It had held little comfort, a bed for her parents and one for herself, a table, a cupboard; yes, the physical comforts of life had been lacking but there had been no shortage of love, that had ever been present. Her father and her mother . . . they had been filled with it, filled with a love for each other so obvious it had shone in their faces, sung in their voices, and the fulfilment of that love was a daughter they had both adored. But now both were dead and their daughter was alone.

The sound of hammer on anvil, the hiss of bellows being

pumped, filled the communal yard with the sounds of nailmaking, the hard manual labour which the Poveys and others
worked at from dawn to near bedtime.

'*You knows you can lodge along o' me* . . .'

Ada's words quiet in her mind she turned away, the sound of
her boots lost amid the noise from the brewhouse which served
as the Poveys' workshop. It had been genuinely meant but how
could she place an extra load on kind shoulders? For all their long
hours of toil they barely earned enough to feed themselves; handmade nails could not compete with the price of machine-made
ones and their livelihood was as threatened as her own.

'. . . *but where'll you go?*'

Ada's question had been one she could not answer. Where
could she go? She had no relative to whom she could turn, no
one to offer a helping hand . . . but there had been one. Shawl
held across her nose and mouth, the brisk breeze plucking at the
skirt she had patched, she left Trowes Court. The bailiffs had
come early in the morning and with them had been Oswin Slade.
He had watched while the only possessions she had were carried
to a waiting handcart and all the while he had smiled. The tallest
of the two men sent to evict her, a brawny man whose jacket did
little to disguise the muscles bulging beneath, had come to speak
with her when the last item had been loaded; he had murmured
an apology then had pressed two threepenny pieces into her
hand. Too numbed by unhappiness it was not until some time
later she had become aware of the coins and then it had been too
late to return them.

'*The Lord be good to them as be good to others* . . .'

Ada had smiled on seeing the small silver coins but the smile
had faded, her next words dark with feeling.

'*And the devil be good to them as thinks o' none other than their-
self . . . may he show that goodness to Oswin Slade by the soon takin'
o' the snipe-nosed swine* . . .'

It was wrong to think badly of another. Charity of heart is

valued more by heaven than charity of hand. So her father had taught but remembering Oswin's smile as he watched the last of her life fall in ruins about her feet she had found it hard to abide by that teaching. But she had prayed in her heart the charity of that bailiff's hand and heart would not go unrewarded. She had known Ada would not accept one of the coins, would insist it had been no hardship sharing what they had with her, but feeding one more mouth had meant a little less on the plates of her family. It was not much with which to repay that woman's generosity but it was half of all she possessed. Tuppence worth of scrag-end of neck would provide a pot of broth and a penny loaf would help fill empty stomachs and show her gratitude. So one of the coins given had been spent. The meat left simmering over Ada's fire, the loaf in the food cupboard, she had left without saying anything; goodbyes would mean more tears and they had each shed enough of them.

Coming to the corner of St James's Street she paused. The lowing of cattle being delivered to the abattoir carried on the morning. Were those animals as frightened as she was, did they too wonder what lay before them?

'Was you wantin' summat?'

Startled by the voice Callista's nerves throbbed, spilling words jerkily from a near-strangled throat.

'No . . . no, I . . . no . . . thank you.'

'Then I wouldn't be standin' about if I was you, it be a fair cold breeze, you could tek the influenza from dawdlin' there!'

Wiping both hands over a bloodstained canvas apron the man touched a finger to a grubby flat cap then turned back inside the tall building.

She had sometimes stood here on this spot as a child. Free from school she had listened for a moment to the cries of beasts delivered for slaughter then had run all the way home to Trowes Court, her hidden tears as much for them as for herself.

Her glance was drawn to the opposite side of the narrow street, where it seemed the breeze held a sound not of its own but a hiss of words, the words of a woman filled with spite.

'*I saw . . . I saw him there and I knew . . .*'

Hands shaking, Callista was a child again, a child whose mouth trembled with fear.

'*. . . it was because of her . . .*'

Seeming to hurl against her ears, the hiss now became a harsh grate of sound, Callista's nerveless fingers released the shawl. Caught by the fingers of the breeze, it whipped from her shoulders to fall about her feet but the cold its absence left behind was lost in the deeper coldness that was memory.

'*. . . it was because of her and you . . .*'

Callista's head jerked as the face of childhood felt the vicious slap of a long-boned hand and her own cry mixed with the savage, '*. . . you . . . the spawn of his evil . . .*'

A sudden push sent her off balance, to stumble against the abattoir wall driving away the nightmare. Callista heard the angry mumble of a woman hauling a young girl with one hand, the other carrying a large wicker basket.

'. . . Ain't satisfied wi' trollin' theirselves on the street o' nights, they be doin' it now in broad daylight . . . should be 'osswhipped . . . they wouldn't be so fond o' wheedlin' a man outta his money given a taste of a 'osswhip; strumpets . . . pah! They should all be jailed!'

First the man who had accosted her as she had walked along the narrow alleyway of Paget's Passage and now the woman who had brushed angrily past, they both thought her a prostitute! Had the man from the abattoir had the same thought? Retrieving her shawl, keeping her glance from the dark building that was St James's Church of England School, Callista broke into a run. There was one more thing she must do before leaving Wednesbury forever.

★

He had not seen the young woman again though he had looked for her each time he had gone into the town, and that had been more often than was usual. His visits to the shop of Joseph Glaze had not been those of a man bent on purchasing some rare and costly antique but of an old man bent on seeing again the thin, slightly ragged figure which infiltrated his thoughts more and more often . . . a foolish old man? Phineas Westley opened the cabinet which housed the perfectly sculpted statuette. Taking it into his hand he smiled at the bewitching face.

'She knew all about you,' he murmured, 'knew your secrets; that it was you shot the great Orion with an arrow, you who demanded Autonoe's son Actaeon to be transformed into a stag and torn to pieces by his own hands because he happened upon you bathing with your nymphs, and you who in a fit of pique filled the marriage bed of Admetus with snakes when he forgot to make a sacrifice showing gratitude for your assistance in gaining the hand of Alcestis. Oh yes, my divine one, she knows your dark side as well as she knows your beauty.'

There had been only the brief few minutes of their walk together along Upper High Street but in that short time she had shown a knowledge of the ancient beliefs, of his own beloved mythology . . . and he had wanted those minutes to go on, to talk longer with the girl who it seemed shared something of his passion.

Was it only that? Was it simply their shared conversation brought the girl to his thoughts so regularly? Or was it she had awakened something deeper, rekindled the desire he had thought long buried? Touching a finger to the cold marble face, tracing the delicately carved features, he sighed. 'Would she come to this house?' It was a smiled whisper but it held a longing, a pathos which throbbed.

'Would who come to this house?'

In the seconds of his standing on the threshold of the graceful room Michael Farron had caught the faint whisper, heard the yearning contained in it. His uncle had used the word 'she'; it was a person and not an object he wished to have in his house. Could that person be the girl he had met along the High Bullen? Was it Callista Sanford he wished to share his house . . . to share his life?

12

Breath short and rapid from running, Callista stood beside a cluster of daffodils and narcissus, their colour beginning to peep from the tip of each bud. She had been given the bulbs by an old gardener who had lived at the coach house adjoining the lovely grounds of Oakeswell Hall and her mother had helped her plant them here where her father lay buried beyond the wall enclosing the sacred ground of the church of St James. Yellow had been a favourite colour and whenever he saw it he would smile and say, 'It is the colour of the cloak of Apollo who spreads light across the sky . . .'

She had early learned to say nothing of the stories her father told, had kept them to herself while at school. They would not have gone well with the clergy who came each Thursday morning to give a Bible lesson nor with Miss Montroy who would doubtless have used them as a reason for yet another punishment, another sharp slap to the face of a frightened child.

But he had not taught the myths as truth; he had not allowed them to detract from the Christian faith, but had been careful always to keep that at the forefront of his daughter's mind.

But it is hard to believe. The cry only in her mind, Callista knelt to rest a hand on the gentle rise of ground which she and her mother had visited each Sunday afternoon, then she on her own when Ruth had become too ill to make the journey. It is hard to believe in heaven's mercy when your mother dies in pain, when she is given a pauper's burial!

'I tried, Father . . .' Tears fused the budding flowers, turning them into a tiny carpet of yellow among the green of grass. 'I tried so hard . . . but it was not enough, I should have gone on trying . . . forgive me.' Choked on a sob, the words rested a moment on the breeze, then were gone.

Rising to her feet, her shawl draped across her trembling mouth, she whispered again. 'I loved you, Father; I loved you both so much.'

Sitting on a bench protected from the breeze by the lee of the church Phineas Westley watched a slight figure kneel to the ground then rise again. Judging by the dress it was the figure of a woman but why had she knelt . . . and why was she now running away?

Gloved hands resting on a cane, he watched as the same figure now came along the path leading from the lych-gate which circled to the rear of the building where burial plots were marked, some by elaborate structures, others by simple headstones. But this woman had gone to neither. Intrigued, Phineas allowed his gaze to follow the shawl-draped figure to a corner of the grave-yard close against the wall which minutes ago had separated her from the church grounds.

What was the mysterious figure doing? Squinting against the brightness of the morning he watched the same ritual. Standing several moments, it seemed she stared at the ground . . . but at what? That small area was devoid of any remembrance stone; not even a simple wooden cross marred the unkempt grass-filled patch. A gust of wind found its way around the sheltering wall and Phineas rose. Whatever the woman was about she had chosen a brisk morning to do it. He had heard talk of some scoundrel taking flowers from graves in order to sell them to the next grieving family; if this proved to be that varmint he would thrash the thief himself, woman or no woman!

Grasping his cane firmly he took a step forward, then halted. There were no floral tributes, at least none he could see; apart from a few hothouse-reared lilies and carnations already wilted by the cold the only wreaths were designed with evergreens and berries. So if not the flowers? But yet it was . . .

Phineas's mouth twisted with disgust and anger as the figure knelt to pick up a small posy, the yellow of petals gleaming like gold. How dare she! Phineas furied inwardly. What kind of woman would rob the dead! He must not call out, that would serve only to alert the thief and she would be off too quickly for him to catch.

Ignoring the path which took a circuitous route he picked his way between graves, his steps making no sound as he approached. Almost level he raised the cane then frowned as the shawl-draped figure sank to the ground and kissing the posy placed it upon a patch of fresh-turned earth whose dark colour hidden among the grass had not been visible from where he had sat.

'Miss Sanford . . . my dear . . . I apologise for disturbing you, I did not recognise . . .'

'You are not disturbing me, Mr Westley, I was about to leave.'

Seeing the glance aimed at the still half-raised cane Phineas lowered it, his smile holding a continuation of the spoken apology.

'I should not have taken it upon myself to approach you. It was wrong of me to assume . . .'

The girl deserved an explanation. To find a man standing behind her an upraised can ready to strike was enough to put the fear of God into her. Allowing himself a short cough, a moment to collect himself, Phineas explained why he had approached as he had.

'You acted in everyone's interest – except perhaps that of the thief.'

'Thank you for being so understanding.' Phineas acknowledged the words with a smile. 'However, I might have employed a little more caution, waited until you were leaving, then I would have seen you were not the culprit. But I let anger get the better of me.'

'Any man would have done as you did but I doubt any thief would bother to steal the flowers from my mother's grave. You see they are not real; they are merely scraps of cloth sewn by the children of Trowes Court.'

An unmarked patch of earth . . . a posy of artificial flowers. Phineas glanced again at the tiny offering, its silken petals glistening still with the gleam of dew defiant against the breeze. A pauper's grave! He had known from her shabby clothing, from the fact of her coming to the High Bullen to stand in the line of hopefuls seeking a day's employment, that the girl's family had little money . . . but a pauper's burial! That would indicate they possessed nothing. But she had made no mention of an illness when they had talked that morning. Could it be the woman – her mother – had met with some accident?

'The posy is no less pretty for being made of cloth.' He spoke gently. 'I am sure your mother would have thought the same.'

No, they were no less pretty. Callista's own glance lifted to travel beyond the enclosing wall, resting on the spot where budding daffodils nodded tall among the grass. They would bloom every year but soon the little cloth gift would fade, the silk of petals and the velvet of leaves would fall to the onslaught of weather, they would disintegrate and leave no trace; her mother's resting place would become unrecognisable among the covering grass; there would be no cluster of daffodils, no delicate narcissus to mark where she lay.

'You have my deepest sympathy, my dear. Please be kind enough to extend it also to your father; perhaps in time I may be able to do so in person.'

Her gaze not moving from the tiny island of yellow Callista answered quietly. 'My father would have been grateful for your condolence and honoured, I know, to have spoken with you, but that will not be possible.'

Not possible. Did that mean the man was crippled, maybe bedridden? Phineas felt a momentary stab of disappointment. But that need not bar him from meeting the man, of fulfilling the hope he had held since encountering his daughter, of having the pleasure of talking with him on a subject he clearly loved.

'Perhaps he might be prevailed upon to allow me to call . . .'

'My father would not refuse, he would have taken great pleasure in speaking with you except . . . except he lies there beneath the patch of daffodils.' Callista turned to face the man beside her; her lashes glittered with tears but her voice as she continued held a love which beat in every word. 'Both my parents are buried here; my mother lies at our feet, my father there beyond the boundary of the church. My mother died a pauper while my father took his own life. They were not given the sacrament of church service, not assured of the love of heaven, but my heart will ever be filled with love for them.'

That was what she had been doing at the other side of the wall: she had been visiting her father's grave.

'The world can be very cruel, child,' Phineas answered, watching the tears spill, 'I know for my own loved ones lie here also. My parents,' he pointed to a rectangular structure carved in the fashion of a small columned temple, 'and next to them my wife. I come each day to speak with them to tell them, as you were doing, of my love.'

She had been too preoccupied with her own misery to see the sorrow of his. Shamed by her oversight Callista brushed a finger across her cheeks, wiping away the tears.

'I am sorry if I sounded bitter . . .'

'Don't be. There is nothing more natural. Only by letting bitterness escape can the heart be truly healed.'

'You sound so like my father; those words could well have been said by him.'

'Then it may be we could have held more in common than simply a predilection for the classics and mythology.'

'The Artemis!' Appalled by her own forgetfulness, Callista apologised. 'I had forgotten. Please forgive me, I should have asked about the damage, I . . . I cannot pay the cost of the statue now but if you will give me time . . .'

Looking into wide violet eyes, their lovely colour darkened with dismay, Phineas Westley felt the heart inside him quicken. Give her time! At this moment there was nothing he would not give her.

'There is nothing to forgive.' He smiled. 'The beauty of our lovely goddess is unmarred.'

Walking beside her as she turned to leave, Phineas wished as he had on several occasions that the figurine had been damaged; that way he would have had an excuse to meet with this young woman again, to talk, if only of the cost of repair. The beautiful artefact was genuine, its rarity adding greatly to its value, but he would willingly have sacrificed it to have Callista Sanford . . . to have her what? Beholden to him? To be in his debt for a sum she could never hope to pay? No, no, he did not want that, he wanted the girl as . . . but he must not let his own aspiration show. Not yet.

'It is a great relief to hear the statue is not broken; I could never have forgiven myself had it been.'

'Would it have been so dire?'

Reaching the body of the church Callista looked back to where the graves of her parents lay. 'To rob the world of beauty no matter what its form is always dire, especially when it can never be given back.'

'What we lose to death cannot be given back, my dear, but it can sometimes be replaced.'

Sharp and edged with bitterness, Callista's reply echoed on the still morning air. 'How! How can parents be replaced?'

His own gaze travelling back over upraised stones to rest on the tomb of his family, Phineas answered quietly. 'Of course, those dearest to us can never be replaced nor would we wish them to be; their place in our heart is unique but the love they gave need not be totally ended, it can be, in some measure, passed on, shared with another, for love is as valuable to life in this world as is beauty.'

A hand lifting to touch the bruise dark about her mouth, Callista thought again how like her own father's words were those. He had always looked for the best in everything; said that despite the bad there was always a little good. But what was good about her father taking his own life? Where was the good in her mother never having enough to eat or working every minute she could force herself to stay awake? No, sometimes there was no best!

Their steps accompanied by the tap of the cane on the pathway they walked in silence, then having passed beneath the lych-gate Callista turned, the question which was bothering her finding its way from her tongue.

'Mr Westley, the . . . the statue . . . I would rather you did not hide anything from me, not allow kindness of heart to keep secret any harm done to it. Please, tell me honestly . . .'

'You think I lie, Miss Sanford?'

Dismay stark and real flooded through Callista, shining from the depths of her eyes. She had offended him, insulted his integrity, but she had not intended that. Embarrassed and regretful she tried to answer but Phineas halted the stumbling words with a smile.

'I do not lie when I say that, unlike yourself, the Artemis is unharmed. May I ask what it was caused your face to be so bruised?'

'I . . . it was my own carelessness. I . . . I tripped.'

Now who was not telling the truth? Watching the colour deepen further in that wan face Phineas felt a sharp surge of anger. Had someone beaten the girl – a member of her family – the man at the market place, the one Michael had spoken of? Lord, should that prove so then the man would regret it!

She had already wished him good day. She was turning away, leaving . . . he might not see her again. Phineas Westley's thoughts raced along a fresh path. With her father no longer alive he had no plausible reason for calling at Trowes Court. Maybe she might decide she could not stay in that place. If he were to speak of what he hoped it must be now.

'Miss Sanford.' He spoke quickly. 'Please stay a moment; I have something I wish to say to you.'

They both thought they had got the better of him. Callista Sanford had refused to marry him; true, she had made no spoken promise, but there had been no need, marriage to Oswin Slade . . . what need was there of a promise, it was an honour! He, lowering himself to marry a destitute. She had refused, thrown the honour back at him, but he'd had his revenge, he'd seen her turned into the streets and that was where she would stay. Callista Sanford would starve, die a pauper as her mother had done, and Oswin Slade would laugh at her grave. Sabine Derry was no destitute, neither was she a young girl to be frightened and bullied. But she too had slighted him, treated him with scorn, and that could not be overlooked; like Callista Sanford that woman had crossed the line. Two women had taken him for a fool; one had paid. Oswin smiled. The other would get her reckoning soon. Sabine Derry would find her insults to be costly . . . very costly.

Standing among shadows wrapping a narrow entry which ran alongside the Turk's Head, Oswin pondered his next step. He needed fact, not the gossip of jealous women. He needed to hear from the horse's mouth the facts of Emma Ramsey's immoral carryings-on, and more to the point whether or not Sabine Derry might be playing a part in them. Not that it mattered. He smiled again. By the time he was finished not a soul who could read or hear would believe the Derry bitch innocent.

From the direction of the Shambles a woman's coarse laugh

answered a remark called to her by a street sweeper clearing the refuse from the day's market, refuse already sifted and sifted again by vagrants and beggars, by women with no other way of filling children's stomachs. A second remark was called to follow sharp tapping footsteps; Oswin tensed. Sally Baker would pass in a moment.

But she had not passed. Oswin smiled in the darkness, holding the struggling body close against him. He had not intended meeting Sally Baker this way, he had thought to meet her inside, ask for her services as did so many other men buying their night's pleasure in what, not so many years before, had been the smart hotel such as the George was now . . . the elegant establishment of whose wealthy clientele Oswin Slade would soon be part.

A heel kicking sharply against his shin dispelled the dream and smile; he swore deep in his throat as he slammed the squirming figure face forward against the wall.

'Listen to me, you no good tuppenny trull, you're going to give me—'

'You'll get what it is you wants, you don't need to go knockin' a girl about!'

A girl! Oswin stifled a snigger. Sally Baker was no more a girl than he was an angel.

'You let go o' me, let me turn around and I'll show you a good time . . . unless o' course you likes to tek your jollies from the back. Either way Sally Baker can mek a man's toes curl up to 'is chin.'

Wedged between his body and the wall, the woman pushed her bottom into his groin, moving provocatively against him. Maybe later; Oswin grabbed a handful of hair, snatching the head back, smiling at the gasp of pain in the woman's throat. Maybe he might avail himself later, but first he would relish the pleasure of hearing what this trollop had to tell.

13

It looked so still, so peaceful. It would take away the pain, end all sorrow. Callista stared into the green waters of Lea Brook. Just a few minutes and it would be over, she would be with her beloved parents again . . . just a few minutes. Eyes fixed on the dark ribbon she stepped forwards, her feet sinking slightly in the damp sedge of the bank . . . just a few minutes . . .

'Ain't yoh got no more sense than to go plodgin' in that there brook!'

A voice, sharp and accusing, rang over the still afternoon.

'A wench yohr age should ought to know better, that don't be no kids' paddlin' pool yoh be steppin' to, set yohr feet too close an' yoh'll like to wish yoh 'adn't for that there brook 'as a undertow as would 'ave yoh sucked down afore yoh could blink . . .'

As if the voice had woken her from a deep sleep Callista looked with dazed eyes at a woman clad in dark skirts and shawl, a bulging sack balanced on her head, small girl clutching her black apron.

'That brook be dangerous!' One hand steadying her burden the woman continued her reprimand. ''Ow do it be little 'uns is expected to learn when they sees others yohr age actin' like it don't be? Huh, I 'ave no knowin' what yohr mother learned ya but I thinks her wouldn't be 'appy seein' what yoh be doin' now! Yohr time be better spent pickin' coal.'

Balancing her own sack of coals salvaged from pit heaps rising like black hills in the distance the woman turned on her way irate mutterings fluttering behind like startled birds.

. . . I thinks 'er wouldn't be 'appy seein' what yoh be doin' now . . . the words repeated loud in her brain.

But her mother would be happy were they together. Callista looked down at the water rippling at her feet. The hunger would be gone; the misery would be ended; just a few minutes . . .

. . . I 'ave no knowin' what yohr mother learned ya . . .

It was not this . . . it was not this! Callista tore her gaze free of the hypnotic spell of the brook, the enticing peace offered by its soft velvet waters. Clambering free of the muddy sedge she stood breathing deeply. Her mother had taught her never to give in, taught the easiest way often proved the harder but always the more worthy. She would never have seen suicide as an answer; it had broken her heart when her husband had chosen that path. How much more so should her daughter choose the same?

But your mother is dead. How is she to know . . . how is anyone to know?

A few yards from her the brook seemed to whisper, to call softly its promise of peace. Glancing at the malachite ribbon, its jewel-like colour stretching a ribbon between dark banks, Callista's heart answered.

I will know . . . I will know.

He had asked her to come live in this house! Michael Farron's fingers tightened about the fragile William IV baluster wineglass. Phineas had asked that girl to make her home here at The Limes!

'. . . she pointed out the burial place of her father . . .'

Above the rim of his own exquisitely engraved glass Phineas Westley observed his nephew with a steady gaze. Michael had listened, displaying none of the scepticism he had shown while hearing of that first meeting with Callista Sanford at the High Bullen, and none of the faint mockery which had coloured his conversation when relating his own meeting with the girl in

Paget's Passage. Sipping the excellent Tuscan vernaccia, savouring the dry crisp taste on his palate, Phineas was not misled in his judgement of wine or man. Both were without equivocation, both bore a candour he found trustworthy, but beneath the sophistication was a sharp cutting edge. The fact of not allowing his inner thoughts to show did not mean his nephew entertained none.

Swallowing the wine, the taste a shimmer of perfection in his throat, Phineas lowered his glass but though his glance left the face so painfully like that of his beloved sister his perception of the moment was crystal-clear as the wine.

'It was covered with daffodils and narcissi,' he went on quietly, 'a golden carpet laid out just beyond the boundary wall.'

Beyond the boundary wall! Michael forked a mouthful of Veal Apricote, the piquant bouquet of ginger, coriander and cumin as delectable to his nostrils as the flavour of the meat to his tongue. *Beyond* the wall, that meant the man had been a suicide, he had taken his own life!

'They made a beautiful picture.'

And the girl? Michael chewed slowly, making no reply. Had she been clever enough to cover what no doubt lay beneath her heart-rending account of her life, had she presented an equally beautiful picture. A tearful child alone in the world? Maybe alone; definitely appealing; but no child. A picture of a small heart-shaped face, angry eyes blazing back at him, flashed into Michael's mind. No, Callista Sanford was no child.

'I had hoped to meet with her father.' Receiving no response Phineas was speaking again. 'From the little she told of him he was well versed in the literature and mythology of the ancient world; one does not often meet with a man of such erudition in this town. To learn he was no longer alive was quite a disappointment to me.'

But not the girl! Taking a sip of wine Michael met the penetrating gaze, giving no indication he knew the discerning capabilities contained in it. Was the fact her father no longer lived a drawback to her aspirations or was it a bonus?

'But the girl herself seems well educated . . .'

She does indeed! Michael's sardonic thoughts ran unchecked. But in which school? Madame Falsehood's Academy of Deception . . . Deceitful's School of Trickery . . . and was her favourite subject fraud, was her education that of how to delude an old man?

'She spoke of the Artemis as though it were an old friend.'

Here was the crux of the matter. Phineas Westley had friends, he was well liked and respected within Wednesbury and outside of it, but of all his associates none held his own passion for the world of yesterday; they were businessmen and their interests reflected that world. Laying aside knife and fork Michael looked across the smaller two-pillar Regency table his uncle favoured whenever they dined together. Though not elaborately laid it sparkled with silver and crystal; Crown Derby plates and dishes gleamed their beautiful colours in the soft light of candlelit chandeliers. Everything in the house was an object of grace and beauty, many lovingly chosen by Phineas and Rachel. His Aunt Rachel! The deep sorrow he had felt at her death, the anger of a young boy robbed twice of loved ones, echoed in the deepest reaches of his heart. Since her passing his uncle had turned even more to the past, to a world which brought him solace from a pain that had been and sometimes even now was unbearable. There, among the ancient long-gone people, in a society today known only in books and ruined architecture, lay Phineas Westley's joy . . . was the joy about to be snatched by some charlatan, a girl pretending an interest when her true interest lay only in securing for herself a husband who in doting on her would not see his wealth slipping away?

'Phineas.' Michael's fingers twiddled the crisp damask napkin lifted from his knee. 'This girl . . . I agree it sounds as though she has been given some degree of education, and if her account of her parents' death is the truth then she has my sympathy but . . . well, what I mean is . . .'

'What you mean, Michael, is can it all be fiction? Is the girl spinning a web of lies in which to catch an old fly?'

'There's no hiding anything from you, is there?' Michael's smile was rueful. 'I learned that long ago yet I still give myself headaches bashing my skull against a brick wall; but in all honesty, Phineas, you know precious little of the girl apart from a name which you yourself must admit is one thing designed to catch your attention: and was it? Is the name Callista her true given name or one specifically chosen as a starting point for that web you spoke of?'

Above the neat silver-flecked goatee beard Phineas Westley's grey eyes reflected the smile his mouth did not reveal. Michael Farron's veiled accusation was not one of jealousy for his own standing in this house or his place in an old man's affections; it was a reflection of the love and concern the lad had always shown for the uncle he loved. Looking directly into the vivid blue eyes Phineas thought again of the mother of this man he loved as his own child, of the sister who had been half of his world, a sister who had the same fierce protective love for him as had her son, and with the thought his mouth received that inner smile, displaying it gently with his answer.

'Birth name or contrivance? That, my anxious nephew, I will make no effort to determine.'

'But why!' Perplexity and doubt creasing his forehead, Michael flung the napkin aside. 'You investigate the authenticity of the smallest of objects you buy, you scrutinise the credentials of every purchase you make with all the care and precision of a coroner, you cross-examine the claims made for everything you acquire with the ferocity of the Spanish Inquisition yet you apply none of these precautions to that girl . . . you ask her to come into your life, to share your home, while all you know of her could be written on the back of a postage stamp! Why, Phineas? Why?'

In the gleam of crystal-shed candlelight Phineas Westley read the concern registered on his nephew's handsome face. He spoke as he did because of that concern; one certainty in all of this was that Michael Farron did not hold any selfish motive.

His voice quiet and even, contrasting with the sharp tone of his nephew, Phineas answered. 'Firstly, Michael, I do not consider Callista Sanford an object, I do not look upon her as a thing and I most certainly do not see her as a purchase. As to my reason for not investigating her background that is simple to understand. I like Callista Sanford, I like talking with her, I like her company. Being with her gives me pleasure . . . and most of all I trust her.'

As men of his famous chronicles trusted the enchantress Circe, who rewarded that trust by turning them into swine! Or did his uncle see himself as Odysseus, who was impervious to the charms of the sorceress? But there was no Hermes to aid this man, no watchful god to protect him from a woman's poison; there was only his nephew. Watching the face which resembled his own so closely Michael Farron knew his warnings would be mist in the wind; fleeting and easily forgotten they would count for nothing against the pretty face and soft words of Callista Sanford.

No, this was not the way he had thought to meet with Sally Baker. Oswin slid a hand over the mouth of the squirming woman. To speak with her inside the tavern had been his plan but then caution had made its voice heard. The Turk's Head was much frequented; not all of its customers were there solely for ale and those that came for the use of a woman could be choosy. They would look around, notice which woman was with which man and Sally Baker might be popular with a number which could mean Oswin Slade being noted. That he did not want; being associated with a common prostitute would not sit well with the life he had set out for himself.

A boot catching a second time against his shin, he caught his breath. This slut was stronger than he thought, if she broke free . . . ran into the tavern . . . then it would be all up with him. There was like to be many a man in that place would be only too happy to help cripple Oswin Slade. But he could not question her here. Uncover her mouth so she could answer and the bitch would scream; even now the sounds of her struggling might be overheard.

Thoughts turning rapidly detracted for a moment from his concentration, but a moment was all the struggling Sally needed. Feeling the hand clamping her mouth relax she twisted loose, then bit hard on the grasping fingers.

His reaction one with the yell he buried in his throat, Oswin's hand withdrew from the woman's face. Snarling with rage and pain he twisted his fingers savagely in the hair at the back of her head then smashed her forehead hard into the brick wall.

Christ, what had the whore done! The figure slumped in his arms; Oswin listened, weighing every sound against the thumping of his own heart. Had they been heard? Had his own strangled cry been detected? Blood pounding, veins racing, he stood poised. He could drop her and run . . . at the first sound of a voice he could run; this alley gave onto unused ground, he could be across it and lost among a warren of houses bordering it before anyone realised he was here.

The beat of his heart boomed like a drum in his ears as he waited. What if the trollop were dead? Should he leave her? His grip slackening, the inert figure slid lower against his body. But if the blow had merely stunned her, so that when found she wasn't dead but alive . . . alive and able to tell who it was had attacked her . . . God Almighty, the bloody whore could see him sent to the gallows!

Beyond the narrow opening the sound of a carter's wagon rumbled on the night. In a few minutes it would have pulled into the yard, there would be ostlers and stable lads buzzing about like bees around a hive and that yard looked out over the derelict ground. Weight pulled on his arms as the senseless figure slid a little closer to the ground. Beads of perspiration trickling into his eyes blurred the buildings opposite the narrow alleyway into an unrecognisable whole. Christ, what did he do! Blinking his sight clear he stared at the opening which gave onto the street. This alley, no more than a three-feet-wide space separating the tavern from an adjacent poulterer's shop, was, he knew, regularly used as a short cut across the empty space to Camp Street, and any minute now somebody might take that shorter route and find him with Sally Baker . . . a dead Sally Baker?

Liquid beads gathering together trickled wetly over his cheeks and down the sides of his neck, burying themselves damply into a stiffly starched wing collar.

Dead! Not now . . . not yet . . . the trollop couldn't be dead, he hadn't asked . . . she hadn't told him . . .

Unreasoning anger blinding him to the risk any noise would elicit, his hands clamped on the slumped shoulders; the woman's boots scraping the hard earth, he dragged her towards the open ground.

Luck had been on his side, luck or the devil and he didn't care which. At home in Loxdale Street, doors locked and curtains drawn against the night, Oswin Slade listened nervously for any sound other than the thumping of his own heart. That slut of a prostitute hadn't died . . . well, not from that strike of her head against the wall.

Fingers still shaking fumbled with the single row of buttons fastening his chequered coat.

He had hauled her to the open ground intending to ask his questions there but a full moon had it lit up like a circus ring; a bloody field mouse couldn't have stood there unseen! He had thought of bringing her here to this house then had ruled out the idea. Spotted bringing a woman home, one seemingly so drunk that he needed to almost carry her, would arouse talk among neighbours. 'Oswin Slade never entertained a body in his 'ouse, now 'ere he were wi' a wumman, a drunken wumman, an' 'twere none but whores drunk theirselves stoopid . . . so Oswin Slade had fetched 'isself a trollop 'ome.'

Oswin flinched as if hearing aloud the words sounding only in his mind. How the tenants whose rents he rarely failed to prise out of them would relish that bit of gossip! But that was a pleasure they would never taste. Buttons freed, he laid the jacket across his bed then slipped from his trousers. He must make sure no sign of that struggle showed on his clothes. There was nothing to link him with that accident but it would do no harm to be careful. Reaching for a clothes brush from the marble-topped washstand confiscated from an evicted tenant he brushed coat and trousers thoroughly before hanging them in a tall cupboard.

Sally Baker had told him all he needed to know. More than he needed. Hands and face rinsed, he smiled at himself in the cheap mirror hung above the washstand.

It had been a heart-stopping exercise half carrying, half dragging her to that empty ground but once there he had realised the impracticality of it. Not only brightly lit as if by a beacon, it was edged around by buildings, the rear of shops with living quarters upstairs, houses knitted together tight as stitches in a jumper, and all had windows any one of which could have someone watching him. He had been as badly burned as scalded dragging the slut there.

Slipping his nightshirt over his head he climbed into bed. He had contemplated abandoning the whole thing, of simply leaving her there, but again the thought of her regaining her senses, of naming him her attacker, had that idea nipped smartly in the bud. So he had hauled her to her feet, his own head lolling on his chest, pretending they were both well under the influence of alcohol, had proceeded to stagger through the maze of constricted streets strangled with condensed rabbit-hutch houses.

Several people had passed, women muttering about drunken louts while men grinned and referred to the hangover that would be his the next morning. But none had interrupted his journey or the thoughts racing in his head. He couldn't haul the woman far, which ruled out the open heath, nor could he risk standing about where they were easily seen. It had been a problem but he had solved it on coming to the Holyhead Road. Opposite him the municipal buildings reared black and heavy against the shadows. That place was no delight to the folk of Wednesbury during the day; at night it was as welcome a place to be as was a graveyard.

Lying in the darkness of his bedroom Oswin smiled again. The rear of the Town Hall had proved the perfect place.

Sally Baker was already moaning by the time he had hauled her there and a few stinging slaps and a threat of strangulation should she utter so much as a whimper had her fully conscious and listening.

Yes, she visited Acacia Villa, yes, she knew the acquaintances of Emma Ramsey. Sally Baker was a strumpet but she was no fool. She had replied to every question he had put and those replies . . . the smile widened . . . they had been all he could pray for. She had given him what he wanted, offering more besides if he let her go, but the thought of tumbling her even for free no longer held any appeal. But yes, she could leave.

Watching moon-chased shadows play over the wall of the bedroom Oswin gave himself to the pleasure of remembering.

'*I aint a blabberer.*' Sally Baker had peered at him in the darkness. '*I won't go tellin' nobody about you, I won't go tellin' nuthin'.*'

'*No, you won't, you won't be telling anything.*' Softly spoken, the words were almost lost beneath the clatter of a steam train coming along from the junction of the White Horse.

'*G'night then.*'

She had wished him goodnight! The smile locked to his mouth, Oswin stared at the dancing shadows. The stupid slut had wished him goodnight! And he had answered in like vein as his hands had closed about her throat.

It had taken only minutes for the body to slump against him, for his fingers to tell him no pulse beat in that throat, but the minutes had been long enough for the sound of the train to say it was not many yards from where he stood. It had been a case of move or lose the chance. And he had not lost it. Hauling the lifeless figure upright, holding it so it shielded him, he marched it to the front of the building and as the train drew almost abreast flung it beneath the wheels.

There was no danger of her saying anything . . . ever. Oswin's satisfaction sat like a warming poultice. Clothes torn, a face marked by the blows of a fist . . . the woman was obviously a prostitute strangled by a client. The constables would be right on two counts; two out of three wasn't bad.

But Oswin Slade had been right on all counts. What he had only surmised, Sally Baker's terrified answers had proved correct; and tomorrow . . . tomorrow he would begin to count the profits of the night's labour.

14

She could still end her hunger, buy a beef pasty . . . would that be so wrong?

Callista left the waters of the brook behind and sank to the heath, resting her back against an outcrop of rock which helped shield her from the freshening breeze.

It did not have to be a pasty. She swallowed the saliva the thought of hot meat and crusty pastry gathered in her mouth. A stale loaf, bread a few days from the baking, could be had for a halfpenny; she could buy one of those and still have twopence halfpenny.

But what if twopence and a halfpenny were not enough? What if the least it would take was threepence?

Taking the silver coin from her pocket Callista stared at it. It was so small lying there in her palm . . . so small to buy so much. But would it buy that which she had promised or would the pangs twisting her stomach be no more than a useless gesture? Maybe. Pushing to her feet she returned the tiny coin to her pocket.

She need not go on. The thought echoed with every movement. She could go back, live in a home filled with warmth and comfort, know the pleasure of seeing so many of the beautiful antiques, of reading those same books her father had loved.

Phineas Westley had smiled when making that proposal, a smile in which she had seen more than friendship.

A home, no more worries of finding work in order to pay rent or buy food, no more Oswin Slade! But all of those things were her gain, they were to her advantage; what would be Phineas

Westley's gain, what advantage would that man get? Pulling her
shawl close against the gathering wind she thought again of that
smile and what she had seen behind it. He was a kind man, the
episode of the Artemis had shown that. He could easily have
claimed it had been damaged due to her carelessness, could have
taken her before the magistrate and pressed for a long custodial
sentence on finding she could not reimburse him the cost of the
statue; instead he had dismissed the whole thing and now in
addition to all of that he was offering her a home.

Head bent against the sudden flurry of raindrops Callista
heard the words play in her mind.

'. . . *with your parents gone you have no other call upon you, you
are alone in the world and believe me, my dear, that world can be a
heartless place. . .* '

She did not need to live another day to find that out; hadn't
she already had very long and first-hand proof of that?

'. . . *I promise you there will be no sorrow for you at The Limes . . .
make my home yours and give us both happiness. Make the choice,
my dear, come with me now. . .* '

A shake of her head had halted him and the look which had
come to his eyes, the veil through which she had seen disappointment peep, had a sharp prick of guilt tightening her chest. She
had not wanted to appear ungrateful, to seem to be throwing
such a wonderful offer back at him, but the promise she had
made in her heart must come before anything.

He had listened as she told him, disappointment fading from
his eyes as she held the threepenny piece for him to see, and once
more the kindly smile had found his lips as he offered his help,
showing his understanding when that help was refused.

'*Do what you must, Callista . . .*'

He had taken both hands, holding them between his own as
he spoke.

'. . . *do what you have set your heart upon, and when it is done
come back . . . my home will be waiting.*'

What was it had urged Phineas Westley to ask what he had? Callista drew the shawl across the lower half of her face, protecting it from wind-lashed rain. They barely knew each other; two meetings, a few minutes' conversation in each, could hardly constitute being called friends, passing acquaintances maybe but not friends in the true sense of the word . . . yet he had asked her that . . . had asked her to . . .

'Won't you bide a while from the rain . . . it seems fair set to give a body a soaking.'

The call had come from a woman stood at the open doorway of a low built cottage, the honey-pot shape of a pottery kiln rising in the background.

'There be tea on the hob should you care to share it.'

A cup of hot tea! Callista's heart seemed to expand, to widen at the thought. A cup of tea! At this moment it seemed to outdo all the promised luxury of The Limes.

'Standing there be doin' no more than adding to the water soakin' through that there shawl; wherever it is you be 'eading for won't go no further away should you bide for a sup of tea.'

Beneath a frilled cotton bonnet a rosy-cheeked face smiled and Callista's hesitation melted.

'Be a real April shower and no mistake.'

Taking Callista's shawl the woman shook it, scattering droplets of water in a silver shower over her doorstep, then draping it over a chair set close to the hearth proceeded to pour tea into cups decorated with scarlet poppies.

'How pretty.' Callista could not keep from admiring the cup passed to her, the scarlet vibrant against the pale cream body.

' 'Tain't nothin' special, it finds work for the hands once the day be done; my Daniel says it be a frippery but I enjoys the doin' of it.'

'You painted these flowers? These cups are your work?'

Bonnet frill bobbing as she shook her head, the woman offered a lace-covered jug, pretty green glass beads tinkling against its sides. 'Not altogether they don't be, the flowers they be done by me but the cups theirselves they be the work o' Daniel.'

'They are beautiful.' Callista balanced the delicately fluted jug in her hand, admiring the same decoration of scarlet poppies. The man's work must be in great demand.

'Was a time Daniel made many crocks such as these,' the woman said, seeming to answer Callista's thought, 'but not no more, folks wants only that which stands up to 'ard wear . . . not that I blames them for that for pennies be too few and far between these days to go spendin' any on china set to break should a child bang it to the table. No, there no longer be a call for crocks thin as this, it be the thicker pottery folk of Wednesbury buys.'

Setting the jug aside Callista drank gratefully of the hot sweet tea, letting the warmth of it flow through her.

People like herself, the inhabitants of Trowes Court and Drews Court, the close-packed tiny houses of Lloyd Street and Manor House Road, of Chapel Street, Dudley Street and so many more where people lived a hand to mouth existence, those she could well understand would not buy delicate china of this sort for the very reason this woman had given, but there were others of the town who were wealthy: people such as the Ramseys and the Derrys, a growing number of industrialists and businessmen who showed a fondness for decking their homes with the trappings which marked their success. And then there was Phineas Westley, who appreciated beauty and workman- ship; his breed might not be so thick on the ground in Wednesbury but Wednesbury was not the only town in England.

Voicing what had sped through her mind, Callista saw the fleeting look she felt marked a certain sadness before the woman smiled again.

'There might 'ave been a time Daniel would 'ave thought as you just does but not no more; oh, the skill, that ain't never left his 'ands, but the love o' potting, that be long faded; now he makes the pots folks asks for, an' they be all such as you sees there along the shelf.'

Glancing where the woman's hand indicated Callista understood the fleeting, quickly submerged sadness which had passed across her face. She too judged the delicate beauty of the poppy-decorated cup against the thicker undecorated straight-sided mugs and jugs and she too preferred the former.

'How could he lose such a love?'

The woman's quiet laugh telling her she had inadvertently spoken aloud, Callista blushed.

'No need for your cheeks to take on that colour though it brings life to that pale face.' Reaching for the teapot she had placed on the bracket before the fire the woman refilled both cups, offering milk and sugar before resuming. 'It be easy to lose a love for the work of your 'ands when the love of your heart be took from you. That were what robbed Daniel, took from 'im the desire to create things o' beauty.'

'But these cups, the jug—'

'Made many a year since.' Her interruption soft, the woman opened a cupboard displaying plates and dishes all painted with the same motif of scarlet field poppies. 'Daniel made the whole set against my comin'-of-age day. They was plain cream ware but over the next year I painted each piece and Daniel took 'em to the pottery for to 'ave the glaze fired on. I might 'ave done more for there were still a few folk who comin' to the pottery left orders for the finer china but with the comin' of the children my time were all took up.'

. . . when the love of your heart be took from you . . .

Did that mean this woman and her husband had lost the children born to them, seen death take them, was that what had robbed the man of the desire to create beautiful pieces like those cups? Callista kept her gaze lowered, not wishing the reflection of those questions to be seen in her eyes.

'My father told me once of the pottery he said was here in Lea

Brook though we never came to see it. Whenever he needed a new clay pipe he went to Potters Lane.' It was almost an apology but the woman smiled as it was said.

'My Daniel has praise for the men along o' that lane but for pots an' dishes the clay there be the wrong sort.'

She had taken enough of the woman's time. Thanking her again for her hospitality Callista reached for the damp shawl, draping it about her shoulders.

'Do you?' She paused, the words awkward on her tongue. 'Do you know . . . ? Do you think the owner of the pottery would sell me threepennyworth of clay?'

'I can't say as to that, me wench, but you could ask.'

'Yes.' At the door Callista turned. 'Yes, I will, and . . . and I won't ever forget your kindness.'

As the thin bedraggled figure walked away, the woman turned indoors. There were few years in the bones of that wench but the sorrow of ages dwelt in her eyes.

Where would the girl have gone? The proceeds of the bailiff's visit to Trowes Court together with the report of his dealings laid on the desk before her, Sabine Derry read through the page again. There had been precious little in the home of Jason Sanford; had it always been like that, sparse of furniture? Of anything worth more than a copper or two . . . or had the years seen his widow sell his property off a little at a time? Property! Leaning back in her chair she stared at the paper. What property would that man have . . . what did any of the tenants of Trowes Court have?

'. . . *the proceeds of their work will be enough to reimburse Mr Derry . . .*'

She had seen the look in Oswin Slade's eyes while saying those words, a look which said he too would be repaid, that some way, somewhere his own reward awaited him. And so it did, but it would not be what the smart little man expected. Smart!

Drawing the neatly handwritten account closer with the tip of one finger her lips clamped in a line thinned with distaste. Yes, smart was the word her rent collector would use of himself. But not Sabine Derry; there were other words she would choose, words such as cunning, wily, sly and contriving . . . yes, she could find many adjectives to describe that repugnant individual, none of which would do him real justice. Gathering coins she had counted twice she slipped them into a cash box taken from a drawer of the desk. The entire value of the contents of that house! Locking the box with a small ornate key she slipped the box back into the drawer. Would the property of a certain Mr Oswin Slade be of any higher value?

He had issued the order of eviction . . . *he* had sent in the bailiffs. The irritation that had burned in her on listening to Slade's obviously self-congratulatory statement of his handling of the affair of Trowes Court glowed again in Sabine. Where would the girl go? What would become of her? That fool had given no thought to questions of that nature, but he would.

Rising to her feet, Sabine left the study. Upstairs in her own room she breathed the anger inside her. Yes, by God, Oswin Slade would think long and hard!

'Threepennorth, you says.'

Whiskers reddened with the dust of clay, fingers daubed with the same, the man sat at a potter's wheel looked at Callista. 'And what is it you expects to do wi' the clay threepence be buyin'? Won't mek you no sets o' dishes for no bottom drawer, 'tain't gonna be 'ardly enough for a teapot an' a mug.'

'I don't want dishes, nor do I want a teapot and mug.'

'Be just as well, for the money you speaks of be nowheres near enough. Pots need to be glazed and fired if they goin' to be any good, 'tain't just a matter of throwin' 'em on the wheel.'

She should have known the money she had would be insufficient. Callista watched the spinning wheel, the deft sure movement of the man's hands lifting and shaping the dull red clay, bringing it to life with a touch of his fingers, creating a thing of beauty where moments before had been only a shapeless lump.

Reaching for a thin wire attached each end to short spindles of wood the potter sliced through the base of the jug he had thrown and in one swift adept move freed it from the wheel, setting it aside on a long bench which held an assortment of freshly worked mugs and dishes.

'Eh up, wench.' She had turned to leave when he called. 'This 'ere threepennorth o' clay . . . what was you wantin' it for? You don't be from a pottin' family, least not from these parts; this 'ere be the last kiln for miles around an' you ain't used it.'

'No sir, I am not of a potting family,' Callista answered with the politeness she had been taught, 'and I have not been here before though I have lived with my parents in Wednesbury all of my life.'

Which don't be many years. Wiping his hands on a crumpled rag the man kept the thought to himself.

Hunger pains dragging at her insides Callista shivered beneath the damp shawl. Perhaps someone back in Potters Lane would sell her threepenceworth of clay. But she must go now before the last of her strength deserted her.

'You lives in Wednesbury, you says.'

He had followed her from the workshop and now stood looking at her, his keen glance narrowing through the mauve of early evening as she answered.

'Not any more. With my mother's passing a few days ago my home was . . . I decided to leave and begin a life somewhere else.'

Maybe not a wholly intended lie, but a lie just the same. He wouldn't be tekin' much of a risk o' losing should he bet a year's income that home had been teken from her, that her 'ad been thrown onto the street like so much rubbish.

'Be your father set on this venture along o' you?'

The wind, sharpening yet more with the fading of the sun, cut through the thin shawl. Trembling with the sting of wet clothes against her skin, Callista could have been forgiven for hurrying away, for leaving the man's questions with no answer, but her upbringing forbade such. Hoping he would ask no more, that with her answer he would return inside his workshop, she replied through lips stiff from cold.

'Jason Sanford died some years ago.'

'Jason, that be a name don't often be given a lad, not in this town it don't.'

Please let him be satisfied, please let him say goodnight so I can leave. Praying silently, she drew the shawl closer using the strength of it to prevent her arms shaking.

'I believe it was a favourite with his father. It seems that like his son, Heracles Sanford too loved the stories of ancient heroes.'

'Sanford . . .' Seeming not to feel the bite of the gathering evening the man stood. 'Then your father would be Jason Sanford?'

'Yes.' Callista nodded.

'The same Jason Sanford who taught along of St Bartholomew's boys' school?'

Why did he insist on keeping her talking! Teeth almost chattering Callista nodded again.

'But I knowed 'im.' The man smiled. 'It were 'im taught my Adam. Never set a task he took no time in the explainin' of afore-hand an' would allus give a lad an answer; a fine teacher my lad said of 'im.'

'Th . . . thank you, my father would have been proud to hear your son say that, please thank him for me.'

The man's face had closed as she said those last words. Why? She had only asked he pass a word of thanks. But the gleam of interest had immediately disappeared from his keen eyes leaving them dull and suddenly empty. Should she apologise even though the reason for doing so was not apparent to her? She would rather do that than leave on a sour note. But before she could bring her chattering teeth to order he had turned from her and was gone into the workshop.

Overhead the sky was darkening. Dusky mauves and lemon-tipped purples were fast becoming deep grey. The lashing rain of the afternoon was gathering its forces for a promised storm. It would be a journey in vain returning to Potters Lane; the men working there would be finished for the day, they would be gone to their homes, doors closed against the cold of the night, and likely none of them would leave the comfort of the fireside to sell her threepennyworth of clay. But she had to try . . . she could not turn her back on all she had promised.

'Eh up!' Like the clang of a bell the shout echoed on the still-ness, bouncing back from the brickwork of the kiln rising like a giant flagon black against a background of pewter sky. 'Was you not saying you was after buyin' 'andful of clay?'

15

Sally Baker had been more than cooperative, she had practically poured out answers to his questions. The stupid whore had thought by telling all he would let her go; 'But that was a mistake, Sally,' Oswin Slade smiled as he whispered. 'That was a great mistake.'

There had been no enquiry following her death. It had happened as he had thought. A prostitute too drunk to watch where she was stepping . . . fallen beneath the steam tram . . . the police hadn't bothered with any line of enquiry other than to ask at various establishments until identity was certified. 'Death by misadventure' had been the finding of the Coroner. Oswin smiled again; it had certainly been a misadventure for Sally Baker.

He had supposed he should thank the slut, lay an anonymous gift of flowers among those her friends along of the Turk's Head had clubbed together to buy from a nurseryman. The idea had faded even more rapidly than the carefully nurtured blooms when laid on the cold earth. Oswin Slade wasted his money on nobody; he wasted even less on a dead whore!

'*Thursday*,' Sally had said. '*I goes there on a Thursday . . . in the afternoon.*' Glancing to the left and right along a street empty of pedestrian or carriage Oswin thanked whichever star shone over him and slipped quickly between tall gateposts and around to the rear of Acacia Villa.

'*. . . why is it Polly Burke be given a full afternoon and evenin' away from 'er job?*'

The words overheard in that smoke-filled room throbbed in his brain; he remembered them all, every vowel and every consonant were etched deep in it carved side by side with those spewed by that trollop as his fingers closed about her throat.

'. . . *it be on a Thursday, I goes there on a Thursday . . .*'

Would Polly Burke have locked the door to the kitchen? Was there a gardener or some other employee of Samuel Ramsey who might see him approach? No, no, Emma would be too wise to allow that, she wouldn't give her housekeeper time away from the house only to have someone else see the arrival of her doxy visitor. Secrecy must be the very essence of those clandestine meetings if Emma wished to save her face in the town, not to mention that of her husband – and Emma Ramsey would very much want to save both. An expensive undertaking! Feeling the door open beneath his hand Oswin's inner smile spread. It would prove a very expensive undertaking!

Apart from the slow tick of a long case clock, the spacious hall was silent. The house smelled of success, gleamed of wealth, but he paid no heed to the gracious furniture, the paintings and ornaments; there would be time for that when they all belonged to him.

Had the death of her playmate halted Emma's little games – was that the reason for the silence lying over the house? Did the wealthy Mrs Ramsey no longer entertain on Thursday afternoons?

'. . . *we all knows her wouldn't give the drip from the end of 'er nose . . .*'

Hadn't those been the words laughed aloud in the Turk's Head? And hadn't he watched that housekeeper leave the house, watched until her well-fed figure disappeared from sight? Why give the woman time away from her duties unless there was something Emma Ramsey wished to avoid being witnessed?

The answer to the dilemma came in a soft throaty laugh. Glancing towards the source of the sound, Oswin's greed found new heights. It was true what that whore had babbled: Emma did like her forbidden fruits served on Thursday.

Feet making no impression on the thickly carpeted landing, he followed the sounds beckoning to him, the moans and gasps he himself knew well, sounds which said Emma thought herself alone with her lover; but this lover was not Sally Baker.

Facing him from the end of the landing, a door stood open; need outstripping caution? Or desire to strip driving it from the mind? Was Emma's ardour for her extramarital amours so strong it suppressed fears of being overheard?

With steps as soundless as his thoughts, Oswin approached the open door, smiling at the scene which met his eyes. His ship had well and truly come in!

A woman lay naked on the large bed, her widespread legs pale against the deep rose of the silk cover, a woman who moaned her pleasure at the mouth sucking at her breast, at the hand stroking long caressing fingers over the dark vee at the base of her stomach. Eyes closed, mouth parted in the extremes of physical pleasure, Emma Ramsey gasped a plea for fulfilment.

'Not yet.' Husky with its own erotic pleasure a slight laugh answered the groan questing fingers brought gurgling from the rapturous Emma. 'Not yet, not before I've done this . . .'

Pulling at the nipple of the voluptuous breast, stretching it to the full before releasing it, a tongue traced the line of pale flesh between the breasts, over the stomach to the thatch of pubic hair to take the place fingers had caressed seconds before. Then the head lifted and with another sensuous laugh, her own nakedness flaunting its mouse-coloured thatch and bobbing breasts, another woman straddled the moaning Emma, one body moving up and down against the other.

'. . . *an' that lover don't be no man . . .*'

Eyes lifting from the two women lost in the throes of passion, Oswin glanced at the dressing table, its surface strewn with pretty jars and delicately shaped bottles. His eye pausing at the centre of the strewn table, he caught the laugh rising to his throat. Yes, Oswin Slade's ship had definitely come in.

It had all gone so perfectly. Sitting beside his own fireplace Oswin gloated over the happenings at Acacia Villa. No one had seen him enter that house, and those women, Emma Ramsey naked and moaning with the pleasure of her lover's mouth and hands . . . and that lover! The triumph that had glowed in him from standing at that bedroom door flared like a beacon. He had hoped Sally Baker's tale of the carryings-on in that house, of Emma's fondness for women, would prove true but he would never have thought to find the sight which had met his eyes.

They had both been unaware of him standing in the doorway, unaware they were being watched. Emma Ramsey groaning and gasping, lifting her buttocks to those long fingers playing in her crotch, begging to be given that exquisite release; and the other one, mousy-brown hair trailing over her shoulder as she sucked that plump breast, her own bobbing as she slid man-like over her willing partner.

This would bring him money. He remembered the thought which had leapt to his mind. Then his eye had drifted across to that dressing table and what he saw among the toiletries spread across its surface had made his thoughts blossom, each giving way to another and yet another like the opening petals of a beautiful flower whose scent was money. Emma and her husband would pay to keep that sordid secret and for such a secret the price would be high. It would have been shameful enough had that mouse-haired lover been a man, but shocking as that would have been to their wealthy friends, it would eventually be overlooked; but a woman making love with a woman – a lesbian affair – that would stick in the craw of society, talk of it would travel to different towns faster than a train. The Ramseys would be glad to pay in order to avoid such a disaster to their comfortable life. Exactly what amount he would demand had been constant in his brain since choking the information from that whore but as his glance had rested on that dressing table he had known he could double what he dreamed of.

Smiling, he stared into the heart of the fire. A wig! The smile widened. A wig placed on that table!

They had not heard his soft exultant laugh above the moans of their lovemaking. The same laugh repeating in his throat, he watched flames leap into the chimney. The woman on top had moved, slid off that pale spread-eagled form, but had not seen the figure at the door, seen who it was standing watching, who was now party to her disgusting little game . . . who could smash her world. Cold ice-glazed eyes would spit their venom. They could spit all they liked; it would make not one penny difference to the sum he would demand.

Emma, silly woman, she would beg him not to tell. The laugh rattled again, low and triumphant. Beg was no word to use to Oswin Slade. The other woman too would make the same entreaty, she too would know the price would have to be paid. What they both did not know was just how often his bill would be presented.

Phineas had not admitted to asking that girl to be his wife. Michael Farron watched the unloading of a narrow boat but his mind played over a different scene. Phineas had talked of seeing her in that churchyard, of talking with her, and his voice had held a warmth and interest not heard in a long time.

Too long a time, and that was the problem! Phineas Westley was no longer in the prime of life and with each passing year the loneliness showed a little more clearly. Michael tried to fill that emptiness, to spend time with his uncle whenever he could, but his days were busy, a business could not run itself. But even were they to have more time together their deeper interests lay in opposite directions. His own interest here at the wharf directing the imports and exports which kept his fleet of narrow boats in operation whereas that of his uncle lay firmly rooted in an altogether different world, one which gave no mind to the mundane business of making a living: a gentler, more peaceful world? Michael smiled to himself. Not if the stories told to him in childhood were anything to judge by.

'That be the lot I reckons, Mr Farron, sir, twenty-eight tons 'as 'er sittin' low; 'er shouldn't ought to 'ave no more in 'er belly . . . not to my mind.'

His attention jerked back to the present Michael ran a glance over the seventy-foot-long narrow boat, its deck criss-crossed with iron girders.

'Your mind tells you right, Moses, the *Ariadne* is carrying as much as she should.'

'Then if you'll set your mark to the paper I'll 'ave 'er boatman tek 'er out.'

Signing his name to the document handed to him, Michael watched the flat-capped figure give last-minute instructions to a man stood at the tiller of the laden boat. *Ariadne*. The name bestowed by his uncle on the water hoss – as narrow boats were commonly called – had raised many smiles among the men who earned their living from working the canals, as had *Thetis*, *Dido*, *Europa*, *Semele* and the rest of the fleet so named by Phineas for his beloved heroines. He had doubted his own common sense, allowing his uncle to choose a name when each vessel was built, thought the men of the cut would resent a title which did not figure in their knowledge, but he had been wrong. Moses had told him of the interest they had shown in learning from Phineas's visits to the wharf the origin of the name painted on their boat, of how they and their families had listened, children with open mouths, wives with smiles of pleasure on their workworn faces, to the stories he had related and of how those same stories were passed along by the women, spread from one boat to another each time they moored for the night.

'D'you want the iron ore seen to next? The *Europa* be tied up a ways down toward Lea Brook Bridge. I sent word for Jos Gibbons to keep 'er there against you wantin' for 'im to be offloaded sooner rather than later for the foundry sent one o' their 'ands to enquire after it.'

Giving consent Michael turned away towards a section of a warehouse he had turned into an office. Moses Turley was a competent wharf gaffer whose experience had come from a life-time of living on the cut; gleaned from the father he had helped as a boy, later as a boatman in his own right carrying all manner of cargo to any part of the country it was required, a knowledge added to by each journey until he knew every aspect of the job as well as he knew his own name. He could be trusted to be left to get on with it.

As that girl could be trusted? Entering the office he sat heavily in a leather-bound chair, his stare following dust motes dancing in the rays of sunlight. She had refused Phineas' offer of a home, refused the comfort and security which went with it. Why? Why would she do that? A girl so poor she picked half-decayed veg-etables from the street, a girl whose patched clothes were held together by a force he could only term magic, why turn her nose up at such a windfall? But more to the point what precisely was Phineas about, what had he hoped to gain from bringing her to The Limes?

Beyond the walls of the small room the shouts of workmen unloading and reloading narrow boats, the calls of boatmen steering flat-bottomed vessels expertly past others pulling into the crowded basin while others jockeyed for moorings at the wharf, went unheard as Michael's thoughts returned to the subject of his uncle and Callista Sanford.

The girl was charming, Phineas had said that night at dinner, she was intelligent, pleasant and talking with her was a delight.

Charming, intelligent, pleasant and a pleasure to be with. All desirable traits in a companion. But was it simply a companion Phineas wanted or was it more? He had not said he had asked

Callista Sanford to share his home as his wife . . . but was that simply a delay in the proceedings, was proposing marriage to that girl his true objective?

And what of her negative attitude? Was that a ploy on her part designed to make the grass on the other side appear even greener? Did she see a refusal having the effect of making her more desirable? Playing an old man for a fool was as ancient a story as any of those contained in the literature of bygone worlds. Was that what the girl was about, playing Phineas Westley for a fool?

He had wanted to give words to that fear, to voice his idea to his uncle, but thought of hurting the man who had given him so much love had deterred him. Phineas Westley might not be young but the pride of the man had in no way diminished with the years and to insult him – it would be seen to be an insult to his uncle's intelligence by virtually accusing him of behaving in a foolish way – was out of the question. So he had said nothing of the doubt niggling at his mind but that did not mean he would take the same stand with Callista Sanford!

'*She will most surely return to the churchyard, visit again the graves of her parents.*'

Phineas's voice had held a wistful note when saying that but his eyes had gleamed with determination when adding, '*When she does I will be there to meet her.*'

Picking up a pencil from the desk in front of him Michael twisted it between his fingers. There was little room for doubt; Phineas was infatuated with the girl. She had told her hard-luck story, her pretty tear-stained face demurely downcast, and his uncle had responded as she had intended he should.

'. . . *what we lose to death cannot be given back . . . but it can sometimes be replaced.*'

Was that a marker, a foreword of what was to follow? Was Phineas saying it was his intent to replace what he had lost by taking Callista Sanford as his wife?

A suicide father . . . a pauper mother. The girl had played her game well. Adept and skilful as any spider she had spun her web and almost willingly Phineas had become the fly at its centre.

It was not the fact of his uncle's wealth being given to another that made him so strongly against such a union; the inheritance that should be his going instead to someone else. That fact he had analysed over and over again, rejecting it as inconsequential. So what was it? Phineas Westley would not be the first elderly man to take a young bride; maybe the marriage would be a happy one, fulfilling the closing years of his uncle's life. Winter and spring . . . so different, so far apart. Would Callista Sanford truly love Phineas as a woman should love a husband?

Love! Michael Farron's lips thinned over clenched teeth, the pencil snapping in his fingers.

16

Breath held behind quivering lips, hands trembling against the possibility of sound, the small girl placed several lumps of coal into the cast-iron stove.

'*Do you delight in stupidity or is it you, like him, have no care for what other people say, like him you place no value upon any feelings but your own . . . well, maybe this will help change that . . .*'

The hand slicing down caught the pale frightened face, the sound of its slap echoing in the quiet room.

'*Did I not say no more than four pieces of coal?*'

Weight of the heavy half-full coal bucket causing the slight figure to lean to one side, the child stammered its fear.

'*I . . . I put only three pieces . . .*'

'*Three!*' Glittering with hate cold eyes stared from a sharp-boned face. '*Is three the same as four?*'

Her own eyes watching the hand, its fingers curling against the palm, the child shivered her answer. '*N . . . no . . .*'

Above her bent head the tightly held mouth of a woman gave way to a momentary smile, a smile holding all the poison of a cobra.

'*Did I not say four?*'

The metal handle of the bucket cut into her fingers but, afraid to set it to the ground, the child whispered, '*You . . . you said no more than four . . .*'

'*Did I say less than four?*'

It would make no difference what answer she gave. Head lowered, the child remained silent.

'*Insolent as well as sly* . . .' Hard and vicious the hand struck, sending the child falling to the ground, coal from the spilled bucket falling over her legs. '*Sly like him but I found him out* . . . *found him and found you* . . . *you* . . . *you* . . .' The hand fastened like a claw about her thin arm as the child cried out.

'You . . . wench, wake up . . . it be all right, I don't be going to harm you.'

Eyes blinking dazedly against the morning Callista let out a sob. It had been that same nightmare. Herself alone in that class-room, alone with that woman's spite.

'There be no need of you cryin' out, you stands in no danger from me, wench.'

Still half lost in the fear that dream had reawakened, Callista brushed her hands across her knees, sweeping away imaginary coals.

'No need of askin' 'ave you been 'ere all night for I sees you 'ave.'

The voice was wrong; it was deeper, not so high-pitched, so scratchy.

'Please, Miss Montroy . . . I . . . I'll put another piece on.'

'There be no Miss Montroy 'ere and I don't be knowin' what it is you'll be puttin' on what, I only knows you'll be catching your death sat there on damp ground so if you allows I'll give you a hand to you standin'.'

The hand closing on her arm, it was not a claw, not the long-fingered hand of that schoolmistress. Another sob, this time of relief, catching in her throat Callista blinked the wraiths of night-mare from her brain only to flinch as something solid fell at her feet.

'Pay no mind to that,' the deep voice said as she stepped instinctively back, 'it be no more than the threepennorth o' clay you bought last evenin'.'

Threepennyworth of clay! Memory rushing in on her, Callista bent to retrieve her purchase.

'Be no use to you the way it is. Whatever you was wantin' to mek from it you won't, least not unless you sets it to rest in water for a week or so. Do that, then set it to drain for a while an' it'll be workable; it be that or buy a new lump altogether.'

A new lump! She could not buy more clay, those three pence were the only money she had, her one last chance . . . disappointment adding to hunger and cold, Callista could not stem the tears.

' 'Ere, there be no need o' crying over a lump o' clay.' The deep voice took on a note of concern. 'There be plenty more where that come from.'

Warm and rapid tears slid unchecked, Callista beyond caring her grief be public. Plenty more clay but not for free, nothing was ever free.

'I should 'ave knowed, I seen from the 'alf-starved look of 'er, from the clothes . . .'

'Don't do no good to go blamin' yourself, I reckons the wench would 'ave refused any hand were offered.'

'But I med no offer.' Daniel Roberts looked at his wife busily setting bowl and spoon onto a gaudily enamelled tray. 'I should 'ave done but I d'ain't. It were obvious to a blind man 'er had no place to go . . .'

'And it be obvious to a blind man I be busy enough without 'aving to pick my way about a man sat in my kitchen, so you be off back to your work and leave me to mine.'

'But the wench . . .'

'Won't be going nowhere for a while yet so there be naught you can do as ain't already been done.'

'I should 'ave offered but I let 'er go, same as I let them go.'

Seeing the slump of those once-fine shoulders, the droop of the head once held high with pride, Abigail Roberts felt the heart twist in her chest. He was still paying for those few hasty words, the pain of their consequence deep inside.

'You were both headstrong.' Going to his side she touched a hand to his face, a gentle tender touch which spoke the heartache of years. 'He as much as you.'

Grasping the hand touching his whiskered cheek Daniel Roberts pressed it to his mouth, whispering against the fingers. 'You've bin my strength, Abbie, my stay. Without you I couldn't 'ave gone on, forgive me . . . forgive me.'

A sheen glinting over soft brown eyes, Abigail smiled into the blue ones lifting to her. He must not see her tears, they must stay locked away until he was gone, to be shed as they had been shed for so many years: in secret.

'I've never judged there be any need of forgivin' you, Daniel, and I've never stopped loving you,' she answered softly. 'We are each other's strength and while it is in me to give mine will always be yours.'

'Abbie . . .' Pressing his wife's hand once more to his kiss Daniel left the kitchen.

He was a proud man and that pride had been hurt. Abigail watched the man she had married thirty years ago, a figure slightly stooped from years of bending over a potter's wheel. But pride had exacted a terrible price, one Daniel Roberts would never cease to pay, one like to be taken with him into the grave.

Turning once more to the business of setting a meal onto the garish tin tray she stroked a finger over its too-brightly painted surface.

'. . . *it be a bird* . . .' Words returned from the silence of memory sounded clear in Abbie's brain. '*The pedlar said it were a feenix, he said it be burned but rises from its own ashes, be that true, Mother . . . be it true?*'

A phoenix. The Reverend Allis had smiled at the child asking that same question after the Sunday service at St James's. It is what we call a myth, he had said, a kind of fairy story, no more than that.

'*Well, I believes it!*' Mary's defiant answer had waited only until they were clear of the church gate. Mary, her pretty wide-eyed daughter. She had carried her father's spirit.

Ladling chicken broth into the bowl she had set on the tray, Abbie felt the tears she had withheld slide slowly over her cheeks.

Mary had carried that same spirit until the day she had whispered of something else she had carried: the child in her womb. She was barely sixteen and the man? The man who had placed a child in her belly had gone without trace.

Daniel had flown into a rage. Abbie's eyes followed the knife slicing through the loaf fresh drawn from the oven beside the fire. How could she have done so wicked a thing, how could she cast such a slur on his name?

That had been the moment Adam had spoken. Twenty-one years old and every inch of his six-foot frame shouting its strength, he had faced his father across this very table. Unflinching and unafraid he had stared with the same fire which burned in his father's eyes.

'*Mary be little more than a child.*'

The voice of her son had been so firm. Setting the knife aside Abbie stared through blurred eyes at the picture so real in her mind. Straight as a young oak, brown hair touching his forehead, blue eyes clear as spring water, he had faced Daniel.

'*Her knows naught of the ways of the world.*'

'*Her knows now!*'

His father's fist had struck the table and, clutched in her own arms, Mary had whimpered but Adam had shown no fear.

'*Yes, her knows now,*' he had answered, '*and I know what you and Mother must be feeling, but it be Mary's feelings we should all be considering.*'

'*Her feelings!*' Daniel's angry response had echoed through the house. '*And who was her considerin' when her were lying with some no good? A babby be her dowry, a child with no name, what man will take her as wife!*'

Adam's mouth had thinned at that, the blaze that swept his

father hardened to blue crystal, but his reply had been more pitying than angry.

'*Perhaps no man will want her for wife, Father, but one man will always want her as a sister.*'

They had exchanged no more. Adam had stridden away to the kiln and Daniel to the potting workshop while she had put a distraught Mary to bed.

The end of the day had seen Daniel full of remorse for his anger. Adam had been right in standing by his sister; tomorrow he would tell him so, tomorrow he would take his daughter in his arms and whisper of a love unchanged, a love which would take care of her and her child.

But the morning had not given Daniel the chance to say anything of what was in his mind and his heart. Their daughter's bed had been empty and in the place where her head should have lain was a note.

Cutting the slice of bread into four squares Abbie placed them on a delicate poppy-painted plate.

Your hearts are broken because of me . . .

The words written on that single sheet of paper, words the years of reading and rereading had engraved on her heart, seemed to take on the sound of that beloved voice, the voice of her daughter, and Abbie's hands trembled.

. . . and the pain I see in your eyes is too hard for me to bear. If by giving my life I could undo what I have done, take this shame from you, then I would do it and give praise to heaven for the granting of such a blessing. But that would replace one slur with another, replace pain with pain and sorrow with sorrow. I cannot face life seeing the shadow of it play on faces I love with all my heart; to leave is my only choice. The guilt is mine, let it not play in any other heart.

Your daughter, Mary

But the guilt had stayed with Daniel. A guilt which was not lessened with the departure of his son. A man grown, Adam could not be denied when he had set mind to following his sister, to search for her; the common sense of his saying one of them must remain to care for his mother and that one should be her husband. Daniel had at last accepted the common sense.

Taking the tray in her hands she walked slowly upstairs.

Her husband had accepted but she knew as he watched her tall son turn from the house that like herself a part of his life had been torn from him, a part which would never be replaced.

Emma Ramsey's face had been the colour of chalk. Sabine Derry fastened the buttons of her wide-skirted black grosgrain coat.

'How could he have known?' Emma's torment had begged an answer.

How indeed! Reaching for the fine kid gloves set out beside a large cloth bag, Sabine remembered the conversation they had shared. She had asked herself that question many times.

'No one knew, no one . . .' Emma had sobbed. 'I told nobody.'

But she must have told somebody; what else would have that toad Slade creeping into Acacia Villa? Emma had revealed her secret and whoever had been the recipient of it had repeated it. To Slade or within his hearing? What matter now! Pulling on the gloves, smoothing each finger down to the palm, Sabine frowned to herself. The damage was done. She drew the heavy black veil draped about her bonnet over her face.

The letter had been delivered by second post. Emma had shoved the envelope into her hand. An identical envelope addressed in the same copperplate hand as the one delivered to Hill House. Slade had written to both. He had been inside Acacia Villa, had stood at the door of the bedroom, watched two women making love, written the very words they had spoken, seen at the centre of the dressing table a wig . . . a red wig.

Her wig! Sabine Derry's wig! Picking up the cloth bag she left the house.

Emma had been beside herself. They had to pay . . . think of the scandal, they had to pay all he asked.

She had agreed. Climbing into the hansom she sat stiff with anger. She had agreed, the damage was done and the piper must be paid.

It had been decided she would hand over both her own and Emma's payment, hand over the money Slade had demanded. Emma in her turn was to say nothing and especially not to Samuel. But that money would not be given to Slade in Wednesbury; the risk of being seen dealing with the man was one she would not take. A viper did not strike once and slither away; Oswin Slade was one such creature. How could she be certain he would not arrange to be seen taking payment from her, providing an accomplice to back his next demand?

Wolverhampton, she had told Emma, Oswin Slade would receive what he asked for in Wolverhampton. He had agreed readily enough; it made no difference where his demands were met, he had laughed, just so long as they were met – and in full.

Behind the veil Sabine Derry's eyes glinted. The man had been obnoxious in her sight as rent collector, now as blackmailer he was anathema. But rent collector or blackmailer, there were ways to deal with both.

The hansom she had beckoned at the High Bullen dropped her at the tram junction at the White Horse. Sabine nodded her thanks to the blue-uniformed conductor. Touching one hand to his cap he steadied her with the other onto the hissing vehicle. Sabine was aware already of the loud chequered suit of the figure following her aboard.

He was taking no chances the agreement would not be kept. Settled in her seat, her glance raked the back of the pomaded head. Slade had chosen his own seat a little to the front of her own; she would have to pass by him to reach the platform of the tram.

'Bilston.' The conductor's call announced the approach of its next stopping place and Sabine's hand closed about the tortoise-shell handles of her large bag. Waiting for the tinkle of the bell which would bring the vehicle to a halt she rose.

'Oh!' The exclamation trembling on her lips, she caught at the iron frame of a seat as the tram jerked to a stop.

'They trams be enough to set a body tumblin' off 'er feet,' a woman edging her bulk ahead of her grumbled loudly. Murmuring her agreement Sabine followed, a smile behind the veil hiding the satisfaction of feeling the blade she had hidden in her sleeve slide easily and deeply into the side of the neck of the figure in the seat against which the halting of the tram had jerked her.

17

'I had meant only to rest a few minutes, the warmth of the kiln. I'm sorry to have caused yourself and your husband so much trouble.'

The wench spoke nicely, 'ad what Daniel would call an educated tongue . . . but the clothes, Lord, they must be near as old as the wench herself; they were clean though; apart from the dust of the clay where her had been crouched against the kiln everything about her was well scrubbed.

'Be no trouble, wench.' Abigail smiled at the girl she had put to bed hours before. 'I were taught that the 'elping of a body worse off than y'self brings a smile to the face of 'eaven.'

'And I was taught not to take what could not be paid for and though I haven't money to offer my hands are willing . . . please say there is something I can do before I leave.'

This wench Daniel had found sleeping alongside of the kiln had come from a good home, a poor one, yes, but money were not the only wealth a parent could pass to a child. Abigail looked at the pale face, wide violet eyes regarding her with a simple honesty. This child had been taught what she and Daniel had striven to teach their children: good manners, frankness of heart and always to give as well as to receive. What greater wealth could be the portion of any child?

To refuse what was asked, to let the girl leave without doing any service, would rankle, the thought of it would plague her mind maybe for weeks.

'There do be summat.' Abigail smiled once more, her decision made. 'I finds it a mite tirin' carryin' them leathered pots for Daniel to stack the kiln; if it be you feels you needs show thanks by doin' summat then I'd ask it be that.'

'Leathered pots?' Callista asked, wondering had she heard all right, but Abigail was already on her way to the scullery with her brightly coloured tray.

Daniel would do the explainin' and take joy in the doin'; it had been long years since he had spoken the ways of the clay to a youngster.

'Means the pots be dried 'til the clay 'as the touch o' leather,' Daniel answered on hearing why she had come to the potting shop. 'You can't go setting 'em to the firing afore they reaches that state or they shatters. They feels strong but they ain't, they needs be 'andled gently lessen they break. That lot,' he pointed to several larger dishes stood on a shelf above a row of mugs, 'they needs be placed in a sagger to 'elp protect 'em from the flames.'

Leathered clay, biscuit firing, saggers, bats, stilts! Pottery-making had a language all its own. The kiln stacked at last, Callista washed her hands in a barrel of water standing outside the workshop, drying them on a clean rag held out by Daniel. His smile said he was well pleased with her efforts. But it was a language she had found intriguing.

'Buyin' threepennorth o' clay were the reason brought you to Leabrook Pottery, be you goin' to leave wi'out it?'

She had bought her clay and her own carelessness had wasted it; if she had not turned back after leaving, if she had gone on; but she had not and now her money was gone and she had nothing to show for it.

As if reading her mind he pointed a callused hand to a lump of fresh clay. 'That be your'n, it be an exchange for that I've set in water . . . the piece you dropped; given a day or so an' it'll be workable same as before an' I can use it, so y'see you ain't teken nothin' as you ain't paid for. Only one thing, tell me 'ow you was intendin' to fire whatever it be you 'ad set your mind to mouldin'?'

She had not thought of that. She had only ever seen the finished product, the long-stemmed pipes made by the men her father would sit talking with; she had played with the clay they gave her but, the visit over, she had politely handed it back.

'Come, wench.' Daniel took the rag from her. 'Bring your clay an' mek what it is that heart o' your'n be hankerin' after an' when it be leathered I'll fire it along o' the rest.'

The tram had pulled away, continuing its journey to Wolverhampton, pulled away with the figure of Oswin Slade sitting silently on its seat. That had been a week ago.

In the sun-filled drawing room of Hill House Sabine Derry scanned the day's newspaper. Nothing! She smiled her satisfaction. There had been coverage, a report of a man having been murdered aboard a tram. But that had been the only information the newspaper had so far printed; seemingly the police had no idea of who had perpetrated such a deed. Nor would they ever find out. Folding the paper neatly, she laid it aside. She had covered her tracks carefully. Taking the hand of the conductor, she had thanked him with a sob in her quiet voice as he assisted her from the tram. He would remember only a woman dressed in mourning clothes and carrying a large black cloth bag, a woman who followed several women passengers towards the busy market. That was the reason for her choosing to leave the tram where she had; Monday was market day at Bilston and she would easily be lost among the many shoppers.

But she had not gone to the market. It had been no more her intention to go there than it had to travel on to Wolverhampton . . . or to pay Oswin Slade the money he demanded. Detestable little man, he had been paid. It was just that he had not been paid what he expected!

He should have known better. Cold unblinking eyes glanced

about the room, hovering on tapestried sofas, glowing mahogany side tables and chiffoniers filled with delicate figurines. The stupid little man should never have dared to blackmail Sabine Derry, to threaten her; now he would never threaten anyone ever again.

Veil drawn low onto her chest, shoulders hunched and spine bent as if with age, she had followed from Oxford Street along Hall Street seeming to any who noticed her to be going to the open market place; but halfway she had taken a left-hand turn that led to the railway station. She had not purchased a ticket directly. First she had gone to the ladies' waiting room, breathing relief at finding it empty. This was the one part of her plan might prove risky. Fingers working quickly, she had whipped off veil, hat and gloves, exchanging them for a mauve-coloured feather bonnet and matching gloves. Somewhere in the distance a steam whistle had shrieked, announcing the arrival of another train. Any moment could see other passengers entering the waiting room. But that was a chance she had to take. Breath caught behind tight lips, she had turned the cloth bag inside out, then slipping off the grosgrain coat, had crammed every trace of mourning into it. Loosing the air from her lungs she had smoothed the mauve velvet suit the wide-skirted coat had covered, then with one final touch, had drawn the tiny velvet dotted veil of the bonnet to eye level; a bonnet set on the same red wig Oswin Slade had thought to assure his financial future. The thought had edged her mouth with a faint smile. The man had no more future! Taking up a bag now seemingly made of mauve silk she had left the waiting room and purchased a ticket to Wednesbury.

It had been a month from her coming to Leabrook Pottery. The small vase she had so painstakingly made from her threepenny worth of clay held close against her, Callista turned out of Dudley Street following St James's Street towards the graveyard.

She would not look at the dark building with its stone-set windows, she would let no memories of her days in that school-room spoil this moment. She had done what she had wanted to do, had kept the promise made in her heart, and in a few minutes her mother's grave would have its marker. But it could never have been achieved without the help and kindness of the Robertses.

'*It has been too long a time since my table were graced by a young face sat at it; you would be doing me a kindness by biding for a meal.*'

The words had been husky, Abigail's eyes filming as she spoke them. But the kindness had been hers. It was she who had suggested staying at the cottage while the vase leathered, she who had said board and keep could be earned from working alongside Daniel at the potting. Had Daniel seen the uncertainty inside her, the argument which said the offer was simply charity? Possibly he had for he had said that next day he was going to the High Bullen to hire a lad who would do the fetching and carrying but if she had a mind to try the work herself then the job and the home which went with it were hers. '*But mind,*' he had warned, '*I'll be mekin' o' no exceptions along o' you bein' a wench.*'

Pausing at the gate to the church she glanced towards a patch of ground which a month before had been covered with the gold of daffodils and now was sprinkled with harebells, their delicate blue flowers mixing with the creamy-throated elegance of stately foxgloves and tall yellow Aaron's rod, seeds she had scattered long ago now covering the father she loved with a mantle of beauty.

'He made no exceptions, Father,' she whispered, coming to the spot beneath the tall tree and kneeling among the wild flowers at its base. 'It was as you would have wished; I worked for all I took.'

Seated on a bench set against the rear wall of the church a man, goatee beard neatly trimmed, hands resting on a silver-topped cane, leaned forward, eyes peering keenly through gold-rimmed spectacles.

It was the same spot; but the same girl? It had to be, hadn't she said she had no kin . . . so who else would visit the resting place of a suicide? Watching the slight figure rise Phineas Westley smiled as the shawl covering the head slipped and blue-black hair gleamed in the perfect light of the June sun.

Michael had scorned the idea of the girl returning to the churchyard, had disapproved of an old man's asking a virtual stranger to share his home – but then Michael was often disparaging of the 'foolish' things his uncle did. But no blame could be laid on the boy, what he said was said out of regard for the longer term of an old man's happiness and though appreciated it had not kept him from coming to this place each day in the hope of seeing the girl he watched now going to the spot she had pointed out as her mother's burial place.

'Good day, Miss Sanford . . . Callista.' He had waited, respectful of her privacy at the graveside, but as she returned he rose, touching a hand to his tall silk hat.

Caught unawares Callista brushed a hand across her face, wiping away the tears lingering on her cheeks, then smiled genuine pleasure at the meeting.

'I was very much hoping to see you again and thought this the most likely place . . . you would not neglect to visit your parents' graves.'

'I have not visited them since last we met here, I . . . I had to find work.'

'And you have?'

'Yes.' She nodded. 'I have worked for a month at Leabrook Pottery.'

'Daniel Roberts' place. I know him well, a fine craftsman; but I thought he had given up since . . .'

Since his children left. Callista did not press the pause. Abigail had spoken of the tragic events of ten years ago, told of the one letter they had received from their son saying he had found his sister and would care for her, that they need not be sad. But even in the few weeks she had shared with that couple she had learned the depth of their heartbreak; Daniel and Abigail would never be free of sadness at the loss of their children, never be free of the anguish unguarded moments revealed on their faces.

'Mr Roberts is indeed a fine craftsman and a fine teacher,' she answered. 'He helped me make the container I have placed upon my mother's grave. I must admit I could not have kept my promise were it not for the kindness of himself and his wife.'

'Abigail.' Phineas smiled. 'As fine a paintress as Daniel is a potter . . . she once showed me a plate decorated with field poppies which looked so real I felt I could have picked them; I told her she could earn a very comfortable living painting the crockery Daniel made but she would have none of it.'

'You were a friend of the Robertses?'

A small shake of the head preceded Phineas's answer. 'Not in the fullest sense of the word but our meetings were always genial. I bought several pieces of Daniel's work. You say he helped you make a piece yourself and to keep the promise you told me of. Might I ask how . . . but that is something you must prefer to keep private, forgive my intrusion. It was not meant as such.'

She could have felt offended at the question, taken it as an invasion into personal affairs, but strangely she felt none of that. Meeting the grey eyes, apologetic behind the spectacles, Callista smiled.

'It is no secret. How could it be out there among the grass for any passer-by to see? The day my mother was laid here I made a promise: somehow she would have something to mark her resting place. I knew I could never buy a headstone with her name engraved upon it but I could buy a small amount of clay, enough to make a container to hold her silk posy. It was obvious to Mr Roberts I hadn't much idea of what went into making the simplest pot, the biscuit or first firing and then the glazing to seal the porous body before firing again; I had not realised the process was so involved but he was patient, guiding me at each step.'

'And now your mother has her daughter's gift. Please, my dear, may I see it?'

Walking beside him to the far corner of the cemetery Callista marvelled at the absence of discomfort. There was none of the dislike she had felt when with Oswin Slade, nor any of the irritation which had filled her when speaking with that stranger while collecting unwanted vegetables that evening in the market place and definitely none of the fear that had filled her when accosted by another in Paget's Passage.

'You have made this . . . and it is your first attempt . . . but this is beautiful!'

'Thank you.' Callista blushed at the praise. 'But it is solely due to Mr Roberts it was made at all.'

'A fine craftsman as I said before, but I can see a different hand in this. May I pick it up?'

Watching him twist and turn the vase in his hands, the clear glaze of it lending a softer mellowed look to the dough-coloured body, Callista thought of the words he had used on making her that offer.

'*Do what you have set your heart upon and when it is done come back . . . my home will be waiting.*'

Would that offer of a home still be there? Would she refuse it a second time?

'You show an appreciation of line and movement; as Daniel has probably said already you have a feeling for the clay.'

'My mother loved the Michelangelo Lamp shown in a book once owned by my father depicting the works of the great artist. I tried to imitate that; the holes in its covered bowl would I thought allow for the arranging of flowers though the figures which support it leave a great deal to be desired.'

'Do not underestimate your work, my dear,' he said, his glance remaining on the vase. 'You have a skill not given to many. I think Daniel Roberts recognised this or he would have dissuaded you from attempting such a piece.'

Daniel had not tried to turn her from the project but had positively encouraged the creating of it and when she had questioned the fact of using more clay than her threepence could buy and then the cost of glazing and firing he had waved the queries aside, saying the work she did alongside of him more than compensated any outlay on his part. Then when it was finally finished he had been lavish in his praise. '*Your fingers be sure and your eye true as was Ad*—' Had he been going to say Adam; had he almost named his son?

Work such as this would find a place in many a house. Phineas turned the piece in his hands, admiring the curve of the bowl supported on the bent shoulders of two figures, their nude bodies partly swathed with a drape of cloth slung across one shoulder following the line of the back, discreetly complementing the shapely leg. Maybe not the standard of Michelangelo but then the great master still stood alone in the world of art; but given time Callista Sanford's work could find its own place in that world.

'You say you have been working with Daniel Roberts since last I saw you?' Phineas said, keeping his thoughts to himself. 'Will you continue to do so?'

Watching as he replaced the vase on the patch of earth becoming slowly green as grass established itself in the rich soil, Callista realised with what was almost a shock she had no longer any reason or excuse for staying with the Robertses. What Daniel said about her work at the pottery paying her board and keep was merely a mask worn to hide his kindness; he had managed the work alone for ten years so why now would he need help? Age? Daniel and Abigail were no longer young but both were strong and well enough able to manage their livelihood without her help.

'I had not given much thought to what I will do,' she answered honestly.

'And the offer I made to you, have you given thought to that?'

Spread about the small churchyard sun-tipped stones seemed to wait for her answer, the spire-topped church listening for her words. She had thought of this man's offer, thought of the comfort of a home such as The Limes, filled no doubt with beautiful works of art, of the pleasure they would afford her . . . but was comfort, the delight of daily being surrounded with all her father had taught her to appreciate and love enough? Should not sharing a man's home hold more than the love of inanimate objects?

'Your eyes tell me you have given my proposal thought, my dear. Now if you will I would like your answer.'

Oswin was dead! Callista stared at the uniformed constable, her brain numbed with shock. Oswin Slade murdered on a tram!

'So you see, miss, I 'ad to come what with you knowin' the victim like, add to that your leavin' Trowes Court quick as you did . . .'

'What do 'er leavin' that house 'ave to do wi' a murder?' Abigail's question was quick and defensive.

'Be still you, woman.' Daniel lifted a hand, bidding his wife to silence. 'The man just be doin' his job so best let 'im get on wi' it.'

'I mean no offence but like I says, miss, what with you 'aving known the victim . . . well, procedure 'as to be followed.' Taking a notebook from a pocket of his tunic, touching the point to his tongue, the police officer cleared his throat with nosy embarrassment. 'I be sorry about all this, Daniel.'

'No cause for any man to be sorry on account o' doin' what he be paid to do so long as it don't go against the teachin' o' the Good Book; an' if the tekin' of a chair, a sup o' tea an' one o' Abigail's scones don't be against procedure then sit you down for you be frightenin' the wench standin' there like the 'erald o' doom.'

'I'll tek a cup and thank you for it, Abigail, it be a trek across the heath.' The constable smiled, settling himself to a chair while Abigail set tea and scones before each of them.

'The time o' this 'ere murderin' . . . you must know—'

'Let it be,' Daniel interrupted his wife. 'There'll be time for our questions when his'n 'ave all been answered; and Callista, wench, try not to be feared; Abbie an' me 'ave knowed John Travers since boyhood and he be no ogre, so you just answer best you can to what be asked and he'll deal fair with you.'

'Do you 'ave any objection to bein' questioned, miss, would you prefer to 'ave somebody else present . . . a lawyer p'raps?'

It was gently said and the constable smiled but Callista could not repress the shudders which rippled one on another along her spine. She was being interrogated about a killing, the murder of the man who had tried to rape her! Did the police think she had done that terrible thing . . . that she had killed Oswin Slade in an act of revenge?

Below bushy eyebrows the constable's dark eyes held a smile but it did not disguise the keenness of the glance resting on Callista. 'Be up to you, miss. Do you wish a lawyer?'

Still dazed by being called from the kiln only to be told by a worried-looking Abigail that a constable was asking to see her Callista stared blankly.

'Her don't be needin' no lawyer, John Travers, for her has nothin' to hide. Now ask your questions so we can see the end o' this!' Feeling the tremble of the girl's thin shoulders beneath her hand Abigail's defensive nature spurred the words.

'No offence, Abigail.' The constable glanced at the irate face. 'But it be the wench must answer for 'erself.'

'Hmmph!' The sound more informative about her feelings for 'procedure' than ever her words could be, Abigail sat beside Callista, taking her hand between her own in a gesture of comfort.

'Abbie, you always did scare me more'n any man I ever come

up against.' Constable Travers laughed, setting bushy side-whiskers jiggling. 'But afore you frightens me to death let me tell the wench her 'as no need o' worryin' why I be callin'. The Inspector took a list o' names from Edwin Derry, names o' tenants on which the deceased called to collect rents, and the Inspector bein' a stickler for things bein' done proper said each o' them tenants must be questioned and they 'ave. So you see, miss, you don't be the only one I've called on.'

Touching the pencil a second time to the tip of his tongue the man went on. 'Would you tell me your full name.'

'Cal . . .' Fright a solid lump in her throat Callista swallowed hard, forcing the words to come. 'Callista . . . Callista Sanford.'

It seemed the questions would never end. Had she lived at Trowes Court . . . who with . . . for how long . . . how well had she known Oswin Slade? With each one her heart had tripped; did this man know what Oswin had tried to do to her? The other people at Trowes Court had been questioned. Had Ada Povey told of that attempted rape? Were all those he was asking now merely a charade, a pretence? The prelude to her being arrested? Callista's head swam but she knew she must continue to answer.

'An' you 'ad been here at Leabrook Pottery at the time the crime was committed?' It sounded more like a statement than a question. Writing her reply in his notebook the constable looked up. 'Just one more, miss. 'Ave you at any time teken the Wolverhampton tram?'

Brows drawn together in puzzlement Callista answered. 'When I was a small child, yes, my father took me to a museum. He was very interested in everything to do with the ancient world.'

'And since you were a small child?'

The thought 'where was this leading' flashed through Callista's mind but her response was frank and honest, 'After my father died my mother found it increasingly difficult to find money enough to feed and keep a roof over the head of herself and a daughter Mr Travers. It was impossible to find the extra a tram ride to Wolverhampton or any place else would take, and following her death my own circumstances remained the same. In fact I think you will already have learned my mother received a pauper's burial paid for by the Parish; and Edwin Derry will most certainly have informed you I myself was evicted from Trowes Court when I could not pay rent due on his property. In fact were it not for Mr and Mrs Roberts's kindness in giving me a home and employment I would probably be in the Poorhouse.'

He had made no answer. She watched him return notebook and pencil to his pocket. She had challenged him and he had given no reply. Was that because he *was* in possession of that information even before she has spoken?

'I be sorry if I be the cause o' frightenin' you, miss. I 'opes you understands it were duty . . . no more'n that.'

It was an apology and the man's eyes reflected the truth of it. Clutching Abigail's hand Callista rose, the quiver still evident in her voice as she replied. 'Of . . . of course.'

'Does what you've 'eard be satisfactory?'

Taking the helmet he had removed before entering the cottage the constable paused. 'I be truly satisfied, Daniel, and I'm sure the Inspector will be. Miss Sanford 'ad already been spoken highly of by Mr Phineas Westley who said her were entirely trustworthy.' Glancing again to Callista he smiled. 'You 'ave some very good friends, wench.'

18

Emma was still in a high state of nerves. The threat of Oswin Slade no longer hung over their heads but the police inquiry would be bound to continue, they would not allow a murder to go unsolved . . . they would find out . . .

'So I'll have to go meet with the man. Lord knows how long that will take.'

Across the dining table lit with crystal-drop candelabra Edwin Derry glanced at a gold hunter watch drawn from the pocket of an elegant amber silk brocaded waistcoat.

'Don't wait up, no sense in both of us losing sleep.'

Forcing herself to smile Sabine followed her husband to the hall, watching him don outdoor clothes, breathing a sigh of relief when the door closed behind him. She had to think!

Going swiftly to her own room she sat at her dressing table staring into the mirror.

He had seen the wig, the wig which hid her own thin mouse-brown hair. How he must have laughed. Resting in her lap Sabine's fingers twisted together at the thought. Yes, how the hateful creature must have laughed . . . but he would laugh no more, neither would he ever again be a threat to her.

But Oswin Slade was not the only threat to Sabine Derry's wellbeing or even her life. There was another with that same potential: Emma Ramsey!

'*The police will find out,*' she had almost screamed with anxiety, '*they will find out and when they do . . .*'

After minutes of trying to calm the cries she had slapped the woman hard across both cheeks.

'*They will not find out,*' she had told her as the shock of those slaps brought instant silence. '*There is nothing can link the death of Slade to either of us . . . all that is needed is for us to remain calm, to say not a word to anyone.*'

'*I said no word to anybody yet Slade found out about our Thursday meetings! How, tell me how he came to know of those when neither you nor I breathed a word? Was it the same way the police will find out about you killing Slade?*'

There had been a truculence beneath the worry but it was the inherent threat behind the fear had caught at her own nerves. Emma Ramsey would never stand up to police questioning; she would fall like a leaf in the wind.

'*. . . the way the police will find out about you killing Slade.*'

The words struck now as they had struck in Emma's sitting room.

'*. . . you killing Slade.*'

There was the danger. The woman could not be trusted. Slowly lifting both hands Sabine removed the wig. Meeting the reflection of her own eyes she nodded as if in answer to a question. Emma Ramsey must follow the path of Oswin Slade!

'It be too much for a young wench an' 'specially so for one not brought up to manual labour; don't be no more needs sayin' 'cept once this firin' be complete then the pottery be closed down complete.'

'But the pottery is your living.' Callista looked at the man sat with leg bandaged to the knee.

'Not no more it ain't!' Half hidden by a wealth of whiskers Daniel's mouth was set firm but Callista heard the faint tremble in his voice. The making of crockery was all he and Abigail had of the life they once shared with a son and a daughter; let that go and the final link would be broken. She was not alone in her thinking; Abigail's eyes spoke the same words.

'But you must let me at least try.'

'Oh ar!' Bright with a moisture he would never admit to being there the man's blue eyes swung to Callista. 'Let you try is it . . . an' let you cripple y'self in the doin' o' it same as 'appened to me.'

'Accidents can happen to anyone.'

'Ar, wench, they can,' Daniel nodded, 'but I 'ave no intention one befall you, least not in my pottery I don't. It be a good 'eart you 'ave but it teks a strong arm an' a stronger back to do the work o' a potter.'

'I am not claiming to be able to do all you do but maybe I can keep the place ticking over until your leg is healed . . . you say yourself Mrs Roberts knows almost as much about making a dish as you and with her help—'

'You 'ave offered the same and many times,' Abigail cut in. 'Given 'elp where you seen it needed, now that 'and be 'eld to you and 'eld with generous feelin' . . . don't turn from it lessen you comes to regret it.'

'But—'

'No buts, Daniel Roberts!' Hands going to her hips, Abigail stared defiance. 'Refuse the offer the wench 'as med and I'll be thinkin' it's 'cause you'll find I *do* know as much of pot mekin' as yourself!'

'I suppose I could get meself to sit alongside.'

'I would need you there, Mr Roberts, with your and Mrs Roberts' guidance then I know we can manage.'

'Ar, Callista wench, I'm thinkin' we can but with one change.' The blue eyes met hers again but this time they smiled. 'It 'as always been the way o' Abigail and me to 'ave friends use our given names when we speaks together and if you stays then that must be the way of it. It be Daniel an' Abigail . . . that be our wish.'

★

Friends! making her way along Lea Brook Road passing light-knit houses built about a shared yard so reminiscent of Trowes Court, Callista felt a surge of happiness well in her stomach. After leaving the Poveys and the other neighbours at Trowes Court she had thought never to find really true friends again.

But hadn't Phineas Westley proved a friend? Not only had he taken no step to prosecute her over the dropped statue he had made that offer, the offer he had repeated again in that peaceful sun-washed churchyard.

'. . . *I would like your answer.*'

He had watched her as he had said it, watched the emotions she had known chased over her face, the uncertainty and hesitation, the indecision and perplexity which had to have shown in her eyes; and she had seen the apprehension in his own, the all-searching consideration of that keen glance, change slowly to a smile.

She had given her answer. Leaving the road, taking the towpath alongside the canal, she walked slowly enjoying the quiet peace of early evening. She had given her answer and Phineas Westley had accepted it.

'Evenin', miss, be there anythin' I can do for you?'

Taken with surprise Callista glanced about her. Lost among her thoughts she had not realised she had reached the canal basin.

'Good evening.' She returned the pleasantry. 'Is this the wharf of Mr Michael Farron?'

'It be that, miss, and I be Moses Turley, wharf gaffer for Mr Farron, but I ain't seen you 'ere afore.'

'No.' Callista shook her head. 'This is my first visit.'

Pretty wench! Moses watched the blue aura the sunlight cast over raven-black hair. Nice way of speakin' to go with her face, but the shabby clothes spoke another story.

'Well, miss,' he replied, 'I 'ave to tell you Mr Farron don't go 'aving no women working on his wharf so if it's employment you be seekin' then I be afraid you've come to the wrong place.'

'It is not employment I came to enquire after, it is Mr Farron. Could you please tell me where I might find him?'

This wench were after findin' Michael Farron! Moses made a play of lifting his flat cap and running his fingers over his hair. But would Michael Farron want to be found by her? Would he want to talk with a wench who it were plain 'adn't two farthings to rub together? Likely not . . . anyway, best not tek a chance.

'Mr Farron don't be 'ere. I can't say where he is to be found.'

'Then as wharf manager perhaps you can tell me is the clay Mr Daniel Roberts ordered brought from Cornwall delivered?'

Moses frowned, his fingers still stroking his hair. 'Daniel Roberts . . . you don't be no daughter to 'im.'

Callista shook her head again, a sprinkling of blue-black lights glistening like gems among her hair. 'No, I am no kin, he is my employer.'

'But Daniel Roberts don't let nobody see to 'is clay. He only ever does that hisself, so why don't 'e come now?'

Callista's glance had wandered to the narrow boats, some tied up at the wharf, others waiting in the basin, but each being serviced by men scurrying like so many ants. This could be another world, a universe away from the quiet afternoon walks she had enjoyed with her parents, her father explaining how the networks of canals were the giant arteries and veins of industry carrying products from factory and workshop to the dockyards, the barges returning with goods from so many foreign countries; while her mother spoke of gentler things, berries in the hedgerow, flowers growing beside the towpath, and she would smile when the naming of one of them would have her husband immediately recounting the myth of which it was a symbol.

'I asked why ain't Roberts 'ere hisself?'

'An accident . . .'

'I have heard of no accident!'

The peace engendered by her thoughts suddenly shattered.

Bringing her glance to the man walking across the cobbled space between canalside and warehouses towards her Callista stiffened. That walk, the way he held himself! She had seen it before, seen the confidence of him, the self-assuredness; but most of all she remembered the voice. It was the voice of the man who had intervened that evening in Wednesbury market place, the same one had spoken to Oswin Slade in the way the rent collector hated, the way which said that was exactly what Oswin was and no more. But this time there was no Oswin threatening her and she definitely required no interference. Pinpricks of irritation glistening amid the soft violet of her eyes, her voice clipped, she answered. 'The fact that news of Daniel's accident has not reached Farron's Wharf does not mean no accident has occurred.'

Daniel! First-name terms! Michael Farron's eyes narrowing slightly was the only intimation of the sudden coldness settling like a stone in his stomach. The girl did not let the grass grow under her feet; the owner of a pottery might not be what she aimed for but it was a precaution should her first choice not prove catchable after all. Daniel Roberts and Phineas Westley, both were men a little past their prime and neither was impervious to the flattery of a young woman. Daniel Roberts was not a widower – but what difference did a wife make to Callista Sanford!

'She be after enquirin' o' Roberts' clay.'

'Thank you, Moses. You may leave this with me.'

Cap replaced on his head Moses Turley turned away to the boats. Weren't often he seen that look on Farron's face but when 'e did 'e were glad it were not directed at 'im for it always heralded a rollockin'.

'Would you care to explain.'

Having reached the wharf office Michael asked the question, the brusque demand of it immediately adding to Callista's irritation. Who did he think he was, what gave him the right to any explanation!

'No!' she snapped. 'My business is with Michael Farron.'

A slight smile accompanying a bow of the head portrayed the very essence of contempt.

'Then that business is with me. I am Michael Farron.'

He had thought to throw her. It was obvious from the look in his eyes. He had thought the revealing of his identity would have her meek and apologetic. Maybe weeks ago it would have; were she still at Trowes Court with a sick mother to put before her own feelings she would do just that; but Callista Sanford no longer lived in Trowes Court. The lessons she had learned from the knocks of constant refusal, the horror of Oswin's attempt to rape her, had worked their transformation. From now on Callista Sanford would speak for herself regardless of whom it was to. Head lifting, determination coloured with a new confidence, she made no indication of his words having achieved any effect.

'I asked your wharf manager had Daniel Roberts' order of clay arrived and now I am asking you. Or do you expect me to bring a note of permission to deal with his business!'

Feisty! Michael smiled to himself. Lord, a man must look out for himself when dealing with this one.

'How Daniel Roberts conducts his business or who he conducts it with does not concern me.'

'Then why ask for an explanation?'

The girl was either changed since her first meeting with Phineas or else she had the abilities of an actress, able to hide her true self beneath a totally different guise. Keeping any intimation of the thought well hidden he looked at the girl who had coldly refused his offer of a chair.

'I apologise for not making myself clear. It is not your association with Daniel Roberts that is the object of my enquiry but that which you have struck up with Phineas Westley.'

How dare he say that! A virtual stranger, how dare he question her personal affairs! Indignation beginning to flare, Callista's look became violet ice.

'It is no concern of yours who I am friends with. Your encroaching upon my private affairs is an affront!'

'Affront!' There was no attempt now to hide the scorn in his voice and any admiration he might have felt for her unflinching answer died an instant death. 'You think it no affront to an old man's dignity to dupe him with your hard-luck stories, to inveigle him into proposing marriage to you by pretending an interest in all he holds dear when that interest is for yourself. A rich old husband is your only interest in Phineas Westley, is that not so, Miss Sanford?'

Indignation now resentment, Callista met the glare of accusation. What was this man's interest in her friendship with Phineas? Was it simply a defending of the older man, an attempt to save him from a marriage he deemed unwise? Or was Michael Farron's reason the very one he had just accused her of having . . . Phineas Westley's wealth?

Animosity which had been hot and flowing a moment before cooled, sitting like lead inside her. This man was arrogant as Oswin Slade had been but where Oswin had had some right to question her motives, Michael Farron had none.

'Bitterness brings no reward other than regret.' She had always tried to live by the teachings of her parents but in this case she would forego that wisdom come whatever may of her answer. Forcing a smile to her mouth she gave it.

'As you say, Mr Farron, marriage to Phineas Westley is my only interest.'

It had been more than a shock; the girl's reply, so cold and hard, had come like a blow to the mouth. She had smiled as she said it, smiled as she admitted her duplicity.

'. . . *marriage to Phineas Westley is my only interest.*'

The words still rocked in his brain; but why should they? Were they not simply a statement of what he had thought . . . had known? Was that girl not what he had guessed all along, a charlatan, a deceiver out to trick an old man?

Standing at the window of the small room lined with shelves filled with ledgers and account books, Michael Farron frowned, his gaze following the shabbily clad figure, fingers of red gold from a dying sun anointing the dark head.

If his assumptions were correct – and had she not just proved them so – then the opportunity of gaining all she sought had been placed within her grasp, given to her weeks ago. Why then had she not taken it . . . what advantage could she get from drawing out the proceedings? He had gone over all of this before and he could continue to go over it, ask himself the same questions again and again and still come up with no satisfactory answer. Who was it had said 'woman is an enigma'? Whoever had said it must have known someone like Callista Sanford for that girl was a walking riddle.

But her dealings with Phineas were not the only mystery in all of this. Her hesitation to draw the net closed about his uncle not the only puzzle; there was another equally obscure, equally veiled from understanding . . . the feelings she aroused in Michael Farron!

Impatient with the truth of it he swung away from the window. Despite what he thought of her, despite what she had said, there was something inside him refused it. Was it simply the compelling beauty of those violet eyes, the prettiness of that heart-shaped face . . . ? God, he'd seen that often enough in his dreams! Was he too being fooled by an innocence which was not real; duped as Phineas Westley had been duped?

Only if he allowed himself to be!

The firmness of that one thought chasing the rest from his mind, Michael strode from the office.

But Michael Farron would not be deluded . . . neither would he allow his uncle to be made a fool of!

19

There must be no variation to what had become their normal routine. Sabine ran an eye over the contents of her wardrobe. They must continue as before so as to give rise to no outside speculation; but afternoons spent in that bedroom would be no more, a nervous twittering partner was not to her liking. Emma Ramsey was no longer to her liking . . . but the visits must go ahead – at least for today!

Not the mauve, she had worn that after delivering payment to Oswin Slade. Dear Emma deserved something new. The honey crepon? Lifting down the walking-out dress Sabine held it against her shoulders. Yes, the colour suited her and the London label would not suit the plump Emma.

The woman had never been able to hide her envy of Sabine Derry's sense of style. Sabine draped the gown across a chair, admiring the sheen of the lovely cloth. It was so easy to disillusion Emma as to her own choice, to make a gown the woman thought attractive and well styled seem like a five-shilling frock from the High Street . . . as that blue dress had been made to look! Poor Emma, she had tried to give the impression the dress that girl had delivered to the house was not the one she had com-missioned, that the design and material were not those she had supplied; but she could have saved herself the bother of the charade for her face had spoken the truth. So had Callista Sanford's face.

Where had that girl gone to? Oswin's replacement had reported no lodger in any house in Trowes Court. She would like

to help her but first things first, dear Emma must take prece-
dence. Fear had the woman beside herself; at any moment she
could panic and blurt everything to the constable. But soon all
of Emma's anxieties would be smoothed away and she could rest
in peace.

The thought etching a smile about her thin mouth, Sabine
fastened the tiny linen-coated buttons of her under-petticoat
then slipped a pale butter silk one over the top. When she
inspected the result in the long mirror of her dressing room the
smile widened. The fall of cloth was graceful, its line symmet-
rical, but would it stay that way when beneath the gown?

She had never employed a lady's maid. Some women of her
social standing might think that strange, the wife of a wealthy
industrialist . . . surely one could be afforded! But money was not
the reason. Sabine slid the gown over her head, fastening the tiny
star-shaped buttons that decorated the front of the palest blue
high-necked silk bodice and smoothing the folds of the honey-
coloured crepon skirt, each of which enclosed a ribbon of shot
silk matching the bodice. No, money was not her reason for
having no lady's maid to help her dress; she wanted no prying
eyes which might see what was not intended they should, things
like the box now hidden in the pocket she had sewn onto the skirt
of her under-petticoat.

Fate could not have been more helpful. Her housekeeper's
sister had fallen sick and the woman had asked could she take
leave to visit her. That had given the opportunity to take the box
of assorted chocolate creams, lift the top of each then insert a few
drops of the aconite tincture she had distilled from the beautiful
deep blue flowers of wolfsbane. Just a small amount in each, not
so much it would taste on the tongue; but to be sure she had
melted a bar of chocolate and recoated the top of each cream
then for good measure had added a sugared fruit, all of which
would prove irresistible to Emma's palate. She indulged herself
with confectionery when her nerves were not on edge; given the

way they were now the woman would virtually wolf them down.

Wolf! Donning a honey-coloured bonnet trimmed with pale blue feathers and silk bow Sabine anchored it to her auburn wig with a pearl-ended pin. An appropriate choice of words seeing what those chocolates contained – and an excellent choice of poison. Emma Ramsey had been warned a year ago of a weakness of the heart following a mild attack. Aconite poisoning gave every impression of the same condition. This afternoon she would no doubt eat every piece of the delicious gift and the box would leave Acacia Villa the same way it arrived; and tonight . . . with the accumulation of that poison and the effect upon the body's system, tonight Emma Ramsey would die of a 'heart attack' and no one would suspect otherwise.

Checking once more the line of the gown displayed no hint of the box, she picked up gloves and the small pochette bag she had chosen to use. Sabine Derry must not be seen carrying anything large enough to house more than a handkerchief and calling cards . . . and most definitely not a box of chocolates.

A sweet way to go. Sitting in the hansom cab Sabine held the thought. That too had been the way she had devised for Sally Baker but the prostitute had stumbled beneath a tram, saving her the bother. It had been a mistake giving that trollop Emma's blue silk dress; it was obvious to anyone that she could never have bought it herself. Sally liked her drink and she had a living to earn. Had the two combined one night, had she told Slade of what went on at Acacia Villa? It was the only way he could have found out. But was that the whole of what she had told him or had she told him the rest, told him what Sabine Derry never mentioned . . . except, it seemed, in her sleep?

Infatuation played with a man's brain, blinded him from facts while allowing him to see what was not there. Michael Farron headed the black stallion away from the busy wharf. Phineas was seeing what was not there, seeing love in the violet eyes of a girl young enough to be his daughter, in the smile of a pretty face, hearing it on a tongue which no doubt could hold the sweetness of honey, while all the time remaining blind to the truth behind it.

'There are none so blind as those who will not see . . .'

How many times had his uncle used that very quotation? Had derided other men for being fools in their business dealings? But Phineas had never interfered. A man's affairs are his and none other's was Phineas Westley's philosophy and one which his nephew was normally satisfied to observe. But Phineas was not just any man: he was his uncle and it was not simply a commercial enterprise was at stake, a contract which if unsatisfactory could be renegotiated, this was a man's heart, his uncle's heart, and he would not stand by and see it broken.

Michael touched the animal's neck, calling softly to it, calming the desire to gallop the scent and stretch of wild heath aroused in the horse.

Phineas would be displeased, possibly angry. The stallion steadied, he let his mind continue to dwell on the older man. As a child Michael Farron had been allowed to develop his own powers of criticism, his own sense of judgement; Phineas had guided but never dictated, offered advice but only ever imposed it where another person might suffer did he not do so. He had passed all of his own perceptions of honour and fairness and morality to the boy he had taken so completely into his life, teaching him above all else to respect the feelings of others.

Was what he was about to do now carrying out that teaching . . . was he showing respect for the feelings of Phineas Westley? A twinge of conscience riffled in his stomach.

'*It is no concern of yours . . . your encroaching upon my private affairs is an affront!*'

The words had been the girl's but they could equally be those of his uncle. Look at what he planned, survey it from any angle you might, the results were the same: it was plain downright interference in his uncle's private affairs and to carry that plan through could bring an end to their relationship; if the feelings Phineas had for that girl proved stronger than the ones he had for his nephew, then it could be that he would turn his back on all they shared together, that he would no longer accept his sister's son.

The thought was bad enough, the result would be worse . . . but not to act, to do nothing at all, would be a thousand times more so; exposing that girl for what she was would cause Phineas pain, but pain eased with time where a broken heart never mended completely.

Ahead of him like a great round-bellied bottle the pottery kiln stood tall against the sky, rising from the heath as he had often imagined some dreaded demon's lair following one of his uncle's tales; but this was no childhood story, this demon was real and he must face it!

Why would Michael Farron want to speak with her? Stepping from the workshop Callista blinked, finding the early summer sun bright after the dimness.

'This will take only a few moments . . .'

Her vision not yet adjusted to the intensity of daylight Callista peered at the figure, which as yet was no more than a silhouette, a dark and somehow threatening shape.

'I think it is Mr Roberts you should speak with; I came to the wharf only as his representative.'

'I know who it is I should speak with and it is not Daniel Roberts!'

Sharp as a pistol shot it snapped across the space separating them. Cold and oppressive, each word seemed to carry the same dark threat as the shape of the figure now coming closer. If it were not Daniel he had come to see then his business here had nothing to do with clay; that meant it was to do with the discussion which they had had in the wharf office. But that had been no conversation – Callista felt a frisson of alarm along her nerves

– that had been a confrontation and Michael Farron could only have come here to repeat it!

'Be there summat as don't be right?'

Turned to face the man supporting himself with rough wooden crutches Callista began an explanation but a brief shake of Daniel's head ended it in mid-sentence, his own voice firm as that of the younger man as he went on.

'Be there a problem o' sorts wi' the transportin' o' the clay or be it the cost be risin'?'

'Good day, Daniel.' Touching a short riding whip to the side of his bare head Michael smiled. 'No, there is no problem of that kind. I came to speak with Miss Sanford on a private matter.'

There had been no 'Good day, Miss Sanford', no smile for her. Callista realised the snub had been intended. The man's manner was as offensive as it had been that evening in the market place and again in his office.

His look saying he held no awe of the man stood in his yard, a man who could end his business with refusing to transport the materials necessary for the working of the pottery, Daniel returned no smile. 'Then private matters should be discussed where no other ears 'ave the listenin' of 'em. Should Callista be of a mind to speak wi' you then Abigail will join me along of the workshop and the two of you can do your talkin' in the house.'

'That is considerate of you, Daniel, you have my thanks.' The intense eyes shifted to Callista. 'If you would come with me, Miss Sanford.'

The slight tremble which had flickered her nerves only moments ago vanished, its place taken by a feeling she had experienced whenever Oswin Slade had addressed her in that vein, a disdainful 'you are at fault yet again' tone to his words. At her sides Callista's fingers clenched and her voice when she answered was cold.

'No, Mr Farron, I will not come with you. Whatever your quarrel with me I will not have it brought to this house nor will

I speak behind Phineas Westley's back, a man who has shown me nothing but kindness and friendship.'

'Friendship yes, but you took that friendship and—'

'I said there will be no discussion here!' Eyes flashing violet lightning Callista hurled the words, using them like missiles as Daniel hobbled back into the workshop. 'How dare you come to this house with your . . . your accusations! A gentleman of quality would have better manners.'

'Were a gentleman of quality dealing with a woman of the same, then his manner might be expected to have differed, but then you are not a woman of quality; you are simply a fortune hunter, a money-grabber with no thought of anything *but* money and anyone other than yourself!'

The answer had been sharp, cutting into her like the slash of knives, while the anger in him had the handsome face hard and chiselled as stone. Callista felt her insides turn. Like Oswin Slade this man had self-interest at heart but unlike Oswin he saw her as a threat to that interest. But why, why see friendship with an old man as in any way a threat to himself unless it was as she had thought and he stood to lose an inheritance should Phineas marry. She had compared him to Oswin Slade in self-interest . . . did he compare also in selfish greed, a greed blind to the needs and interests of the man he appeared bent on protecting; was he too a shallow self-seeking hypocrite?

The thought aroused pain rather than anger, a tightness which pulled on stretched nerves adding to the ache that had stayed with her since leaving the wharf, an ache telling it mattered what this man thought of her.

Fingers still clutched into her palms, using the bite of finger-nails to fight the emotions stirred by the flintlike incisive blue gaze coming back at her, Callista breathed slowly. She must not let his obvious dislike of her own emotions influence or get in the way of what must be said.

'Mr Farron . . .' Callista's head rose in the characteristic way it always had when a decision had been reached. 'I may not be a woman of quality but though my appearance would deny it I have a certain breeding . . . not that of title or wealth but one far exceeding both. I was taught to observe the sense of fair play, of giving thought to the reasons as well as the actions of others. I think I know the reason for your coming here, for the accusation you made while in that office, and though I am willing to answer your questions I feel it only fair to do so in the hearing of the third person involved. We will talk, Mr Farron, but only in the presence of Phineas Westley.'

20

'Emma Ramsey is dead . . .'

In the quiet privacy of her bedroom Sabine took up a heavy silver-framed photograph of a young smiling girl.

'She is dead,' she whispered. 'Emma won't ever speak again, never tell of your secret . . . you are safe my dear, dear sister. I did it, I did it so no one would know, I killed her for you, my darling, I took her life as I took that other . . . I did it for you.'

Pressing her lips to the cool glass Sabine kissed the smiling image.

'You saw what I did with those chocolates.' A laugh murmuring in her throat she touched the smiling eyes with a finger. 'You watched me as you watched that day . . . the day I helped you keep your secret, watched me add the poison which killed Emma. But Emma cannot be the last; there is another yet must pay, one more life before atonement is complete, one more, my dearest, and then you can rest easy.'

Returning the photograph to its place on the French giltwood writing table beneath the window, Sabine smiled to herself. One more life!

It happened as she had known it would: Emma had died a few hours after she herself had left Acacia Villa, died of a heart attack the doctor had confirmed. It had all been so easy, just as taking that first life had been . . . but had killing Emma been as enjoyable? Had it afforded the many hours of pleasurable contemplation, the exquisite thrill of anticipation and finally the hedonistic, almost sensual glow of triumph when that goal had finally been achieved? Satisfaction fading, Sabine turned from the static lifeless smile of the unrelenting young face.

No . . . Emma's death had afforded none of those feelings. There had been no tingle of excitement, none of the delight of planning or anticipating and no breathtaking rush of exultation on learning of success. No, there had been none of those emotions, stupid snivelling Emma Ramsey could not even give that! Her death had afforded security, safety from the reach of justice and the wagging tongues of society, but it had not afforded that deep satisfying sense of victory, the physical feeling that came with revenge.

But the next one would. It would bring all of that, restitution would be made in full, compensation would be complete.

Swinging to the delicate giltwood table again she took up the silver frame but there was no laugh in her throat when she spoke to the smiling face.

'I told you they would be made to reckon, that I would see to it settlement was made in full and I will keep that promise. Two are gone . . . one remains; one only to stain your name, my dearest sister.'

Leaving the room, Sabine repeated the words in her mind, revelling in the pleasure they sent rushing along her veins.

Two are gone . . . one remains . . .

But not for much longer! Titillation rising in a pink flush to her face she took her seat at the dining table.

One remains . . . not for much longer!

'And did she give you her answer?' Phineas Westley's grey eyes twinkled surreptitiously behind gold-rimmed spectacles. His nephew had told him of Callista Sanford visiting the wharf on behalf of Daniel Roberts and of the conversation which had taken place in the small room which served as an office.

'She definitely gave me that,' Michael Farron answered

grittily. 'She told me it was no concern of mine who she was friends with, that it was an encroachment on her privacy.'

'And so it was,' Phineas replied, hiding the smile ready to break onto his lips. 'You had no right to question the girl; her business is her own.'

'But that business becomes mine when it involves making a fool of you!' Lord, that was clumsy . . . he hadn't meant to let it tumble out like that. Michael saw the twinkle die.

'Make a fool of me . . . how?'

There was no remonstrance in the question, no demand; simply the same quiet enquiry which had always had him so embarrassed when as a child, he had felt guilty of doing something not approved of. He felt that way now! Taking refuge in sipping the brandy he and Phineas enjoyed after dinner together Michael strove to find words which might form a plausible answer while not hurting the other man's feelings . . . heaven knew that was the very last thing he wanted.

'I asked, Michael, how has Callista made a fool of me?'

There was to be no let-up; Phineas was as relentless as he had been during the years of his nephew's growing, gentle but relentless, he would have his answer then and he would have it now. Resigned to the fact, Michael lowered his glass.

'By pretending an interest she cannot possibly have . . . ?'

Seeing one well-shaped eyebrow raise, brought the explanation to an awkward halt. Oh Lord, that had made things worse!

'An interest . . . she cannot possibly have; you intrigue me, Michael, do go on.'

Go on! How could he put what he had said, how could he say it without sounding insulting? He couldn't, but say it he must if things were not to go downhill. Downhill! It brought the ghost of a smile. They were halfway down the slippery slope now.

'I told her displaying an interest in the myths was as much a myth itself, that in truth her only interest lay in yourself and what you could give her.'

Lifting his own glass, staring into the rich amber glow of its contents, Phineas hid the returning twinkle. His nephew was perturbed, unsure of the reaction to what he still had to tell. But let him squirm a little longer. Phineas sipped slowly. Serve the young blighter right, teach him the lesson he should have learned years ago, not to go meddling in other people's affairs . . . especially where the affairs were those of a woman!

'And what could I give her, Michael?'

The old rogue was playing him like a fish; he had him on his line and he was determined to reel him in! Despite himself Michael wanted to chuckle, but resisted.

'You don't need me to answer that, Phineas; you are nobody's fool.'

'Is that not a contradiction? Did you not say a moment since that the girl was making a fool of me?'

This could go on all night. Resigned to what must be, Michael met the grey stare. 'All right, yes I said it. I told her she was spinning a hard-luck story, pretending a knowledge of mythology in order to inveigle you into proposing marriage.'

Taking a few moments to quell the feeling rising inside him Phineas held the intense blue eyes with his own gaze. The lad was honest, there had been no self-interest in what he had said to Callista Sanford, of that he was certain; headstrong yes, foolish maybe: his sister's son had shown those characteristics before but his motives had never been those of selfishness. His nephew was concerned for him, anxious he not be hurt by a young woman, a girl who . . . *showed an interest she could not possibly have.*

Maybe he could take affront at that. Phineas smiled inwardly. Take this scoundrel to task for implying he was past the age of engendering love in a young woman. But he was enjoying the moment . . . he would let it go on a little longer.

'A pretended knowledge, you say.' He sipped again from his deeply cut Royal Brierley crystal goblet. 'Can one pretend knowing the classics, the deities of the ancient world and their deeds? Would have thought only dedicated teaching or study to be responsible for that and disagree if you must, Michael, but Callista Sanford knows her gods and goddesses.'

'As she knows her own wiles. The girl would make Circe look like an amateur.'

Well, well! Phineas heard the snap in the retort. If the girl did indeed have wiles then she had used them on his nephew! Admit it or not, realise it or not, Michael Farron's interest in Callista Sanford was not entirely born out of a wish to prevent his uncle from contracting an unfortunate marriage.

'You did ask her, didn't you?' Unaware of the vehemence of the question Michael's lips set tight as his uncle nodded the reply.

'Yes, Michael. I did ask my question.'

So he had been correct in his thinking. Michael watched the light from the chandelier bounce a myriad of colours from the crystal goblet twisting restlessly between his fingers. Phineas had asked the girl to be his wife . . . and she would not have refused. Oh, she had played the shy hesitant little thing, but that was play-acting designed to bring the protective male rushing even faster to take her into his home, to protect her. Protect her! He sipped again at his brandy, daring the fiery liquid to burn more than the heat of blood in his veins. Would his uncle think the girl needed protection had he seen her at Roberts' pottery, saw how she stood up for herself, heard the sharp reprimand in each answer? Would he see her as the shy hesitant little thing then?

'Did Callista tell you I had proposed marriage?'

The question cut across thoughts as yet unfinished but Michael met the grey glint accompanying it. The girl had not said it in so many words yet the implication had been there. But his uncle would not accept an answer such as that; he would insist upon hearing the girl's exact words. Pulling a longer breath he answered.

'I told her I thought her true interest was herself, that grabbing a rich husband was her only interest in yourself.'

'I see.' Phineas nodded. 'And Callista's reply . . . what was that?'

It couldn't be avoided. The answer would be bound to injure this man's pride, to cause him hurt. Michael felt the surge of sympathy rise in his throat. He would rather it were himself must feel the pain . . . but then he did, his heart too ached at the remembered words of Callista Sanford! What he felt was not truly for Phineas but for himself.

'I would like an answer, Michael. What did Callista reply?'

Letting the breath go free Michael answered. 'She said marriage to Phineas Westley was her only interest.'

The sound of voices drifting across the yard brought Callista hurrying from the workshop. She had packed the plates and mugs into wicker baskets, separating them carefully between layers of straw ready for sending to market, but Daniel must not lift them, his leg was not yet healed.

'My nephew told me of your accident; I came to enquire if I could offer assistance.'

'Be kind of you to think, Abigail an' me be grateful, but this 'ere young wench will be all the 'elp we need.' Daniel Roberts' whiskered face beamed as he saw Callista emerge into the sunshine.

Touching his tall silk hat Phineas Westley smiled. 'Good afternoon, Callista, it is good to see you well. I have missed you at the churchyard.'

Following her mother's teaching Callista dropped a faint curtsey as she returned the greeting, adding, 'I have not been there of late.'

'Then I must tell you the silk flowers you placed in your vase are still pretty; their colours are not yet faded completely.'

Why was Phineas Westley come to the pottery? Callista's

nerves tightened. Was it what she had said to Michael Farron, that she would not discuss this man behind his back? Was he now come to take her to task, to demand to know what she thought she was about daring to imply a question of marriage between herself and him?

'Is Abigail's teaset still as pretty? I remember the colour of those corn poppies like the blush of Abigail's cheek when being asked to marry you.'

Was that meant for her, was it his way of intimating the purpose of this visit? But would the man who had been the soul of courtesy and politeness on each of their meetings confront her with his questions here in front of others . . . would he be so rude and embarrassing as Michael Farron had been?

'Them there poppies be bright as ever.' Daniel chuckled. 'But my own cheeks will be brighter than them o' any blushing maid were I to let you leave wi'out invitin' you to a sup o' tea.'

'A sup of tea will be welcome, Daniel, but not so welcome as Abigail's smile.'

They talked together like old friends. Callista watched the ease between the two. It had never been this way at Trowes Court; no sign of friendship had ever been exhibited between the poor and wealthy; it had never been known to exist. Workers were two a penny and the industrialists who employed them valued them no higher; they were kept in their place. But Oswin Slade had seen his place as being not among the employed but side by side with the masters and like many of them he was willing to sacrifice the happiness of anyone he could use to get there.

'Then come you into the 'ouse for if I knows my Abigail the pot will be brewin' right now.'

Michael Farron must have told him. They were obviously of the same social class so it was certain they were bound to have talked . . . it was the only way Phineas Westley could know what she had said that day at the wharf and again here at the pottery and friendly as he was trying to make this visit appear it could only be that which brought him. But she could not bring the matter up, embarrass Daniel and Abigail with so sordid a problem. She would wait, listen for him leaving then follow to beyond the house.

'There be no task as'll fail in the waitin',' Daniel said as she turned back toward the workshop, 'and you knows Abigail will not sup lessen you be there so lend me your arm afore herself comes to see where we be.'

Abigail would not sup without her! Phineas Westley mulled the words as the three of them walked slowly towards a cottage, its walls covered now with a confusion of pink-petalled roses. The Robertses had obviously taken to the girl.

Usually so relaxed with the couple she had come to love, Callista's nerves refused to release their grip, leaving her words and movements taut. Agibail had noticed. She returned her poppy-painted cup to the table. If only she could return to the workshop – but to excuse herself now when both she and Daniel knew there was nothing there required immediate attention would only serve to heighten speculation. She would just have to wait.

'I still envy you, Daniel.' Phineas's words broke across Callista's thoughts. 'You beat me to the best cook in the county and the prettiest; if only I had been a mite quicker off the mark then maybe Abigail would have taken me and not yourself, but maybe it is not too late . . . even for an old man.'

There it was again. Callista's heart jumped. He *had* to have been told . . . Michael Farron had not baulked at speaking behind anyone's back!

'Now you must forgive me . . .'

Had anyone heard the breath she released, seen the look which crossed her face as Phineas Westley rose? Callista glanced at Daniel's wife but the woman's attention was on her caller.

'I have to leave but before I go there is a matter I would discuss with Miss Sanford.'

This was it . . . he was going to accuse her in front of Daniel and Abigail! But what else could she hope for; she had shown no courtesy by speaking of him at all to a stranger. How then could she expect any difference?

'And I think, Daniel, we would both benefit from your advice.'

Feelings which had been almost stunned by anxiety flared into brilliant life. She would not have Daniel drawn into this! Pride in every line of her, Callista rose to her feet.

'Mr Westley,' she said, aware of the tremble in her voice. 'I can only guess you have been in conversation with a Mr Michael Farron and it is a result of such conversation you wish to discuss with me, but I will say to you what I said to him: whatever quarrel you might have with me I will not have it brought to this house nor will I speak of it unless it be in the presence of . . . of the man who carried my words to you.'

She had not spoken the words Michael had said to him. Phineas Westley watched the tilt of the raven dark head, the flash of fire in those violet eyes . . . those honest violet eyes! She had not said she would not speak behind the back of a man who had shown her nothing but kindness and friendship but then the lad was probably not yet aware he wanted only to show the girl those feelings . . . those and more.

'Ah, Michael Farron.' Phineas smiled. 'Yes, my nephew did tell me of his conversation with you. I hope you will forgive him, Callista, he is sometimes overhasty on my behalf.'

His nephew! Callista felt the flush rise to her face. Michael Farron was Phineas Westley's nephew! Yet he had made no mention of that either when here or at the wharf; he had deliberately vexed her, led her into saying what she had and never once hinted at his relationship.

'I apologise for any embarrassment he may have unwittingly caused you as I know he will also should you permit a further meeting between him and yourself.'

Unwitting! There was nothing unwitting about Michael

Farron! Catching the spark of a smile Callista knew her thought had shown and been interpreted. The hasty nephew would know better than to voice his concerns at Leabrook Potteries a second time.

'But to the matter I came about,' Phineas went on. 'The copy of the Michelangelo vase you placed on your mother's grave. I think Daniel will agree when I say it is an excellent piece of work.'

'I does that!' Daniel's grey head rocked back and forth. 'I never seen a better done by a beginner.'

'And would you also agree that given a little expert tuition Callista would be capable of more excellent pieces yet?'

Ready as his smile Daniel's answer was on his lips. 'Ar, I agrees to that an' all.'

'Then what I wish to ask Callista is, should you be offered that tuition by the man I consider to be the best among potters, namely Daniel Roberts, would you consider crafting such pieces and others you have a feeling for? Pieces I know would be valued in many a home.'

This was not what he had come to say. He had come to confront, not compliment. Confusion chasing the blush from her cheeks Callista stood unspeaking.

'Well, Callista?'

Phineas was nudging her silence aside, his eyes on hers calling for an answer.

'I . . . I . . .' She stumbled in the search for words. 'My vase was pretty but in no way could it be called worthy of a place in anyone's home.'

'But I do say it.' Phineas smiled. 'And I believe Daniel would say it also. You have the makings of a craftsman, my dear, your work would sell well.'

'Plates and mugs, yes, but pieces such as that I made for my mother . . . people who know and love the original would never buy a copy made from clay.'

'Have you ever offered people a chance? I can see you have

not; how then can you be so sure? Originals cannot be owned except by a fortunate few but does that mean folk less fortunate should not enjoy their beauty? Should they not also have the joy of a Michelangelo, an Antonio Canova or a Girolano della Robbia in their home even though they be a copy?'

'But those are masterpieces carved from marble. I cannot carve marble.'

'I would not ask you to.'

'But each of those pieces are the work of a master!'

The protest was clear in the answer and it pleased Phineas. The girl was not flattered by praise, she was not ready to jump where her mind told her she should not tread; she showed caution as well as humility. There was more to like about this girl than ever he had thought.

'The work of a master, yes, Callista, but the greatest of them all had to start from the beginning and you are at the beginning. The skills of your hands need refining, teaching until they are sure of what is in them. With Daniel you can reach that stage; you only have to remember not all beauty is portrayed in stone or on canvas; clay too can speak to the soul.'

'He be right, wench.' Daniel added his convictions gently. 'You 'ave the touch I ain't seen in 'ands other than those of . . . well, I ain't seen it more'n once afore; you should pay heed to what be said for it could bring a living the mekin' o' plates an' mugs won't.'

He had been about to say the touch he had seen in his son's hands. From the corner of her eye Callista had seen the quick hand touch Abigail's mouth before the woman turned, hiding pain she could not keep from her eyes . . . pain of losing her children. How could she turn her back on their kindness; but how could she refuse Phineas Westley without appearing ungrateful?

'What you say of my work is pleasing,' she answered, 'and none I'm sure could advance any skill I might have as Mr Roberts would, but even given such expert help I could not produce the works of the old masters.'

'No one could, they are all the works of an individual. They bear the stamp, the hallmark of their maker just as these cups and plates with their painted poppies carry the exclusive stroke of Abigail's brush, of her eye for movement and design. That is what makes a master and you share those same traits; you say you cannot produce the same but that is simply because you see them in their present value . . . as the lovely products of a bygone age. We cannot add to the antiques of the past, Callista, but we can make the antiques of the future. But I will say no more of it until you and Daniel have talked further.'

Shaking hands with Daniel and kissing Abigail on the cheek he turned once more but now the smile was gone from his eyes and Callista felt her nerves quicken once more as he said quietly, 'If you would be kind enough to accompany me to my carriage, Callista.'

21

He had been a fool. Michael Farron watched the girl talking now with Moses Turley. '*He need not take the trouble of arranging for the three of them to meet.*' His uncle had said her tone was cold when she said it, that what his nephew had said had caused her no bother, therefore he need take none in order to apologise.

Nevertheless he must do so and it might as well be now. Seeing him approach the wharf manager touched a hand to his flat cap, its peak shading his eyes from the bright light of the sun reflecting from the waters of the canal.

'Miss Sanford be . . .' He paused as a shout from one of the huddle of narrow boats rang across the wharf.

'See to it, Moses,' Michael Farron answered the other man's questioning look then, 'perhaps Miss Sanford you would allow me—'

'My business here is done!' Callista interrupted, already turning away.

'But my business with you is not!' It had come out sharper than he had meant. Lord he was sunk even deeper into the mire! 'Please.' He grinned ruefully. 'I am already in Phineas's bad books, my name has an asterisk beside it and should he learn I have met with you and not apologised for my atrocious behaviour then it will be erased for good.'

Despite her intention to remain coldly aloof Callista felt a warmth inside her; but she would not let it show, she would not allow him to see she suddenly wanted only to smile.

'I'm sure that is not true.'

'Not exactly.' His grin widened. 'But it was good for a start and I really do need to apologise. It was wrong of me to speak as I did . . . as you told me, it was no concern of mine.'

Allowing herself to be led away from the busy wharf Callista asked quietly, 'Why did you not say you were Phineas Westley's nephew?'

Coming to a halt Michael met the candid violet eyes. Why had he made no mention of that fact? To answer truthfully would have turned her away from him, made her see him as no more than a man filled with . . . what? He was going to say filled with spite and jealousy but there had been no spite to his action . . . and jealousy? Could he honestly claim there had been no jealousy of her association with his uncle?

Wrestling with the argument playing in his brain his answer came stumblingly. 'I . . . I can only say it was anger kept me from mentioning our relationship; I did not want to see Phineas hurt . . . that blinded my mind to all else.'

'I too did not wish to see him hurt.'

'Yet your reply was that marriage to Phineas Westley was your only concern. I thought that meant . . .'

'I intended to get myself a wealthy and elderly husband?' Seeing the flicker of guilt flash across his eyes Callista shook her head. 'You were wrong, Mr Farron, my concern was that your uncle *not* come to regard me as anything other than a girl he once talked with in the cemetery of St James's church. That was one of the reasons I refused his offer . . . not an offer of marriage but a proposal I document and record his collection of antiques.'

She had not spoken acerbically nor with any rebuff but as Phineas had done, almost with quiet sympathy. He could thank her for her understanding, express regret for his hastiness now and leave . . . so why didn't he, why not leave it at that and go? Glancing again at those half-smiling violet eyes Michael Farron knew why.

'You say that was one reason you refused to live in my uncle's house, which implies there was another. Am I permitted to ask what that other might be?' The question provided respite from his thoughts but they were thoughts he knew would return.

Across the cobbled wharf shouts announced the departure of narrow boats and the calls of boatmen bringing their own to moor in their places. Watching them Callista mused on the question. She had no need to answer anything Michael Farron asked but then she had no need of secrecy either. Returning her look to him, the half-smile of her eyes touching faintly to her lips, she replied, 'I could not accept a place in that house being certain as I was Phineas Westley would not look upon me as a member of his staff.'

'You would not have been a member of his staff!'

'In the domestic sense of the word perhaps not.' She answered the quick intervention as quietly as she had replied to his questions. 'But whatever the task I was hired to perform I would be paid help, a servant no matter the title placed upon it. I felt your uncle would not be prepared to treat me as such and therefore I refused the post. Did he not explain that to you?'

'He did not.' Lifting a hand to his face Michael rubbed his beardless chin. 'He said what you had said hours before, that it was no business of mine whom he formed a friendship with; in fact he called me an interfering young pup who needed his tail docked.'

'Ugh!' Callista pretended pain. 'Then you should thank the stars you are his nephew and not his dog.'

'The Pleiades,' Michael laughed, 'perhaps those are the stars you would recommend.'

'The seven daughters of Atlas, the great Titan,' Callista answered immediately. 'They became stars in order to avoid the amorous attentions of Orion the hunter though I fear he chases them still across the night sky. Choose whom you address your prayers to carefully, Mr Farron, for though the daughters of Titan are kind, those of Nyx, the goddess of the night, those we call the Fates, are not always so.'

The Fates were not always kind. On her way back to the pottery Callista repeated the words to herself. Sometimes it seemed they delighted in the opposite, adding to the unhappiness of life as they had the lives of her parents. First her father's suicide, then her mother's death from overwork, constant cold and insufficient food. How could heaven dictate one life be so wretched while others lived in plenty! And her own life? That too had been no bed of feathers. Stooping, she picked a buttercup from the heath, staring into its golden face. There had been those three years when every day Miss Montroy had found some reason to slap her, some reason to drive fear deeper into the heart of a child. But those years had ended. Plucking a golden petal from the tiny flower, she watched it flutter to the ground. So too had her father's life. Freeing a second petal she watched it fall. They had ended but the wretchedness of life had gone on. Her mother's endless toil and then her own repeated failure to secure employment. Taking a third petal between her fingers she let it drop, watching its gleaming downward spiral to where it nestled in the grass. Then, hard on her mother's passing, had come Oswin's attempted rape. The horror of that assault, of his twisted leering face pushing close to her own, the touch of his body pressing against hers, had a shiver run the entire length of her. Fingers trembling, she severed a fourth petal. Shaking it free of her hand she whispered a prayer that never again would she be subjected to such degradation.

Callista touched the one remaining petal, the broken delicate flower gleaming silken gold. Would her future be no different to her past? Would time show her that one or each of these tiny shining gems of nature could represent more misery or had the Fates she had spoken of to Michael Farron had their enjoyment of Callista Sanford?

'They improves every time. Phineas Westley were right when he said you had the touch of a master.' Daniel Roberts picked up the small replica of a woman reclining, turning it admiringly, his keen potter's eye inspecting every fold of the gown, every drape of the veil covering the head leaving only a touch of curls nestling on the brow, the promise of a smile shadowing the finely executed mouth while remaining hidden in demurely downcast eyes.

'I hardly think Antonio Canova or Girolano della Robbia would agree,' Callista answered, taking the finished figure of a small shepherd boy from the saggar in which it had been fired and placing it on a shelf with several other pieces Daniel had helped her create in the time that could be spared from the making of tableware.

'Well seein' as I don't 'ave the knowin' of any Giro . . . Giro . . . him you speaks of, then I can't go disputin' them claims . . . but this I can say, you 'ave a way many a man mekin' pots has the envy of. It hears the call of your 'eart, feels the love in your fingers and responds to it; you should tek heed of what Westley 'as offered for it will bring you more than ever you can 'ope for by stayin' put at this place.'

Watching him place the piece with the others Callista smiled. 'This place, as you put it, is where I have been happiest since my mother died. You have given me more than a home, you have given me back my self-esteem, more even than that . . .' She paused, suddenly shy, then added softly, 'You have given me love.'

His eyes moistening, Daniel set the piece with the rest. The wench spoke truth; Abigail and him had given her their love and in turn she had given them hers; she had brought back a little light into their lives, the light extinguished so long ago when his children had left home, driven away by a father's stupid pride.

'So what be you going to name these 'uns?'

She had heard the tell-tale break in his voice, a break she had come to recognise. He was thinking of the love of two young people, how it had once filled the cottage, that of a daughter coming to womanhood and a son strong and agile . . . children for whom his face often betrayed his yearning though he never spoke these thoughts.

Coming to his side she slipped a hand into his, feeling the skin hardened by years of throwing clay. 'What do you think of David for the shepherd boy and Helen for the woman?'

'Well I knows who be David, but who be 'Elen?'

'Ar, who be 'Elen?'

It was Abigail asking from the doorway of the small workshop, an enquiring frown settling on her forehead.

'It's a long story,' Callista smiled.

'Then it best be told over a sup of tea. I've brewed a pot an' there be a fresh-baked scone an' jam to go along o' it.'

'So who be this 'Elen the both o' you were on about when I come to the workshop?'

Abigail had obviously not given up on her curiosity. She looked at her husband but Daniel simply shrugged.

'The wench gives each piece her meks a name an' 'Elen be what her's christened that reclinin' woman.'

'So why 'Elen? What be special to that name apart from it bein' pretty?'

'Helen was a central character in one of the stories written by an ancient Greek scholar named Homer.' Callista was suddenly in the home of her childhood repeating a story heard from her father. 'She was so beautiful that a prince of Troy fell in love with her and she left her husband in order to be with her lover and the Trojan War was the consequence.' The explanation brief as a young child had made it to her mother, Callista could almost hear her father's reproof. She had kept it so brief he would have been dismayed to hear it but to tell a fuller version would take time and Daniel had already stolen two glances at the clock.

'Hmmph! Be no more to that story you don't 'ear goin' on anywheres 'cept mebbe he were a prince . . . but they gets everythin' they fancies anyway an' that includes women! An' some o' them ain't never satisfied wi' the bargain they gets. Riches and comfort be all well an' good but they ain't everythin' in life an' tekin' a 'usband just so you 'ave them brings shame to a woman!' Abigail gathered mugs and plates, banging them together in her particular expression of what she thought of such a poor story . . . and not a little of her contempt for the heroine.

Following Daniel's lead Callista followed back to the workshop. Michael Farron had held the same opinion of her; he had thought her ready to marry Phineas Westley simply to gain a comfortable life. Had Phineas also suspected the same . . . seen her as a scheming woman currying friendship, using it as a cloak to a truer intention?

The thought hurtful, she tried to concentrate on the stacking of plates into saggars, bedding or separating them with a layer of flint before Daniel carried them balanced on his head to the kiln he was stacking in preparation for biscuit or first firing.

But not by a single word did Phineas ever imply he thought of her that way. It had become a practice for them to talk together each Sunday afternoon when she visited her parents' graves; that too was a benefit afforded by working and living with the Robertses, for she had thought never again to have the opportunity of standing in that quiet churchyard, with the love in her heart flowing out to them. Nor did Phineas speak of the misunderstanding which had occurred between herself and his nephew; whenever he spoke of Michael Farron it was only in terms of business.

Michael Farron too had kept conversation strictly to business whenever she had visited the wharf in place of Daniel; for him also it seemed the past was forgotten.

But she had not forgotten.

'There be room for a couple more then the oven be full.'

Standing a moment watching Daniel hoist yet another loaded saggar onto his head, years of repetition having his balance so perfect he had no need of steadying it with a hand as he crossed the yard to the tall bottle-shaped kiln he called an oven, she felt a rush of self-condemnation. Her thoughts were full of herself, of what she had lost, of her own clash of temperament and misunderstandings. But what of Daniel and Abigail? Their loss could be said to be greater than hers, the misunderstanding which had happened had robbed them of their children; and love and respect the couple as she did she could never replace their own flesh and blood.

She had two more of the heavy clay boxes filled with plates before realising Daniel had not returned. A frisson of alarm rippling the edges of her nerves she went out to the yard. The doors of the 'hovel', the bottle-shaped brick-built outer casing which surrounded the firing chamber or 'oven' of the kiln, were pushed wide on their hinges, a full brick set to prevent their swinging shut; but of Daniel there was no sign.

Something was wrong! Callista's heart seemed to stop then lurch on in a mad race. Resisting the urge to shout his name she ran, twisting an ankle painfully on the uneven sets, but the bite of it went unheeded.

Inside the 'hovel' the gloom after the brilliant sun-filled gleam of the afternoon had her move more cautiously. Trying to keep any note of alarm from her voice she called softly but no answer came from the shadowed depths. But, of course, Daniel had been stacking the oven so that was where he would be. Lifting her skirts as a precaution against tripping over it she mounted the three steps which gave onto the firing chamber. In here was dark as the regions of the underworld. At any other time she would have smiled at the simile but right now she was too concerned with why Daniel did not answer. Waiting until her sight was at one with her surroundings she let her glance rove over the saggars carefully placed one on top of another ranging around the walls in columns she had learned to call bungs, which reached almost the full height of the oven. But where was Daniel?

The ladder he used to reach loads to and from the bungs rested near a partially completed stack. After running a swift glance along the length of it, Callista stifled a half-emitted scream, holding it in her throat. Daniel was at the foot of the ladder, his body covered in broken pottery, the heavy saggar lying in the small of his back.

22

'These are all the work of Callista Sanford?'

'With the assistance of Daniel Roberts.' Phineas Westley watched his nephew touch each of the dozen or so figurines ranged tastefully on elegant tables set in the library of The Limes, a home equally refined providing a setting a background graceful as the figures themselves.

'But I thought she worked in clay.'

'So she does.' Phineas's eyes twinkled behind his gold-rimmed spectacles.

Michael Farron's brow furrowed as he took up a small replica of a woman seated against the flower-twined stump of a tree. 'Clay?' He glanced at Phineas. 'But this looks like marble, it has the feel of marble, smooth and silk to the touch.'

'Doesn't it!' Phineas was obviously enjoying the moment. 'This is what helps to make it special . . . though no one can deny the artistry, the form and rhythm, the absolute quality of the work.'

A woman of quality! He had denied Callista Sanford was such a woman. Michael replaced the delicate figure. But that was yet another mistake on his part, for she was all of that.

Phineas moved to the next table watching his nephew pick up a bust of a young woman, curled hair caught high on a head turned slightly to the left; lips parted, sloe eyes dreamy, it bore a faraway look.

'She is beautiful . . .'

Was his nephew speaking of the woman in his hand or the

woman in his mind? Judging by the number of times Callista Sanford's name managed to enter their conversations he would judge the latter.

'She seems to tempt,' Michael was still looking at the bust, 'yet at the same time remain beyond reach.'

'An apt description of Venus.'

'Is that the name she gave it or is the choice due to a certain Phineas Westley?'

'It was Callista's choice, she names each of her pieces . . . but I confess had she not given the title "Venus" to that one I would have done so myself for it has every attribute and beauty of the goddess.'

'You'll never change, will you, Phineas?' Michael smiled affection at the man stood beside him. 'I only hope that one day you will find the happiness of your Elysian Fields, your paradise of the immortals.'

Unspoken, a whisper in his mind, Phineas's reply was heartfelt. As I pray one day you will have the good sense to reach for your own more earthly happiness.

'So how does Cal— the girl achieve this colouring and effect? Some of the bowls are translucent.'

Had she denied him use of her given name or was it his own stubbornness prevented his speaking it? His inner smile deepening, Phineas turned to yet one more table. More likely his nephew did not speak the name for fear of betraying his emotions.

'Daniel Roberts wasn't giving too much away,' Phineas replied. 'Apparently it is a formula he and his son worked on before the boy left the pottery. He did however say it was a compound of china clay, feldspar, white sand and frit, but the rest of the mixture is a secret he would not divulge.'

'I can't say I blame him. It makes a most desirable object and I'm sure they would find a ready market.'

'My sentiments exactly but we will reserve that judgement until these have been seen by my dinner guests.'

His uncle was moving towards the door but Michael remained, his glance touching again each of the lovely creamy-white groups of figurines, busts and bowls reflecting the light of candles from the overhead candelabra and the smaller standing ones set at intervals about the book-lined room. Phineas was a connoisseur of art who also knew how to present it to advantage.

'Before they arrive,' he said, halting the older man, 'tell me, was this showing an idea proposed by Miss Sanford?'

Why that question? What particular imp of mischief was running around in his nephew's brain?

'No.' Phineas shook his head. 'It was not Callista's idea but then what you see here does not belong to her; that being so I feel I may show them to whomsoever I please.'

The frown which earlier had rested on Michael's brow settled again. 'Not hers! I don't understand.'

'Really Michael, what is there *not* to understand?'

'Why you should have them!'

The reply quickly spoken had said more than the words it contained. Phineas hid his smile. It said there was still a worm of doubt wriggling in his nephew's mind, doubt as to whether an old man's feelings for a young girl were strictly those of friendship.

'I did not buy them . . .'

'Phineas . . . for heaven's sake! You didn't buy them and it is certain you did not steal them and she did not ask you show them so how come they are here?'

'As you say, Michael, I did not steal them. I asked Callista to sell these pieces to me but she maintained they were not hers to sell.' The frown hardening further on his nephew's brow, Phineas went on patiently. 'She said she was merely their creator, that the materials used in their making belonged to Daniel; he had paid for them as he had the coal necessary to fire the oven, so, as with any person employed by another, the articles she produced belonged to the owner of those materials.'

'So you purchased them from Daniel Roberts.'

'No . . .'

'Phineas!'

'Kindly allow me to finish.' Interrupting the outburst with a gesture Phineas looked concernedly at a dish whose covered lid was worked with a delicate tracery of leaves and flowers newly opening from their bud, Michael's hand a shade closer to it than prudence permitted. 'Daniel insisted they belonged to Callista; the state of impasse appeared unbreakable, so I asked could I borrow them in order to enjoy their beauty in a setting more suitable than a shelf in Daniel Roberts's workshop.'

'I see.' The note of relief was clear though not intended. 'And do they know you have arranged a viewing?'

His look saintly, Phineas smiled before opening the door. 'I see no reason to inform anyone of my inviting guests into my own home.'

It was an evasion, but one he could not argue with. Following his uncle to the drawing room where they would await those guests Michael could only admit himself defeated. What Phineas had said was totally logical but how would that logic be interpreted by Callista Sanford should she come to hear of his evening's activities?

The lengthy preparation of dressing completed, Sabine Derry looked at her reflection in the long oval-framed cheval mirror of her bedroom. This new gown looked well . . . very well indeed. It had cost a small fortune, coming from the London fashion house of Jacques D'Albe, but it was certain no other woman at Phineas Westley's dinner party would be gowned so splendidly. The Limes. She half turned, watching silken flounces of the skirt glide behind her. She had chosen the design well: a décolletage and off-the-shoulder short puff sleeves showed off her throat and shoulders while the skirt, flounced and cut into a train set off by a generous ruching of lace and velvet with a finishing of bows of the same material, emphasised the stateliness of her figure. The colours too were well chosen. Deep yellow silk edged with apple green, a sash of green not about her waist but falling from one hip to be gathered into a large rosette before being draped elegantly to a lace-frilled hem. Teamed with the emerald necklace and long drop earrings Edwin had given her on their marriage day the whole presented a picture of wealth and prosperity. And that was what she wanted to be seen: Edwin Derry as a wealthy and successful manufacturer. The Westley family had always been looked upon as squires of the county by the people of Wednesbury, the landed gentry, but tonight would show that though they might be the old money they were not the only money; tonight everyone who was anyone in this town would see and would know the Derrys for what they had and for the place she intended them to hold in society. From this evening onward Phineas Westley would see the challenge to his being regarded as sole 'Lord of the Manor'.

Somehow they had got Daniel to the house. The first moment of seeing him lying face down at the foot of that ladder she had been struck dumb and motionless, her feet seeming to root themselves in the floor of the dark oven. She had tried to call his name but sound had died before it could leave her throat. How long had she stood there fastened by ties of fear . . . fear that Daniel was dead? Then from somewhere had come a sound; a movement, a shifting of a pot not quite settled in its place? She had not known or cared. It had broken the bands holding her to the spot and she had run to the figure lying on the ground. He had been so still. Lying in her own bed Callista watched moon-born shadows dance in the silence. She had been afraid to touch him yet had known she must. She had lifted the sagger from his back, the weight of it, even though empty now of its contents, pulling on his arms. With it pushed aside she had bent over the unmoving form whispering his name, willing him to answer. But Daniel had not answered.

Beyond the window an owl hooted, its cry echoing on the still-ness. Her father had told her owls were the night watch of the gods sent to safeguard sleeping children and to bring pleasant dreams, releasing them to drift in at a window. How he had always comforted her fears! But there had been no father to comfort her in that kiln, no steady voice or reassuring hand, no strong arms to hold her until her fear was gone. There had been only herself, Daniel and that terrible overwhelming mind-shattering silence.

At last the shreds of sanity had collected together enough for her to realise she could not move Daniel alone. She had tried to keep her anxiety hidden but the clatter of her running feet on the cobblestones of the yard had brought Abigail hurrying from her kitchen, their story told before she could speak.

She would never forget the look that had come to the woman's face. Callista's eyes closed on the memory but the pictures played on behind her eyelids. Abigail's lips had formed a ques-tion but the words had not come, only her brown eyes had asked, had screamed an inner torture as she had raced past and into the oven. She had been on her knees, her face pressed to the cheek of her husband. Callista watched the scene playing in her mind, showing the moment she had re-entered the kiln. Then Abigail had lifted her head. The gloom of the interior had shrouded the anguish she had seen smouldering seconds before the woman had run past her, the gnawing agony she had known still played in the depths of her soul, but the tremble of the voice could not be concealed by shadow, or swallowed by darkness; that had spoken the fear, the terror clamped about the heart.

'We can't lift 'im wi'out help.' Tears had made each word quiver, testifying to the grief tearing at Abigail. 'To try might give rise to . . .' She had broken off the thought too impossibly painful to voice, then after moments had said, 'Go you to the 'ouse, wench, bring me pillow and blankets enough to keep 'im warm then get you to the wharf . . . it be nearer than the town . . . you'll find men there as'll come.'

She had done as requested and though loath to leave Abigail had run to the wharf. The owl hooted again, the sound nearer this time. The bearer of a dream? The bringer of sleep? Callista's head turned restlessly on the pillow. The gods had chosen unwisely; sleep was a comfort worry denied her.

It had been minutes only before, led by Moses Turley, a group of men called from their narrow boats and carrying a door they could use as a stretcher were racing across the heath, but each of those minutes had proved a lifetime.

Left a short way behind by the speed of their travelling she had reached the yard as the unconscious figure was being carried across to the house. *Daniel was alive.* She had trembled as much as the woman she had held in her arms when given the news by Moses Turley. '*But,*' the wharf gaffer had continued gravely, '*he be bad 'urt, there be no tellin' 'ow bad 'til he be seen by the doctor. If it be all right wi' you, Abigail, I'll send a man to fetch 'im along to the 'ouse . . . and p'raps it be best we men gets Daniel to 'is bed, he be heavy for you to wrestle wi' the undressin' of.*'

They had stayed, all except Moses sitting in the yard, stayed there talking quietly among themselves. Strange how the thing she remembered most was the shafts of sunlight! They had streamed from a sky so blue, so perfect, their golden beams seemed to hover above each bared head as if in blessing, a recognition of the kindness and sympathy of men who would not leave until knowing they could do no more.

Daniel had had the devil's own luck. The doctor had smiled after making his examination. *The saggar had bruised the spine fairly severely but it had not broken it. Daniel would recover but his days of stacking the kiln were over.* Taking a cup of the tea Callista had brewed and served to the boatmen the doctor had given his diagnosis finishing with, 'What has happened today will most certainly happen again should he continue in the potting and next time, Abigail, your man might not be as lucky. He has escaped a very serious injury and we all thank God for that but you must make him see he cannot tempt providence twice.'

His days of stacking the kiln were over . . . should he continue in the potting . . . he cannot tempt providence twice!

Callista's eyes opened as the words echoed in her mind. Abigail had realised the enormity of them; it had shown in her gentle eyes, in the tremor of her voice as she had thanked the doctor, displayed the new fear nestling in an already overloaded heart; one which told her Daniel would be as a man condemned to a lifetime of misery when learning he could no longer work the pottery and she, his wife, must be the judge to pass sentence!

The boatmen had left with the doctor's leaving. Each had spoken with Abigail, assuring her she need only to ask and help would be given, but those men could not throw pots.

Clouds drifting across the moon gave the shadows on the walls of her room fresh life, a new dance to twist and glide to. A new beginning! A silvered ray reaching across the bed like a shimmering finger touched the frown drawing Callista's brows together from the irony of the thought. What new beginning could there be for Daniel and Abigail? All they had ever known had been the making of crockery, their whole lives had been given to the one occupation. What else could they do, what could they turn to now?

Nothing! The answer breathed from its own shadowed seclusion, whispered from each darkened corner like some harbinger of doom. There was nothing for Daniel Roberts except a potter's wheel. With that taken from him the man's heart would break; he would be as a man whose will was drained and lost, a man without purpose.

And Callista Sanford, what of her? She too must face a new

beginning for without work in the pottery she could no longer remain in this house.

So many beginnings . . . so many endings. The moon becoming obscured by cloud, its silver light swallowed by shadow which seemed to creep into her heart, Callista closed her eyes. Why was it misfortune followed so closely in her wake, ever ready to devour any happiness she found?

The Fates are not always kind.

She might have meant those words for herself.

23

'Moses Turley told me of what happened when I returned to the wharf this morning. You must allow me to help.'

'Ain't nothing you can do, Mr Farron, but I thanks you kindly for the offer.'

'What exactly happened? Moses said Cal— Miss Sanford came running to the wharf and when he and the men reached here they found Daniel unconscious on the floor of the kiln.'

Trusting to brewing of tea and setting of scones on a plate to find work for restless fingers and a diversion to an agitated mind Abigail took the pot from the hob, filling it with boiling water.

'Seems the leg he injured a while back don't be healed as Daniel believed. He were halfway to the top of a bung . . . that be a column o' saggars set one on another . . . when the leg buckled beneath 'im an' down he come wi' the pots he were carryin' coming' down on top of 'im.'

'Is he badly injured?' Taking the pretty poppy-painted mug and plate with its fresh scone Michael caught the flicker of pain crossing the woman's face before she answered.

'Daniel be badly bruised but his spine be in one piece, praise be to God; but while bruises fade the pain o' the 'eart remains to chafe.'

'Pain of the heart?' Michael Farron's brow creased in a frown. 'I don't understand, Abigail.'

'Nor would you, with not 'aving the years on you. But men like my Daniel, men who 'ave given a lifetime to one job . . . 'ave never known aught else but that one way of mekin' their livin'

. . . when it be snatched away so cruel like then it teks the heart wi' it and leaves naught but pain in its place.'

Was she saying Daniel would be a cripple as a result of his accident? That for all his spine had not been broken by the fall he might be unable to walk again? Politely drinking his tea Michael denied the urge to ask. The woman might find the question too harrowing to answer and he did not want to be the cause of more tears; Abigail Roberts had most certainly shed more than enough of those already.

'Doctor said as Daniel shouldn't go stackin' bungs no more.' Abigail supplied the answer to his unspoken question, her hands busy with setting mug and scone on a wooden tray set with a pristine while cloth. 'Said as the leg 'ad a weakness, that it wouldn't stand the strain o' climbin' ladders wi' a saggar whether or not it were an empty one . . . so there you 'ave it . . . Daniel be finished in the potting.'

Extracting a promise they would ask for any help they needed now or in the future Michael rode slowly back to the wharf.

He had hoped to see Callista Sanford but there had been no sign of her nor had Abigail spoken of her. Had she already left the Roberts's house? She would have known of the doctor's warning as to the stacking of the kiln. She would also have realised that if the man could no longer operate the pottery then her living also was snatched away! Had she not waited to find out?

Fingers tightening on the rein Michael stared ahead but saw nothing of the wild flowers splashed like tiny jewels amid the rough grass of the heath.

Had Callista Sanford cut her losses and run?

Dinner at The Limes had been a success. Sabine Derry paused in the entry she was making in the accounts ledger. Her dress, as she surmised, had brought envious glances from the female guests and several of approval from some of the males. How the

gown would have affected poor plump Emma Ramsey . . . !
Sabine smiled at the neatly written page. If she were not already
dead she would have died of jealousy; she should have waited a
little longer before seeing Emma into her grave, given herself an
added satisfaction of seeing that jealousy which would so clearly
have played over those puffy features! But she could not have
everything, and the evening had been a complete fulfilment of
all she had wanted, of all she had hoped to portray. Edwin Derry
was a man of prospects.

But there had been more . . . more than she could have hoped.
It had come with the ending of the meal. Phineas had craved the
men's indulgence, asking that they delay cigars and brandy for a
few minutes as he had something he would like them to see. He
had led the way to the library and there, displayed on exquisite
stands and tables, had been figurines, busts and delicate, intri-
cately patterned bowls, each quite remarkable in its own right.
But what had been most remarkable of all had been the statement: 'They are all the works of Callista Sanford.'

Callista Sanford! Sabine laid the pen aside, closing the ledger.
The girl from Trowes Court . . . it seemed she had ability for
more than scrubbing floors. Phineas Westley had been lavish in
his praise of her pieces and of her talent, saying it was one such
as is seen only rarely, that one day in the future they would
become as collectable as any crafted by the old masters.
'Antiques of the future' had been the note he had ended on.
Pushing the ledger across the desk she leaned back in the chair,
her eyes glinting at the thought drifting quietly into her mind.

The trouble with the future was it was always a day away!

How long since that accident? It seemed a lifetime ago, a lifetime
when all the help she could give had been like no help at all. But
in reality it had been only weeks. Her head beginning to throb
with the headache which, returning so regularly, now seemed
just another part of her life, Callista placed a hand over her eyes.

They had worked the pottery together, herself and Abigail. The woman knew almost as much about the process of wedging the clay as did Daniel, kneading and rekneading it until no air pockets remained to burst in the kiln and ruin a hard-worked pot by leaving a hole in it or shattering the piece completely. Abigail could throw a vase or jug on the wheel, press a plate or dish in a mould with a skill to challenge Daniel's own, but his strength she could not match. She did not have the strength it required to carry loaded saggars up and down a ladder; consequently the oven was fired each time with only a third of the crockery it might have held; even then Abigail and herself were exhausted.

But tonight it had come to an end. There would be no more firings. She had seen the pain in Daniel's eyes, the tight clutching of Abigail's hand as he had said it.

'*The work were too 'ard for a couple o' women alone, it were set to kill 'em should they try to carry on. You 'ave done your utmost, God knows I've watched you slave 'til you've fair dropped from weariness, and I'll watch no more. The fires will be left to go out . . . there'll be no more crockery comes from Leabrook Pottery.*'

It had been an effort for him to say it. Callista's inner eyes played again over the whiskered face, the tight-lipped mouth, the eyes blue and pained behind the façade of courage.

They had both impressed upon her that her place with them would be unaffected by the decision, that she was welcome to remain at the cottage. But with no way of paying for her board and keep that was impossible. Daniel and Abigail would find it hard to feed themselves with no sales from the pottery; she would not add to their burden.

Her hand covering her eyes closed out the silver moonlight but it did not shut off the remembered sight of a buttercup denuded of all but two of its petals or of one more fluttering to join its fellows in the short turf of the heath . . . one more mark of the misery of Callista Sanford's life!

★

Standing in the yard of Leabrook Pottery Callista glanced at the bell-shaped cone, its round-bellied bulk rising dark against the sky. There was no more to be done. It was said so easily but the words held a finality she had not realised fully until this moment. The plates, bowls, mugs and dishes loaded now into large round wicker baskets and stored neatly against one wall were the last that would be fired in that oven. There had been a potter on this same site for hundreds of years. Daniel's voice had thickened while telling her the history of his workshop. In the seventeenth century the town was famed for its salt-glazed vessels, pottery his forebears had made and marked Wedgbury Ware.

'. . . *more'n two 'undred years as we knows to* . . .'

Callista seemed to hear the words again, hear the pride and the crack in the voice which told of heartbreak.

'. . . *and 'ow many before that* . . . *the Robertses 'ave always worked the clay, but now it be finished* . . . *done. I'd thought once to see the place go on, to see it grow 'neath the 'and of* . . . *but I be the last.*'

The last! Callista felt tears rise to her throat. Daniel was a proud man with a proud heritage; he felt badly at being the Roberts to have broken that line, it had hurt him more than had that fall from a ladder and though the latter hurt would heal the former never would.

I tried to help! The cry silent in her heart she walked slowly into the workshop, its wheel and benches sponged and tidied, the empty saggars stacked in columns higher than her head. She and Abigail had taken it in turns to stack the thick clay containers but even though they were empty they had proved too weighty for them to haul more than three steps up the ladder. Daniel was right in saying the work was hard; p'raps he was right also in saying it was too hard for women to do alone, but she would have gone on trying.

Unable to stem the flood in her throat she stared through tears amid the silent workshop. She had tried reasoning with him, tried to argue they could manage somehow. She had already learned some of the processes; all she needed was time and she would learn the rest.

'*Ar, wench, you've learned.*' Daniel had smiled from his chair beside the hearth. '*And though you've learned well it be as a drop in the ocean. I been in that workshop daily since I could put a dozen steps together an' I still be learnin', no . . . your 'eart be good but it teks more than goodwill—*'

'*I am not afraid of hard work!*'

'*Nor you ain't, you've gied proof of that already.*' Abigail had smiled at the interruption. '*But what Daniel be sayin' be truth, to know all that be needed teks a lifetime in the learnin'.*'

Common sense had affirmed what she heard but love for the couple had driven it away. Yet even as she began to speak Daniel had shaken his head.

'*Listen to me, wench,*' he had said, '*the good Lord touched your 'ands givin' to them the skills of a potter, your eyes He blessed with a sharpness which sees the clay from the inside . . . you see not what it is but what it can be . . . an' in His goodness He added to them blessings a quickness o' the mind, but He give you only two 'ands. You learns, ar, an' you learns well, but answer me this: given that you knows each an' every process it teks to mek a pot 'ow many o' them processes can you do at any one time? Ar, you can wedge clay, you can throw on the wheel an' you can fashion by 'and but that don't be the all. Who will act as saggar-maker's bottom-knocker, makin' the base you need by beating the clay inside the iron hoop which will give the shape you need . . . and who will be frame-filler, beating out a flat sheet of clay which will be the sides o' your box, and then who will be saggar-maker, the one who joins sides to base, an' who the carrier tekin' them to the drying place? That be only one process; then who will mek the moulds you needs for cups an' cup 'andles . . . who will be jiggerer, he be the plate- an' saucer-meker, an' who the jolleyer, the one who meks bowls an' basins? Then there be the makin' o' slip, the mixin' o' clay an' water 'til they be as cream, you needs that for* casting o' jugs an' such from moulds. Then o' course there be glazes; lead, soda an' borax be the main fluxes for low-fired glazin' but for high-fired glazin' you needs add others an' then you needs think about oxides to be used for colourin'. But that don't be the all for when the oven be full an' ready for firin' the clammins – that be the doorway – must needs be bricked up an' plastered over so as to keep heat loss at a minimum: then an' only then can the fires be lit an' these needs be fed wi' coal every three to four hours 'til the right temperature be reached, that teks about forty-eight hours, an' maintained for four more an' most o' that time sees a body shovellin' coal into the fire-mouth. But that only be the work o' the potter's shed. On top o' it you needs think o' the buyin' an' transportin' o' clay o' the sort don't occur local, o' buyin' oxides an' fluxes an' then o' sellin' your wares . . . no, girl, it don't be work for a couple of women, for even that which I've told don't be near all there be to potting.'

But he and Abigail had managed! Somehow they had kept the business going! She had wanted to cry out both of those reasons for continuing to try but she had said neither. She had known deep in her heart that try as she might for as long as she could she could not succeed.

Heartbreaking as it was the facts had to be faced. Daniel was right in what he said: Leabrook Pottery was at an end.

Phineas Westley had said the tiny silk and velvet posy she had placed on her mother's grave had not faded. Maybe then, a few months ago, they had still held their colour but now with the effects of sun and rain the tiny flowers and leaves were colour-less bedraggled shapeless bits of cloth.

As she knelt beside the grass-covered patch, Callista removed the tiny offering, replacing it in the vase with the wild flowers she had picked while crossing the heath. There had been several glances from other visitors to the graveyard, frowns and whispered remarks from people bearing their own costly tokens. But beautiful as the sheafs and bouquets were, with their lovely blooms, they were not laid with more love than these wild violets and kingcups or that posy the children of Trowes Court had made.

Trowes Court! Callista stared at the wisps of faded cloth. It seemed so far away, as if she had lived there in some distant past. But Trowes Court and its poverty was not far away nor was it a memory of a distant past; the place and all it stood for was close at hand. Her leaving there, finding happiness and what she thought to be security, had been another illusion, a whim of the Fates she had spoken of to Michael Farron; with the same cruel twist her life was once more in turmoil. Yet it was not empty of love as it had felt on her mother's death; Abigail and Daniel had removed the loneliness, had treated her as a daughter. But once she was gone from the cottage, once she was no longer with them, then the loneliness would return. The worst cruelty of all would be not being able to come here on Sundays, not being able to kneel here beside the resting place of her mother or there beyond the wall where her father lay.

'. . . so long as you remembers . . . the two of them will always be with you . . .'

The words told her by Ada Povey whispering again in her mind Callista placed the weather-worn posy next to the vase of wild flowers. She would leave it there, the token of respect made by the hands of the children of Trowes Court; her mother would have wanted to keep it always. Touching her fingertips first to her lips she rested them on the soft turf. It was a last goodbye kiss. Tears gathering behind her lids she rose and turned quickly along the path which would take her to the street.

'Miss Sanford . . . it is Miss Sanford?'

Her head bowed, Callista had passed the figure dressed elegantly in pale grey but now as her name was called she turned.

'Mrs Derry, good afternoon.'

'My dear, I hoped so very much to find you. I did attempt to contact you, poor Mr Slade was making enquiries and then . . .'

Letting the sentence trail away Sabine held a gloved hand expressively to her lips while her eyes lowered in pretended grief.

'We heard at Lea Brook of Oswin's death. It was a terrible thing to have happened.'

'Terrible,' Sabine echoed, her glance still lowered, 'how . . . how could anyone do such a thing, and to such a nice well-mannered young man. The dreadful business fair has folk afraid to leave their homes.'

Well-mannered . . . yes, Oswin Slade could be the gentleman when it suited him, but nice! Could she in any honesty say she had ever found him nice?

'Of course what alarms most is the fact the culprit has not yet been arrested. The constables made enquiries, of course, but so far they have come to nothing. Tell me, my dear, did they come to . . . where did you say you are moved to?'

'Leabrook . . . Leabrook Pottery. Yes, the constable did call.' The sickness which had risen in her throat as the man had told them of Oswin's murder blocked Callista's throat again.

Obviously the girl had what the newspapers termed a water-tight alibi. Sabine lifted her glance.

'That was something they had to do, my dear. It was possibly because you had known him. I believe they spoke to everyone from whom Mr Slade collected rents; you must not allow it to worry you, they can in no way believe such a monstrous deed could have been done by a woman . . . the whole idea is too horrible to contemplate.'

'The Robertses said it would be no more than a matter of procedure and it seems it was for no constable has called since.'

'The Robertses?'

'They own the pottery,' Callista supplied in answer. 'Daniel . . . they gave me work and a home.'

'That was kind of them and fortunate for you, my dear . . . will you remain there with them?'

Her glance straying to the small patch of colour among the

grass at the furthest corner of the graveyard Callista's fingers curled tight against the rush of emotion.

'I . . . I had hoped to but the pottery is to close and I cannot stay; without employment with which to pay for my keep.'

'Then my dear you must allow—'

'No!' Callista replied sharply. 'You were kind enough to offer me financial help after the death of my mother . . .'

'Which you did not take.'

Bringing her glance back to eyes grey as the hat perched on fiery red hair Callista was surprised by the hardness of them and of the features the Poveys would have called wire-strung, referring to the sharp nose and taut thin lips. It gave entirely the wrong impression of the woman who had offered only kindness.

'Which I could not take seeing I did not earn it, though I was grateful for the thought, and once more I thank you for it.'

There was a dignity in the girl, the dignity of . . . Sabine thrust that thought away. Sentiment had no place in her life.

'Then if you will accept only what you work for allow me to offer that work. My husband has agreed we are in need of a second clerk to keep the accounts of rent collections; if you would care to take the position then I feel certain Mr Derry will appoint you; as for somewhere to live . . . that would not present an insurmountable problem. Think it over, my dear, there is no hurry for an answer. Now I must go lay these flowers on poor Emma's grave.' Taking a handkerchief from the bag hanging from her wrist, pressing it suitably to the corner of each eye, Sabine sniffed. 'Dear Emma, such a wonderful friend . . . how very much I miss her.'

Emma Ramsey – what had caused such a change in her? Wishing Sabine goodbye Callista left the churchyard, keeping her glance deliberately from wandering across to where the windows of St James's School seemed to be watching her.

For years Emma Ramsey had been delighted with her mother's work, congratulating her on the fine stitchery and delicate execution of each gown, petticoat or nightdress; in fact the woman had never found fault with any garment her mother had made . . . except with that blue dress. But the dress had been perfect, the pattern followed exactly, the stitches neat as they had ever been . . . yet it had been rejected!

Why? Callista walked on, her thoughts on that awful night. Her mother had sat staring at the ashes of a fire long dead from want of coal, the fevered cough which grew a little worse with each day racking her thin body. The talk of her work being rejected with such callous and unfair words seemed to have had little impact; it seemed only Emma Ramsey's visitor interested her; she had insisted Callista try to recall every detail of her appearance. But why should she have persisted as she had? And equally puzzling was the relief which had seemed to settle over those flushed features on hearing of Sabine Derry's rich copper-coloured hair.

It had been her own intention to ask her mother to explain, to give her reasons for wanting to elicit a description of a woman who was a stranger to them both, but that opportunity had never come, nor had the chance to kiss that dear face before life had left it.

It was that same woman, that stranger, who had offered a gift of money and now had offered employment, a chance so many in Wednesbury would give much to secure. Waiting for a wagon to rumble past she crossed over Dudley Street directing her steps towards Lea Brook.

A chance so many would give much to secure . . .

So why the feeling she did not want it?

24

‘I saw . . . I knew . . . it was her . . .’

Eyes glinting like grey ice, a sharp-featured face glared at the child cowering in fright.

‘. . . it was because of her . . .’

Whimpering, the child drew back into the corner of a room shadowed in darkness, a small figure curled against the blow of a long-fingered hand, while above its head the venom and hatred hissed on.

‘It was because of her . . . the spawn of evil . . .’

‘No . . . no, it’s not true.’ Held fast in the net of sleep, Callista cried the denial.

‘I saw . . . I saw what was done . . . I saw her do that . . .’

‘No . . . I didn’t, I didn’t!’

Trapped in her nightmare Callista’s head tossed on the pillow.

‘. . . it was her . . . she did that.’

The tight mouth drawing back in a feline smile, the lizard-cold eyes gleaming triumph, a long finger pointed to a coffin visible in the gloom and the figure which rose from it to point a pale hand at the trembling child while the dead face grinned . . . the face of Oswin Slade.

‘I saw . . . it was her . . .’

The child in the corner lifted terrified eyes to the advancing shape, a half-strangled cry staying on the small quivering mouth.

‘Please, I didn’t kill Oswin.’ Callista’s sob whispered on the grey dawn filling her room while in her sleep she watched the burly figure of Constable Travers reach for the child.

It had been a dream, a nightmare . . . but only a dream. Yet even now with the warm sun of midsummer warming her body the memory of it sent shivers along her spine.

The nightmare of childhood, the dream which relived the fear and the abuse of that teacher, recurred often and that she could understand. So much unhappiness in so young a life was not easily forgotten by the subconscious mind; maybe it would return at intervals for the whole of her life. But why the part about Oswin Slade? The constable had made no further call at the pottery and no word of her being involved in that killing had been levelled at her; yet the dream had been so real, so frightening, the policeman reaching for her . . . but was that the real fear her nightmare had contained?

Pausing in the task she had found for herself numbering and recording each of the many plaster of Paris moulds, their design and use, she stared at the book in her hands.

The real fear! No, it was not of the constable but of the woman, the woman whose grey, almost vulpine eyes had watched her as they had talked together in the churchyard: the eyes of Sabine Derry.

That was ridiculous, fantasy! Callista breathed deeply the perfume of wild flowers and tufted grass of the heath filling her nostrils.

A tired body results in a tired mind and a tired mind could jumble facts and occurrences together and that was what had happened: a plain and simple mixing of one thing with another; as for Sabine Derry being the tormentor of those school years, that was too idiotic to contemplate.

Reaching the wharf she dismissed the thought, leaving her mind clear for the business Daniel had entrusted her to carry out.

Unable to see Moses Turley among the figures moving between wharf and narrow boat she waited a moment but when there was still no sign of him she approached a figure bent over a large basket container. Touching the man's shoulder she stepped back in surprise when, straightening, he turned to face her.

'Mr Farron! I . . . I thought . . .'

'I was one of the men?' Michael Farron grinned. 'Well, so I am. I believe a man should not ask others to do what he himself is not prepared to have a go at, and sometimes that means getting one's hands dirty.'

Holding them out for her to see he laughed, a light unconcerned kind of laugh . . . something else which haunted her dreams. A flush of colour followed the thought and Callista turned her glance quickly along the busy wharf.

'I was looking for Mr Turley.'

'Moses?' Michael Farron had not missed the sweep of pink. 'He's at the basin alongside of Wiggins Mill Pool and won't be back until tomorrow, hence my dirty hands; but if it is nothing of a personal nature then I am willing to help.'

If it is nothing of a personal nature . . . The words seemed to sting. Was he telling her Michael Farron could never be anything other than the businessman where she was concerned?

'It is not personal, Mr Farron,' she answered, watching him wash his hands in a barrel of water then dry them on a strip of cloth hung beside it. 'I am here on behalf of Mr Roberts.'

'Daniel . . . how is he? No setbacks, I hope. Phineas was saying he was recovering; I would have visited myself more often but . . .'

But what? For what reason? Was it because she was there, the girl he thought interested in his uncle's wealth, a girl not to be trusted?

'So what can I do for Daniel?'

The smile which accompanied the words, the slight tilt of the mouth were so reminiscent of Phineas but unlike his uncle Michael Farron felt no friendship for her. Disconcerted by the strong pull at her stomach resulting from the thought she glanced away to where narrow boats nosed into the wharf replacing others which, now loaded, were leaving. To go where?

'You said you were here on behalf of Daniel.'

When she looked at him again she saw the smile was gone leaving a hardness where it had been, a hardness which seemed to say she was wasting his time . . . or was it saying she was not welcome here!

She nodded, fighting the churning inside her. Michael Farron must never see, never so much as guess her feelings, emotions she should not have. Chest tight with the effort, head lifting almost in defiance, she replied. 'Daniel cannot yet walk so far and Abigail is unwilling to be more than a few yards from his side, therefore I was asked to come here in their stead. I have been asked to tell you there will be no further requirement for clay from Cornwall.'

'No more clay! But I thought Daniel was on the mend, that he had suffered no permanent damage to his spine!'

'The bruising was severe though thankfully that was all, but the doctor says it would be wiser for him to no longer carry on the work of potting.'

'No more potting!' The clear brow creased. 'Lord, that'll just about do for Daniel. According to Phineas the Robertses have been potters at Lea Brook for years.'

'More than two hundred,' Callista sighed, 'and he believes it goes back much further than that . . . he was so proud when telling me of Wedgbury Ware.'

'Heritage like that makes a man proud.'

It can also break his heart when he has to let it go. Callista kept the thought silent in her heart as Michael Farron continued.

'So what will the Robertses do? Daniel has never known anything other than potting.'

That was a question she knew had plagued the Robertses as it had herself but it was not something to be discussed with others. Daniel's business was his own and she would speak no further of it. Meeting the eyes which now showed concern she answered quietly.

'I was asked to inform you there will be no more orders for clay, silica or any other ingredient you formerly delivered for Leabrook Pottery. I have done that, Mr Farron.'

'Wait!' Catching her arm as she turned away Michael almost gasped at the effect of touching her, a piquant yet intoxicating rush that had his heart thumping like a sledgehammer, but even more heart-stopping was her pulling free and taking a step back from him. Torn by his own emotions his face hardened, his eyes resuming an earlier look of coldness.

'Forgive me, Miss Sanford.' He too took a step backwards. 'I was not thinking . . . the news of Daniel closing his pottery . . . I did not mean to touch you.'

That was obvious. Callista felt the weight of sadness deep inside. The look on his face said it for him. That Michael Farron, a man of breeding and substance, would actually touch a pauper's child! Oh, there could be little doubt he knew her background. Phineas would have told him of their meetings at the cemetery, of her frank disclosure when he had asked she catalogue his collection of antique art; yes, Michael Farron knew her past, but he did not want to know her future. Looking at him now, her lips compressed to stop their trembling, she felt the world in which she had come to feel secure and happy drift further away. He had called her to wait. Was there something else he wished to know, something he needed to ask? As if reading her thoughts he spoke quietly.

'I asked what the Robertses intent was, how they meant to make their living with the pottery closed; you did not answer.'

Had he not remembered, had he chosen to forget or was this a way of testing her loyalties? Drawing in a breath Callista met the incisive blue gaze head on and when she answered it was cold.

'I believe, Mr Farron, I once told you I would not discuss

another man unless that man were present. I place the same restriction upon a man's business; you wish to know of Daniel Roberts's plans for his future then I advise you ask him.'

A flash of annoyance drawing his handsome brows together, a quick intake of breath a witness to his anger, Michael Farron stared.

'You cannot answer for another,' he said after a moment. 'That I accept; but perhaps you can speak for yourself. What will you do now there is no work for you at Leabrook Pottery?'

Why should he ask that, what possible interest could it be to him what she did? But then again she had nothing to hide. Still holding firm to his gaze she answered, 'I have not given thought—'

'Then perhaps you should have!' It cracked across the wharf like a pistol shot, causing several heads to turn.

'Perhaps I should.' Callista's reply was marked in its quietness. 'But my immediate concern is for the people who befriended me when I needed it most.'

'But you must have some idea . . . some place in mind.'

Was he thinking that place might be his uncle's house, that she would go back on her refusal to live there, that she would accept the offer if only for the time it took to list and record details of Phineas Westley's collection? Was he thinking that once more his inheritance stood in jeopardy?

For once not caring about the emotion showing on her face, Callista replied witheringly. 'You need have no fears, Mr Farron, I shall not be seeking the help of your uncle!'

He had seemed to snatch air into his throat, his stare becoming blue ice as she had said those words, and his hands had part lifted as though he would strike her. Michael Farron's irritation was clear as if it had been painted on his face; evidently he had not expected the answer she had given. Resentment flying high, Callista harboured no regret for her recent censure. He had taken her words as a snub, a reproach, as indeed they were meant to be. Hopefully this time he would have learned from the encounter, learned she was not to be accused of something she had never tried to do, something which existed only in his mind.

How clear did she have to make it! Part cry, part shout, the question rang in her mind. He had no right to any knowledge of what she did or did not do. It was not like he was family, he was not even a friend; Michael Farron was nothing to her.

But that was a lie! Brought to a standstill by the admission Callista stared across the heath. He was not family . . . he was not friend, but she could not truthfully say he was nothing.

Then what? What was the feeling inside, the emotion that sped through her like heath fires whenever they met? A light breeze rippled across the tranquil sun-warmed heath, carrying with it the delicate musky fragrance of wild flowers, but it was the murmur as it brushed her face, the faint sigh which seemed to whisper it was love . . . the feeling she had for Michael Farron was love!

'Appears we be in the same quandary as we was afore.'

Daniel's voice drifted through the open doorway of the cottage. Still dazed by what her heart and mind had told her minutes ago Callista had not noticed the bay horse quietly cropping grass beside the house.

'But be sensible, Daniel. What was said was fact, the materials used were yours.'

'Ar, right it were in that, but it were not my 'ands done the creatin', it were not my work an' I'll tek neither credit nor payment.'

'That is simply foolish.' Phineas Westley's well-modulated voice was followed by the gruffer one.

'Foolish it might be but I 'olds to it. I'll tek no money I feels don't be earned by me an' that be an end to it.'

'But what about you, Abigail, what do you think?'

This was eavesdropping. Listening to other people's conversation was wrong, it was as much an intrusion into their privacy as Michael Farron's questions had been into hers. Turning quickly Callista moved towards the closed door of the workshop, Abigail's reply following her.

'I thinks decisions made in this 'ouse be them o' Daniel Roberts, beggin' your pardon. It be 'im be master an' 'im will 'ave the say.'

Pulling open the door, Callista slipped inside the cool workshop, the lingering smell of clay filling her nostrils. She would wait here until the visit were over and Phineas Westley gone. But why come at all? True, he had visited several times while Daniel had been confined to his bed but that was no longer the case. So was this a social call? But surely a social call would not entail talk of payment. Business then. This was as bad as openly listening to the talk in the cottage! Impatient at her inability to control the thoughts crowding in on her Callista moved restlessly about the shadowed workshop, but try as she would to prevent it the thoughts spoke in her mind.

Was Phineas Westley's visit one of business? After all he would not yet have heard of Daniel's decision to close down Leabrook Pottery. He had often said the tableware produced by the Robertses was the finest to be bought so maybe he was here to place an order, one which would mean Wedgbury Ware and Daniel going on at least a while longer.

Her glance caught by the columns of neatly stacked saggars, columns only half the height Daniel would have built them, Callista felt the joy of that thought drain from her. Supposing the unbelievable had happened, that Phineas had come with an order; who was there to produce it? Hadn't Daniel made it clear it was impossible for Abigail and herself?

Outside the calls of goodbye drifted to where she stood, her hands touching the wheel on which so many pots had been thrown.

. . . two hundred years, an' 'ow many afore that . . .

It was more than a reflection of the mind, it was an echo from the ancient walls themselves, a reverberation from every corner of this building steeped in time and history, a cry for life; yet it was the whisper of death, a sentence she could do nothing to commute, nothing to revoke.

It was over! Within the shadowed walls Callista's glance touched the stool where she had sat listening to the teaching of Daniel, following the guidance which had developed her understanding of potting and the skill of her own hands. But there would be no more teaching, no more of the satisfaction of creating a piece of tableware or the wonder and delight of seeing a figurine gradually take life beneath her fingers; even deeper than the disappointment of that was the pain of having to leave the people she loved.

25

The girl had not come to Hill House, she had not taken the offer of second clerk. Sabine Derry smoothed violet-scented cream over her face, her eyes on the mirror of her dressing table searching keenly for signs of wrinkles. Had Callista Sanford received a better offer? Pausing in the task of nourishing her skin before retiring to bed Sabine felt a ripple of annoyance. Had the girl been approached by someone else and if so who might that someone be? Was it a person known to herself? No! Sabine resumed her creaming. Were that the reason for the girl not showing up here she would have known of it. So why then had she not come? She had said the pottery was to close, that she could not stay there without the employment with which to pay for her keep.

It was something of a mystery. Her nightly ritual completed, Sabine moved to the bed, the bed she had slept in alone for so many years. Staring at the blue silk cover, her eyes saw the blue of a silk gown, a gown lying at the feet of Emma Ramsey. The woman she had killed. But she had had to die; no chance could be taken of her babbling to the police what she knew of Oswin Slade's death. Nor could the risk of her talking of that other thing she knew. Now it would never be spoken of.

Glancing across the room Sabine smiled at the photograph on the giltwood table. 'I did it for you,' she whispered. Picking up the heavy frame she looked once more into the past, into those distant years before coming to Wednesbury, at a young girl who smiled up at her from a bed of grass. Julia Montroy, her sister, her pretty sister . . . her lover! She had never quite recalled when childish games, the tumbling together down a grassy bank, had become play of a different sort, when her hands had first touched that tender figure, stroked flesh hidden beneath layers of clothing, but gradually, slowly, one piece at a time, the clothing had been discarded and deep among the copse of trees close to their home, both naked, they had made love. All of one summer they had visited the copse, two innocent sisters walking hand in hand, but in the secret shelter the innocence had dropped away. They had both been hungry for the pleasure the touching of breasts could bring, for the ecstasy of fingers stroking a stomach, of probing into the soft warm moisture of the vee at its base. The ending of summer had meant no more excursions into the copse but the heady pilgrimages to the altars of passion had not ceased. As sisters they had shared a room, and in the night hours as the rest of the house slept they had shared a bed.

They had been such satisfying days and nights, she and Julia exploring new and exciting paths to pleasure, until one day Julia had found a new interest, one they could not share. She had found a man.

Sabine's eyes closed on the memory, on the pain which had turned to anger, on the jealousy which had become a poison in her blood. Then as memory flooded her mind once more with words, she looked again at the photograph.

Jason Sanford was a fine man, Julia had said, *he had asked her to marry him and she had said yes.* Julia had been flushed with the joy of it. Sabine's lips pressed hard together. Sitting on her bed Julia had prattled on about what was to be, of the happiness Jason Sanford had brought into her life and the love he would bring to her future. That had been the moment she, Sabine, had asked the question, the question that had brought the babbling to a sharp halt.

'*Have you told him about us?*'

The span of years since putting that query was wide but the satisfaction of it felt as real as on that night.

Julia had stared at her with wide eyes. Her fingers stroking the smiling face, Sabine watched yesterday's scenes play again.

'*How could I tell him that!*' Julia had cried. '*Jason must never know. Maybe he would not understand that what had begun in that copse was simply a game, a perfectly innocent game between two young children.*'

The laugh Sabine had given on hearing those words rang again in her mind.

'*A game!*' she had answered. '*Immoral conduct . . . the indulgence of lewd and carnal behaviour . . . that can hardly be called a game and in no one's eyes could we be seen as children. Maybe in that first month or so what we did might be viewed as a silly childish prank . . . but at seventeen years old? No, Julia, at that age it becomes an obscenity, a gross uncleanness. In the eyes of society we have committed a social evil; to them incest is worse than harlotry, and when it is practised between two women then it is seen as being a thousand times worse.*'

The picture in Sabine's mind showed a pretty face crumpling with distress while another slightly older and far less pretty smiled in triumph.

'*Think of it, Julia.*' The words with which she had pressed her case returned as if said just moments ago. '*Think of your fiancé should he find out his wife is a lesbian.*'

'*But he won't.*' Julia's eyes had filled like lakes. '*Nobody knows but us and we will never speak of it. Promise me, Sabine, promise me you will never tell!*'

'I did promise you, my dearest.' Sabine touched her lips to a mouth parted in a smile. 'I promised, and I kept my word, I never told Jason Sanford of what we had done together. But I could not let him have you, my darling; the thought of a man's hands touching those sweet breasts, his mouth taking the nipples my mouth had taken, his fingers stroking where mine had stroked between your legs; that he should enjoy the delicate pleasure that was mine, that should always be mine.'

Holding the frame at arm's length, Sabine stared at the pretty image, her grey eyes glinting. 'I tried to tell you, Julia, to tell you he could never love you as I loved you, but you would not listen, so you see, my dearest, I had to do it. You ate the chocolates just like Emma did. I sat with you, I held your hand until the end came and when you slipped into your endless sleep I put the rope about your neck, I hung you from your bed post. But it was *his* fault!'

Bringing the frame hard against her chest Sabine held it close, the gleam of her eyes brightening.

'I never told him you had agreed to release him from his promise of marriage as you asked I should. That was too easy for him. He had taken your love from me and I wanted him dead, but before I could act I saw him go into the railway station and I knew, I knew he was leaving Willenhall, that he was going away with that slut. It took me years to track them down but at last I found them . . .' Sabine laughed again, a hint of mania mixed with triumph. 'I found them, Jason Sanford, private tutor to a boy . . . my letter finished that. They moved to Wednesbury, I followed and again I saw to it he lost his post as teacher, that he could not secure another. Poor Jason Sanford.' She clutched the photograph, the laugh in her throat tinged with hysteria. 'Poor intellectual Jason Sanford, reduced to slaving in a steel rolling mill. But that was not the end. I tortured him with threats, threats to tell his wife they were the cause of your "suicide", that his withdrawing from his promise, his setting aside of your engagement had been too much for you to bear, that during the course of the night you had taken your own life. Oh it was sweet, my dear one, sweet to watch the joy of living fade from his eyes, so gratifying watching the spirit die within him until he walked into the path of an engine carrying molten slag from that same mill. He thought his death would remove any threat from his family.

But he was wrong, Julia, your handsome fiancé was so very, very wrong!'

Bringing the photograph to where she could see it, Sabine smiled, her voice dropping to a conspiratorial whisper.

'He thought his death would wipe out his debt to you but it was only a down payment; there would be many more before it could be finally written off. The slut he married, the child which was the spawn of his evil, they also must pay; but not so quickly, not in a few short months but for years as Jason had.'

Drawing the tip of a finger along the line of the smiling mouth, stroking it across a pretty cheek, Sabine's threatening madness glistened in cunning eyes.

'It was so clever, Julia, so clever the way I made them pay. I had secured a post at the child's school and for three years I made her life a misery, but with Jason ending his life I resigned. But I did not forget that woman and her daughter. I was in no hurry; revenge was sweet and the longer it was in the mouth the longer the enjoyment lasted. I left Wednesbury and I waited, waited until the time I guessed the pain to have eased for Jason Sanford's family. It was during that time I married Edwin Derry and it took only a little persuasion on my part to get him to move his business to the town I had left. No one connected the wealthy Mrs Derry with a long-gone schoolmistress. I soon became a woman highly regarded for her taste in all things and every woman of consequence followed my lead, so when my housekeeper obeyed my instruction to let it be known to the tradesmen I would not buy from any who gave the Sanford girl employment then the misery of that woman and girl began all over again. And I saw the girl . . .'

Sabine's high-pitched laugh rang in the quiet of her bedroom.

'I saw her at Emma Ramsey's house but she did not recognise me. You knew about Emma . . .'

The laugh died, Sabine's voice becoming low and heavy with remorse.

'Oh my dearest, I'm so sorry! But you have to try to understand. Making love to Edwin – to any man – could never be the
same as it was with you. A few minutes of groaning and pushing
and it was over. There was no thought of giving pleasure to me;
that a woman too needed satisfaction was beyond his compre-
hension. It had been so long since the rapture I shared with you,
the ecstasy you had given; so many nights of longing for the
delectable touch of a woman's fingers on my body, delight of a
soft breast in my mouth, for the passion sending fire along my
veins or the arrows of desire piercing my every fibre as your
fingers slid along my legs to play between them, to satisfy that
wonderful pain, that exquisite ache of pleasure. It was a relief
when Edwin no longer came. I would not have to pretend any
more; he had his pleasure elsewhere and I eventually found mine
with Emma.

'Emma!' Remorse switched instantly to anger; Sabine's mouth
thinned. 'We both enjoyed the afternoons spent in her bedroom.
We could both give rein to the passions which boiled the blood.
It was following one of our sessions I fell asleep. Emma said I
talked of a sister, of lovemaking in a copse of trees, of you, Julia;
but she vowed the secret would never leave her lips, made a
solemn promise no whisper of it would ever be spoken. But when
I learned of Sally Baker, the prostitute who had come to share
those Thursday afternoons, of her having a blue silk gown, then
I knew Emma must have broken her word, that the gift of that
dress was a bribe for the trollop to keep her mouth shut. But
prostitute or not, the woman had a brain, the bribery would not
end there; sooner or later she would come to me. I would have
killed her as I killed Emma and the foolish greedy Oswin Slade
except a tram did it for me.' Pausing, Sabine stared at the image
in her hands, a slight frown creasing her brow as though
listening, then shook her head.

'No . . . no, my darling sister, your secret is not yet safe. Yes,
those we are certain knew of it are gone but can we be so certain

they alone knew it! What if they are not? What if Slade told Jason Sanford's daughter? I was informed he was interested in the girl, that he intended to marry her; it is unbelievable he would keep secret the information he must have got from Sally Baker, or the sight he saw in Emma Ramsey's bedroom. I cannot allow you to be jeopardised, your reputation must not be sullied . . .'

Touching the photograph once more to her lips Sabine smiled. 'So you see, my dearest, Callista Sanford must die.'

'I came to see Daniel. One of the boatmen up from Liverpool asked did I know of a Leabrook Pottery. He had been asked to deliver a letter there and seeing as I was coming there myself I said I would deliver it for him.'

Glancing at the handsome face of Michael Farron Callista felt a surge of disappointment course along her veins to settle heavily in her stomach. He had been to the cottage to see Daniel and not herself. But why would he come to see her? They did no business together, they had no background of friendship that might give rise to a social visit; in fact they had nothing in common. Pushing a faint smile to her mouth she answered.

'That was kind of you, Mr Farron, I know the Robertses will have appreciated it.'

Damn her, couldn't she see! Couldn't a blind man see! Michael Farron's fingers curled with the effort of controlling the feelings welling inside of him but he managed evenly.

'It was not only Daniel I hoped to speak with; I hoped also to speak with you.'

A sudden weariness adding to disappointment was too much for Callista's self-restraint and she snapped.

'Mr Farron, if you came to discuss my intentions . . . as to how I will live or where then I must tell you bluntly it is no concern of yours! I have already said I will not be seeking the help of your uncle.'

'Look, let's leave Phineas out for once . . . please!' Sharp though his answer had been, Michael Farron's eyes held a kind of plea. 'I know I acted rashly with regard to his friendship with you and so does my uncle, only he puts it a little more strongly than that: he says I have behaved like an idiot and if I am honest I can't disagree with him; but I have apologised and will go on doing so for as long as you wish, only please . . . don't make it a lifetime commitment.'

The grin which broke across his face, the wide, almost boyish grin melted all of Callista's carefully constructed resistance. 'A truce?' she said, a smile returning to her eyes.

Feeling as he had so often as a boy on being given Phineas's forgiveness for some misdemeanour, Michael nodded. 'A truce.'

'So, Mr Farron, what did you wish to speak to me about?'

His grin fading to a smile he shook his head ruefully. 'It seems I have already said it. It was to say I am sorry if my asking about your plans for the future was untoward. I did not mean to pry, it was simply my intention to offer help in any way I could and if you do not find it insulting then I make that offer now.'

Blue stars! Callista looked into eyes smiling their repentance. They were like blue stars!

'You do find it insulting!'

Cheeks flooding with colour at what she had been thinking, Callista's answer was flustered. 'No . . . no, not at all, but there is no need . . . I mean I don't . . .'

'If it will help then like the rain children sing about I'll go away and come again another day.'

'I don't want you to go away.' It had come out too quickly, the hint of desperation, of wanting him to remain must have rung in it! Embarrassed, Callista felt the tide of colour deepen. Now who was behaving like an idiot? The cottage door opening was like a blessing, providing her with a reason for not looking at him. Taking advantage of it to regain a little of her composure she went on.

'What I mean is, although I appreciate your offer I have no

need of it. I have been offered employment with Edwin Derry.'

'Derry?' Michael frowned. 'But he's in coal mines.'

'Hardly.' Callista's glanced stayed on the cottage. 'But I know what you mean, Mr Derry does own several coal mines.'

'But a woman can't work in a colliery!'

She had to look at him; she didn't want to for she knew the strange emotions at the pit of her stomach would churn again the moment her eyes met his. But to continue avoiding his gaze would indicate rudeness.

'I have to differ on that point.' She smiled briefly. 'There are women in Wednesbury find employment in that business, though not underground.'

'But you aren't going to push bogeys!'

If he were not so serious the look crossing his face would have been amusing. But the man seemed to catch every nuance which played on her face, every inflection colouring her tone, and was misinterpreting most of them. Deliberately keeping the smile from her voice she settled for a shake of the head.

'No, Mr Farron, I am not going to push wagons loaded with coal . . . or empty ones for that matter. Edwin Derry has interests other than coal mines, several others, so Abigail informs me. One of them is houses. My employment is to be as an accounts clerk recording the amounts of rent paid by his tenants.'

Turning his glance past the dark hulk of the kiln, letting it ride over the heath striped with gold where the sun's rays played tag with puffball clouds, Michael took a moment before asking quietly, 'Is accounts clerk for Edwin Derry so much more agreeable than recording an antiques collection for my uncle? Why accept one and refuse the other . . . is it because of me?'

The question was a quiet shock, the prick of a knife against skin; the truth it threw at her a sharp slap catching the breath in her throat. All these weeks, all of the time spent here at the pottery, she had told herself she had not accepted Phineas's offer lest it create a fondness between them but that was not all of the truth. It was because of Phineas's nephew. She could not take employment at The Limes for fear of Michael Farron, of meeting him there . . .

Watching the shadows play across her features, Michael Farron's mouth clenched like a steel trap. She had told him what he wanted to know; she had given her answer. Turning abruptly he strode towards the cottage where Abigail had appeared in the doorway.

Watching him go, Callista's lips trembled, the remainder of her thoughts ringing in her mind.

. . . for fear of him seeing a love she would be unable to hide!

26

She had watched him enter the cottage and she had watched him leave, his body tall and straight, flickers of sunlight gleaming like drops of liquid amber among his brown hair. He had not glanced at her as he strode to the horse tethered at the gate, not given a nod in her direction or cast a look across his shoulder as he rode away. He had ignored her completely. Only minutes ago they had stood together on the brink of friendship and now it seemed they were as far apart as ever.

Dejection brought smarting tears to her eyes; Callista dashed them away. Had he thought her taking work with Edwin Derry a slight to his uncle? If he had only waited before turning away, if he had come to speak to her after leaving the cottage, she could have explained, told him she had not yet accepted the post Sabine Derry had spoken of, that in truth she had no liking for it. But he had not waited! Callista stared at the round-bellied kiln, its bulk casting a great shadow on the ground. Like the shadows of her life: moving with her, dark and obstructive, hiding any gleam of light, destroying every hope of happiness. A life of shadows! Was it one on which no dawn of joy would ever break?

Brushing her fingers across her cheeks, ensuring no mark of her misery rested on them, she walked slowly across the cobbled yard. She would not take the post of accounts clerk; tomorrow she would leave Lea Brook and its brief interlude of peace and contentment behind, tomorrow she would begin a new search. That much she could promise herself, but there was no promise the shadows would not follow.

★

Was this a result of Michael Farron's talk with Daniel? Callista stared at the scene in Abigail's bright living room. The fire, lit as it must be every day for the cooking of meals, slumbered lazily beneath a gently bubbling pot, poppy-painted crockery smiled from the tall three-shelved dresser and the sun glinted through windows sparkling behind pretty flower-strewn curtains. Everything was normal . . . so why was everything so different?

Confused, Callista stood in silence, her mind trying to come to terms with what her eyes were showing her yet attesting to the reality of difference. Daniel was sat in the chair he always occupied. In the hearth beside him a brown-glazed pot shaped to a laughing face held paper spills which lit the long-stemmed white clay pipe kept on the mantelpiece above his head; Abigail, grey-streaked chestnut hair caught in a neat bun, brown skirts covered with a snowy apron, stood beside the table covered with a spotless cloth slicing crisp freshly baked bread. Nothing was wrong. It was the same as greeted her whenever she came into the room. But it was not the same, they . . . Callista's brain seemed to become still, the breath to halt in her lungs. *That* was what was different; was what was not the same, Daniel and Abigail . . . neither of them had looked at her, neither had spoken!

What had she done to cause such a change in them? Why were their faces turned from her? Only minutes before Michael Farron arriving here the three of them had laughed together yet now they behaved as though she were not there.

In the silence broken only by the tick of the clock Daniel wound every night before going to bed, Callista felt as alone as the night her mother had died. Ada Povey had been in that room as the Robertses were in this, but for her the world had been empty, filled only with unhappiness, and she the one person in it.

But there had been no death here; whatever had happened to cause the atmosphere of this house to alter so suddenly could not have the finality of death. It could be discussed, explained, apologised for it necessary, but it must be clarified. It would break her heart to leave Leabrook Pottery and its owners under a cloud; she would spend the rest of her life wondering what it was she had done had taken their love away from her.

A deep breath lending her courage she began quietly. 'Is . . . is anything wrong? Have I done something which displeases you . . .'

The clatter of the knife falling from Abigail's hand, the anguished cry breaking from deep within her, swept away the rest of Callista's enquiry, reaction to that sharp agonised broken sob almost hurling her to the woman's side.

'Abigail!' Too concerned to recognise she used a first name, Callista threw her arms about the sobbing figure. 'Abigail, what's wrong? Oh please, if it is something I have done then I'm sorry . . . believe me, I'm sorry.'

In his chair at the fireside Daniel dropped his head into his hands, his voice muffled with emotion he did not wish to show. ' 'Tain't nuthin' be done by you, wench, ain't no fault o' your'n.'

'Michael Farron . . .'

A question or an accusation. Callista did not know or care.

'Not 'im neither,' Daniel answered. 'The cause be mine an' mine only.'

'No.' Pulling Callista gently aside Abigail went quickly to her husband, dropping to her knees beside his chair, her hands covering those held about his head. 'No, Daniel, that don't be the way of it, weren't you alone let them go . . .'

'But 'twere me as drove 'em! My stupid pride had 'em leave.' Grief bitter as aloes coloured Daniel's reply.

'And mine which kept me from followin' after, from tryin' to bring them back.'

Daniel suppressed a sob as he shook his head. 'That don't be truthful, it were loyalty kept you in this 'ouse, loyalty to me over-rode the love you 'ad for your children but it broke your 'eart 'an mine. I were wrong, God forgive me I was wrong.'

'We was both wrong . . . the Lord pardon us both.'

Callista watched the tender kiss touch the drooping head. There was more than loyalty Abigail had for her husband: there was love, a deep, exonerating love.

'The Lord might forgive.' His head lifting, Daniel's arms went about his wife. 'But I'll never forgive myself for drivin' your children from you, for never seekin' them; an' now it be too late.'

Callista caught the strangled words. *Your children.* That could only be a reference to the son and daughter Abigail had told her of, the two who left the cottage together! And 'too late', did that mean . . . ? Oh no, not that, Abigail's children could not be dead!

Feeling her presence to be an intrusion she turned to leave but the quiet movement was seen by Daniel.

'Don't be goin', wench.' Releasing Abigail, he stood up. 'Abbie an' me 'ad no wish to worry you, it . . . it be a bit o' news . . .'

Too overcome to continue he reached for the clay pipe and tin of tobacco, leaving Abigail to continue. Wiping her tears on her apron the woman followed the custom of ages in times of grief, her hands shaking as she reached for the teapot.

About to take it from her, to press her to a chair while she herself made tea, Callista remembered the words of her mother and the other women of Trowes Court whenever some disaster struck. 'Let her do it for herself, best her keep busy, it holds the mind together.'

'Michael Farron, he brought a letter.' Her voice trembling as much as her fingers, Abigail sniffed back fresh tears.

'Please, Abigail . . .' Callista set the mugs she had reached from the dresser onto the table. 'I have no right to hear what is private to you and Daniel, I am not your—'

She had almost used the word 'daughter'. Regret for what had so nearly slipped from her tongue brought a flush to Callista's cheeks.

Looking at her across the table Abigail either did not see or else refused to see the colour staining the pretty face or the apology in soft violet eyes, only answering in that same heartbroken voice. 'That be right, Callista wench, you be no daughter to Daniel and me but the gladness that come along of you helped ease the soreness that sits in our 'earts. Your being in this 'ouse don't remove the pain entirely, 'twould be a sin of mine to say it does for nothing could do that, short of the comin' of my own two children through the door and that won't never be . . . not now!'

How could she reply to that? How could she ask a mother that dreadful question: are your children dead? Knowing she should answer, that to make no reply could be construed as unsympathetic, Callista struggled to find the right words but none would come.

Seeming unaware of the silence which had Callista feeling so awkward Abigail stirred sugar into Daniel's cup. 'Be too late,' she murmured, 'be too late.'

'The letter tells it best. Read the letter, girl, and then you'll know.'

Refusal came swiftly to Callista's lips. She could not violate their privacy. Dear as this couple were to her, love them as she did, she was not kin and the prerogative and privilege that accorded was not hers. Whatever was contained in the letter lying on the table she could not be privy to; it was something she could not share.

The feeling the thought carried with it was one of separation, a rift between herself and the people who mattered most to her, a space her love could not cross.

Wearing a shawl draped over her cotton nightgown, Abigail sat beside the hearth, the letter in her hand. As with that left on a pillow so long ago, she knew every word of it by heart. She had lain with it against her breast. Her daughter had written the words, Mary's hand touched the paper and maybe Adam too had held it. Adam, her tall strong-limbed son; Mary her pretty brown-eyed daughter; their touch on the sheet of paper was the closest she would ever again come to the feel of their dear hands.

Near-spent coals settled deeper into the bed of the smouldering fire and in the cascade of sparks rising from it Abigail watched a young boy, dark hair falling over bright intelligent blue eyes, a laugh breaking on a strong handsome face as he chased a younger girl, her own hair, the colour of ripe chestnuts, streaming out behind her, a beautiful fluttering veil of colour. Mary . . . Mary, she had been so pretty, so loving. A sob quiet in her throat, Abigail lifted the letter to her lips. Why did it have to bring such news? Why did it have to add to heartbreak?

Dearest mother and father . . .

The spark of the settling coals had died into darkness but the words of the letter pressed against her quivering mouth shone like tiny beacons in her mind and in her mind Abigail read them again.

Dearest Mother and Father,

It might be you will not read this letter but still I must write it, tell how much Adam and me both love you. It doesn't be a letter asking forgiveness of the sin I committed, of the pain my wrongdoing caused you, but just a telling of love. Our mother and our father have never been a day from our thoughts and their names never missed from our prayers. Nor those of their grandchildren who speak it nightly in their own and who longs as we does to hold you close as you once held Adam and me. It was you, my dearest mother, I cried for in the pain of childbirth, you I longed to hold my hand and my father not far away ready ever to comfort his little girl, but that could not be. Next week we leave England. Adam won't never settle while he be close to Lea Brook but never can return, and as for my husband and me we won't never leave him to go alone to America. Adam and me won't know the joy of looking upon your dear faces again but we carry you with us, our beloved mother and father, we will carry you forever in our hearts.

Your loving daughter and son.

'Mary . . . Adam . . .' In the silence of the small living room Abigail's sobs trembled against the paper held to her mouth.

She had been disrespectful. The thoughts she had entertained before entering the cottage had been discourteous to Michael Farron as well as to the Robertses. She did not know Michael Farron very well, in fact she knew him hardly at all, but thinking clearly she realised he was not a man to go skulking behind her back making trouble. Hadn't he faced her openly with regard to his uncle? As for having thought Daniel and Abigail acted as they had out of hearsay, that was even more disparaging. How could her thoughts have gone that way even for a moment! They were the kindest of people and she . . . ? She was unworthy of their friendship.

All around her the heath lay in the hush of afternoon, the only sound that of bees investigating the blossom of slender pink rosebay and stately yellow Aaron's rod standing guard over the deep blue cornflower and delicate blooms of creamy woodbine. It was a world of beauty edging a town hidden beneath the dark haze of steel mills and iron foundries, the black dust of coal mines, but at the heart of it were the people, people like Ada Povey. Daniel and Abigail, they had hearts of gold. And she had judged them harshly!

Guilt brushing her face Callista walked on, passing the squat low-windowed Boat Inn and the huddled houses of Pitt Square, answering a pleasant 'good day' as she passed the tall brick malthouse. Taking a right-hand turn to follow along Great Western Street, the rumble of carters' wagons and the quicker snap of trotting horses pulling carriages to and from the railway station invaded the earlier peace of the heath, growing in sound and density as trams added their own cacophony; but immersed again in her thoughts she paid little heed.

She had left her bed early, the light penetrating the little bedroom as yet barely strong enough to battle the shadows. She had slept fitfully, waking several times to feel the guilt which was with her yet, the inner sense of blame she could neither condone nor excuse. At last, draping her shawl about her shoulders, she had slipped quietly downstairs. A drink of water might help her settle the storm in her stomach. But there she had found Abigail, seated beside the fireplace, a folded sheet of paper pressed to her mouth. The sight of that loved figure, the sadness and heartbreak portrayed by the bent head and slumped shoulders, had struck through her with the force of physical pain. Whispering the woman's name she had thrown her arms about her, feeling the dam of Abigail's resistance break. She had wept quietly, the despair of years in her tears, and Callista's own had merged with them. They had clung together, friends in heartbreak, held each other until the weeping was done. Then over a mug of hot tea Abigail had told the contents of the letter and she had listened, hoping the therapy of talking would take some of the bitterness from the blow.

Her son, her daughter, the grandchildren she had never seen, were leaving England. She had heard boatmen along of the canal talk of ships they had seen in Liverpool docks, of the weeks of sailing it took to reach that far-off country that was America and of the money it cost to take passage there. Adam and Mary must have saved every spare farthing, worked each of the years since leaving Lea Brook, managing on none but the basic necessities in order to scrape together money enough to buy their tickets; money she and Daniel would never have. Her prayers, her nightly beseeching of the Lord to bring her children back to her, had been of no avail. In a week they would be gone, as lost to her as if they had never lived.

' ''Tis the finish, wench,' she had murmured, placing the sheet of paper beneath her nightgown, a hand pressing against her breast. ' 'Tis the end of a dream.'

Glancing behind her, into the distance which held Leabrook Pottery, Callista knew the exact meaning of those words. She too had lost what she loved; for her also this was the end of a dream.

27

Phineas Westley glanced at the figure his housekeeper had shown into the sitting room of his home. The skirts were faded and patched and the shawl threadbare and drab but the head was held high. The girl was a pauper's child in her clothing but in bearing and manners, in her quality of speech and intellect, she had all the hallmarks of a lady.

'Thank you for seeing me, it is kind of you to give me your time.' Callista dropped a small curtsey.

'I am pleased you came.' Offering her a seat Phineas touched a brocade bell pull hanging beside an ornate marble fireplace. 'May I offer you some refreshment?'

Concerned that her skirts, dusty from crossing the heath and walking through soot-clouded streets, might leave a mark upon the beautiful tapestry covered chair, Callista shook her head, saying hastily, 'Mr Westley, I came to ask about the figurines.'

'Ah!' Phineas's hand dropped away from the bell pull. 'And here am I hoping you had at last decided to accept my proposal you catalogue my collection.'

Glancing at the several beautiful pieces placed about the elegant room she recognised the exquisite carving of Cupid pleading Psyche to become his lover, a marble Christ comforting a weeping Madonna, while yet another depicted a peasant couple sat together, the hand of the man held in that of a smiling wife, and in a glass-fronted cabinet the serenely beautiful Artemis.

Each was breathtaking in its skill of design and creation, each a work of sublime beauty, and these she guessed represented but a few of the treasures this house held. Treasures she had not learning enough to deal with.

Watching her, guessing at the thoughts behind the nuances of expression crossing her face, Phineas was struck again by the unassuming dignity, the quiet acceptance of what she was, the pride which upheld her while preventing her accepting a post she felt was offered only as an act of charity. But what was she? What was this Callista, a girl named for the gods? Deep inside Phineas smiled. His nephew would call him all kinds of a fool, laugh at his description, but for Phineas Westley the girl was a woman of quality.

'So you are here to discuss the pieces I was so kindly allowed to borrow; but may we not do so sitting down?'

Reluctantly Callista perched on the edge of the costly chair.

'Daniel . . . Mr Roberts . . . said you had spoken to him.'

Taking a chair facing hers, Phineas nodded. 'Spoken yes, persuaded . . . no. Daniel Roberts is a stubborn fellow. I told him of the praise each received from guests I had to dinner, of the money they were prepared to pay could they purchase them. He said, as he had in our previous conversation, the pieces were not his to sell, he would take neither credit nor payment; that they belong to you. Do you now wish them returned to Leabrook Pottery?'

Hands twining self-consciously in her lap, Callista thought of the reason for her coming to this lovely house. Would Daniel understand or despise her as a liar, a girl who could not abide by her word? But there was no other way; she hadn't a penny to her name, it had to be done!

The words almost choking in her throat she forced herself to meet the grey gaze. 'No.' She paused then pushed the rest out before they could die on her. 'No, I do not want them returned to Leabrook Pottery. I want them sold and the money paid to me.'

*

She must not act hastily; time would be her ally, time would help her plan her moves carefully.

Sabine Derry settled the carefully coiffured wig over her faded mousy hair. She had taken to using it just prior to the return to Wednesbury, a precaution against being recognised . . . but who would connect the wealthy Mrs Edwin Derry with the nonentity of a mistress teaching in some backstreet school? But to err on the side of caution, however, could be no bad thing. The wig securely pinned, she studied her reflection in the mirror then turned her glance to the silver-framed photograph.

'I was too smart for them, Julia,' she laughed, 'too clever for our so efficient police inspector. He has no idea it was me, no clue as to who plunged a knife into Oswin Slade's neck. Oh, the police called, they came with their questions and their apologies. A matter of routine, that inspector told Edwin, simply a call to ascertain the names of tenants Oswin Slade collected rents from. He hoped his coming to the house would not alarm Mrs Derry. What . . . what was that, my dearest?'

Leaning closer to the photograph Sabine stayed silent for several moments before laughing again.

'No.' She drew back but her eyes remained on the pretty smiling face. 'No, of course Edwin does not suspect! But then neither does he suspect I know those so-called late-night meetings at his club are simply a way of covering his evenings with a prostitute of his choice. Edwin is as gullible as that police inspector. They were both so easily duped, just like Emma Ramsey. Poor Emma! So very foolish.'

Sabine giggled, the tone of it rising. 'If . . . if I told her that black was white the woman would have believed me. Yes,' she nodded to the photograph, 'yes, dearest, just as she believed what I said about that blue dress, that it was poorly made and of a design outmoded years ago, but hush.' Holding a finger to her lips Sabine stifled the giggle.

'Shh, Emma mustn't know the gown was really very pretty and excellently stitched. Ruth Sanford did . . .'

Pausing, Sabine's eyes seemed to glaze, to lose their focus as they lifted to the mirror.

'Ruth Sanford . . .' It was a snarl, drawing the mean lips into oblivion. 'It was she hurt you, it was because of her and him, Jason Sanford . . . it was what he did, leaving you for some trollop. But I took revenge, I hounded him and his, harried and thwarted him until he took his own life. I made him pay for what he did . . .'

Her gaze still locked on the mirror it seemed Sabine saw a scene other than her bedroom, a scene that had her smile, a vindictive rancorous twist of the mouth.

'But that was not enough. You!' She jabbed a finger at something the mirror showed only to her. 'You took my Julia from me, you took my beloved . . . you ruined my life so I ruined theirs; your wife and daughter went on paying. The child suffered in the schoolroom, your trollop suffered in a house not fit for dogs to live in and then . . . and then, Jason, she died of consumption and your daughter . . . she will follow very soon.'

A laugh, a high-pitched crazed sound, bubbled in Sabine's throat then was quickly stifled, her attention caught by people moving and speaking only in her mind.

'You didn't know, either of you, you didn't know and you never will. You see, Jason, my sister gave you your freedom from your promise, she held no malice when you asked the engagement be broken. But I could not allow Julia to become the object of people's talk, of fingers pointing, the jilted fiancée; do you know what that means to a woman . . . the pain of it! There was no one to help her . . . no one but me.' Gazing at the unreal, at illusive mind-created shadows, her brow creased in a puzzled frown.

'No.' She shook her head. 'No, it will not be murder, it will be justice; an eye for an eye, Jason, you killed my darling Julia so I must kill your daughter.'

For a silent moment Sabine smiled into the mirror, a venomous spite-filled smile which of a sudden was gone, replaced by a look of pure hate.

'That is a lie!' Serpent-like it hissed about the quiet bedroom. 'An evil lie. I did not harm her, I could never harm her.'

Snatching up the heavy frame Sabine pressed it to her breast, the eyes shining into the mirror aflame with the frenzied light of insanity.

'You lie, Jason Sanford,' she snarled, 'it was not murder. I did not kill Julia . . . I helped her!'

She had thought the transaction to have taken time, that the people Phineas had spoken of as showing a keen interest in her work when viewing them during the evening of his dinner party would require to see them again, to examine them in detail before undertaking an obligation to purchase.

But it had not happened like that. Phineas had simply looked at her, his glance behind gold-rimmed spectacles neither questioning nor disapproving, but she had felt a sense of shame. Had she not told him that those pieces were the property of Daniel Roberts? Said she would never accept money for them? Phineas must have remembered those words yet disrespect her as he must now his face had shown no sign. He had simply informed her of the offer made for each item and finally totalled the amount. It had left her bemused; how could they be worth so much!

Thinking the business finished she thanked him again and made to leave but Phineas had opened a drawer of an ornate walnut bureau. Taking out a small metal box and opening it with a key attached to his watch chain he had counted out twenty-four five-pound notes.

The money tucked in the pocket of her skirt Callista walked quickly along Wood Green and down the sloping Spring Head and across the market place, ignoring the cries of stall holders exalting their wares.

Phineas Westley had paid her one hundred and twenty pounds, asking only she put her signature to a bill of sale. There had been no enquiry as to Daniel, what he thought of her decision to sell, whether he was in agreement, had he been consulted? Only that bland look, that polite, refined essence of a smile . . . a smile which no longer held esteem? A smile which said Callista Sanford no more warranted the approval of Phineas Westley? And Michael Farron, he was already of the opinion she was not worthy of his uncle's friendship, that she was no woman of quality. What would be his opinion once he heard of what she had done?

Hurrying in the direction of the Great Western Railway station, Callista's hand touched against the pocket which held the folded notes.

She had gone back on her word. She had not only sold the statuettes, she had done so without telling Daniel. But what would it have achieved talking with him? Hadn't he said the pieces she created were hers to do with as she pleased? So she had said nothing. She had simply walked away from that cottage, called at Phineas's home and sold them all.

There had been no other way; she needed money.

Across the street people came and went, through the entrance to the station. Where did they all go; where did they all belong? Where would she go? Would she ever belong anywhere?

But what did it matter where she went, what did anything matter any more. Phineas Westley, Michael Farron, Daniel and Abigail, they were part of the past.

Hearing the plaintive call of a child Callista glanced to where a woman dressed neatly in a dark blue gabardine skirt and jacket hurried a child towards the high-arched entrance to the station.

The girl had dropped her posy and was scrambling to pick them up. Joining them quickly Callista scooped up several of the flowers already wilting from being held in a warm tight hand. Thanking her, the woman's smile was harassed as the child handed a buttercup to Callista. Murmuring about a train and friends waiting to meet them she scurried into the station, the child's feet pattering as she trotted to keep up.

Glancing at the tiny gift Callista's mind flew to another golden flower, picked from the heath, her inner vision seeing four spots of gold nestling on the ground and one remaining on the flower held in a young woman's hand: her hand.

Four petals she had plucked, each a token of the grief which had afflicted her life. They had lain at her feet like the tiny golden arrows of the Fates which had robbed her of the joy of childhood, stolen all but precious memories of her parents.

One remaining petal! Callista stared at the image in her mind, the words she had thought then returning now.

Would her future be no different to her past?

Phineas Westley, Daniel and Abigail, they had been her friends, perhaps even Michael Farron . . . but where was the hope in dreaming, of thinking on what might have been? They like every other thing of value to her had been snatched away.

The daughters of Nyx had played their final trick. The last of the petals had fallen.

'Callista wench, you shouldn't 'ave done what you 'ave!'

Eyes wide with distress, Abigail Roberts stared at the railway tickets and money lying on the table.

'Abigail be right, you acted wrong!' Daniel's time-beaten face clouded in a frown. 'You shouldn't ought to 'ave sold them there pieces.'

Anxiety which had built in Callista since going into the station and purchasing those tickets overflowed into her answer.

'But you said they were mine, I could use them as I saw fit!'

'Ar, I said that an' it were that I meant. Them pieces was your'n, med by your own 'ands an' meant to be used to benefit you an' no other. I 'olds no argiment with your sellin' o' 'em, but the money be your'n. Abbie an' me will tek no part o' it!'

'Please . . .' Dismay reflected in the film of tears, adding brilliance to the violet, Callista turned her glance to Abigail. 'I did it for you . . . I did it so you could go look for Adam and Mary, try to find them and your grandchildren. Please don't tell me that was wrong. You both love them as my mother and father loved me and your hearts cry for your family as my own heart cries for mine. Selling those figurines was the only way I could think to help; please don't turn your back on the chance. Go to America, at least try to find your children.'

'Oh wench!' Flinging her arms wide, Abigail smiled through her own mist of tears. 'What you offers be the blessing I've long prayed for,' she murmured, folding Callista close. 'You come to me out of nowhere. you be no kin, I never carried you in my womb, no blood of mine flows in your veins, but our 'earts be bound by chains no force of earth will break; you be no child of my body but you be a daughter of my soul, one I will love as I love them you 'ave med it possible for me to seek and I asks the Lord bless you for your goodness.' Taking Callista's face between her hands she kissed the tear-strewn cheek then turned to face her husband.

Taking only time enough to dash a hand across her own wet cheeks she stared at him. 'Daniel Roberts,' she said, determination throbbing in every word, 'I ain't not never gone against you in all the days of our bein' wed but as God be my witness, I'll go against you in this! Refuse what the wench offers if you will, cling to your stubborn way if that be what pleases you, but I accepts what her gives. If it be as I must travel by meself then so be it for I don't reckon a chance such as this to be given a second time.'

Nonplussed by the outburst Daniel shook his head. 'Abigail, be sensible, woman. America don't be like Wednesbury, it don't be a small place where everybody knows everybody else, it be a vast country. Searching for Adam an' Mary'll be like lookin' for a needle in a mountain of hay!'

'I am bein' sensible,' Abigail sniffed, 'an' though America be vast it were med as Wednesbury were med, by the Lord's hand, and I reckon if He 'as sent me the chance to go looking for my children then He'll guide my steps in safety 'til I finds 'em!'

Taking his clay pipe from the mantelshelf Daniel reached for the tobacco tin, filling one slowly from the other.

'You truly means what you says, you will go by y'self if needs be?'

A sob rattling up from her chest, Abigail nodded. 'If needs be, Daniel.'

'Then there be no more to say.'

Callista felt her throat tighten. She had meant only to help the couple, provide them with the means with which to go in search of their loved ones, instead she had brought disagreement.

Holding a paper spill to his pipe Daniel puffed until the tobacco in the tiny white bowl glowed scarlet; then his glance sought Callista's through the gauzy veil of grey smoke and he said quietly, 'Abigail's mind be med up, that be the all o' it . . . all savin' one thing!'

28

'She came to this house alone? Daniel Roberts was not with her?'

'As I told you, Michael.' Phineas Westley nodded.

'But didn't you tell me she had flatly refused when you told her some weeks ago those pieces would sell? Didn't she say they did not belong to her?'

Pouring two glasses of brandy Phineas handed one to the younger man then carried his own to a favourite tapestried chair.

'They both disclaimed ownership.' He settled comfortably. 'Daniel and Callista each maintained the statuettes, busts and bowls all belonged to the other; neither would take full credit for their creation and neither would sell.'

'But she did! She came alone and that means Daniel Roberts knows nothing of what she intended!'

The lad was hurt. He had never said anything of the feelings he had for that girl yet they showed in his face. He cared for Callista Sanford, cared for her deeply. Doing what she had puzzled his nephew; he had thought her a woman of her word, yet that word was broken. However, hurt as he might be, he should not make accusations of which he had no proof and certainly no justification.

'That is unfair, Michael,' Phineas remonstrated gently. 'We have no reason to believe she did not come here with Daniel's full approval.'

'Then why was he not with her? We both know full well Daniel Roberts is not a man to let her come to you without his being there to support her word!'

Phineas sipped his drink, savouring the richness on his tongue. Cognac had ever been his choice and this was a particularly fine bottle.

'True.' He sipped again. 'But do we not both know also fully well that Daniel Roberts has suffered two injuries in fairly quick succession? Given that fact, is it not feasible to assume the walk from Lea Brook to Wood Green and back again might as yet prove too much for him to attempt and it is because of that Callista Sanford made the journey alone?'

He wanted to believe that. Michael stared into the amber liquid in his glass. It was feasible . . . but why then had she made no reference to that as a reason for coming to The Limes alone, why had she made no mention of Daniel Roberts? The question filled his eyes as he looked across at his uncle; behind it there was another. With enough money to start a life somewhere would she have returned to the Robertses cottage?

The question and the answer it provoked caused fresh doubt to add fuel to the flame of disappointment flaring inside him, Michael remained silent.

'You say you delivered a letter to Daniel?' Replenishing both glasses, Phineas revitalised the conversation.

'Yes.' Michael took his glass. 'A boatman up from Liverpool said a fellow at one of the basins along from the docks there asked was he travelling to the Midlands and on finding the boat was calling at Wednesbury paid the bargee half a crown to deliver a letter to Leabrook Pottery.'

'Half a crown!' Phineas's eyebrows lifted. 'Quite a sum. Whoever has written to Daniel was anxious it reach him. Did the man say an answer was expected?'

'Not so far as I know. He spoke to Moses Turley so I can't be certain of his exact words but Moses wouldn't forget to mention if an answer were called for.'

Holding the brandy beneath his nose Phineas breathed the bouquet before replying. 'Moses is most dependable; he would not forget had an answer been mentioned, but half a crown for a letter her Majesty's post would have charged a penny to carry! Does it not strike you as improbable no answer would be required? And do you suppose Daniel Roberts might prefer a reply to be taken back in the same way . . . namely by way of the canal? Perhaps, Michael, it would be a kindness to enquire.'

Had Phineas guessed the uncertainty inside him, guessed what thoughts troubled his mind? Michael sipped slowly. His uncle had always shown quite a proficiency in that, a skill almost, and it seemed the years had not robbed him of it. Using the same guile he had used with a young child and later with a mettlesome teenaged lad he was offering a solution. Michael smiled to himself. His uncle was a wily old bird. Without actually saying he was pointing to a means of settling the doubt.

'You may be right.' He nodded. 'A call enquiring after Daniel's progress would be welcome from you, and an enquiry as to the need for sending a reply; you could offer to bring it to the wharf for him.'

His nephew had not simply acquired a sense of business, he had gained a dexterity of mind! Phineas's inner smile was warm. Michael was his equal in most things but when it came to artifice he was dealing with an old campaigner! Holding his glass between both palms Phineas twisted it slowly.

'Would that be wise, Michael?' he asked musingly. 'Enquiring about a reply to a letter, I mean. To do so would prove we two had been talking of the man's business and that may not sit well at all with Daniel Roberts. In fact he might take you to task for disclosing it to me, and he would have every right in doing so. No, it is best I do not go to Leabrook Pottery – at least not for a day or so.'

He should have known better than to try. Phineas could still tie him in knots when it came to deviousness. Michael hid his own smile in his glass. He had turned that particular table very neatly. Now it was up to himself to accept the suggestion he had made, go to the Robertses place and find out whether or not Callista Sanford had returned there, or not call and live with his own doubts.

It had come again last night. It had slid silently across the darkness of sleep, winding about her, trapping her brain in the coils of fear. The same dream, the same terrifying nightmare.

'. . . *it was her . . . !*'

Spat like venom from a striking snake the words had seemed to sting like knife points while a woman's hard, unblinking, ice-cold eyes held a small child immobilised with fear.

'. . . *it was her and you, the spawn of his evil . . .*'

The long-fingered hand had lifted as it so often had, remaining poised above the mousy-brown-haired head while those dreadful lizard eyes glared raw hatred; then it had lashed downwards, the force of its blow sending the thin figure sprawling backwards . . . falling against a coffin from which rose a grinning Oswin Slade, a skeleton rolling from beneath him.

The horror of it had stayed with her throughout the grey hours of dawn and was with her still, cold and clammy against her skin. Stood on the platform of the railway station Callista felt waves of the night's terror eddying in her veins. It was only a dream, she had told herself on waking, nothing more than a dream. Both the teacher and Oswin Slade were gone from her life; neither could hurt her any more.

'I dislike trains, 'tain't no natural means o' travel, mebbe's we should go to Liverpool by way of the cut, there's many a narrow boat would give passage.'

Seeing his wife flinch as the screech of a steam whistle heralded an approaching train Daniel took her hand.

'Be nothin' about 'em can do you 'arm,' he said consolingly. ''sides, it'll 'ave we to the docks quicker'n any coach.'

'If you says so!' Far from convinced Abigail withdrew her hand, glancing embarrassedly the length of the platform.

Touching in public! Whatever would her dear mother 'ave said to such! 'An' you,' she turned to the girl stood at her side, 'you ain't said two words together since leavin' your bed this mornin'. Be you sure you be all right? You still 'ave time enough to change your mind, to come wi' Daniel an' me.'

'You knows you be more'n welcome, wench.' Daniel's gruff affirmation accompanied a film of brightness in his eyes.

A pull at her stomach threatening the strength she had striven a week to maintain, Callista forced a smile, then as the train steamed to a halt hugged Daniel. 'Thank you for everything,' she whispered against iron grey hair. 'I love you.' Then Abigail was in her arms, the trembling of their emotions mingling as they clung to each other.

'I love you.' Despite all of her resolve Callista sobbed the words. 'I will always love you.'

'My 'eart 'olds the same for you.' Abigail's hand stroked the ebony-dark head nestled on her shoulder. 'It'll call to you across the vast ocean, across the miles that lie between you an' me; it will speak its words in the darkness of the night an' in that darkness I shall hear you answer. God keep you in His merciful 'eart as I'll keep you forever in mine.'

They were gone. Once more her life was empty. From the distance the whistle of a steam engine added to the isolation which had swept over her as she had watched the train pull away. Abigail's hand fluttering at a window had seemed to add to the awful loneliness already enveloping her like some stifling cloak.

Emerging into Great Western Street, Callista's downcast glance caught the gleam of buttercups. Daring the station-master's wrath they danced among carefully planted borders that brightened smoke-dark walls. The golden markers of fate! The glittering emblems of decisions taken by the daughters of Zeus! But for Callista Sanford the tally was complete. Her life had been deprived of every happiness, the last petal had been plucked.

She could have held onto that last thread, accompanied

Abigail and Daniel to America, made her life afresh with them secure in the knowledge they loved her. But there had been something inside her, something stronger than herself. It had fought against that desire for security, held her back from agreeing to go with them, even though that something had all the time remained elusive, stayed beyond the borders of her recognition. And now it had come too late. Raising one foot she lowered it onto a tiny glistening flower, pressing it beneath her boot, crushing it as the Fates had crushed her life!

First her father taken from her by his own hand, then her mother dead from a disease they had not the money to combat; neither of those events had been within her power to avoid but parting from the Robertses . . . ! That had been her own doing as had losing the friendship of Phineas Westley. Moving her foot Callista stared at the crumpled patch of gold, its former beauty twisted beyond recognition, then, stooping, plucked the tiny pulverised flower. Her life in her own hands! She stared at the delicate broken remnants. The Fates must indeed be laughing. But Michael Farron had not laughed; he had not even smiled at her when he had called to visit Daniel. She had not known he was at the cottage. She had walked in after yet another check of the silent workshop to find him just arriving. He had glanced once in her direction, his face impassive, his blue eyes unreadable, then he had turned from her, the action dismissive. It had needed no words. Clear as any speech it had told her he knew of her taking that money, that he despised her as he would any thief. That too had been her own doing. She could have owned to the truth of her selling those figurines, the beautifully crafted bowls; she could have seen him smile. Now he would smile at her only in her dreams. A pauper's child! Parting her fingers she let the fragile broken petals fall to the ground. Callista Sanford was a pauper, she had not a penny to her name, no home to return to, nothing but the patched clothes on her back. But all of that counted not a scrap against the destitution in her heart, the poverty of spirit that had come of Michael Farron turning away.

'Miss Sanford . . . Callista.'

The sound of her name cutting the cloud of dejection she looked to where a smart burgundy-lacquered pony trap stood at the opposite side of the street.

Phineas Westley! Nerves drying her throat she stared as the coach moved. He was coming to her. What did he want? It could only be . . .

Her heart beating nineteen to the dozen Callista remained glued to the spot. Had the sales he had spoken so confidently of fallen through, had her work proved unsatisfactory? If so he would require the return of the money he had paid her. Hands tightening into painful balls, she watched the pony trap manoeuvre between two laden carts. She no longer had that money, it was gone . . . every last penny of it!

Bringing the animal to a stop beside her, Phineas alighted. Unsmiling, he looked at her when he spoke. Did she imagine it or did his voice hold none of the warmth she had come to know?

'I was hoping to find you.' He touched his hat, the air of politeness a little distant and withdrawn. 'Would you come with me? There is something I have to discuss with you.'

There would be no more pretty bowls, no more delicate figurines no more busts.

Sabine Derry looked at the statuette her husband had purchased from Phineas Westley. It had taken his eye that evening of the dinner party. The Limes! Sabine stared at the lovely creamy figure. The house was filled with beautiful things: furniture, paintings, works of art each more desirable than the other . . . and she desired them all. With a home like that everyone in Wednesbury would look up to Edwin Derry; he and not Phineas Westley would be the most important member of the town, and as Edwin's wife she would share the glory . . . and that glory she meant to have.

Edwin had spared barely a glance for any other of the exhibits Westley had shown them, but then would Edwin ever look at anything when a naked woman was on display . . . even one made of clay! Naked, lying on a bed, preferably with her legs spread wide was her husband's ideal picture of a woman, a taste reflected in his purchase of this flimsily draped piece. But Edwin could have all the prostitutes he wanted, all the women his libidinous appetite might crave, for while his attentions were held elsewhere her own liaisons would continue to go undetected. And they would continue. She would find another lover, another to replace Emma Ramsey, another woman to bring delight and relief to the longings which plagued her nights. But first she must rid herself of that one threat, remove the menace to her peace of mind. Clear away the dregs of the past. Phineas Westley had said there would be no further pieces, that Leabrook Pottery had ceased the production of pottery of any sort. With no earnings Daniel Roberts would not be able to feed another mouth, to keep another dependant beneath his roof, and the girl had not taken the offer of employment with Edwin. That could only imply Callista Sanford had no intention of remaining in the town and once she was gone then so also might be the chance of silencing her, of preventing her ever revealing what she might have learned from Oswin Slade . . . of taking the final revenge that must be taken for Julia.

She could not afford to wait much longer. Leaving the sitting room Sabine climbed the graceful staircase which curved to the wide landing of Hill House, following along its deeply carpeted length to her own bedroom.

She must take the first opportunity, the first chance that arose, to kill Jason Sanford's daughter.

29

Taut with anxiety Callista glanced at the man seated beside her, at the handsome aristocratic features of Phineas Westley. He had not said what it was he wished to discuss with her but then he didn't really need to, she knew . . . knew he would ask for the return of that one hundred and twenty pounds . . . the money she no longer had. Every nerve tingling with apprehension she waited for the inevitable, her mind churning with the thought which had played in it all during the drive to Leabrook Pottery. How could she ever repay so large a sum?

'I thought this the best place to hold our discussion; I felt you might be more at ease here than at The Limes.'

At ease! Callista's tight throat seemed to close altogether, making it difficult to breathe. She would never be at ease again!

'You saw the Robertses off to Liverpool?'

'They have a long journey ahead of them.'

Why this talk of the Robertses, why not say what he had to say and be done with it! Callista's nerves sang with tension.

'It is not at all certain—'

'Mr Westley!' Unable to bear the strain Callista jumped to her feet. 'You do not have to prevaricate. I am fully aware of why you waited outside the railway station, of what it is you wish to say to me. I can only tell you I no longer have any of the money you gave me; now that it is said I will go with you to the police station.'

Phineas Westley's eyes were sympathetic behind his spectacles. 'Is that what has had you so nervous all the way here? The fear I am bent on recouping that money?'

Standing at the small window Callista looked out over the cobbled yard half covered by the shadow of the kiln, then to the small patch of garden with its herbs and flowers. Soon the silence it knew now would deepen; the garden would be swallowed by the heath and Leabrook Pottery would fall into desolation, forgotten in its loneliness. But she would not forget; she would never forget. Emotion it had taken so much effort to suppress threatening to overcome her failing resistance, she answered quietly.

'Please, say what you must and then be kind enough to let us leave. I would rather not be here when the men come to empty the house.'

'Did Daniel tell you who that would be?'

'I did not wish to know. Whatever the Robertses decided was not my business.'

'I see.' Phineas's expression was thoughtful. 'And you ... have you decided what you will do?'

She had tried to think of that. For all of the few days it had taken Daniel Roberts to finalise his affairs, days Abigail had asked be spent with them, she had tried desperately to think of her own future but her mind had remained a wilderness, any thought attempting to flourish being quickly swallowed into an empty void. Keeping her glance to the garden she shook her head.

'Mrs Edwin Derry told me her husband might consider me for a post of accounts clerk.'

His reply quiet as her own, Phineas asked, 'Is that what you want?'

Misery of sleepless nights filled with the pain of yet another parting from people she loved showing stark in the violet of her eyes, Callista turned.

'It doesn't matter what I want, Mr Westley. I must take whatever Fate has in store!'

'Ah yes!' He smiled briefly. 'Those fickle daughters of Zeus. I fear we are both victims of their whims.'

Yes, he too had known the heartbreak of losing loved ones, his wife, his sister . . . parents; like her had felt the cruelty of what was called fate. Looking now at that kind face Callista felt the stones she had tried to erect about her heart, the barrier she had built to contain her emotions, crumble and fall. Tears she had prayed she could hold back glistened like sheens of silver as the thoughts flowed in her mind. This man had known the same hurt she herself knew and maybe the same loneliness. Had it been that loneliness had prompted him into offering her a temporary home and employment? Was it an emptiness of life he had hoped to fill for a few short weeks by having her catalogue his antiques . . . and could it be some miracle that had brought him to the station?

But his life was no longer empty; he had his nephew, he had the company of Michael Farron! That last thought shattered the flimsy skein of comfort beginning to form inside her. Hoping he had anything in mind other than recovering his losses was simply wishful thinking, a fantasy like so many other of her hopes had been, shadowed illusions that faded in the strong light of reality. Clutching the last threads of self-control, breathing deeply against emotions that filled her throat, Callista made what she feared would be a final effort. She could not bear to stay in the house where she had known peace and happiness, which now held only memories.

'Mr Westley,' she began, 'I spoke the truth when I said I had nothing left of the money you paid me . . .'

'I know that, Callista!'

Quiet, well modulated as always, Phineas's reply struck her mind with the sound of thunder. He knew! But how?

'Yes Callista, I knew.' Phineas smiled. 'And if you would be good enough to sit down I will explain just how it is I knew.'

Waiting until she was settled, he drew a paper from his pocket. Opening it, he handed it to her. 'Daniel came to see me the day after you sold your creations. He told me what you had done, of the tickets you purchased for himself and Abigail to travel to Liverpool, of your insistence he accept the rest in order to obtain steamship passage to America and have an amount to live on while they searched for their children. He wanted to show his appreciation and that is why he came to The Limes, to ask my assistance in drawing up that paper; it deeds Leabrook Pottery, this house and all they contain, together with the land around them, to yourself.'

'To me!' Callista's gasp sounded loud in the hush of afternoon. 'But . . . but he can't, I won't . . .'

Phineas's smile deepened and behind the gold-rimmed spectacles his grey eyes gleamed respect. 'Daniel knew that would be your response and it was for that reason he did not tell you of the decision he and Abigail made together. The deed of gift which that document attests had of course to be legally drawn up. That was done by my lawyer the next day and was signed by Daniel in the presence of that same lawyer, and witnessed by Michael Farron and myself. Leabrook Pottery and this house is yours, my dear, and believe me, Daniel Roberts would have it no other way.'

This cottage was hers! The pottery was hers! Sitting on the bench that Daniel and a young Adam had constructed years ago from thick tree branches, Callista stared at the small patch of garden crowded with herbs and vegetables and the flowers which Abigail loved. It was all hers . . . but it was wrong, Daniel should never have signed such a document. The pottery had been his life.

'. . . *but the pottery is no longer viable, it is obsolete, my dear, no longer a going concern . . .*'

Phineas Westley had been so kind telling her Daniel was loath to hand her what in fact was an almost worthless property; a kiln she could not operate; but it did not alter what she knew deep inside, that parting with the kiln was like parting with his heart.

Puffs of cloud drifting across a sky tinged pink with approaching sunset chased small shadows across the garden but Callista's mind blocked all but her thoughts.

She had begged Phineas Westley to have the document rescinded, declared null and void, to have everything returned to Daniel, but Phineas had shaken his head, though the refusal which had answered her was sympathetic.

'*I understand your feelings, Callista . . .*' He had taken her hand, holding it gently. '*Now you must understand those of Daniel and myself. Daniel is a proud man; he could not accept what he knew was all you had without giving something in return, and worthless though it is Leabrook Pottery was all he owned. He assigned it to you but it was done out of more than obligation, it was done from the love he and Abigail have for you; as for myself I honour a promise even more: I gave Daniel my word not to help in any way which might result in having his wishes overturned and that promise I shall keep.*'

He had left her then, his only other words being to repeat the offer of employment. Callista's eyes followed the infant shadows of evening tumble playfully across the ground, but their movement did not register in her mind.

There was food enough for a little while but soon she would have to earn money for more; she could not go to Phineas's home . . . to a house where she might be in the presence of Michael Farron, a man who had shown quite clearly that, unlike his uncle, he had no sympathy for Callista Sanford. He had not spoken to her on that last visit; apart from glancing once in her direction he had totally ignored her. But it was not like they were friends, no true amity existed between them; so why should his disregard of her hurt as it did? Why the dejection which pressed on her heart like a stone? There was no reason – except she loved him!

'Excuse me . . .'

Immersed in her own world, Callista did not hear until the words were repeated more emphatically; then, her glance a little blank, she looked to where a tall wide-shouldered figure stood at the edge of the garden.

'I'm sorry to have startled you . . . I did speak twice but you did not hear.'

'I . . . I was lost in thought.' Callista rose from the bench.

'I was rather hoping to see inside that kiln.' The man smiled, showing strong teeth. 'Do you think the owner would agree?'

The owner! That was her. She was the owner of the kiln. Bemusement which the hour since Phineas Westley's departure had not lessened still clinging to her senses, Callista stumbled over her reply.

'The kiln . . . it's not . . . it isn't working . . . the pottery is closed.'

'Closed?' The man's smile disappeared abruptly. 'Why . . . I mean where . . . When did it close?'

Her mind clearing, Callista recognised a note of disappointment in the man's voice while the look flickering across his eyes caught an echo inside herself, a reflection of the pain the closure of the pottery had caused to her, and suddenly the man did not seem like a stranger.

'It shut down finally a week ago,' she explained. 'Mr Roberts had suffered an accident which made stacking the kiln impossible. His wife and I tried to keep the work going but being able to lift the saggars only barely above head height we had to fire the kiln less than half full and that meant a loss which could not be sustained therefore Daniel – Mr Roberts – was forced to close.'

'An accident!' He glanced beyond her to the house and again Callista caught the flicker cross his eyes. 'How serious?'

There was no need to explain, to tell this stranger any more than she already had done, but watching that strong face Callista felt instinctively she should.

'Some of the saggars fell when he was stacking the kiln; he was knocked to the ground but the injuries he sustained were not as serious as they might have been. However, the doctor advised against his continuing with the potting.'

His glance had turned from her during the telling to wander over the brilliant blue cornflowers nestling at the feet of purple heavy-belled foxgloves and cream delphiniums standing tall over a medley of sweet william mixing boldly with deliciously scented carnation, but as she finished he looked back at her.

'Would you ask Mr Roberts if I might see the kiln and his workshop?'

'That will not be possible. Mr Roberts and his wife no longer live here. They . . . they have left for America.'

She had not envisaged the hurt of saying that. It was almost the same pain she had felt when smoothing the soil which had been thrown roughly over her mother's grave, a dead hopeless feeling of finality.

'I see.' The stranger had smiled briefly. 'My apologies for having disturbed you.'

He had not enquired the reason for the Robertses' journey to a foreign country, had not pressed his request to be shown the pottery, but had simply turned away.

'I could show you.' Suddenly alive to her lack of courtesy Callista called after the departing figure.

Why had she called? Why had she not just let him go? She had asked herself that question while she waited outside the kiln and again when coming with him into the workshop, but watching him now Callista knew why. He had a knowledge which intimated he was familiar with the craft of the potter, but there was something which went deeper; he touched the wheel with fingers tender as those which might have been caressing a beloved child, he lingered beside Daniel's stool, touched tools with what might almost be termed a reverence. In fact his whole mode of behaviour was that of a man with a feeling which matched her own, a feeling of respect for the clay, an embrace of the beauty which could be created from it. Remembering her own emotions when crafting her figurines Callista waited, leaving the stranger to drink his fill, patiently answering his questions.

'And these?' Coming to the baskets she had packed with crockery left from that last and final firing, he paused. 'These are waiting for collection?'

Callista shook her head, briefly explaining their being where they were.

Asking permission he took a plate in his hand then carried it out into the yard, inspecting it in the stronger daylight. When satisfied he asked, 'If Mr Roberts has left for America then who do I see regarding buying the rest of these?'

For a moment Callista was lost for an answer. The crockery was Daniel's property . . . but he had given everything to her! The realisation of what that meant becoming clear at last she looked at the tanned face, the blue eyes now watching her keenly.

'You see me,' she said quietly. 'I am the owner of Leabrook Pottery.'

30

━ ﹀ ━

They had talked together for an hour or more sat on Daniel's bench while the sun had dipped toward to horizon. Callista watched the baskets of crockery being loaded onto a wagon, each of them carefully placed on a thick bed of straw as extra protection against the bumping of the cartwheels over the rough road which led to the wharves and basins of the canal.

The man had taken every last piece of crockery and had shown considerable interest in the figurines and groups that had been left standing on a shelf of the workshop. He would have taken them except they had not been fired. That had been when, accepting a glass of Daniel's apple cider, sitting with it on the bench, he had asked would she set the pottery working again. He would buy all it produced, especially her figures.

She had told him all of what Daniel had said, explained the need for other people to operate the various processes, finishing with what she had heard from the bargees who had delivered goods for Daniel and taken his products on to various towns, that he could buy pottery in quantity from the towns of Stoke-on-Trent, that they could provide all he wanted.

Yes, he had agreed, *the five towns between them produced many forms of pottery and the tall narrow-necked bottle ovens with which they were replacing the kind Daniel had operated could fire hundreds of pieces more at a single firing, and though he bought these and was happy with their work this from Leabrook Pottery would fill a special niche.*

He had not said what that niche was and she had not asked;

what use was there in doing so when what he had asked could never be?

He had finished his cider, then, telling her he would arrange collection of the purchases he had made, he had taken his leave.

She had watched him go. Tall and broad-shouldered, dark against a fire-red sky, he had taken the path across the heath and with his going she had felt a strange sort of unrest. Had she known that stranger longer she might even have called that feeling the sadness of parting.

'That be all o' them, miss. I've shut the doors along o' the workshop so if you've nothin' more to go on the cart I'll be away.'

Smiling her thanks to the burly wagoner Callista climbed onto the front of the horse-drawn cart. Daniel had always insisted he see his crockery loaded onto the narrow boat, watching it was carefully handled, and this time would be no different.

Michael Farron glanced at the invoice in his hand. Delivery of ten baskets of crockery to Bristol.

They had been collected from Leabrook Pottery – from Callista Sanford! But who did she know who would buy crockery to send on to Bristol? He would know were it anyone in Wednesbury. Who had bought those baskets now being loaded onto the *Persephone*?

Crossing to the window overlooking the wharf he watched the slight figure, daylight wreathing the ebony-black hair with pinpoints of blue. Callista Sanford had learned more from Daniel Roberts than the art of throwing pots; she had also learned how to sell them.

But why should that irritate him? Turning away from the window he threw the invoice onto the desk. Why should he feel anything at all? Callista Sanford was nothing to him.

But that was the crux of what had gradually grown inside him, the Gordian knot that shackled his days and bound his nights, refusing to release his mind to sleep. Callista Sanford was nothing to him! But he wanted her to be, Lord, how he wanted her to be!

He had not spoken to her the afternoon he had visited Daniel on the pretence of enquiring if the man wanted an answer sent to the letter he had received; he had not spoken because he could not trust himself not to blurt out the feelings twisting in him now. But he could not reveal what was in his heart, tell her he loved her. She had agreed to friendship between them; she would never feel more than that for him. Hadn't he thought the worst of her, accused her of trying to dupe Phineas into marrying her? What girl could forgive that . . . what girl could love such a man! He had blundered from the very beginning, from accosting her in the darkness of Paget's Passage and later in the market place when he had humiliated the man who called himself her fiancé. But she had not married the pompous little man; nor would she marry Michael Farron.

Restless, unable to curb the thoughts which in turn riled then depressed him, he crossed again to the window, his glance sweeping the busy wharf. The *Persephone* had already pulled out of the basin, another narrow boat moored up in her place; Moses Turley was talking with the boatman while at the same time checking one of a sheaf of papers which he carried so often they seemed as much a part of the wharf gaffer as did the cloth cap covering his head. Everything was normal, everything as it should be. 'Right as ninepence' would be Moses' description. Smiling ruefully to himself he turned back to the desk. But Moses' description could not be applied to Michael Farron! For him life would never be 'right as ninepence', never again be that way without Callista Sanford.

It had been three days since she had ridden with that crockery to Michael Farron's wharf. Callista plumped pretty chintz cushions Abigail had made and filled with goose feathers she had kept several days in the hovel, the outer shell which protected the oven and helped conserve its heat during a firing.

'Doin' that makes sure there be no mites left in 'em.'

Callista smiled, remembering the explanation. She had enjoyed Abigail's company, enjoyed working with Daniel. She had not realised how empty this house would be without them. Where were they now? Somewhere in the middle of an ocean? Had they reached America? She had no way of knowing, just as there had been no way she could have known how lonely she would really feel once they were gone.

But that was not the only reason for the emptiness inside her, for the misery she could not shake off; some of that at least was the result of her trip to the wharf.

She had hoped he would be there, to catch a glimpse of his face. Michael Farron need not smile at her, need not cast a look in her direction, need in no way acknowledge her presence. Just to see him would be a comfort to the unhappiness which dogged her like a shadow. But there had been no comfort for her; Michael Farron had not appeared and she had asked no reason for his absence.

He might have been away on business, he could have been visiting his uncle; she turned to the dresser, rearranging cups and plates she had rearranged a dozen time since returning that day from the wharf. There could be any number of reasons for his not being there. A plate held in hands suddenly motionless, Callista stared unseeingly at the scarlet poppies decorating its centre. There were many causes could account for Michael Farron not being present but there was only one reason could be attributed to the pain it caused in her heart . . . she was in love with him!

How had it happened? A sigh rose from the very pit of her stomach as she replaced the plate among the rest. He had given her no ground to believe, no incentive to fall in love with him. The opposite was nearer the truth and she must never show she dreamed otherwise!

Across the soft silence the sound of hooves caught Callista's attention and she moved to open the door, a quick rush of blood surging in her veins at sight of the tall bare-headed figure tethering the rein to a wide-spreading elder tree.

Swallowing disappointment she smiled a response to Phineas Westley's greeting.

'It is a very tempting offer, but . . .'

'But what, my dear? No journey can ever begin without the first step being taken.'

Words were so easily said but could they be lived up to? What Phineas was asking sounded easy, but the practicality of it? That was a different matter.

'I know what you are thinking and of course you are right, Callista. To produce something like Abigail's plates and cups needs years of practice.'

'And running a pottery requires years of experience: experience I do not have and even if I did I could not do it alone.'

'You would not have to,' Phineas answered. 'There are men would be glad of the opportunity to work here at Leabrook Pottery.'

Excusing herself Callista went into the scullery for milk. Staring at the small metal churn that stood in a cool shaded corner she thought of the events of the morning. She had bargained with Herbert Cox the milk-seller in Pritchard Street, exchanging a vase for a pint of milk, then again in Union Street she had haggled with the baker William Hinton; he had accepted a jug for a loaf of bread. But how long before they refused . . . how many jugs or vases would they want? It was not only men who stood in need of employment; she also must find work.

'I have given a great deal of thought to the prospect I have put before you.' Phineas watched as she placed the jug with its pretty glass-beaded cover on the table then reached for the poppy-painted teapot from the hob of a fireplace blackleaded until it shone like silver.

He may have thought a great deal but Phineas Westley was no potter. He was kind and his offer was generous but he didn't understand. Callista filled the cups with tea, then returned the pot to the hob. Phineas did not appear to have taken into account the fact of Daniel Roberts being the only maker of tableware in Wednesbury for many years. The skills potting required no longer existed in the town; true, the men of Potters Lane still used clay but they only made tobacco pipes; it was also true there were men, and women also, would thank heaven for the chance of employment here but they would need direction and she could not give it.

'I do understand there are problems.' Phineas spoke over her thoughts. 'But they are not insurmountable. Skilled people can be brought in, men who understand the intricacies of firing and timing the oven, of mixing oxides for glazes and for the many specialist processes involved, people who can train our own local folk. By reopening the pottery we could give at least a few of the young of this town a chance to do something other than toil underground dragging coal from the bowels of the earth of smelting iron in foundries the like of which could only be matched in hell itself.'

It was a wonderful idea. Callista watched as he stirred sugar into his tea. But what he proposed was impossible for her, for even had she the skills of Daniel himself she could not accept. 'Take nothing but what you earn' had been the teaching of her parents. How could she ever earn what Phineas Westley was offering, a partnership with himself.

Eyes lifting to hers as he returned cup to saucer showed understanding. She had a pride that was admirable, a pride he appreciated, but it could not be allowed to stand in the way. The girl needed help and she would not take charity.

No trace of the sympathy he felt colouring his tone, Phineas repeated his offer that they become equal partners in Leabrook Pottery, adding, 'I understand your feelings, Callista. You think you have nothing to offer in return but you are wrong, my dear. Plates and dishes are all very well but useful as they are and provide the work as they will, they cannot bring to this venture what you can bring. The figures and groups you create are what will draw buyers to this place. It is the beauty and grace of your pieces, the skill of your hands, that make the whole of the rest viable. That is your contribution and without it my own is worthless.'

He had thought . . . but not of everything! Callista felt the dream he was kindling die. Her pieces had sold well but it was not simply the form they took, not just the skill of her hands had caused those people to buy; in part that was due to the clay from which they were constructed, the additives which produced a silky cream-smooth texture. And Daniel Roberts alone knew what these were and how much to use, a recipe he had not completely shared.

31

Phineas had insisted they go ahead. It could not be so difficult to discover what it was produced the marble-like finish to a dish or figurine, he had declared. What Daniel Roberts had discovered could not be a once-and-for-all-time miracle. She knew some of the constituents; maybe someone who had known Daniel in his earlier years, someone still living in Wednesbury who may have worked with him, would know the others.

Maybe he was right to believe, maybe Phineas Westley would find a man who was privy to Daniel's secret, but she could not share his faith. It seemed from Abigail's confidences in the time they had worked alone in the workshop or stacking the kiln that her husband had worked only with his father, grandfather and later with his son, so who was there with knowledge of the complete formula Daniel had used?

Glancing up from weeding the patch of garden, she looked across to the kiln. It had been heart-wrenching for Daniel to leave all he had known, the work of a lifetime, but it was best he had for it would have broken that heart to see the place so silent and empty of life. Phineas would try to revitalise Leabrook Pottery but she feared he was building castles in the air.

Had he discussed those castles with his nephew? Callista turned back to her weeding. Had Michael Farron been consulted, and if so, what had been his response? His uncle and Callista Sanford partners in business! Would he place the same interpretation on that as he had on the proposal she catalogue his uncle's antiques? Would he think joining with him to reopen this pottery was merely another ruse on her part, to inveigle herself deeper into Phineas's life?

If only Daniel had not passed the property to her this problem would not have arisen; she would have been gone from Wednesbury by now and Michael Farron and the thoughts he had of her would no longer be a thorn in her flesh. But that was unfair! She jabbed the trowel into the ground. She must never lay her sorrows at Daniel's door. He had given this cottage out of the goodness of his heart, provided her with a place to live, a place where he thought she would be happy.

'Ouch, that looks painful . . . poor old weed, whatever has it done to annoy you so?'

A shadow falling across her Callista looked up into a strong, faintly smiling face.

Sabine Derry fastened the buttons of the wide-skirted black grosgrain coat she had worn for that tram ride. It had helped hide her identity the day she had plunged that knife into Oswin Slade's neck and it would do the same today. She had given her housekeeper the afternoon and evening off; the woman would not return to Hill House until morning and as for Edwin, his lady of the night would keep him occupied until the early hours. That left plenty of time. Settling the black bonnet on her head Sabine smiled at her reflection. No one would guess it was the mistress of Hill House swathed in this monstrous costume; were she seen leaving she would be taken for some washerwoman or widow seeking employment. No one would give her a second thought, nor would folk she passed in the town for she would be only one of many women dressed like this.

Taking the black kid gloves she had set out on the bed she hesitated then tossed them back. No washerwoman or widow poor as she wished to look would possess kid gloves or a sapphire engagement ring. Removing it, she placed it on her dressing table. Cotton, they would wear cotton. But she did not own a pair of cotton gloves. None then . . . she would wear none. Bare hands would be a stronger sign of poverty, stronger proof if any were needed that the woman shrouded in 'widow's weeds' was not Sabine Derry. Lowering the veil over her wig she inspected the result closely in the mirror. The colour must not show through the flimsy chiffon. Maybe it would be prudent not to wear it at all; avoiding the risk of recognition was the very reason for these distasteful clothes . . . but not the wig. Picking up the black cloth bag she had placed with the gloves she left the bedroom. She had a special reason for wearing her wig!

Not this way! Her hand already reaching for the heavy door that was the main entrance to the house, Sabine halted. No servant would ever be seen entering or leaving by a front door. She must be careful, keep her mind on what she was doing; a slip such as she had almost made would bring attention. Recrossing the wide hall she entered the kitchen. Something was not right! A niggle of doubt edged into her brain. What had she forgotten, what had she overlooked? Behind the veil her eyes probed shelves and dresser then, coming to the cooking range, took on a satisfied gleam. The coat she was wearing, the boots, they were too clean, too obviously rarely worn; a woman who was poverty-stricken, who wore the same clothes day after day, was the picture she wanted to present, a figure who would command no second look in a town rife with poverty and stained with labour.

Fetching a cloth from the adjoining scullery she dipped it in the ash of the fire then smeared several streaks down the skirt of her coat before rubbing it over her hands. Next she stubbed first one foot and then the other into the hearth, rubbing their sides well into the gritty residue of burned coal, breathing satisfaction at the way a film of the disturbed ash settled along the hem of her coat. Now she had overlooked nothing.

She must not take a hansom. Head slightly lowered, Sabine passed along the streets. Nor could she ride on the steam tram.

Women such as she aimed to pass for wouldn't spend money on riding when they could walk, and walking would give her time to go over what she had planned. It had not been difficult to find out where Jason Sanford's daughter was living; Phineas Westley had talked to Edwin when selling him that statuette of a reclining woman, had said it had been made at the pottery belonging to Daniel Roberts along of Lea Brook.

She had somehow got herself installed there, that had been easy to deduce, but how long would she remain there? That was not so simple to surmise and to fail now, to break the promise she had made to Julia, sweet darling Julia, her beloved sister . . . Sabine's long fingers closed tighter around the handles of the cloth bag. She must not fail, she would not fail!

She had gone over everything again, she had made doubly sure that all was in its place. Daniel would be happy with the workshop. Running one last glance over shelves and workbench, seeing the throwing wheel and small array of potter's tools clean and free of any trace of clay, Callista smiled satisfaction. She had cared for the workshop as she cared for the cottage; Abigail and Daniel would approve. If only she had a way of telling them what Phineas Westley hoped, that Wedgbury Ware would once more be produced at its age-old home, if—

A sound at her back ending the thought she turned, breath catching in her throat as the workshop door closed behind a black-draped figure.

'I have waited so long . . .'

The words seemed to hiss across the shadowed workshop.

'So very long. But it was not an onerous wait, it was enjoyable; all those years, all those long pleasurable days of knowing how you suffered.'

The woman had obviously made a mistake; her clothes said she was a widow; perhaps grief had caused her to lose her way.

'I think you mistake me for someone else,' Callista said gently.

'And perhaps you are looking for some other place. This is Leabrook Pottery.'

Like stones thrown against a wall the answer hurled itself at Callista.

'I know where I am and no I have made no mistake . . . it is you I came to see, you I came to kill!'

Kill! Callista's nerves vaulted. Whatever had happened to this woman had her seriously disturbed. Realising that to try running past and out into the yard might add to the woman's mental suffering she tried to keep her own voice steady.

'Why would you want to kill me? I don't even know you.'

'Oh, you know me. You know me very well!' Her raucous laugh accompanying the words Sabine threw back the veil. 'There,' she snapped, 'didn't I say you knew me?'

'Mrs Derry!' Callista stared at a face distorted by hatred. 'I . . . I don't understand. What have I done to make you wish to kill me?'

Lips drawing back in a snarl, eyes glittering like grey ice, Sabine's answer hissed from the shadowed doorway.

'You were born . . . you were the spawn of his evil.'

The spawn of his evil.

Callista's brain rocked. They were the words of her nightmare, but how did this woman know them?

'You,' it continued, spitting like cobra venom, 'you were the result of his unfaithfulness, you the reason he left, but I saw him, I saw him and I knew . . .'

They were the words which came in the night . . . the same which had her wake in fear, fear she had known in childhood! A trickle of cold ran along Callista's spine.

'Please . . .'

'No!' A long-boned hand rose, the shriek that was denial drowning Callista's attempt to speak. 'Did he give the chance of saying please? Did he listen to any plea? No he did not. Like a thief in the night he left, no explanation, no apology, no care for the heart he broke . . . and why did he do so? It was because of her . . . her and you, the spawn of his evil.'

Every word was the same: a carbon copy of those which she heard in her nightmare! Watching the woman glaring at her, loathing blazing with the cold flames of madness in unblinking eyes, Callista felt the trickle of fear which had run along her spine flare along every vein. But Sabine Derry had never heard them . . . how then could she repeat them verbatim?

'I promised . . . I promised I would take revenge and I did, a long sweet revenge.'

Fright real as ever it had been on waking from the horror of that recurring dream held Callista's body rigid, the hate in those crazed eyes snaring her senses until it was an effort to force words past her throat; but somehow they came.

'You . . . you promised revenge, but on whom?'

'On him! On him who took my beloved from me . . . but not only him.' Sabine laughed, a high hysterical laugh. 'No, not only on him, that would not be enough, those he loved must die too.'

She had thought this to be a woman mistaken in her grief, one who had misjudged her direction in the unhappiness of losing a loved one. But beneath the hysteria Callista discerned a woman of purpose, one who knew exactly what she was about. Praying her nerve would hold she said quietly, 'Perhaps we could go to the house, talk over a cup of tea.'

A dry rasping cackle erupted from across the room. 'Sly as ever, sly as the child I tormented, yes . . . yes it was me, I was the teacher who made your young life miserable; look . . . look and tell me you remember!' Snatching bonnet and veil from her head and flinging them aside Sabine hesitated, then with a serpentine smile stretching her mouth, she lifted away the wig.

'Ah,' she breathed as Callista's eyes widened, 'I see you do remember.'

Suddenly Callista was back in the classroom, her lips

trembling, her throat locked with fear, her hand rising to ward off a blow from a long-fingered hand. 'Miss Montroy . . .' she whispered.

'Yes, Miss Montroy.' Letting the wig fall alongside the bonnet and veil Sabine took a step forwards, a look of fiendish delight playing over her hard features. 'You never guessed, never suspected Sabine Derry was the teacher you were so afraid of. Oh, I relished that fear, relished it as I did that of Jason Sanford. His wife did not know, she thought it was the unhappiness of losing those teaching posts, of being forced to work in a steel foundry, but she was wrong, it was me. I brought her husband to the brink of despair, I drove him until he took his own life.'

What was she saying? What had she to do with her father's death?

As if reading the questions reeling in Callista's mind, Sabine laughed. 'You didn't know, they didn't tell you, didn't tell their darling she was the fruit of his infidelity, the reason for breaking the promise he made to Julia. A promise he broke when he met that strumpet, the whore who made him forego the pledge of marriage he made to my sister. But I made him pay, I caused him to commit suicide as he caused Julia to do. I never told him, I kept it secret . . .'

The laugh which had been shrill and manic dropped to a secretive giggle.

'Julia forgave him but I never told him so, I made him think he caused her suicide, that Julia died sooner than face up to the shame of being left in the lurch; each time he secured a post I wrote to the Board of Governors saying I would reveal to the newspapers they were exposing children to the influence of a killer. That was all it took, a few words written on paper and he was dismissed. Then he got work in an iron foundry . . . he thought that would satisfy me.' She giggled again, her grey serpentine eyes glistening. 'But the clever Jason Sanford was wrong, I told him I would shame his wife before the whole town, tell how she had used her body to entice him away from Julia . . .'

. . . a few words written on paper . . .

The words burned through the horror of the rest. This woman had driven her father to his death, had simply blackmailed him into ending his life! 'But he could not have killed her, my father could never kill anyone!'

Callista did not realise she had whispered the last aloud but the insane gleam in the eyes that watched her, the demented giggle curdling in Sabine Derry's throat, said it had been heard.

'Not Jason . . . he did not help . . . it was me . . . I helped my darling.' Suddenly, with the swiftness of a lightning flash, the gleam of madness was gone and the voice which continued was steady. 'I could not see my sister laughed at behind her back, see the finger of ridicule pointed in her direction, so I had her poisoned, and when she was dead I hung her body from the bedpost, then I wrote the letter which made her death look like suicide.'

'Why?' Callista gasped her revulsion.

'Why?' Sabine's mouth twisted, the hate inside her a torch on her tongue. 'Because he took her from me! Took the love that was mine and that I could not allow; Julia was mine, she could only be mine, her lovely body must never be touched by any hands but mine. I was her lover and that was how it must always be.'

She had been her own sister's lover! Callista felt a sickness rise in her throat. A sister she had murdered!

'I could not risk her turning away from me.' Sabine's voice fell, the soft words seeming to be said only for herself. 'Julia had known the kiss of one man; maybe it was a kiss she would prefer to mine, a kiss she would look for elsewhere, maybe in a husband. I could take no chance of that happening so I killed her. Then I killed the man who had spoiled my life. Jason Sanford paid for what he had done to me and so did his whore of a wife and the child their evil produced. I tormented you, made three years of your life a misery, before Miss Montroy left that school. But I did not forget and when I returned to Wednesbury I took up the task again. Oh, it gave me so much pleasure watching your mother slowly die . . .'

A frown appearing between her brows Sabine paused, peering enquiringly through the gloom of the workshop before asking, 'Did you not wonder why things always went so badly for you until in the end you were not even given a job scrubbing floors? It was all so simple. A word from Sabine Derry's housekeeper saying her mistress would not take supplies from any tradesman who employed or dealt in any way with the Sanford woman or her daughter was all it took.'

'You did that!' Callista stared in horror. 'You let my mother die!'

'Oh yes.' Sabine nodded, her answer almost nonchalant. 'She had to, you see I had to be certain she would not speak to anyone of my sister, of your father breaking off his engagement to her; that is also the reason for my killing dear Emma and the odious Mr Slade and why I must now kill *you*.'

She was mad, the woman was out of her mind! She had murdered three people and been instrumental in the deaths of two others; now she was bent on taking another life. Callista's brain reeled under what it had learned. Sabine Derry was here to kill *her*!

The realisation could have sent her brain spinning into a frenzy but instead it had an instantly calming effect. Drawing a long breath Callista summed up her position. The woman was insane; there was no doubt she counted the daughter of Jason Sanford not only in part responsible for her sister's death but saw her as a dangerous threat to Sabine Derry's future. She would kill, there was no question about that . . . but the door was only yards away. If she could draw the woman from it there was a chance she could reach it and once outside . . .

Intuition or the sixth sense born of madness seeming to tell her what was forming in Callista's mind, Sabine snatched a heavy plaster mould from the workbench and, the shrill scream of lunacy ripping from her throat, hurled it at Callista.

32

'It will be as it was before my dearest . . . before he came.'

The voice came from the darkness, a soft soothing whisper brushing against the pain throbbing in her head.

'We will go back home, back to our secret place in the woods, spend the afternoons in each other's arms, love each other as only we know how . . . oh my dear love, we will be so happy . . .'

Deep in the darkness of a pain-filled world Callista listened to the soft voice, her mind reaching for its comfort. Her mother was murmuring to her, they would go home . . . they would be happy.

'We will be together, no one else will share you, you will be mine again, only mine, and in the hours of night we will delight in each other's body . . .'

They would go home, her mother was telling her they would go home. But that was wrong? Callista moaned, struggling with the conflict between what her ears heard and what her brain was saying.

'Hush, my darling, you are safe now.'

The whisper answering the moan was gentle as the hand caressing her breast and for a moment Callista gave herself to it. The darkness was warm and pleasurable and her mother's voice . . . but her mother was dead! The thought was a blow, a weapon which smashed her dark world, flooding it with the light of reality. Her mother could not be speaking to her, and the hand fondling her body . . . her mother would never touch her like that. Her eyes, flying open, met the deranged gleam in those of Sabine Derry.

'Don't touch me!' Heedless of the ache pulsing in her head Callista tried to hurl herself from the woman bending now to kiss her breast, but a snatch at her throat had her gasp with pain. There was something around her neck, something which had pressed chokingly when she moved . . . and her hands . . . Callista's mind screamed in terror. Her hands were bound, tied at the wrists and secured behind her back.

Everything that had happened before she had awakened in a world of darkness rushed into her mind, remembered words falling into and over each other, finishing with 'why I must now kill *you*'.

She had thought to run but Sabine Derry had seemed to sense the thought and had hurled a plaster mould which must have knocked her unconscious. Now she was tied and helpless.

The woman's hand was stroking her legs, the mouth was touching her breast; Callista shuddered. She was at the mercy of a woman whose mind was deranged, a lunatic who believed she was her sister, a woman who had unbuttoned her blouse and chemise, lifted her skirts.

'Please!' The cry choked from her. 'Mrs Derry, I am not your sister; please, you have made a mistake I . . . I am Callista Sanford, I am Jason Sanford's daughter.'

Sabine Derry's head lifted and in the shadowed light Callista caught the glitter of eyes lost in madness. 'Jason.' The laugh was low, a cunning machiavellian sound grating in the throat. 'The so handsome Jason. He thought to rob me, to steal that which was mine, but he didn't succeed . . .' She laughed again, the harsh screech of mania echoing around the walls of the workshop, sounding a chorus of frenzied lunacy. 'He didn't succeed but I did. I did . . . I was more clever than him, I killed him, I killed them all. I did it to protect you, my dearest, to save you from scandal, and now I will protect you again, help you as I helped you that other time except I did not bring chocolates. Poison would take too long, but I have the rope. I tore the cloth I placed in my bag, knotted the strips together, they are strong enough to bear your weight. Do not be afraid, Julia . . .'

Mousy hair trailing behind the lips tracing a line of kisses along her neck and across her breasts brought a wave of revulsion shuddering along Callista's body but as she tried to twist away from it the cloth around her neck bit deep against her throat. Snared in her own world of delusion Sabine Derry paid it no heed.

'Do not be afraid,' she went on, her wild laugh ringing whenever she lifted her mouth from the trembling body, 'I am taking you home, home to the delectable joy, the ecstatic pleasure of our lovemaking, of—'

'Miss Sanford!'

A shout from outside had the crazed laughter die on Sabine's lips, the snarl of a cornered animal taking its place.

'Miss Sanford!'

The second shout had barely ended before Callista screamed. Whoever was in the yard let them hear her . . . please God, let them hear! Drawing breath to scream again the air choked in her throat as the cloth rope jerked taut.

But her one scream had been enough, the door burst open crashing on its hinges.

'What in God's name . . . !' Michael Farron stared at a black-garbed figure bent over the body of another.

'Go away!' Sabine's eyes glittered, the face she turned towards the doorway distorted with hate and rage. 'You can't have her, Jason Sanford, she's mine . . .'

Gasping against the stricture of the cloth circling her neck Callista tried calling but Sabine's shoulder pressed deliberately down on her chest.

'What the hell are you up to, woman?' Michael Farron took a stride forwards. 'I'm not Jason Sanford.'

Completely taken by the insanity which clouded her mind Sabine hissed between clenched teeth. 'You shan't have her, Julia is mine, she is my love . . . you killed her, Jason Sanford, you killed my darling Julia . . . but I will help her, help her like I did before.'

Moving with a speed that took Michael unawares, Sabine was on her feet, the hand which held the end of the cloth rope flinging it up and over a beam that was part of the roof, then, a maniacal laugh bursting from her, she pulled at it with all her might.

Dragged upwards, the rope biting savagely into her neck, Callista felt the world sway and twist; the breath choked from her as she heard a shout from a universe away, then a chasm, black and bottomless, opened beneath her.

'It's all right . . . it's over, it's all over.'

Who was intruding in her world of silent darkness, disturbing her peace? Why was someone infringing on her comfort, trespassing on her privacy? She did not want them here in her quiet seclusion, in her own intimate place, she did not want . . .

'Callista . . . Callista . . .'

Drawn by hands she could not feel, dragged towards a world she did not want to see, Callista moaned softly.

'Thank God!'

Somewhere above her in the surrounding blackness the voice which had been urgent, compelling and afraid became a sigh of relief. But she did not want to answer, did not want to leave the placid tranquil space in which she was floating, this world of soundless dark.

'Callista, oh my love, thank God . . . thank God.'

Who was thanking God, and why was someone calling her name? Slowly, unwillingly, Callista watched the blackness turn to grey, felt the ease of her body become pain.

'Callista my darling . . . I might have been too late.'

It could not be her that voice was murmuring to; she was nobody's darling, she was a pauper's child. A slight whispered laugh rested on her lips. A pauper in money . . . a pauper in love!

'Stay still, don't move just yet.'

Listening to the quiet words Callista did not want to move. Her body ached and her head throbbed and she never wanted to move again. Eyes still closed, she rested her cheek against a warm firmness and the encircling bands which held her were strong and gentle. No, she never wanted to move again.

'God damn the woman, why in heaven's name did she want to hurt you?'

It was whispered, muffled against her hair, but Callista heard. Woman? Woman! Instantly torpor cleared, leaving her mind clear. Sabine Derry . . . Sabine Derry had wanted to kill her, she had bound her wrists, put a cord about her neck, fondled her breasts and now . . . Eyes flying open she struggled free, almost sobbing when she saw her blouse had been fastened and her skirts lowered.

'It's all right, you are safe now, she won't hurt you again, but let's get you out of here and into the house.'

'Mrs Derry?'

'Mrs Derry will not be bothering anyone – ever!'

'She . . . she . . .'

'I know,' Michael Farron answered, his heart twisting at the sight of the face he loved crumpling with tears. 'I know, but it's over now.'

'I had no idea Edwin Derry's wife was the same Miss Montroy who taught at St James's School.'

Ada Povey looked at the girl sat beside her hearth. The wench 'ad been through the mill, that was clear to see. 'Nobody 'ad any idea who 'er was,' she answered, 'the woman 'ad everybody fooled what with 'er red wig an' fancy clothes. A whited sepulchre were what Sabine Derry were, clean outside but black with filth inside; the world won't suffer for 'er 'aving left it!'

No, the world would not suffer. The real tragedy was a life given to hatred and revenge.

'It be fittin' what 'appened to 'er,' Ada went on. 'I reckons we all need be grateful to that Mr Farron. Told me all about it 'e did when 'e brought you to me, said as 'ow that woman 'ad tied your 'ands and put a rope about your neck . . . said 'er would 'ave throttled you if 'e 'adn't arrived when 'e did. Well, thank God be all I can say . . . thank God 'e come to that there pottery.'

Tied her hands and placed a rope about her neck. Was that all Michael Farron had told Ada; had he said nothing of Sabine Derry's unfastening her clothing . . . of touching her? He must have seen when he entered the workshop. Who else could have buttoned her chemise and blouse?

Bustling with kettle and teapot Ada continued non-stop. 'Eh wench, when 'e brought you through that door my 'eart fair turned over, I thought you was done for and no coddin', but thank the Lord I were mistaken. Said 'e 'ad wanted to take you to his uncle's 'ouse but you was set against that, said the only place you would 'ear of were Ada Povey's 'ouse over to Trowes Court and seein' the only alternative to that were for 'imself to stay along o' you in that cottage then 'e give in and brought you 'ere. More seemly that . . . 'e be a gentleman.' She nodded, pouring tea into two thick china mugs. 'Ar, Michael Farron be a gentleman, said to let 'im know should anythin' be needed for your comfort and no accountin' o' the cost . . .'

The cost! The Poveys were as poor as herself. Callista watched the lined face, the hands veined and worn from constant labour. Ada had always been kindness itself but kindness did not feed a family and it could not be stretched to feeding her. She must pay for the food which had been given her . . . but how? She hadn't any money, she had been forced to barter crockery for bread and milk. The money for those baskets of mugs and plates . . . but there had been no money.

'Left a couple o' sovereigns 'e did.' Ada swallowed a mouthful of tea. 'I told 'im it were not necessary, that you was welcome to what my 'ouse 'eld an' no payment needed, but 'e wouldn't listen; put the coins on the table 'e did and said were I to permit then 'e would call again to see 'ow you fared . . . ar, like I says, that one be a gentleman.'

Two sovereigns! Callista's thoughts whirled. Where could she find such a sum, how could she ever earn that amount? Yet somehow she must; she had to repay Michael Farron.

'I could not have gone to anyone but you, you were always so good to Mother and myself.' Callista's eyes misted. 'I can't thank you enough.'

'Bain't no call for thanks, your mother were like a sister to me an' you . . . you was like one o' my own children.'

'Oh Mrs Povey, it was so awful.' Unable to stem the tears she had held so long Callista sobbed against the woman's shoulder.

Like to be a lot more awful than either this wench or Michael Farron had told and it was like to take longer than the three days the girl had spent beneath her roof for the pain of it to fade completely. Holding the shuddering girl Ada Povey's mouth tightened. No the world would not suffer for Sabine Derry's leavin' of it!

Ada had argued against her leaving. It was too soon, she had declared emphatically, wait a few more days . . . she shouldn't be alone.

But hard as she had found it she had known she had to leave Trowes Court. Michael Farron had asked could he call at Ada's house again but she must not be there when he did. She could not face him, not after what he had seen in that workshop, seen what Sabine Derry was doing to her.

Her hands had been tied, a twisted cloth choking her throat, she had not been responsible, not able to push the woman away . . . she could not be blamed! But that would have no meaning to Michael Farron. He would believe only what he saw: Callista Sanford lying half naked, another woman's mouth on her breast, and that would forever disgust him.

One half of her mind competing with the other half Callista walked along Holyhead Road, her glance going to a tall building, pale stone mullioned windows contrasting against smoke-darkened brickwork. St James's School! Would the unhappiness of those three years ever leave her, ever be forgotten?

Passing quickly she walked towards Union Street, passing the Dartmouth Arms, the inn locals referred to as the 'Bottom Wrexham', passing its counterpart, the George Inn, known familiarly as the 'Top Wrexham', as she turned to cross the market place.

Callista, my love . . . my darling . . . Memories chased through her mind. The words drifted through the darkness but the fog encompassing her mind must have caused her to hear wrong; she had been barely conscious. It had been easy for her brain to play tricks, to tell her not what was said but what she longed to hear said. But Michael Farron would never call her his love . . . his darling, he would never whisper such words to her, to a pauper's child. Yet it had been his arms that had held her, his eyes that had held such concern as he had looked at her. Or had that been another product of her half-conscious mind? Whichever they were she must forget those words, she must not let herself believe she had heard them. It was agony enough knowing Michael Farron was so near yet would always be worlds above her, agony feeling the love she had for him while knowing it could never be returned.

She must thank him, of course, for his helping her, give him her word she would repay the money he had paid to Ada Povey, but she would do so in writing. There would be no need for them to meet again.

33

'Callista, my dear.' Phineas Westley smiled his genuine welcome. 'I am so very happy to see you, but are you fully recovered, should you not be resting?'

Her own smile warm as unhappiness inside her would allow Callista accepted the seat he ushered her to. 'I am quite well, thank you, your nephew has been most kind.'

'Ah, Michael.' Phineas nodded as he too sat down. 'Though I admit to being a bit biased I have to say he is a good chap. He told me about that wretch Sabine Derry trying her best to hang you; Michael says the woman was completely out of her mind, that had he not rushed at her knocking her away she might well have succeeded. It is a terrible shock for her husband but the man could be forgiven for feeling grateful she bumped against a shelf bringing a load of heavy moulds down on her head. Had she lived the shame of what she did would have been harder still for him to live with; and the woman herself . . .' He shook his head. 'No, no, it's better this way. But you, my dear, what of you? You cannot go on living at Leabrook Pottery and no one there with you. I blame myself, I ought never to have let you remain there.'

'It was my choice, as is leaving.'

'Leaving?'

The quietly spoken word lanced through Callista, flaying her nerves, adding to the still-painful tightness of her bruised throat.

'Michael.' Phineas's smile broke again. 'Come in, my boy, I hadn't thought to see you today.'

'I have been to Trowes Court; I wished to assure myself of Miss Sanford's recovery.'

Miss Sanford! Callista felt the sting of formality. How could she have imagined that in the workshop he had called her by her given name?

'She tells me she is quite well.' Phineas's reply followed her own quiet answer.

'Well enough to be leaving Leabrook Pottery? And what of the contract you made with each other?'

It was an accusation, Michael Farron's face thunderous as he made it.

'Nothing was set down on paper, Michael. Callista is breaking no contract. Should she wish to leave then she is perfectly at liberty to do so.'

'No written contract? But a promise is a promise; you were to set that place going again . . . work together, she was to make those figures while you saw to the production of everyday ware!'

His nephew was not annoyed at the breaking of a contract nor was it Callista Sanford's broken promise which had caused the anger on his nephew's face, it was the fear of his losing the girl herself. And she? Phineas looked across to Callista, seeing the droop of her head, the hands twisting in her lap. Her feelings matched those of Michael. The two were in love. Understanding the emotions running through the couple, Phineas's remonstrance was gentle.

'If Callista wishes to leave then that is her business, Michael; we must not try to influence her in any way.'

But he loved her, how could he not try to influence her? If she left that cottage he might never see her again! He wanted to shout those thoughts, to tell this woman what he felt for her even though she held no love for him. But that he could not do, he would not embarrass her that way. Forcing both thought and anger away he spoke quietly.

'My uncle of course is right and I apologise, Miss Sanford. If it is your wish to leave Lea Brook then you must do so.'

'I don't wish to leave . . .' She lifted her violet eyes soft with the threat of tears, to Michael and he felt his heart contract. She must not cry! Lord, if those tears spilled he wouldn't have strength to hold his feelings in check!

'Truly I don't wish to leave,' Callista continued, 'but I cannot stay. Leabrook Pottery is no longer mine.'

'Not yours!' Michael was incredulous. 'Do you mean you have sold it?'

Her voice trembled but Callista's reply was steady. 'No, Mr Farron, I have given it away.'

'Given it away!' Flinging up his hands Michael looked to where his uncle sat. 'Phineas . . . can she do that?'

The older man smiled. 'She can do what she likes with her own property seeing she is without any legal guardian. But if you must ask questions would it not be polite to let the answer be heard fully?'

'There is nothing to add.' Callista made to rise but Phineas raised a hand.

'Forgive me, my dear, but that is not so. I believe you had a visitor before that unhappy incident with Sabine Derry. You were weeding your garden, were you not?'

How could he know? Callista lifted puzzled eyes.

'The man who visited you visited me.' Phineas answered her unspoken question. 'It was that man to whom you have given the property Daniel deeded to you, am I not correct?'

What could be gained by evasion? Callista repressed a sigh. She had not wanted it known why she had done what she had but Phineas would discover a way to find out. Perhaps after all she owed him an explanation.

'If you were threatened . . .' Michael's hands curled convulsively.

'No.' Callista shook her head. 'I was not threatened. I was

happy to give the pottery away, to return it to its more rightful owner; I gave it to Adam – Daniel Roberts's son.'

'As you freely gave those baskets of crockery.' Phineas smiled.

'They belonged to Daniel, therefore they belonged to Adam; I could accept no payment where I had earned none.'

'But how could you know the man you speak of was Daniel Roberts's son?' Michael could not contain the question.

Callista looked at the man she loved. If only their stations in life were not so far apart. But thoughts like that could only increase the unhappiness inside her, add to the heartbreak.

'I felt it the day of his first visit, the day he asked to purchase the baskets of crockery. There was such a love in his voice when he asked of Daniel and Abigail, a love that showed when he touched Daniel's tools, when he paused at his stool; it was some-thing more than a love of potting. But it became truly obvious when he caught sight of a small statuette that had failed in the firing. He picked it up and smiled as he ran a finger over it then said, "He still believes in Parian ware, I see." '

'Parian ware?' Michael glanced at his uncle.

'I believe it was a term I used when seeing one of the first pieces Daniel tried with his special formula,' Phineas answered. 'I said the creamy ivory of the glaze reminded me of the marble I saw being worked on Paros, a Greek island I visited with my wife. Daniel seemed to like the term, using it several times while I was there, but I should not interrupt. Please continue, my dear.'

Hands still twisting nervously together, Callista went on. 'I told him of the pieces which had been made and he asked would I be making more. I explained that was not possible for I did not know the complete range or amount of constituents which needed to be added to the body of the clay but that Mr Westley hoped to find someone who did. He did not hesitate or have to think, he simply reeled off oxides and their proportion to clay, temperatures to which the kiln should be fired and how long it must be allowed to cool. It seemed he had lived and breathed that particular process. But it was not until his second visit he revealed his identity. I felt then it was fate had sent him to the pottery but he said he and his sister's family were leaving for America; he found it impossible to live any longer in this country while being unable to return to Lea Brook but then it was equally impossible to leave without seeing the home of his childhood once more and to find out for himself the health of his parents. That was almost identical to the contents of the letter you, Mr Farron, delivered to the cottage, a letter written by Mary Roberts, Daniel and Abigail's daughter.' Sending her glance to Michael she finished, 'What more proof could I ask?'

'None,' Michael answered and now he smiled. 'I apologise if I offended you with my scepticism, my uncle will vouchsafe it has ever been a failing of mine.'

Rising to her feet Callista could not force the smile she knew she should return saying instead, 'Let us not say it is a failing, let us say it is the Fates you laughed at taking their revenge.'

The Fates taking their revenge! His heart crying out inside him Michael Farron watched her walk from the room, watched her leave his life.

Adam had called with the news; he had contacted his sister, told her of their parents travelling to Liverpool. She would know of the canal boats, the basins they pulled into, and would leave word at each. Abigail and Daniel would see their children again and if heaven were kind they would be reunited. Now Adam had gone, but if fortune smiled he would return, bring Abigail and Daniel back to the home they loved.

Callista stood in the living room which had not so long ago been filled with the sounds of Abigail's cleaning, the aromas of baking bread and simmering meat, and she felt the happiness of the couple's hoped-for return mix with the sadness of her own departure. If things went as she prayed, then Abigail and all her family would return to Lea Brook and there would be no room for Callista Sanford. But the fact he had written to his sister was not all of what Adam Roberts had called to say.

He had visited The Limes as Phineas Westley had said, but Phineas had not told why. It had been to leave with him the written list of materials for and the method of making the form of pottery he had called Parian ware, saying should his father refuse to return to Lea Brook then the work he had begun could live on beneath some other hand.

But surely Daniel could not refuse, not once he saw the love in his son's eyes, heard the pride he had for the work they had done together. He had smiled his gentle smile as he had looked at her. '*You must continue with yours,*' he had said, '*you have a skill in your hands, share it with the world.*' Then he had taken from his pocket the paper she had insisted he keep that second time he had come here. Daniel Roberts's decision would not be challenged by his son; what his father did with his property was his right; his parents' happiness was all he and his sister desired.

She had taken the paper, holding it in her hand while she asked, '*Then Leabrook Pottery is mine alone and I have the same rights, the prerogative to do with it as I will?*'

The blue eyes had held hers, the face so like Daniel's had smiled as he had answered, '*Yes, Callista, you have that same right.*'

She had not hesitated then but had torn the paper into shreds. '*Then I choose to return it to your father.*'

He had taken her hands, cupped them with his own strong ones, preventing the shreds of paper falling to the floor. '*Work with us, Callista,*' he had asked quietly, '*let your pieces carry the Wedgbury mark alongside your name.*'

She had made no promise as to that; it could be Daniel would prefer to follow tradition in producing only tableware, but she had given her word to stay until his parents' return. She would care for the cottage and the tiny garden but the workshop . . . she shuddered at the memory of what had happened in there . . . no, not the workshop.

'Callista . . .'

The soft calling of her name, the tenderness in the voice which had spoken it, that was not part of memory, it was part of a dream, a dream in which Michael Farron smiled at her with love . . . a dream she should not long for yet nightly yearned for it to come.

'Callista . . .'

No, not now, the dream must not come now, she could not deal with the misery its fading left in her heart. The fragments of paper falling in a cloud of white about her feet she covered her face with her hands.

'Callista . . . Callista, my love.'

The voice was a breath in her mind, the whisper against her hair a fantasy, the arms holding her a figment of imagination, but unreal as they were she did not want them to end. Caught between the torment of knowing it was a waking dream and the desire to let it play on she could not repress the sob rising in her stomach, the shudder of it travelling every inch of her body.

The arms dropped away and the voice which a second before had been soft against her hair was husky with apology. 'I should not have done that, I should not have touched you . . . said what I have. I vowed I would not let that happen but a man's vows count for little when he knows he is losing all his soul's desires, the one thing in life he craves. Once more I have to apologise for my treatment of you.'

Lifting her head Callista's reply was soft as that first whispered 'my love'. Eyes silvered violets behind a gauze of tears she shook her head. 'Don't apologise. What you said was no more than a slip of the tongue, sympathy . . .'

'Sympathy!' Michael Farron's laugh was harsh with emotion. 'Lord, if only that were all I felt, if my words were no more than a slip of the tongue . . . but they are not, God help me they are not. I love you, Callista Sanford; it seems I've loved you forever.'

'No!' Callista stared. 'You can't! Do you know what I am! My father was a suicide, my mother a pauper. You cannot love a pauper's child!'

For a moment the intense blue eyes were again chips of stone. 'Don't,' he breathed, 'don't you see it does not matter. It is what you are, not what your parents were, and though they may have been poor they must have been wealthy in love to have produced a daughter with . . .' He turned away. 'I've been a fool, I can see in your eyes you could never share the love, you could never have those feelings for me—'

'Then you have not looked properly,' Callista interrupted gently. 'Look again, see in them what I truly feel, see the love I have for you . . .'

She could not finish all she had wanted to say, to tell him the depths of that love, for she was in his arms, his mouth claiming her, their hearts telling each other of paradise found.

Looking down at the lovely face which had filled his dreams for so long Michael Farron's eyes gleamed the love he need no longer hide.

'You have torn the deed Daniel Roberts had drawn up . . . shhh.' He touched her lips with his, cutting off her reply. 'And also you agreed to my uncle's offer of a partnership producing pottery. Now I ask you will you form one with his nephew, a life-long partnership. I'm asking, my dearest, will you be my wife?'

A kiss her answer, Callista gave herself to the happiness flooding her soul. The Fates, those daughters of night, had smiled. They had not placed her among the stars but they had lifted her into heaven.

They had given her the man she loved.